D1264317

1st Book

THE KINGPIN

THE KINGPIN

By TOM WICKER

THE KINGPIN

WILLIAM SLOANE

ASSOCIATES · *Publishers*

New York 1953

To
NEVA

THE KINGPIN

Chapter One

Everybody who read the *Capital Times* that Sunday morning could see that Tucker had been defeated.

Everybody but Tucker.

Actually his name was hardly mentioned in the paper. Its headlines merely proclaimed in triumphant type—so it seemed to Tucker—that Colonel Harvey Pollock had been defeated by the incumbent, Ralph Anson, in the State primary election for a seat in the United States Senate. Defeated, to be more exact, by almost forty thousand votes.

The paper did say, while listing those with more than a voting connection with the event, that one William Tucker was campaign manager for Colonel Pollock.

So that meant, of course, that Tucker had also been defeated.

Tucker himself was contemptuous of the *Capital Times'* triumphant ink. (The *Times* was an ardent Anson backer, and one thing people always said about the *Times* was if they were for somebody or against somebody they didn't hesitate to say so, no sirree, not the good old *Times*.)

In fact, as Tucker read the story, he was not even thinking of defeat. He was thinking, We did it. We did what we had to do.

He took a large pair of shears and snipped from the front page of the paper a two-column box which set forth the unofficial returns, by counties, of the previous day's election. He put his feet up on the desk and leaned back in the swivel chair. The Sunday morning stillness and the chaos around him magnified its squawk in treble.

The figures from the tabulation registered on his mind like a small boy's initials in setting concrete. He knew that he would

· 1 ·

seldom, if ever, look at the clipping again. The figures were already a part of his consciousness.

The stories people told of Tucker's memory were fabulous. The Governor, for instance, swore Bill Tucker could tell you how many votes Al Smith got in 1928 in Nut Gap Precinct way out in Paulding County, without even looking it up in the State Almanac. And Tucker, the Governor would add, had been just a tyke in 1928.

Of course, Al Smith didn't get many votes in *any* precinct in 1928, but that was beside the point. One number was as hard to remember as another, the Governor would say.

Christ, Tucker thought now, putting the clipping down on the desk. That Anson. He sure did rack 'em up.

There was almost satisfaction in the size of the whipping Anson had handed them. Because that makes it just that much better, Tucker thought. The bigger they come the harder they fall.

Yesterday was just an archive now; it was over with and done. All of yesterday. Not just the election. All of it.

I never thought I'd run into Katherine again. But there she was, big as life, when I went down home to vote yesterday. After eleven years. Twelve.

That sly little bitch.

He took a worn leather wallet from his pocket. The money compartment was well-filled and he thumbed the bills idly, not counting them. He reached into the card compartment with blunt, abrupt fingers, nails short and stubby, and began to draw out the various papers it held. Driver's license, Social Security, auto club, State Employees' Retirement Fund—this one he threw into the wastebasket—car registration, YMCA gym card, Selective Service, coming at last to a newspaper clipping, almost in tatters, its print fading to illegibility on the flimsy paper. He unfolded it carefully.

"Mr. and Mrs. Daniel Saunders Sprague announce the engagement of their daughter, Katherine Ann, to . . ."

He chuckled again and the clipping followed the retirement fund card to the wastebasket. Ashes to ashes, he thought.

He replaced the cards in his wallet and the wallet in his pocket, relaxing, his feet and legs sprawled on the desktop.

He closed his eyes and wearily rubbed at his temples. Somewhere in the basement of his mind an invisible hand waved, beating time. Voices echoed through him in response, swelling to an off-key chorus:

> *Oh—I—wish I wa-as in the land of cot-*TUN
> *Ol times there are not for-got-*UN
> *Look-a-*WAY
> > *Look-a-way*
> > > *Look-a-way*
> *Dix-ee-land—*

That goddam song, he thought. I thought I'd go crazy last night if they sang it one more time.

He shut his mind to the sound of it. But still it came, faint and faraway, swelling, unceasing, bursting through his concentration.

You get a tune on your mind like that, he thought, you can't get it out no matter what. Like *The Music Goes Round and Round.*

> *Look-a-*WAY
> > *Look-a-way*
> *Dix-ee-land—*

He swung his legs to the floor in one long motion, the big hands levering his body from the chair. He walked around the desk and across the well-tramped carpet to a long table upon which many whisky bottles stood.

There were dozens of dirty and unemptied glasses, white crockery bowls in which crushed ice, now reduced to worse-than-tepid water, had risen in gleaming cones, saucers of the same white hotel crockery spotted with browning, drying half-moons of lemon and wooden bowls containing the limp remains of potato chips.

Tucker found a bottle of Kentucky Tavern which was almost half-full. He took a glass from the table, wiped its edge carefully upon the inner side of the tablecloth and poured a small drink. He sniffed at a bottle of ginger ale which had been uncapped since the end of the revelry. He shook the greenish bottle violently and a few answering bubbles made their way to the surface.

Flat, he thought. His lip wrinkled. The hotel ought to have cleaned up this mess by now, the rent they get.

*Ear-lee on wun fros-*TEE *mor-*NIN
*Look-a-*WAY
    Look-a-way
        Look-a-way
Dix-ee-land—

He cursed the song again and put the ginger ale bottle down. As he tipped his head back to drink the whisky straight he looked at the face of Harvey Pollock. He shuddered.

The face stared at him from the wall, from between two tall windows. It—the face—was as long from chin to hairline as Tucker's body from waist to crown. It was neckless, bodiless. Its eyes beamed benignly at the room and its lips—the width of Tucker's head—pursed solemnly.

Beneath it in red letters—the height of Tucker's extended hand —outlined in blue and interlined with stars, Tucker's own words boasted:

A VOTE FOR POLLOCK IS A VOTE
FOR REAL SOUTHERN DEMOCRACY

Tucker threw the whisky underhand at the picture, holding on to the glass, the liquid dashing across space, glittering in stray sunlight, splattering against the fleshy chin, dribbling in slow, damp globules across the slogan.

Tucker thrust his hands in his pockets and rocked up on his toes. His face was passive, undisturbed. The other face regarded him with equal lack of emotion.

Tucker turned away. As he did so his eyes fell on an inch-long cigar butt which lay on the rug. I hate a goddam cigar, he thought. Especially the stinking dead butts.

His nose wrinkled at the stale, heavy atmosphere of the Bright Leaf Room, the fetid rancidness of dead cigars, the thinner trace of many crushed cigarettes, the sour reek of whisky, compounded with the scented remembrance of sweating men, of perfumed and powdered female-smelling women, sweating too, and the faint nauseous taint of burning oil and gasoline and rubber and baked asphalt from the street two floors below.

Tucker walked rapidly to one of the windows flanking the huge face of Harvey Pollock. He leaned far out and drew great gulps of air. Beneath him was the black-iron roof of the hotel marquee. Along its outer edge, in yard-high letters, he read backwards: HOTEL STONEWALL JACKSON.

He felt the sun jolt against his head. Another scorcher, he thought.

On the wide street below cars moved, their sounds subdued as befitted Sunday morning. Across the street stores and shops, neon lights still burning before some, waited quietly for Monday, blank and empty and useless.

He could turn his head to the left and see the gray stone pile of the capitol building, the green, pigeon-limed dome surmounting it, the centuries-old trees and the grass and brick-cobbled walks paying homage to its eminence. Two flags fluttered from its highest point, Old Glory on the right, the State flag on the left.

A door opened behind him. He pulled his head in from the window and turned.

"About time you came around, Sid."

"Yassuh. Gret day! Look at dis mess!"

"No wonder. Must have been ten thousand people in here last night."

"Uh-uh!"

"There really were. We had them climbing up the walls."

They stood, side by side, looking down the long room. It was the pride and joy of the Stonewall Jackson. Here were held banquets, balls, receptions, all the tinsel events which fell to the lot of the leading hotel in Capital City. It was an immensely long room, running nearly the full length of the hotel at the second-floor level. Eight-foot-high windows were at their backs and a row of similar openings were spaced at regular intervals down the wall to their right. Between each pair was, at present, a poster of Colonel Harvey Pollock.

The far wall, facing Tucker and Sid, was occupied by a tremendous mural of a field of bright leaf tobacco, a farm house and tobacco barn in the background, with an overalled farmer driving a mule between the rows, the mule pulling one of the sledlike drags common to the tobacco field. From this mural, signifying one of the State's chief industries, the Bright Leaf Room took its name.

Now, at the far end of the room, two teletype machines looked glassily at them. The long threads of paper which they had issued had been ripped and torn and wadded, hurled toward the wastebasket which stood by the machines and overflowed its contents to the rug. Around the machines old and forgotten paper littered the carpeting.

Sid kicked at a wastebasket which had overturned. The spill of trash included a man's bow tie, a twenty-five cent book from which the cover had been torn and half of a stiffened hot dog.

"You got a job, all right," Tucker said. "Hope they pay overtime, Sid."

"Yassuh! We got us a union now."

I should have a union, Tucker thought. Something like the International Brotherhood of Political Management Counselors. IBPMC. We'd be terrific at collective bargaining with our employers.

He became aware of an unlit cigarette between his fingers. He did not remember taking it from his shirt pocket, but he stuck it between his lips and held a match to it.

"You should have seen it, Sid. They started coming in here about six o'clock. They kept coming till about eleven. By that time it was all over. But they sure did raise hell in the meantime."

Sid chuckled.

"I heerd um. Work late las night. Some racket, dat singin an all. Up in the yuther place too."

Sure, Tucker thought, up in the other place too. Naturally. Anson's crowd was singing too.

But not *Dixie*.

The song still throbbed inside him. For a moment he could hear it all again, the shouting, the singing, the kids' rebel yells cutting through the mass of sounds (And I organized that bunch of half-grown fiends, he thought, I should have had my head examined.), the ever-present jumble-grumble of the talk and the women screeching their laughter into the haze, all the people—

· 6 ·

noisy, drinking, sweating, laughing, hoping, stupid, lousy people —who had crammed themselves into the Bright Leaf Room to celebrate the election of Harvey Pollock to the United States Senate.

They celebrated all right, he thought. The fools. They actually thought we would win. Even Pollock. Even Joe. Even *Cousin*, for God's sake.

I told them and told them and *told* them. And they still thought we were going to win.

Sid methodically began to clean up the room, working out in widening circles from his wheeled refuse container. Tucker watched him begin to gather up the mass of bottles from the long table.

Where are they all now? he thought. All the people who drank our whisky and whooped and hollered and yelled about Colonel Pollock, that great man we have to have in Washington to save the nation.

"Huccome you down here all alone, Mis' Tucker? Sunday mawnin an all?"

Tucker laughed. A good question, Sid, he thought. I approve of that. How come indeed?

Because I alone out of all that stinking mob you are cleaning up after and will clean up after again, I alone have the brains of a brass billygoat. I alone know that this morning, right now, is really the time for the singing and the yelling. And the work.

This morning. Because now is when we start to win.

"Sid," he said, "man's work is from sun to sun. A politician's work is never done."

Sid laughed. Two gold teeth gleamed in his mouth.

Tucker went to the desk to look for the clipping from the *Capital Times*. It was the reception desk for Pollock-for-Senate Headquarters.

Tucker deliberately ground his cigarette out in the exact center of its mahogany surface. He did this carefully, methodically, twisting the cigarette between his fingers until even the paper lay in white flakes upon the wood.

Childish, he thought. Uncalled for. But eloquent. Oh exceedingly eloquent and exceedingly gratifying.

He went out through one of the many sets of French doors lining the inner wall of the Bright Leaf Room. He walked down the carpeted hall to a large room which he and Harvey Pollock shared. He opened a door marked *Private* and went in.

Two large desks similar to the one he had just used for an ash tray, several comfortable chairs, a floor model radio, and a row of filing cabinets occupied the room. It was dominated by another huge portrait of Colonel Pollock.

Even in here, Tucker thought, I have to look at that fat face.

He reached for the phone, then checked his watch and discarded the idea. She won't be up yet, he thought. She was around here last night until the last vote was in.

Nevertheless, he wanted very much to talk to Vivian. Now that she would be leaving there were a million things to tell her. With an effort he decided to let her sleep. Beauty rest for tonight, he thought.

He dropped wearily into the chair behind his desk and placed the clipping on the bare expanse in front of him. I could have slept all day myself, he thought. The empty desk across the rug from him suddenly mocked his burning eyes and his tired muscles.

The lousy bastard. Here I sit and where the hell is he? Tucker glanced at the gold watch on his wrist.

In church. That gut-bellied hypocrite. I can just see him putting on his act.

The martyr. Beaten by a cruel world forgetful of all the old values. But not disillusioned. Oh no. Head high. Chin up. Grave. A little sad. Small jokes. In very good taste, of course.

"Good Christ," he said out loud. Did he just imagine that the portrait of Pollock was smirking at him?

He shook his head. Of course it was imagination. I've got to cut this out, he thought. No use letting him get under my skin.

His mind roved back to its picture of the Pollock church activities. The only thing wrong with it, he thought, is Fred. I wonder if he was sober enough to get there. Had to pour him out of here last night. But I guess he'll be all right. His mother can keep him in line all right.

Figures from the clipping flashed in his mind.

Ralph Anson had polled 231,328 votes. Tucker did not need the newspapers to tell him that this was within a hairbreadth of a total majority. I didn't think he would get that many, he admitted to himself. I knew it would be a lot, but not that many.

Harvey Pollock had also exceeded his expectations. The Colonel had rolled up a total of 194,312 votes, a highly respectable figure against anybody but Ralph Anson. That Anson, Tucker thought. I knew he was popular. But not like that.

His mind moved on to what actually surprised him most about the returns. Rooster Ed McDowell, the third candidate, had polled 38,692 votes. Tucker shook his head, amused. The old banty-rooster, he thought. He's still got plenty on the ball.

That was the best day's work I've ever done, getting the old sot to run. I knew he could pull those hillbillies out of the woods and get us in the second primary. Where we had to be.

A pity we couldn't take over some of those votes now he's out of it. But we can't. Nobody could. Not even Anson. Those are Rooster Ed's votes. They always were and they always will be. Maybe we'll get some of them, but not enough. Most of those people never voted for anybody but Ed in their lives and they won't start now.

Tucker smiled.

There was a politician, he thought. He knew what a vote was, just how much it was worth and how to get it. He could tell you a lie to your face, admit it was a lie, and you knowing all the time anyway it was a lie, and when he got through with you you'd swear to it for Gospel and hit the man who said it wasn't.

❈

1924

It is spring.

He feels the ecstasy of the dust and sand between his toes, because it is the day after his mother's birthday and it is always on the day after his mother's birthday that he is allowed to go barefoot for the first time.

The dust and the sand are warm and the sun is not yet blistering. It will be, but not yet.

It is spring and Bill Tucker is nine years old. He runs along the narrow road, behind the old rubber tire which he has found on the mill junk pile, controlling it with a bent wire, curved like a shepherd's crook around the scarred and broken rubber.

The houses, small, gray-painted, as like to each as the beads of an abacus, fall behind him now, and still he runs, the old tire bouncing on the washboard road, the boy's exultant feet stirring small plops of gray dust at each step. The road begins to drop before him and suddenly he is on the crest of a hill.

The boy slows, stops. The tire slows too, stops, wavers, then pitches sidewards, breaking the grip of the thin wire, striking flat against the earth and bouncing in circular jerks into stillness.

The boy sees beneath him, swarming over the bald clay and the soft green grass of the ball park, surging around the frail platform pitched over second base, a black crawling shifting murmurous crowd, a crowd larger than he has ever seen. But it is not the crowd he watches.

It is the man striding across the platform, his arms waving, his claw-hammer coat swirling behind him. It is the menace and the power of this antlike figure he watches, this figure which, even far below him, seems to tower and loom in contempt of mere physical size.

Above the swelling bass of the crowd, above the beckoning whisper of the softly stirring air, above the suddenly beating thunder of his own heart, above all these, the boy hears the high-pitched and inexhaustible current of the voice, against which it is impossible to swim, to resist, against which the will and the knowledge drain out of him—the voice of Rooster Ed McDowell, rising and falling to rise again and yet again, like a mill whistle blaring across the sky, howling of defiance and damnation and outrage.

He moves down the hill, the tire forgotten. He enters the wide gate, moves across the yielding grass; the crowd is bigger now, less mobile, but the voice is still commanding, still piping, still screeching the defiance and the call, drawing him across the earth like fire draws air to feed itself.

And then it stops. The voice stops. The restless feet halt and the arms drop, hang limp and motionless. The hair flops across the forehead. The eyes hold them.

No man moves. Except the figure on the platform. No eye blinks, no breath catches, no finger twitches, as the man leans forward and swivels his shaggy head upon its wattled neck.

But still it is the voice, not heard, contained within him now, but casting out upon them the foreknowledge of its coming, already seizing steel-trap-hard upon them before the head goes back and the lips open:

"I got eyes. I got eyes like you got. I got eyes to see with an read the Good Book with. I got me a nose to smell stink with. I got me a tongue to talk with an guts inside of me to hate with, an I got the sperrit all over me to git up an claw an scratch an tromple over them what stands agin me an mine!

"An I got somethin else too. I got the sense to know the Yankees an the Jewboys an the niggers is a-marchin down on us like I been tellin you all day. I got the sense to know the Yankees and the Jews is a-thinkin an a-schemin an a-foamin at the mouth to get the niggers in our schools an our front doors an our jobs an our daughters' beds. I got the God-given common sense to see the pattern a-shapin an a-formin in front of me. Like you can see it."

Slowly his hands rise from his sides, together, the fingers pointing, pale and gleaming.

"The Jews," he says. "The stinkin Christ-killin Jewboys own the mills an the stores an the money. They tell the Yankees what to do, an the Yankees er so runny-butt scared of losin a penny they tell the niggers what to do, an the niggers er so dumb an lowdown they ain't got the sense to know they ain't fit to walk the same dirt a white man spits on an they do what the Yankees says to do.

"Oh it's all as clear as glass iffen you only got the guts to git up on your hind legs an look it in the eye. They want to mongrelize the race, brothers an sisters! They don want no white man down here a-thinkin an a-plannin an a-bellyachin to get a decent wage an a house of his own to live in, an maybe a day off an a car to ride in iffen he gits it.

"They want us all like black niggers is what they want! They

want us all gutless black-hided baboon kinky-headed nigger-smellin darkies what ain got the brains or the sense even to know they ain got no brains or sense. That's what they want! That's what's a-comin! The Book says the wicked er in power an a-spreadin like the green bay tree an that's Gospel! Gospel, I tell you!"

The voice rises again now, imperceptibly creeping up the scale, slowly, surely, pulling every man with it, until every man is leaning forward, up on his toes, head thrust forward, fists clenched.

"But the Book it says too ther swords they shall enter into ther own hearts an ther bows shall be broken. Ther bows shall be broken! An I will be the one! The *one*, brothers an sisters! I'll lay about me with the jawbone of an ass like the mighty Samson in the days of old, an I'll call upon the Lord on high from whence cometh my help an smote round about me, an I'll lie an I'll cheat an I'll steal when I have to, an by *God* I'll fight! And by God ther bows they *shall* be broken!

"I heerd the call like the preacher in the pulpit to go forth and lead my brethrun outen the wilderness. I heerd it a-singin in the midday sun an a-howlin in the night an a-screechin in the blood, an I have answered it! I have answered the call to tromple under foot them what sits on the seats of the ungodly!

"An I'm a-goin to keep on a-answerin an a-fightin an a-whoopin an a-hollerin. I'm a-goin to keep on so long as you let me, brethrun, so long as you git up offen your blood-runnin backsides an send me back up there to Washington to smote them what's a-stealin your birthright an your God-given messuh pottage, an a-schemin an a-lyin to mongrelize the race with the niggers so they can keep on a-gettin fat on your sweat an a-growin rich on your rightful money an a-layin up with your daughters, when they got a mind to go a-slummin—"

The voice stops, chopped off, sliced in midscreech. The words seem to hang above them, like doom, like a sword balanced delicately upon a string. And then, low and even and malevolent and deadly, drawing from them the teeth-clenched jaw-aching blood-racing blind-mad rage of a thousand years of shame and fear and dirt and poverty and outrage:

"I ABOMINATE the Christ-killin Jews! I DESPISE the money-grubbin Yankees! I HATE the filthy niggers!"

A mutter rolls across the crowd. But his hand sweeps upward, stills the rumble, pulls each eye to that hand, flashing palely upward like a falcon sweeping down the vast and fierce heavens.

The boy's eye too. It is the first time he has seen the rooster perching on the high pole, on the red-painted cross bar of a twelve-foot pole vaulting into the air; the rooster, held, framed, seized in the invisible rays emanating from that upraised and magnetic arm; the rooster, white and gleaming and prideful, the red beak and comb and eyes outlined like blood of old and unstanched wounds against the sky.

"Rooster!" the voice screams. "Crow for JESUS CHRIST!"

And jerked by some demanding and resistless string, the wings spread wide, embracing them all, the gory and indomitable head arches back on the proud neck and the beak opens and the sound —shrill and defiant and outraged—hurls forth and splits the atmosphere above them.

And now the roar comes, a seething boiling undertow of sound rolling from the bottomless sea of faces and people and bellies —and stills, quickly, obediently, expectantly, as the hand moves, twitches, the barest part of an inch.

"ROOSTER! CROW FOR THE SOUTH!"

Again the wings spread, the neck arches. Again the outrage shrills above their heads. And again, the rumble rises to meet it.

The hand flicks. Silence drops.

"R O O S T E R! C R O W F O R W H I T E S U P R E M-A C Y!"

And now there is no crowing and no roar, only a steadily rolling tumbling torrent coming out of the bowels of the trompled, the bellies of the shamed, the souls of the undefeatable, not rising, not punctured by shrillness, a massive inhuman growl of fury and unbending defiance.

The boy is lost in the sound. He is not aware of it. He is of it.

He looks away now from the white bird, preening and wingspread, steadily crowing above them all, away to the looming and implacable figure on the platform. He sees the upraised and outstretched arms, the face flung forward to the sky, the exultation and the triumph and the doom.

I have heard the trumpets sound, he thinks. I have seen Glory Hallelujah.

Tucker chuckled.

He leaned back in the swivel chair and swung his long legs to the desktop. He sure had me going that day, he thought. He had us all going.

That damned rooster.

He chuckled again.

Good thing he ran out of roosters, he thought. None of us would have had a chance even now. There never was anything wrong with the old boy's methods. The tune was all right, he just never learned to change the lyrics.

There was a short rap at the door, not questioning, merely a brusque announcement of entrance. The door swung open and Fred Pollock came in. Tucker turned his head to look over his shoulder.

"I thought you'd be in church," he said.

Fred flopped into a chair in front of the desk.

"I was. But church is out."

The remark pleased Fred. He was pleased all over himself this morning. The bright spring day and the wonderful thing that had happened made him feel as he had once felt when he had come close to fighting with a drunk at a football game—a very large drunk—and the drunk had surprisingly backed down.

"You look mighty cheerful for a man who had a night like you did."

"This, friend Tucker, is the happiest day of my life. I do believe it is. I don't even feel my hang-over."

Tucker grinned.

"You love that father of yours, don't you, boy? You really think a lot of him."

Fred didn't answer. I'm going to spit right in that smart face of his someday, he thought. The bastard. He sees too much.

He took a silver cigarette case from the inside pocket of his well-tailored, collegiate-cut gray suit. His puffy face relaxed somewhat and lines became evident about his eyes. His lips were a trifle too loose.

"Mother sent me down to get her pocketbook," he said. "She left it in his desk drawer and didn't have time to get it before we left last night."

"Help yourself. How is your mother today?"

Fred squinted his eyes at Tucker. Cigarette haze veiled about his head and the loose lips pursed. I wish I knew what he meant by that, he thought. He always means something, every time he mentions her. I wonder if—hell, no. She wouldn't look at the bastard twice. She better not.

He rose and went over to Pollock's desk. He was not very tall and he gave the impression of continuously stretching his whole body upward in search of height. He stood in front of his father's desk, gazing at the huge campaign portrait. He felt an urge to draw a mustache upon it.

Suddenly he backed away, stretched his arms over his head and bent forward in a low-comedy obeisance.

"O Great White Father," he intoned, "forgive them for they know not what they did to you."

Tucker laughed harshly behind him. "They did it, though," he said.

Fred straightened abruptly.

"Bless 'em all," he said. "The long and the short and the tall."

He went around the desk and opened the wide center drawer. He took from it a gaily colored woman's pocketbook and held it aloft for Tucker to see.

"Highly symbolic. Do you see the significant parallel here, Tucker? Her moneybag in his desk. Very probably without a cent in it."

"Cut it out," Tucker said.

"No, seriously. It's very apropos, or something. Where would he be without her money?"

"Where would she be without his name? For that matter where would you be without both of them?"

Fred felt warm blood pour through the vessels and veins of his face. Suddenly the bloom was off the day. He hated Bill Tucker more than he had ever hated him before. He spoils everything, he thought. Just like the Colonel. Everything they touch.

"You just watch what you say to me," he said. "You're not so smart."

It was a very poor answer and he knew it and said it anyway. He could think of nothing else to say. Sometimes he worked for hours on devastating squelches to deliver upon the crushed head of Tucker or of the Colonel. Maybe at night when he lay alone in his room at college. Or driving down a country road with the top down on the Ford. At times like those it always seemed easy to find an answer to Tucker or to the Colonel.

But all he could think of when the time was at hand—a time such as this—was the sort of childish and petulant rejoinder he had just made. Despair touched him. They always win, he thought. Always.

"Forget it, Fred. We're all on edge."

Fred tried to recapture the earlier brightness of the day.

"I'm not," he said. "I'm not on edge." He came across the office, the pocketbook in his hand, and stood in front of Tucker's desk. "I am vastly pleased with the world. The world has more sense than I thought it had."

"Never in your life," Tucker said. "You just believe what you read in the papers."

"He got licked, didn't he? He was slaughtered, wasn't he?"

"All right, all right. You enjoy it, Fred. It's all you'll be able to enjoy for a long time."

"You mean the second primary. You still think he'll win? After the licking he took?"

"Yes."

Fred rolled his eyes back. His voice became hollow and sepulchral.

"Faith," he said, "what follies are pronounc-ed in thy name."

Tucker laughed, too sharply. Fred was surprised. I got a rise out of him, he thought, I do believe I did. I stepped on a sore toe that time.

"Listen, Fred. You hate your father. That's okay with me, hell, go ahead and hate him. But hate him in private for the next month, you hear? Your summer holiday begins next week and the Colonel says he's going to put you to work here in the office. I don't want you, of all people, geesing up the works."

Fred saluted smartly. He was beginning to enjoy the exchange of words. It was seldom that Tucker so obviously showed annoyance.

"No sacrifice is too great," he said. "No hardship too onerous. The demands of the Pee-Pul of this Gra-yut Sta-yut must be served. Colonel Big Belly Pollock must be elected so that Big Brain Tucker can get a cut of the swag. I shall endure."

Tucker stood up. Hot damn, Fred thought, why wasn't I able to do this a long time ago? I haven't had so much fun since Grandma fell through the johnny-seat.

"I ought to kick your ass out the window, Fred. You made your joke. So get out of here. Just get the hell out of here."

Tucker's eyes bored into Fred's. The boy blinked. He knew that he now held a definite advantage. His goads had prodded Tucker into intemperate language, into losing his temper, and now was the time for the crushing counterattack.

But something curled inside of him. The soft deadness that had come into Tucker's eyes, the low-pitched malevolence of the voice, the blunt threat wiped out the contempt and the enjoyment and the cool precision he had for a few moments felt. He knew these to be dripping out of him and he sought desperately to hold them to him, to stand face to face with this man, and then it was all gone, all lost in an unreasoning fear of the eyes and the voice and the words. He was a boy again.

He backed hastily toward the door.

"I'll tell you what I'll do," he said. "I'll get me a whore and bring her up here on next election night, and lay her right in there in the Bright Leaf Room in front of God and everybody. That ought to get him a lot of votes."

His voice rose toward a shriek. Then, horribly, Tucker grinned at him.

"You do that," Tucker said. "She can bill your dad for the two bucks."

For a moment the boy thought he would hurl himself across the room at the grinning man. Just for a moment.

Then he whirled and went out. The door slammed loudly after him.

Chapter Two

Joe Harrison was insulted. It showed in every line of his handsome square-cut face. It bristled from his cropped brown hair.

His whole body was erect and angry under something that seemed to him to be more than anybody should be required to take.

He glared at the glossy menu in his hand and let his eyes fall down the right-hand side of it. Joe did not need to order from the right-hand side of the menu. It's just the goddam principle of the thing, he always thought. Dollar-fifty is plenty for a meal even with the goddam inflation.

The dollar-fifty items—three of them—were grouped together a little more than halfway down the list of entrees. They were Salisbury Steak Smothered in Onions, Broiled Veal Chops and One-Quarter Milk-Fed Tender Southern-Fried Chicken.

"I'll have the Salisbury steak," Joe said, his voice disapproving, not so much of the steak as of its position on the menu price list. "And skip the onions."

"You get soup or tomato juice and two vegetables, tea or coffee, rolls or muffins."

"All right. Just hold your horses, can't you?" His glare reproved the waitress briefly, then fell back to the menu.

"Gee, Mr. Harrison, I didn't mean—"

"I'll have the soup and French fries and string beans. Iced tea and rolls. And don't let it take all day."

"Yessir. Right away, Mr. Harrison."

Her speed at scribbling down the rest of his order, taking the menu from his hand and setting off for the kitchen of the Stonewall Jackson Hotel Coffee Shop failed to soothe Joe's wounds. Nobody lets a man have any peace, he thought.

His belligerent eyes took in the other Sunday diners. Fools. The goddam fools. They don't know. They don't even realize. Sitting there chewing their cud like that.

He shifted impatiently on the deep leather seat of the booth. He felt the newspaper crackle as his weight crumpled it. He remembered the gloating headlines and swore under his breath.

Forty thousand votes!

How could they *do* it? How could they do that to the Colonel? After all the work we did. I thought maybe we had shown them. I thought maybe for once they'd be able to *see* what's happening to this country.

Forty *thousand!*

Joe Harrison took the defeat of Colonel Harvey Pollock personally. He felt in his entrails that the deepest, blackest outrage of history had been perpetrated upon his person. And upon the Colonel.

This was in part because Joe was sure that Harvey Pollock ranked among the Greatest Living Patriots. It was also because he was equally sure that the Colonel's avowed program—not only what he was for but also what he was against—contained within it the Salvation of the American Way of Life. Joe entertained serious fears for the American Way of Life.

In his rigid outrage Joe was hardly aware of Tucker sitting down in the booth. He nodded stiffly at Tucker's greeting and lit a cigarette.

"Glad you're here," Tucker told him. "There's a lot for you to do this afternoon."

Joe regarded the glowing tip of his cigarette.

"What's the use?" he said.

Tucker smiled.

"They sure did shellac us, didn't they? But things could be worse, Joe. A lot worse."

"I don't want to talk about it. I get sick to my stomach just *thinking* about it, for Christ sake."

Tucker chuckled again.

Two girls came in and sat at the table beside their booth.

They were brilliantly dressed, and they were very assured and walked well in their high heels.

Their hats were perched confidently on their heads and their faces, brightly observing the Coffee Shop and its patrons, reflected no uncertainty or shyness or reserve and held no concern of any kind at all. Obviously the only thing that might even remotely concern them was their own appearance and, just as obviously, in their beautiful and fashionable Sunday attire and their ordered and exact make-up and their healthy and blooming youth, this was a worry which at least for the moment could not possibly be more pressing than perhaps a faint feeling that a stocking seam might—probably not but might—be ever so slightly crooked.

"Nice," Tucker said. "A little on the college side but nice."

Joe grunted.

"You *are* in bad shape, Joe. I never saw you just grunt at a woman before. Two lookers like that, anyway."

Joe allowed his eyes to sweep boredly over the girls, who were now chatting swiftly over the tops of their menus.

"How can you talk about things like that?" he said. "After what happened last night, I mean."

Tucker began to feel the impatience that Joe Harrison sooner or later always aroused in him.

"All I said was there are two nice-looking girls. What's wrong with that, for God's sake?"

Joe again looked at the girls. Identical cigarettes now extended at identical angles from identical red-tipped fingers. Joe looked at them for a long time and one of the girls returned his stare coolly for a moment before turning her head to look at a passing foursome of young men heading for one of the rapidly filling tables.

Joe turned back to Tucker.

"Not one good tit between 'em," he said.

Tucker stared at him.

"Who the hell said anything about their bosoms? All I said was—"

"It's just typical, that's all. The whole world is gone to hell. Everything that used to be worth anything is dying out. It even applies to women. You don't ever see any big knockers any more.

They all got to be like in *Vogue* and *Charm*. If they got a bust they got to strap it down so it won't show too much. And most of 'em don't have anything up there to start with."

"I didn't mean to get you started on a philosophical rampage," Tucker said. "I know your philosophy too well. And will you kindly not talk so loud about people's bosoms? This booth isn't soundproof."

Joe leaned forward slightly.

"I saw something in the *Reader's Digest*, Tuck. This doctor said women ought to go back to breast-feeding their kids. Now that makes sense to me. That's one of the things that's wrong nowadays. Kids aren't brought up the way they used to be. This doctor, I forget his name, but he was a big wheel in the AMA, said if mothers would breast-feed their kids again the kids would grow up a lot better off."

"And women would have big knockers again?"

"Stands to reason, doesn't it? But what I'm driving at is none of 'em *do* have 'em nowadays. It's just *typical* is what I mean. Everything's gone that made us what we are—"

"We're losing our freedoms," Tucker said.

"Sure we are. Those girls there. Do they care what happened last night? Hell, they don't even know what happened last night."

Joe waved a hand.

"Well, don't get me started, Tuck. I could go on about it all day."

That's the second time he's called me Tuck, Tucker thought. The things I have to take to get along with this guy. What I ought to do if I didn't need him, I ought to boot his fanny right back to that goddam radio station.

"I remember once I was in the Army I had me a woman down in Texas. Now there was a woman. Listen . . ."

But Tucker did not listen. He knew that if he had not heard this particular story before then there had been plenty of others like it from Joe.

"Of course, she was a little loose with men," Joe said, ending his verbal orgy. "You wouldn't want to marry a woman like that. But she was a real woman, all right."

I wish I hadn't said all those things to Fred, Tucker was thinking while Joe spoke. I wish I hadn't said any of it. He can't help it. None of it is his fault.

The snotty little punk. He sure does get under my skin.

The waitress arrived and began placing Joe's food before him. She took Tucker's order and departed again for the kitchen. Joe inspected her legs as she departed.

"They sure do have lousy-looking waitresses in this place," he growled.

"Let's forget about women for a minute. You're planning on working this afternoon, aren't you?"

"I wasn't. I was planning on eating an inch-thick steak and doing absolutely nothing but celebrate this afternoon. Before last night, that is."

"I told you all along," Tucker said.

"I know. But things looked so good. Tuck, tell you the truth, I thought it was in the bag. In the *bag!*"

"You shouldn't have. I told you and told you and told you. He didn't have a chance this trip."

"It's terrible. Just awful. I was thinking just yesterday how swell it was going to be for a real American to win over that pinko. And now it's all smashed up just like that." He endangered his iced tea glass with a sweep of his huge hand.

"Nothing's smashed," Tucker said. "You haven't listened to a thing I've tried to tell you in the past three months."

"Forty thousand votes. That's all I can hear. Forty thousand ostriches with their heads in the sand that can't see what that Anson is and voted for him instead of the Colonel. You never thought it would be that bad, yourself."

"No. I didn't. But I never thought the Colonel would get as big a vote as he did either. He racked up a few too, you know. One hundred and ninety-four thousand three hundred and twelve to be exact. Unofficial returns."

"Things have gone too damn far," Joe gloomed. "I should have known it. This country was sold down the river too long ago. Too many people given too much to know what anything's worth any more. Creeping socialism. They don't even know a real American rugged individualist like the Colonel when they see one now."

How corny can this guy get? Tucker thought.

"Joe, listen. Look at it this way." I have to be patient with the slob. He makes me want to puke but nobody can grind crap out of a typewriter the way he can. I have to be patient with him if it kills me.

"I haven't got the exact figures down to a decimal point. But this is pretty close to it. If everybody that voted in this last election votes again—they won't, you can bet on that, but if they do—all we have to do is to change less than one hundred of them out of every one thousand from Anson to the Colonel and we're in."

"Fat chance."

"Or look at it this way. If we can change only four hundred voters in every county, we're in. And that's if everybody votes again."

"We couldn't do it in the past three months, could we? How the hell do you expect one more to do any good?"

Give me strength, Tucker thought. Let me bear up under the stupidity. Don't let me blow up and spread my guts all over this coffee shop.

"I haven't got time to go over it all," Tucker said. "But one thing I know you've forgotten. Hartsville."

Joe's gloom failed to lift.

"We may not get the decision in time. We can't be sure."

"That would be the only thing that could hurt us. But we'll get it all right. Listen, Joe, get your chin off your chest, will you? You know Judge Benton kicked in for the Colonel. Heavy sugar, too."

Joe frowned. "Judge Benton is a fine man," he said. "He's a real American. Even if the Colonel would let you, you couldn't influence one of his decisions."

"I didn't say I could. Hell, I don't even have to. It's an open and shut case. But we can make sure the decision is announced on time. There isn't anything wrong with that, is there?"

Joe weighed the matter.

"I don't think the Colonel will like it."

Tucker mentally rolled his eyes heavenward.

"The Colonel doesn't have to know, Joe."

"Listen, Bill. I know we've pulled off a few deals. That's the way it is in politics. You have to be realistic. But the Colonel doesn't know. And you better not do anything to get him in trouble. He's too—"

Tucker cut him off quickly. No eulogies, he thought. That I absolutely could not take.

"You're just upset," he said. "But I give you my word on it, Joe, things are just beginning to break our way. You been kicking around in politics long enough now—you ought to know that."

"Christ, I guess I got to believe that, all right. I've burned my bridges now. I guess I got to believe it."

Tucker relaxed. You had to handle the damn fool like an only child, spoiled rotten. You had to do it because he had a special sort of value to you. But some day. Oh there would come a sweet lovely day of reckoning some day, some sweet lovely day.

The waitress arrived again, bringing his food. He ate quickly. Joe had finished his meal and sat watching Tucker, much to Tucker's annoyance. He hated people who watched him while he ate.

He finished more quickly than he otherwise would have, and decided he would skip dessert.

"I left a note on your desk, Joe," he said. "Might as well tell you now, though. We've got to get up a lot of stuff for the press. You know, cliff-hanger stuff. He's making up his mind. He's talking to his advisers. All the campaign funds are gone, but the Colonel may dip into his personal bank roll. That kind of crap."

"Sure, sure."

"Thousands of telegrams rolling in. Urging him to run. Actually there *are* a hell of a lot of 'em up in the office. Quote one or two of the real corny ones. Say the Colonel still has faith in Democracy, but get it over without saying that after yesterday it's damned hard to keep that faith. And put in a little something about this nigger single-shot voting. Don't give that one to Pollock. Say I said it."

"You want a press release or a novel, for Christ sake?"

"I want about three good stories. For the morning and afternoon papers tomorrow. For the radio stations. Try to get a little different angle in each one. You—"

"Don't tell me my business, Tucker, goddammit, I'm the publicity director, not you."

"Get your fanny out of gear, Joe. We got too much to do to get in each other's hair."

"I'm sorry," Joe said. "But you just remember I gave up a damn good deal to come in on this, because I believed in it. I've sacrificed a lot and you ought not to talk to me like I was some flunky after all I've done."

"Hell, I'm sorry. You get to work, Joe, and I'll drop in about five. Don't give the press a thing before then. We'll give your stuff a quick check and then hand it out."

He stood up, fishing in his pocket for change.

"Where can I call you, if I need you?"

"I'll be at the Colonel's. We've got a lot of work to do."

Joe's sensual lips pouted. For a moment Tucker was viciously gleeful. Joe would give his right arm to be going along for what he knew was a top-level strategy meeting. Joe worshiped the Colonel almost as much as he worshiped himself, and such an occasion would be the perfect opportunity for him to court both of his great loves.

And the Colonel doesn't give a hoot in hell for you, Tucker thought. When there's thinking to be done, he calls me in, not you. Even if you are the typical one hundred and twenty-five per cent red-blooded All-American Jack Armstrong of the airwaves.

This feeling passed through Tucker like a dose of salts, and he immediately admitted to himself that the end result was the same as if it had been salts.

A sensation that was almost as much fear as shame came over him. I got a hell of a lot to do, he thought. Getting into a popularity contest with this ass kisser. Especially when it's Pollock's ass. Like I was another of the fools we got hanging around. Like I don't know what Pollock is, and what all of this is and just how much the goddamned conference means anyway.

He threw a quarter on the table.

"I'd rather be home in bed," he said.

"Yeah? Who with?"

Tucker walked away. Oh Jesus, he thought, oh Jesus, just let the day come soon. Just let it be soon.

⚜

Martha Pollock straightened the seam of her stocking, her leg stretched before her from the little dresser bench. She critically examined a faint network of blue veins showing on her thigh. No bathing suits this summer, she thought. Just shorts. I hate swimming anyway.

She turned back to the mirror and began to brush her hair. A flush of pride went through her at the youthful reflection she saw. The only place it shows, she thought. Those damn veins in my leg.

The door opened behind her. In the mirror she saw her husband enter the room.

"You might knock," she said. She stood up and reached for her dressing gown.

Pollock watched the gown envelop her figure.

"I no longer take the slightest interest in that sexy little body, my dear. You don't have to cover it up on my account."

"Not on your account. On mine."

Pollock sat down cautiously in the flowered bedroom chair.

"Did you want something? I'm dressing."

He crossed his legs and inspected the tip of a gleaming cordovan.

"A matter I thought we should discuss."

Strictly Harvard tonight, Martha thought. He's always so posed. If he was speaking to a bunch of farmers, he'd make you think he had hay in his hair.

She returned to the dresser bench. She looked at her fingernails and picked up an emery board.

"How much this time?" she said.

Pollock laughed.

"Always thinking about money," he said. "Or sex. A two-track mind."

"Maybe I have too much of both." She filed a nail. "There was a time when you didn't complain."

"A short time. And a long time ago."

"Not long enough ago."

He shrugged. "Do you want to hear what I wanted to talk about or not?"

"Suit yourself."

"Tucker thinks I should go to the beach this week. Put on an act as if I were thinking over whether to run again."

"Why tell me? Go where you please."

"He thinks you should go along."

"Damn Tucker."

"You get harder to get along with every day, my dear. Tucker says it'll look good for you to go along. The helpful wife sort of thing."

Martha looked at him coldly. Tucker this and Tucker that, she thought. I married a real man all right. A big wide smile and a big loud voice and a handshake. That's what I married. A hotel greeter with a fox's brain.

"Harvey," she said, "you know I don't want to go to Washington."

"So you've said. But I do."

"Haven't you got enough now? Of everything?"

"Just money, my dear. Just money."

"Well, I don't want to go to Washington. I don't want to go to the beach either."

"But you will."

"No."

"Yes, you will. You'll go to the beach and you'll go to Washington too, when the time comes. We'll leave for the beach in the morning."

Rage shook Martha with frightening force. But she did not lose control of herself. Experience had taught her that he would only laugh and she would only grow more furious.

She rubbed at another nail. "You're a common stinking blackmailer, Harvey." Ice edged her voice.

Pollock took a cigar from his vest pocket.

"You will be vulgar, won't you? Goes to show. Can't make a silk purse out of a sow's ear."

"Get out, will you? I've had enough of you for one day."

"No breeding. My dear, you are only about one million dollars removed from the cotton patch."

She stood up.

"It's my million dollars, though."

"And it was my cotton patch." He chuckled and lit the cigar.

"All right. You're a goddamned aristocrat. God knows you've told me often enough. And my father sharecropped for yours. You've told me that too. Just get the hell out of here, will you?"

He rose, puffing easily at the cigar.

"Since you brought it up," he said, "maybe you'd better have five thousand transferred to my personal account before we leave. For—ah—contingencies."

"I'll make it ten thousand. So you won't have to bother me again any time soon."

He chuckled again.

"Suits me. By the way, you *will* be ready to go in the morning?"

"Maybe."

"I don't have to remind you, do I?" His voice was suddenly harsh.

No, she thought, you don't have to remind me. But you keep on doing it. You and your brief case.

She cursed him viciously. He heard her out and laughed again.

"No breeding," he said. "No breeding at all." He went out, closing the door gently behind him.

Martha sat down on the dresser bench again. She reached for the hairbrush, then let her hand fall to her lap. The miserable son of a bitch, she thought.

She found herself looking at the framed photo of her father on the dresser. I wish you'd never invented your damned tobacco whatever-it-is, she thought.

The photo was not signed because Martha's father had not been able to read or write. "Never had the sense to learn when I was young," he had told her once.

He had had, however, a good deal of sense. Enough to figure out and build a simple device to make the curing of tobacco simpler and cheaper. Enough—and this was the most remarkable thing of all—to seek out an honest lawyer to handle patents, marketing, and so forth. He claimed later that it took him two years to find one.

The honest lawyer was rewarded and became one of the richest men in the State, but not so rich as Eben Turner, a sharecropper on old Randolph Pollock's Cumberland Plantation.

The money didn't do Eben too much good. He wasn't used to it, didn't want it, and rarely touched any of it. The one big expenditure of his whole life was the purchase of Cumberland from old Randolph Pollock. And that, as he freely admitted, was a matter of pure spite.

Old Randolph had been cheating him at the plantation commissary as regularly as spring came on each year. When Eben found out that Randolph could no longer meet the plantation taxes, he had the lawyer draw up a check, not too big a one at that.

"Take it or leave it," he told Randolph. When the old planter took it, Eben ordered him off the place by sundown.

The money had been more liberally, if not wisely, used by Martha, a ten-year-old at the time of Eben's ascent to wealth. The best in schools, clothes, cars, and entertainment became hers. The looks had been there all the time.

In much the same way that Eben had purchased Cumberland from old Randolph, she obtained Randolph's handsome son, Harvey, as her ticket to the considerable number of things money could not buy. Harvey, in return, was given all the things that money could buy.

Well, I made my own bed, Martha thought now, staring in the mirror. And it wouldn't have been too bad either. Only he turned out to be a little smarter than I thought. A little smarter and a little harder and a hell of a lot more expensive.

She got up and finished dressing. I should have left him a long time ago, she thought, I should have walked out when I could. Now I've got him around my neck for good. Him and his brief case. The bastard.

I wonder if he'd really use it, she thought. I wonder if he'd dare.

It didn't really matter whether he would or not. She couldn't take the chance. That was what mattered. There was too much at stake, too much to give up, too much never to have again. Too much dearly bought respectability.

She couldn't take the chance that he'd use the brief case. The affidavit from the overseer at Cumberland, now ten years old. That was the first one. The New York private detective's report. The pictures from Miami. What the bellboy told Harvey the time they were in New Orleans for the Sugar Bowl. The chauffeur's sworn statement about the Major, the one when they'd been in Japan. All that and God knows what else.

No, she thought, leaning toward the mirror to apply lipstick. He's got me over a barrel. I've got to just keep on being the perfect wife in public and doing the best I can in private.

She surveyed herself in the mirror. At least she still had that. At least he left her strictly alone about that, let her have what little there was left, have it where she could find it. Even if he did take notes on it for the brief case.

Cold terror suddenly took hold of her. Before her, like a prophecy of death, shimmered the delicate tracery of a single blue vein showing through white flesh.

She looked at her reflection in the mirror. She clasped her hands to her breasts and lowered her eyes to look along her body.

What then? she thought, the terror coming stronger now. What happens when this goes too?

Joe Harrison stayed in the booth for a long time after Tucker had left. He smoked cigarettes and thought.

There was no doubt of it, he thought. He had his back to the wall. Not since his discharge from the Army had the career of Joe Harrison been in such danger.

The career of Joe Harrison was not a thing to be taken lightly by Joe Harrison. It was too real. It had been, up to now, too brilliant in conception and execution.

The first twenty-two years of that career had been singularly ordinary, except for the fact that during them Joe's father had steadily accumulated wealth.

He had provided for his son a college education, a convertible, a sizable allowance, and his own absolute belief in the American Way of Life and in free enterprise.

The American Way of Life, he taught Joe, in deeds more than in words, is getting ahead on your own. Free enterprise is what you use to get ahead on. Doesn't much matter in what field of endeavor you apply free enterprise. That is, so long as you get ahead in it. So long as you hit the old bull's-eye. In the American Way of Life, it's the old bull's-eye that counts.

Joe's practical application of this education had to wait for four years, which he devoted to the armed defense of it—in a Texas training base, a Pennsylvania advanced training base, an English rear-echelon post, a French rear-echelon post, and finally an occupation billet in Berlin.

The last three months of the forty-eight comprised all that ranked in Joe's mind as profit from his patriotism—excepting the fact that he had been in the service at all, a fact which alone was invaluable.

As it happened, in those three months in Berlin, as a clerk-N.C.O., Joe occupied a desk in a police outpost back-to-back with a Russian N.C.O. named Vaya. Vaya was an amiable fellow, put politically obnoxious.

As it further happened Joe became accidentally acquainted with a fräulein who lived in the Russian zone. Visiting her secretly, he became the cause of a minor international incident when her Russian lover discovered him, not only in the Russian zone of Berlin, but also in the Russian zone of the fräulein's bed.

Joe was in Russian hands for two days, was questioned interminably, fed badly, not allowed to wash, and royally chewed out by his commanding officer when his release was effected.

When he returned to the States, Joe's mind had already turned these events over and over and had fastened on the possibilities. (Bill Tucker once told Harvey Pollock that that was probably the only act of imagination of which Joe had ever been guilty.)

Joe talked these possibilities over with his father. His father continued the discussion with a banker, who took the matter to the manager of a radio station in Capital City. Thus was begun the career of Joe Harrison.

His baritone voice, crew-cut good looks, considerable charm—at least when he felt the necessity—thorough indoctrination in the American Way of Life, and intimate and revealing knowledge of the Russian Mind, gained at first hand through harrowing wartime experiences as a prisoner of the Reds, within the space of a few short years made him the State's most-listened-to radio news commentator, its most eagerly sought Chamber of Commerce and Rotary Club and convention speaker, and its most publicized and vocal opponent of Creeping Socialism, Government Interference in Anything, Radicals, Communists, Red Spies, High Taxes, the Welfare State, and all other things Evil and Subversive.

Joe was also for a lot of things, most of which he lumped together in such words and phrases as What Our Forefathers Stood For, the Things That Made the Nation Great, Rugged Individualism, Self-Reliance, Freedom, Democracy, and his old stand-by, the American Way of Life. But it was the things that he was against that made his reputation.

The times were made to order for his orations. Joe couldn't miss and he knew it. Self-Reliance was going to pay off.

It did. When Bill Tucker approached him about handling publicity for Colonel Harvey Pollock in his campaign for the Senate, his fifteen-minute, five-day-a-week broadcast was heard over a twenty-three station network in the State, he was asking and getting $250 for his convention appearances, and his income was about $25,000 a year.

Tucker's proposition, even backed by an offer of a place on the future Senator's staff, with all its attendant possibilities, probably would not have interested him, involving as it did considerable financial sacrifice and the loss of his beloved radio forum.

But Tucker (who was perhaps the only man in the whole State who had taken the trouble to investigate Joe's exact activities while in Berlin) turned the negotiations over to Colonel Pollock.

For Joe, it was love at first sight.

The bluff, hearty Colonel personified the successful American male to him. The program which the Colonel outlined to him struck him as being the exact thing he had been driving at all along. Could he, Joe Harrison, do less than his all to replace that pinko, Ralph Anson, with this real American?

Now, consuming cigarettes in the booth in the rapidly emptying coffee shop, Joe was more or less rid of his blues. What Tucker had said had made its mark—how he had acted had made more of one. When Tucker was sure of something, Joe had found, nine times out of ten whatever it was he was sure of usually worked out.

And Tucker had been sure that the Colonel was going to win the runoff election. No doubt of that. Therefore Joe's outlook on that matter had brightened considerably.

Joe harbored, without admitting it, a rather nervous respect for Tucker. This was in part due to Tucker's demonstrated abilities, but more so to the fact that Tucker had been at pains to let fall certain hints that left in Joe's mind no doubt that Tucker was well aware of the exact extent of Joe's harrowing experiences as a prisoner of the Reds.

It was Tucker who bothered Joe now. A vague worry had begun to grow in him not too long after he took his post with the Pollock forces, but it had been swallowed up in the tremendous pre-election excitement, had been shoved to the back of his mind in his mistaken elation at the prospect of victory.

This worry was the fact that Joe knew—or realized now—that he was being used for what could be got out of him and at the same time was being pushed to the background in matters of decision and policy. He was becoming—no doubt about it—a flunky.

He did not blame Colonel Pollock for this state of affairs. In fact, he suspected that the Colonel himself was also being used. They were both becoming tools in the satanic hands of Tucker.

I'm in a corner all right, Joe thought. That Tucker is just riding the Colonel and me for what we're worth. And if I don't watch my step, I'm going to find myself out on my ass.

It was clear that something had to be done. He, Joe Harrison, had to take his rightful place at the Colonel's side. Tucker had to be put in his own place and the Colonel had to be protected against this sharper.

But how?

Joe didn't know. For one thing—and Joe didn't hesitate to admit this fact—Tucker and Tucker alone could win the election for them. Therefore it was not so simple a problem as simply getting Tucker out of the way. He had to be kept on to do his job, but at the same time he didn't have any business cutting Joe Harrison out of the limelight, either. Not by a damn sight.

But there was a way, somewhere. After all, Tucker wasn't perfect. In fact, nobody was. There was a flaw in Tucker somewhere. As Joe saw it, if this flaw could be discovered and judiciously exploited, when the last vote was counted and Colonel Pollock became Senator Pollock, Tucker could be, so to speak, exiled to Siberia.

Like I'll be, Joe thought. Just exactly like I'll be if I don't watch my goddam step.

So, sitting there smoking innumerable cigarettes and staring moodily into the ash tray, Joe made up his mind to find the flaw in Tucker. It was not, he told himself, entirely self-protection. After all, the Colonel was above the more earthy details of the political game. The Colonel had to be protected too.

There was a fine man for you, all right. Too bad he had to get tangled up with a cynic like that Tucker. I'd like to see the Colonel this afternoon, tell him I know he's still going to win in spite of all the stinking pinks that voted for that Anson.

Suddenly Joe was ashamed of his earlier discouragement. The Colonel wouldn't have been thinking that way. He had too much faith, too much courage. And if the Colonel hadn't lost faith, who was he, Joe Harrison, to give up without a fight?

I'm glad I got on to Tucker, he thought. I'm glad I finally see him for what he is, for the Colonel's sake. It doesn't matter much about me, but I can't let anything happen to the Colonel. I don't know what I'm going to do yet, but for the Colonel's sake, I'm going to do something.

He no longer thought of his own motives for mistrusting Tucker. His concern for the Colonel's well-being swallowed up his concern for himself. There was not a selfish bone in Joe's body.

He paid his bill and went upstairs to the Bright Leaf Room. With a sincere sense of dedication to a worthy task, he sat down at his typewriter and began to work.

Chapter Three

The ringing of the telephone woke Vivian.

For a moment she could not remember where she was. She lay on her back, her scalp itchy and tingling from her tumbled hair, and looked with dazed eyes at the uninspiring off-white of the ceiling.

The phone rang two more times before she was able to focus on the light fixture in the center of the ceiling and recall that this was Number Fifteen at the Motel Toledo. The fixture had been her landmark every morning during her stay.

She had never become used to sleeping anywhere but in her own airy, high-walled room at home, and she often woke up with this same puzzlement as to her whereabouts. A whole series of lighting fixtures, rug patterns, wall-paper designs, and plaster cracks existed somewhere in her mind, identifying places in which she had slept for more than one or two nights.

The phone rang again, beginning to sound a little impatient. She rolled over on her side and immediately became aware that she badly needed to go to the bathroom. She fumbled at the phone and got the receiver to her ear in time for the ear-splitting buzz of another exasperated ring.

"Hello?" Her eyes roved toward the traveling clock on the glass-topped dresser. My God, she thought, it's one o'clock.

"Vivian?"

"Yes?" Her eyes seemed to be trying to inspect one another.

"This is Bill."

"You woke me up, you fiend."

"I'm sorry. I thought sure you'd be up by now. Started to call you earlier, matter of fact."

· 36 ·

"Good thing you didn't. I'm not like some people. I *need* sleep."

The telephone harshened his laugh, but she could tell he was pleased. He's got two kinds of laughs, she thought, and that's the amused one.

She rolled over on her back again and let her head relax against the pillow. Her mouth suggested that she had been chewing an Angora sock.

"I'm sorry I couldn't take you home last night," Tucker said. "I just couldn't get away. They were running me crazy."

She groped on the bedside table for a cigarette.

"I'll never forgive you. But you'd have just had to take a taxi back to your place. I had my car."

She found her pack of Chesterfields. It was empty.

"What are you doing this afternoon?"

"Packing. Tucker, have you got a cigarette?"

"Sure."

"Smoke one, will you? I'm all out, but maybe if I know you're smoking I can imagine how it tastes."

"You sound hard up."

"I am hard up. If I don't have a cigarette in the morning, I eat my young."

"You don't have any young. Do you?"

"I can't carry on a witty conversation at this hour of the night, Tucker. Is this call business or pleasure?"

"Social, purely social. Official reminder that you're having dinner with me tonight. And it's one o'clock in the afternoon, case you didn't know."

"Delightful. Will you please hang up now so I can go buy some cigarettes?" And so I can go to the bathroom too and comb my hair and bathe my eyes and brush my teeth, she thought.

What a time to be talking about a dinner date.

"All right," Tucker said. "Be that way then. Wish I could help with the packing but I'm already overdue out at the Colonel's house."

"Is he crushed today?"

"Haven't seen him yet."

"He ought to be. And you too. I thought you'd be off drowning your sorrows somewhere."

"Not me. I'm always cheerful. Especially in adversity."

"How revolting."

"Oh, go on and eat your young. I'll hang up. See you about seven?"

"Fine. 'By, Bill."

She hung up and got quickly out of bed. Three minutes later she emerged from the bathroom, combed, face-washed, teeth-brushed, but still cigarette-less. She wore a white Tommy-coat, trimmed in red, which barely reached below her hips.

She peeked through the drawn Venetian blinds into the court-yard of Motel Toledo. It was a bright, hot day and she did not particularly enjoy the prospect of spending much of it in Number Fifteen, packing to return to Jamestown.

But tonight—now that she was over the hump of awakening —would be fun anyway. Bill Tucker was an interesting man and she liked him, even if they had sort of started off on the wrong foot. And even if . . .

But that's his business. That's the way he is, and if there's one thing I know it's that you have to take people the way they are and either like them or not like them. And I like Bill. I guess I like Bill.

She tossed the Tommy-coat on the rumpled bed and glanced at herself in the mirror. As always, she wished that she were not so tall and that her breasts were not so large. This morning, however, she decided to skip her usual calisthenics. The hell with how much I weigh, she thought. She began to dress.

As she selected her clothes and hurried into them, the night before began to recall itself to her. It was not so much the licking administered to Colonel Pollock and Tucker that came back to her as it was the thought of the tremendous hurly-burly and excitement of the two political headquarters at the Stonewall Jackson.

They get a real bang out of their politics down here, she thought. I'm glad I'm a neutral so I can watch both sides.

And drink with both sides and get shoved around with both

and smoke in my eyes and my feet stepped on with both, too. That was some night you had yourself, sister.

Still, it had been fun. It had been exciting to watch the returns come in, slow at first, then faster and faster, until finally there were new totals every few minutes.

You wouldn't know there were that many people in this State, till they all voted yesterday, she thought.

And the way the crowd's excitement and tension grew and got a little louder and a little wilder every time they chalked up another precinct on the blackboard. The way they kept getting happier and surer and more sweatily victorious in Anson Headquarters, and the way, finally, in Pollock Headquarters people just began to stand around the blackboard and shake their heads and then to drift away to wherever they had come from.

It had been about that time that Fred Pollock had said what he did to her.

The drunken pup! He ought to have his mouth washed out with soap. Lye soap.

She had just come back from a quick tour of the victorious Anson establishment and was mixing herself a highball at the Pollock bar.

Fred had sidled up to her and watched, slack mouth grinning, his breath reeking of whisky. His tie was awry and she remembered feeling surprise at that, for Fred, if nothing else, was usually a good dresser and a neat one.

She had finished mixing her highball and tipped the glass to him.

"Mud in your eye, Fred."

Fred was still grinning.

"Are you sleeping with Tucker?" he said.

Well, I'm no high-school girl, Vivian thought. I wasn't hearing something that shocked my innocent mind. But to have that weak-livered little sot say that to me—I wish I'd slapped him.

At least, she told herself, I didn't act shocked. I was pretty good in there. What I said was a pretty good squelch, if I do say so myself.

She had looked at him coolly and measured him up and down

· 39 ·

with her eyes and said calmly, "No, I'm not. Would you like to sleep with him?"

If Mother could have heard that one. Oh well, it served him right. It got rid of him in a hurry.

She was dressed now and she gave herself a final check in the mirror before going to the Motel Toledo lunchroom. Her blue eyes were a trifle shadowed from the long night and her face was somewhat peaked under her dark hair.

No, she thought, I'm not sleeping with anyone, Mr. Fred Pollock. Least of all with Bill Tucker.

She turned to get a profile view of herself and laughed softly.

Tucker should be so lucky, she thought. And was immediately amused at her own vanity.

Or maybe I should be so lucky. After all, I've already admitted I'm no high-school girl. And I haven't ever, not once, denied that I'm like every other woman I ever knew when it comes to wanting a man of my own.

And there's the rub, she thought. I never did like excursion trains.

When she stepped into the courtyard the bright sunlight made her blink. She hurried across the asphalt, a tall young woman with long, fine legs, who might have been rushing to meet her husband for a late lunch.

Actually, she was hurrying to buy cigarettes.

Harvey Pollock's home was in Forest Park. The route to it lay past the Capital Country Club, of which Tucker was a member. The country club had originally been a mile or two out from town, but the city had gradually expanded in its direction. Now the golf course was surrounded by suburban homes, paved streets, and on one hole electric wires provided an overhead hazard.

Tucker was an expert golfer. This was not because he enjoyed the game, which he considered somewhat silly. It was because it was a definite social, business, and political asset that he played it at all, and it was because he never played anything, or did anything, which he was not able to play or do well that he consistently scored in the high seventies.

The fourth tee was at the corner of Sunset Drive and Oakmont Avenue, and the fairway stretched out along Sunset, then curved away on a dogleg to the green. As Tucker turned slowly from Oakmont onto Sunset, a foursome was just coming up on the tee. Tucker knew one of the men by sight, but the others were strangers.

The foursome had employed two caddies, each carrying two bags. Tucker did not approve of overburdening caddies. Anybody that belonged to the club didn't, in his opinion, have to pinch pennies that way.

You'd never have caught old man Sprague at anything like that. Tucker could remember how the old man had always had a fifty-cent piece ready for his caddie after a round. And that was a lot of money in those days. A hell of a lot of money. Not ever a quarter or a couple of dimes but always a shiny new half dollar.

If that old bastard had stayed on the golf course all his life he wouldn't have been such a louse, Tucker thought. He was all right to caddie for, at least. And that's more than you can say for most folks, at that.

1926

The boy is in sight of the house when he turns the corner. It sits at the end of a dead-end street—gray-painted, wood-shingled, a square-sided box, a porch in front and a chimney rising to the left.

The street is not paved. It need not be, for not a man living on it owns an automobile. On each side of it stand four houses, none of them differing at all from the ninth house, which faces them from the end of the street. The boy's house.

The yards are different, however. Five of them are of bare sandy earth without blade of grass or bush to hold down the dust that swirls from them in summer. Since the street has no curb, these yards are indistinguishable from the street and the street only stops at the steps of their houses.

A sixth house has a chinaberry tree to the left of its door. From a gnarled branch of this tree hangs a single strand of frayed rope which is knotted around a rubber tire. The tire now hangs motionless and plumb, but it is a satisfactory swing when in use. The ground beneath the tree is littered with yellowing and malodorous chinaberries.

Two more houses have hedges in front of them. One hedge is recently trimmed, with an arch of green rising above the break which leads to the steps of the house. The other hedge, which is actually a continuation of the first, is untrimmed and nearly hides its house from view. The line between trimmed and untrimmed is as plain as a deep scar across a man's jaw.

The boy approaches his house. The ninth house. It has a lawn. At least it has, in patches, sun-yellowed grass struggling in the dry sand. It has a spiraea bush at each side of the steps and the walk from the street to the steps is lined with bricks, half-sunk in the sand and slanting at a forty-five degree angle toward the house. This border forms a saw-toothed but not unpleasing effect. On the outer side of each row of bricks, verbena is green against the gray sand.

Over this street of nine houses triumphantly hangs the hum and whine and roar of Sprague Number Two. This street belongs to Sprague Number Two and its nine houses belong to Sprague Number Two. The people who live in them also belong to Sprague Number Two.

The only one among them who will not admit this—and he from birth a man who has faced fact unblinkingly—sits upon the single two-by-four railing which encloses the porch of the house beyond the brick and verbena walkway. The boy from the moment of his entrance upon the street has been aware of the man sitting there, one lank leg drawn up under his chin, the other extending easily to the porch floor, the head turned, tense, rigid, almost as if to pick from the omnipresent song of the cotton mill the individual sound of one machine or of one man.

The boy enters the brick-edged walk. The man does not move. The boy's foot touches the bottom step, the second, the third. He does not look at the man.

"Where you been, boy?"

The man's voice is flat and toneless. It is hardly distinguishable from the sound of Sprague Number Two. He still does not move.

The boy stops on the top step. He looks at his father's back, at the gaunt profile, the dark stain spreading away from his armpit.

"School," he says. "Some of us got up a ball game."

"No, you ain't. You ain't been at no school."

The boy is silent. He moves onto the porch. His face turns sullen, it comes out in the corners of the mouth, the slight narrowing of his eyes.

"Where you been, boy?"

The boy knows from long experience that he cannot lie. It is not that he will not lie, but rather that he knows it is no use to lie. Not to his father. Nor is it that his father can automatically tell lie from truth. It is rather that, and soon now, his father will look at him and his eyes will compel the truth from him.

The long leg swings to the porch floor, and the man stands. He is tall, but a lifetime at the loom has robbed him of his rightful height. His shoulders hump forward and the blades protrude against the back of his shirt. He turns and his thin arms hang straight, clear forward of his narrow chest. His neck, long and scrawny, pushing out from the shoulders, seems to be eternally stretched to the rigid, expectant head.

"I ask to know where you been, boy. I ain't a-goin to ask no more."

"Golf course," the boy says. His voice takes the hint of sullenness from the mouth. He meets his father's eyes steadily.

These eyes seem to bulge from the protruding bones of the face. They are blue, above a sharp, angular nose and pale, angular lips. They seem, like the eyes of a fly, to see in all directions.

"Cut school, I reckin?"

The voice is neither harsh nor gentle. It has no tone and gathers force from the lack, the way a single unvarying note of sound gathers force with prolongation.

"Teacher send you a note?"

"Nope. Came by an talked to your ma."

"Bitch," the boy says.

The hand seems to flash from the man's side, huge, thin like the rest of him, its knuckles and joints and fingers knobs and lumps and angles. It cracks across the boy's face. The boy takes a step backward and puts his hand to his jaw. His eyes do not leave his father.

"Dirty mouth. Ain't I learned you yet?"

The boy does not answer. Bitch, he thinks, dirty old bitch.

"Tole your ma you been cuttin evry afternoon."

The boy nods.

"Goin to the golf course evry day?"

He nods again. Again the quick, explosive flash of the hand. This time the boy does not move.

"What for?"

"Make me some money. Caddyin."

The man's face does not change, but his shoulders seem to straighten slightly.

"What's that?"

"You carry the bags with the clubs. They pay you so's they ain't got to carry them for themself."

"Who you carry bags for?"

Ain't none of your business, the boy thinks. Ain't none of your goddam business.

"Lots of them," he says. "Mister Sprague mostly."

The man nods. In motion his head does not lose the tense expectancy.

"How much you make?"

"Fifty cent today."

"Fifty cent. Work an hour for that in the mill."

"I ain't goin to work in no mill," the boy says.

"I know you ain't. You ain't goin to carry no more bags for Dan Sprague neither."

"All right. I just wanted to make me some money."

"You ain't got to make no money yet. I'll feed you an put cloth to your back."

The boy does not answer. He puts his hands in his pockets. The half dollar is moist and warming against his palm.

"You goin to school, boy. You goin to learn."

"All right. I ain't said I wasn't."

"Sam Tucker's boy ain't a-goin to be no mill hand. You hear?"

The man's body turns to the sound of the mill.

"I been carryin Dan Sprague's bags all my life. You ain't a-goin to do it. Not even on no golf course."

The boy is still silent. The screen door of the house pushes open and a woman comes out on the porch. She is not tall, nor is she short. She wears an apron and her hair is gray. Her eyes are squinted and myopic for the want of glasses.

"You ought not to devil your pa, Billy," she says.

"He ain't devlin me. He's devlin hisself is all."

"I was only tryin to get me some money," the boy says.

"I got some supper ready now." The woman peers from one to the other.

"Give your ma the fifty cent, boy."

He looks at the man. The bulgy eyes pound at him. He takes his hand from his pocket and gives the woman the round and shining coin.

At the table he eats hungrily. The woman brings the food from the stove to the table, and he and the man are half-through before she sits down to eat.

Once the man lifts his head from his plate. He chews solemnly on a piece of corn bread, and his head is cocked and listening.

"He work you pretty hard, boy?"

"Naw. Jus carryin that bag."

"Treat you like dirt, hey?"

"Naw. Bought me an ice-cream cone today. Mister Sprague's mighty nice, pears to me."

He hears his mother's quick intake of breath. I don't care, he thinks, I don't care what he says. Mister Sprague *is* nice. He *is*.

The man does not seem to have heard the words. He lowers his head and begins to eat again. His jaw moves rhythmically and his chewing is audible. Then, once more, he speaks, "He wouldn't miss a hunnurd ice-cream cones."

Later the boy lies in bed. He thinks of Mr. Sprague and the other men who play golf with him. He sees their clean and beautiful clothes and their smooth tanned skin and he hears the laughter; he sees too, atop the long hill that slopes away to the golf course, the cool whiteness and greenness of the country club and the deep chairs upon its veranda that looked, from the caddie shop, as if they might enfold all of you and smother you in ease.

He sees the shiny automobiles parked behind the club, the steel and chrome of them, and the vast wide expanse of their seats. He has never ridden in an automobile.

But as his mind sees these, his eyes pierce the darkness and he sees also the drab gray of his room and the hard iron bed and the bare floor and the single framed picture of Jesus on the Cross hanging on the wall. He hears his father's belligerent snores; the smell of supper lingers in the house. He turns over and the rusty springs of his bed squeak.

And coming in the window and through the walls, like night mist, he—not hears—is conscious of the biding and triumphant sound of the spindles and the looms, the enduring humming rumble of the mill.

I'm going to get out of here, he thinks. I'm going to be like Mister Sprague. I'm going to play golf and have me an automobile and fine clothes and caddies and fifty-cent pieces.

And then, like floodlights flashing across the mill yard, he sees his father's bulging eyes and his mother's squinted ones and is ashamed, reproachful of himself, and suddenly full of love for them. They have to work so hard, he thinks.

But I can't help that, he cries to himself. I can't help it!

Hate fills him for Mr. Sprague and all the other men at the golf club. The bastards, he thinks, the bastards, the *bastards!*

And yet . . . and yet . . .

They can't be all bad. It can't be all their fault either, because they can't be all bad.

They live too beautiful, he thinks. They can't be all bad.

At last he sleeps. Clutched within his hand, still warm and

moist and beckoning, is the fifty-cent piece which, like the price of a pulled tooth, he has found beneath his pillow.

Tucker parked his car in the street in front of Harvey Pollock's white colonial home. The driveway was already occupied by Cousin Hadley's green Buick, Steve Gary's black Cadillac and Zeb Ruggles' robin's-egg blue Cadillac. Directly in front of Tucker's car was a black Ford convertible which Tucker knew belonged to Fred Pollock. The Colonel's own black Packard was not in evidence and Tucker guessed it to be in the garage.

Asphalt stepping-stones led across Pollock's lawn to the wide veranda. The Colonel's lawn was green, despite the hot sun, and his grounds were trim and well-kept. Comfortable porch furniture was scattered across the flagged veranda and green window shutters seemed to radiate coolness.

Tucker punched the doorbell and chimes sounded inside the house. In a moment Fred opened the door.

"Well," he said, "the mob's all here now."

Tucker could not decide if this was pleasantry or sarcasm. He decided to accept it as the former. He stepped inside and Fred closed the door after him.

"I'm a little late, Fred. Had to make a phone call."

"Well, they can't start without you. Nothing does."

No doubt about that one, Tucker thought. But let it pass, let it pass. I've had my argument for today with him.

"Where are they?"

"The library."

The house was shadowy and cool. From the wide hallway in which they stood, the curving stairway vanished into the second story. A double door to the right led to the sitting room and on the left another double door opened into the library. The hallway was spacious and uncluttered.

Tucker never failed to marvel that Martha Pollock could provide a home like this—or even want to—for the Colonel. Or that he could inhabit it.

"I'll go on in," he said. Fred shrugged.

Tucker stepped to the library door.

"Hello, Bill," Martha called from beyond the open doors of the sitting room.

That goddam voice, Tucker thought. Everything she says is like something you whisper in bed.

He turned and crossed the hall to the sitting room.

"If I'd known I was going to see you," he said, "I'd have worn my best suit."

She laughed. That's worse, Tucker thought. That laugh is worse than her voice. He looked at her and his stomach went shivery and empty.

"That one is fine," she said. "How are you today?"

She sat in a deep easy chair, a dark-haired woman with dark eyes, something misty lurking in them, her skin startlingly white and smooth, her knees crossed before her, and her curving calves and slim ankles visible. Her lips were parted in a cool and serene smile, and a pearl necklace was white and still and rich around her finely boned neck.

"A little the worse for wear," Tucker said. "It was a pretty tough night all around."

"I'll bet he hasn't gotta nother suit," Fred said.

"Fred!"

Tucker looked at Fred. The boy was leaning against the rich wood of the mantel, a highball glass cool and frosted in his hand. His eyes were bleared and hostile.

Martha Pollock stood up.

"I think you'd better leave the room, Fred."

"Going anyway. Goddam house beginning to smell."

"The goddam house can do without you for a while," she said.

What the hell do you do in a case like this? Tucker thought. Stand around and look silly like I'm doing? Or bash the bastard in the mouth like I want to? This kid is psycho. Absolutely psycho.

"All right. I'm going. All *right*."

Fred walked to the door. He bumped against the arm of a chair on the way. Martha and Tucker stood watching until he had gone out.

"I'm sorry," Martha said. "I'm afraid Fred drinks too much sometimes."

"Forget it. He just doesn't like politicians, I guess. Can't blame him, at that."

She nodded.

He was standing close to her and he looked steadily at her, and in her eyes and her face and her manner, he made a discovery.

He discovered that Martha Pollock was saying and doing what seemed to be the required things after a social nuisance had been committed in her well-ordered and impeccable house, and by her son at that, but that she did not really give a damn, either for what Fred had said or for what Tucker had felt, or for that matter for either of them at all.

Tucker discovered this, surely and indisputably, and it immediately changed his whole outlook on the matter. It switched him instantly from the embarrassed if unwitting object of the social nuisance to an angry man who had been cheapened, not by the nuisance, but by her disinterest.

Crudely, obviously, he let his eyes fall over her body. He watched her high, firm breasts move with her breathing and he looked down to the slim hips, rounded under her tight skirt, and on to the silken and enticing legs.

She watched him as he looked at her.

"Nothing bothers you. Does it, Martha?"

"Some things."

No, they don't, he thought. Nothing bothers you because nothing interests you. Maybe not even yourself.

"What bothers you?" he said.

"A man looking at me like that."

"You're worth looking at. But it ought not to stop there."

"It will though. With you anyway. And I think it's time for you to go too."

He smiled.

"You don't have any call to pretend you're mad at me, Martha. We understand each other too well for that."

"Do we?"

"That's what they say in books and movies. It's a silly question and you're not a silly woman."

She smiled now, not with mirth. Not with mockery either. But it was as near to that, Tucker knew, as to anything that could be defined.

"What kind of woman am I?"

"A beautiful woman. A rich woman. Lots of kinds of woman."

"Including a married woman."

"Touché. I almost forgot that."

"That's not smart politics, is it? And you're a smart politician."

Tucker smiled and turned toward the door.

"Well," he said, "you're right about that."

He was almost to the door when she spoke again.

"You're right about something too."

"What's that?"

"I'm not angry."

"I knew that. You probably don't know how to be."

They looked at each other a long time, she calm and expressionless, Tucker smiling slightly. The best-looking woman I ever saw, Tucker was thinking. I wonder how much it costs her to stay that way, at her age. If she had a heart inside of that body she'd be something. She'd really be something.

"Actually," she said, "I'm not even interested."

"Well, I knew that too," he said.

Chapter Four

Heah's Cousin Tuckuh now!"

The drawl-dripping voice of State Senator F. Warren Hadley
was the first to greet Tucker as he stepped into the library. It
was usually the first voice to lift itself on any occasion.

"Hello, Cousin," Tucker said. "Sorry I'm late."

"Tha's all right," Hadley rumbled. "Been drinkin some good
Pollock likker to kill time."

Steve Gary turned from the portable bar at the far end of the
room and came toward Tucker with two glasses in his hand.

"You need a drink, Bill. We all need a drink."

"Thanks, Steve."

There were four men in the room, besides Tucker. Colonel
Pollock was at his desk. Cousin Hadley had spread his ponderous bulk over an easy chair and placed his feet on a has-
sock. Steve Gary had returned to the little bar. Zeb Ruggles
sprawled at full length on a brown leather sofa, his shirt open
at the neck, his hands clasped behind his head.

"Give Cousin another one, Steve. Oil his creakin old bones
up a little," he said now, his Adam's apple bobbing visibly in
his long thin neck.

Cousin peered amiably at Ruggles. He was used to sly cracks
at his whisky capacity and he was used to the lazy mockery of
Ruggles' voice.

"Cousin," Hadley said, "tha's the best idea I heard yet." He
held out his glass and Tucker handed it to Gary.

"Look at that man," Hadley said, pointing to Ruggles and
glancing about the room. "Ain't a muscle in his body. You ever
done a day's work, Zeb?"

"Hell, no. Neither have you, you old bastard."

The men chuckled. Gary put the glass, refilled, in Cousin's hand.

A real nice boy, that Zeb is, Hadley thought. Real smart, too. I do believe he's got more on the ball than his old daddy had. And that's saying something. Leastways the old man never had that power company making money like Zeb has got it. Best stock I own. Damn f'it ain't.

Looks lazy. Lying around like that, even in his own office. Like he wouldn't move if his britches was on fire. Nothing working about that boy but his brains.

"When I get as old as you," Cousin said, nodding at Zeb, "maybe I kin afford to take it easy like that."

"Go way, ol folks. My grandpappy knew you when you were a full-grown man." Ruggles was twenty years younger than Hadley.

The men laughed again. Steve Gary cleared his throat.

"To get down to business . . ." he said.

Zeb Ruggles' brown eyes turned to the neat little man in the gray suit. That bastard's going to make trouble, he thought. Just as sure as hell. Trust a goddam zealot to make trouble sooner or later.

He wiggled deeper into the leather sofa, watching Gary, listening to the talk of the others.

"We were saying," Colonel Pollock said to Tucker, "that yesterday was a little worse than we figured on."

Tucker nodded.

"A *little* worse!" Gary said. "My God."

"But on the other hand we didn't do too badly ourselves."

Tucker nodded again.

"Thanks to Rooster Ed," Ruggles chuckled.

"Well, we did all right by ourselves," the Colonel insisted. "We got a lot bigger vote than we planned on."

"Everybody did."

"And that," Ruggles said, "ought to prove something."

"It proves that Anson is a vote-getting sonofabitch."

Gary's voice was flat and carefully toneless, but Ruggles caught the nervousness behind it.

"I don't think any of us ever doubted that," Tucker said. "If we did, we were fools. Personally it looks to me as if everything is coming along just the way we figured."

"That's what I was saying when you came in." Pollock was smiling broadly.

"Well sho now," Cousin said. "We in the second primary, ain't we?"

"By the skin of our teeth." Gary's voice now held a plain hint of annoyance, Ruggles thought.

He studied the little man, who sat tensely in a deep armchair. Gary's steel-rimmed glasses and conservative suit, Ruggles decided, made him look more like a history teacher than the czar of a rayon-weaving empire which branched out over half the world from the precise little town he owned and operated as his company headquarters. Even his voice seemed to be coated with classroom dust.

"I don't know. We may have underestimated Anson. Even after all the planning we did. Too many people see the man as Santa Claus. Or Jesus Christ himself. It's hard to beat a man who promises things."

"On the other hand," Ruggles said, "who the hell wants Jesus Christ in Congress? Or Santa Claus?"

"Steve, are you suggesting we're on the wrong track?" Tucker said. "Because if you are—"

"I'm not suggesting anything yet. I'm just saying how it looks to me."

Gary glared at Tucker and his glasses seemed to flash angrily. I don't have to take anything from you, Mr. Mastermind, Gary thought. I don't have to take anything from anybody.

"Keep your shirt on," Tucker said. "No call to lose your temper."

"How much money do you have invested in this thing, Tucker?"

"None. And don't tell me how much you've put in either. I don't want to hear it. I don't want—"

"Now, now," Colonel Pollock said. "You two cool off. This is no time for bickering."

Tucker grinned. "Go on, Steve," he said. "I won't interrupt."

You'd better not, Gary thought. I could break you, Tucker.

I could fix you good. You and that tongue of yours and that God Almighty air you put on and the way you act like nobody has any sense but you.

I'd like to see you spend one day at my desk. Just one. It'd take me a month to straighten things out afterward, but it'd be worth it. Just to see you sweat for once in your life. You cheap lint head.

"The point is," he said (that was a favorite phrase of his—Tucker had heard him declare that "the point" was a half-dozen different things, all in the same session), "that so far we've concentrated—at your direction, Tucker—on yelling about Anson being for a welfare state and socialism and being tied up with the unions, and we've hinted around that maybe he's pretty close to the Communists too. All those organizations he joined and all. Well, to my way of thinking, it hasn't worked so well. Look at the vote he got anyway."

"It was a big one, all right," Tucker admitted. Let the bastard talk, he thought. Let him get it all off his mind.

"Well—maybe we *should* change tactics a little. Maybe we ought to lay off the welfare state and the socialism angles. The truth is—and I never thought I'd live to see the day—the people just aren't scared of that kind of talk any more. Too much welfare. Too many handouts. All that sort of thing." He shook his fist angrily. "It looks to me like the old American backbone and spirit of independence, the things that made this country what it used to be, are just about shot to hell!"

And right there is where you are as wrong as you can get, Tucker thought. Not about the backbone. You've got a point there. You're wrong about what's happened to it.

The Communists scared it out of us is what happened to it. They've got us scared. They've got us climbing up the walls right here in the richest, biggest, strongest country in the history of the world.

They've got us scared because we think they aren't human. Everybody else this country ever fought—hell, they were just people. They put their pants on in the morning and took them off at night, one leg after the other.

But the Men in the Kremlin—nobody wears pants in the Kremlin. Can you imagine Stalin sitting on the john?

They only have supermen over there, we think. Only supermen who know what we think before we think it, who have a spy planted on every city block and a hand in every train wreck, only supermen who planned twenty years ago what is going to happen tomorrow.

And these supermen, following the design of some vast, undefeatable plot, have, we think, a party member in every government agency in this country, from the State Department down to the County Sheriff's office. They have, conservatively, five hundred million men under arms, each of them nearly eight feet tall and a raper of women. They have bombs full of germs and wagonloads of atom bombs and God only knows what else.

No, the Communists—which is to say the Russians—aren't human. They're the kind of supermen we laughed at the Nazis for claiming to be. They're the Reds, the cruel brilliant crafty scheming invincible Reds.

And they've got us scared for the first time in history. The Indians couldn't do it and neither could the wilderness. The Redcoats couldn't scare us, our own people couldn't do it in the Civil War, and the goddamned galleys of Spain couldn't do it either. The Germans and even those creepy little Japs couldn't make us turn a hair. But the Russians have got us just plain scared shitless.

That's where the backbone went, Mr. Gary, and that's where you begin to be wrong. Because we got ourselves into this fix. The Russians couldn't do it alone. We had to help them.

Us with our investigating committees and our big-mouthed Senators and our Joe Harrisons and our loyalty oaths and our lists of subversive organizations and our probes and counter-probes, and our everlasting goddamned certainty that every man who says out loud that maybe the doctors are bringing social-ized medicine on themselves, or who once sent a bundle of old clothes to Spain or said a good word for Old Age Assistance or even hinted that the government might have a right to stick its nose in business every now and then to see what's going on— that everybody who ever said or even thought anything like that, anytime in his life, is a cog in the plot, a member of the party, with a private built-in-telephone line right to the desk where Stalin sits, the old superman himself sitting there, smirking and planning and scheming and reading over the plot again and knowing what we're thinking before we think it.

Oh, we did it to ourselves, all right. Because we began to doubt. We began to doubt that we could fight the Reds on our own terms, in our own way. We began to think our way was all right only when nobody threatened it. We began to think maybe we had to do it their way if we wanted to live and do well and save democracy. And then, slowly, surely, the probers and the loudmouths and professional flag-wavers began to do it their way, the Red way.

And now anybody who won't go along, who won't play it that way, who thinks we had enough guts and muscle and brains in this country to beat the Reds with our own weapons, who has enough guts and muscle and brains left to say so—anybody like that, Mr. Gary, is maybe a Red himself.

Don't tell me we can't scare the people. Don't tell me they aren't already scared. Don't tell me Harvey Pollock got all those votes because he's got a pleasant smile. Two months ago he wouldn't have got ten thousand. Ralph Anson would have got ninety per cent of the whole damned vote.

Only not now he won't, and not ever again. Because every day we scare them a little bit more and every day more of them decide maybe he's a Red too.

Given enough time you can even prove Santa Claus is a member of the party. He wears a red suit, doesn't he?

All of this kaleidoscoped through Tucker's mind in the time it took him to set his glass down on an end table, get out a cigarette, light it, and drop the match in an ash tray. He recognized that it was a protest pitched in too high a key, a little shrill, a little unjust.

But he knew also that it was essentially true. We're all a bunch of bastards, he thought.

He rubbed his jaw reflectively. And then he realized they were waiting for him to speak.

Tucker could not help the pride which, quite suddenly, twitched at his stomach, moving other thoughts rudely aside. A candidate for the Senate, a powerful politician, the head of an industrial empire, the president of the largest power company in the State. They were waiting for him to speak, waiting for his opinion.

A long way, he thought. I've come a long way. I've waited a long time. And I'll never be without this again. Never in this world.

He caught a swift wink from Zeb Ruggles, saw the slight frown of worry shading the Colonel's eyes, watched Cousin Hadley placidly licking at a Churchillian cigar. Then he looked straight at Steve Gary.

"I could give you an argument, Steve. A damn good argument. But it's not necessary. We never planned to beat Anson on the Red issue alone."

The room was very quiet. They've been waiting for this, Tucker thought. They've been waiting for me to say it, for me to start it. They haven't got the guts.

He puffed slowly at his cigarette, letting it dangle from his lips, caressing his chin with his fingers.

"A second primary," he said, "is where you separate the sheep from the goats. You don't serve pink lemonade in a second primary."

Cousin Hadley chuckled hugely around his cigar. Tucker grinned at him.

"You all know," he said, "how we originally conceived this thing—"

"Let's not be modest," Ruggles said. "You wrote the whole damn book, Tuck, and we all know it. We're just the publishers."

The Colonel's frown deepened slightly and Gary seemed to stiffen in his chair.

"That doesn't make any difference, Zeb. The idea was to get enough mileage out of the Red angle—with old McDowell's help —to get us in the second primary. So far that's exactly what we've done."

"All right," Gary said, "but I—"

"Let me finish," Tucker said. He did not see the prim lips tighten. "We didn't stop there. We had this second primary figured too. We had our Sunday curve all planned. I don't see any reason to change now."

"Amen," Ruggles said.

"We were going to keep right on with the Red stuff," Tucker said. He leaned back in his chair and took the cigarette out of his mouth. "And we were going to yell nigger."

The room was still and contained. Cousin Hadley emitted an immense cloud of blue smoke.

"Not the old McDowell kind of race-baiting," Tucker said. "Maybe you can still get away with that in some places but not where white folks wear shoes."

"You're not answering my question," Gary snapped. "I—"

"You never asked me any questions, Steve. But I'm going to give you some answers. In this campaign we keep on charging that Anson is pro-Red. That keeps the ground we've already won, maybe grabs us a little more. We trot out FEPC and antilynch and civil rights, and when the Hartsville decision comes out, we really get rolling on segregation. That was the original plan and far as I'm concerned that's the way it's going to be."

He snubbed out his cigarette in the ash tray.

"That is," he said, "if you want a return on that investment you're worrying about."

Gary stood up.

"I've had enough of your snottiness," he said. "It's time you learned who's—"

"Oh, for Christ sake!"

Gary's head swiveled sharply around. Zeb Ruggles was shaking his head in mock disgust. He still slouched on the sofa.

"Steve, you remind me of when my old man bought his bi-focals, damn if you don't. First day he had the things Ma found where the old boy had peed all over the bathroom floor.

"She asked him what was the idea and the old boy said, 'Mary, those damned bifocals, I had 'em on and I was standing there and damn if I didn't get so interested in looking at the big one I forgot all about what the little one was doing.'"

Cousin Hadley belched into wheezing laughter, and Tucker heard the Colonel's hearty voice chime in. Tucker felt the tension go out of Steve Gary. Even he can't be pompous on top of something like that, Tucker thought. Good old Zeb.

"Now, Steve, goddammit, you're acting just like my old man. You can't see the target because you're worrying about something that doesn't matter any more. I'm not saying there's not some truth in what you said. But Bill's right, too. We got a Sunday curve coming up that's going to make the fast ball we've been throwing look like nothing."

"Maybe so," Gary said. "Maybe so. I just thought I ought to explain the way it looked to me."

He sat down again. That's that for now, Tucker thought. But only for now. The little bastard.

Pollock cleared his throat.

"Then there's no question," he said, "about our going on into the second primary?"

"Hell no," Cousin Hadley said.

"And . . . ah . . . then you gentlemen are willing to keep up the . . . ah . . . financial—"

"Don't worry about money," Gary said. "We're in too deep. We have to go on now."

"Well now," Cousin Hadley said, "down my way folks are mighty long on getting a dollar's pay for a dollar's work. Sort of an old custom, you might say."

Tucker stared at him. The long cigar protruded clownishly from the bald, cherubic head. The pale blue eyes placidly looked at the ceiling.

Why, the old son of a bitch! Tucker thought. The fat old slob is getting ready to pull something. You get off one hot seat onto another.

"Cousin," he said, "I'm surprised at you."

F. Warren Hadley was always called Cousin. He also called everybody else Cousin. This custom dated back to his maiden speech in the State senate—a few old-time newspapermen could still remember the occasion—when he had sweepingly and emotionally declared every citizen of Jasper County his cousin. Not

many elections had passed before he had so designated practically every citizen of the State.

He was the prosperous owner of a string of tobacco ware-
houses in Jasper, one of the easternmost counties of the State.
But Tucker well knew that by unceasing compliance with the
whim of every farmer who brought tobacco to his floors, un-
flagging courtesy to their rawboned and string-haired wives, and
a peculiar ability to see both sides of a political question, become identified with neither, and placate the proponents of both,
Cousin had expanded his political sway from Jasper to Twiggs,
Appling, Shelby and McNairy counties, all of which were nearby
and from all of which farmers brought their tobacco to him for
sale.

Now he sat, rotund and smiling, pink-jowled and gleaming-
scalped, one of the upper hierarchy of Colonel Pollock's campaign command. Tucker did not need to be told how hand-
somely the tight block of counties had come through for Pollock in yesterday's voting; the majority Cousin had delivered for
the Colonel had been a big factor in the second primary project.

Cousin was far from being unaware of the same fact, Tucker
saw, and they both knew that a similar majority in the next
election was a necessity if Harvey Pollock were to go to the
Senate. Cousin was undeniably in a strong bargaining position.

"Why, Cousin Tucker," Hadley said now, "you know I ain't
talkin about myself. It's all my cousins down there round home
I mean. Takes money to turn 'em out."

"We've already poured a lot in there, Cousin. You know that."

"Long way to go," Hadley said, puffing smoke at the ceiling,
"tween now and votin time. Long way to go. Lots of things
could happen."

Tucker considered the problem. With a man like Ruggles you
were always sure of where you stood. Pollock you just had to
show what to do. Gary, well, you had to watch your step with
that dedicated type, sort of baby them along. Like that goddamned Harrison.

But Cousin Hadley was a horse of a different color. He always had one foot in the band wagon and one hanging over
the tailgate. The trick was to keep an eye on that dangling leg

and be all set for the time when it started feeling around for dry land.

Tucker could see Cousin Hadley's toes twitching now. He had never believed it his business to inquire as to how the fat man delivered his territory. So long as he delivered it. But this time, he thought, it's pure blackmail. I don't mind what he's already zilched out of the campaign fund. But I'll be goddamned if I'll sit here and let him force me into paying blackmail.

"How much money would you say all your cousins down there need this trip?" Tucker asked. The words were light and bantering.

Hadley puffed at his cigar. His voice was bland.

"Bout the same as before, Cousin. Like you say, a second primary is sort of where you separate the sheep from the goats. You sure-God do."

"My God!" Colonel Pollock said. "That was for four months. This campaign won't last but a week or two, Hadley! You must be joking. We can't afford—"

"Why, no, Cousin. Don't believe I'd say jokin. Don't believe I would."

Tucker looked at Steve Gary. The prissy lips were pursed tightly and the man's glasses glinted angrily toward Hadley.

Brother Gary, Tucker thought, you were going to tell me, when Zeb shut you up, that it was time I learned who's boss around here. And you're right. It's time everybody did.

"Now, Cousin," he said, his voice still bantering, "be reasonable. Just because you got us by the balls you haven't got to get piggish. You know we can't afford to spend money where it's not needed."

"Sho now. Wouldn't dream of it, Tuck. Fact is, I figure I can cut a corner here and there and scrape by on no more'n I had last time. Wouldn't want any of the folks to switch over to Anson, though."

How quiet it gets in here, Tucker thought, when the chips are really down. How willing these big rich successful men are to let me do the dirty work. He felt his anger rise.

"Cousin, you promised your folks a hospital come next legislature, didn't you?"

The fat man's head, which had been nodding in pleased be-musement, halted suddenly. His eyes remained on the ceiling, teeth clenched on the shortening cigar.

"Pity if they didn't get it," Tucker said.

"They'll get it."

"I don't know, Cousin. People get funny ideas. Lots of folks think the State's spent enough on hospitals already. Fact is, I know some of 'em myself."

A car eased along the street outside and the swish of low-pressure tires seeped into the room. Harvey Pollock cleared his throat. Tucker lit another cigarette. Smoking too much, he thought.

Through the flame of the match he saw Steve Gary's eyes flick rapidly from Hadley to him and back to Hadley. Zeb Ruggles moved easily on the leather sofa.

Cousin Hadley's head came down and a pudgy hand removed the cigar from his lips. Pale blue eyes peered over fat cheeks at Tucker and looked away.

"Come to think of it," he said, "I believe there *was* an un-expended balance in the fund. Clean forgot about it."

"Sure," Tucker said. "Right big balance, wasn't it?"

"Right sizable, Cousin."

Zeb Ruggles sat up suddenly.

"Easy to forget a thing like that," he said. "All we have on our minds. Anybody want a drink besides me?"

"Good idea," Pollock said quickly. "I'll be bartender this time, Steve."

He jumped to his feet and busied himself at the bar, his face carefully expressionless. Tucker puffed thoughtfully at his cig-arette. Hadley sat silent a moment, then began to tell Gary about the vote he'd turned out down his way yesterday. Ruggles slumped back on the sofa.

Chalk up one more, Tucker thought. Another moosehead for the wall of my den. If I had a den. Only that kind of a moose you just have to hope it stays dead.

He felt his muscles aching and forced himself to relax. First Gary, then Hadley. When you were playing for table stakes like that, it took a lot out of you.

And no help at all from Pollock, that bastard. This crew would pluck his eyeballs if I weren't around.

"Say, Tuck," Colonel Pollock called, "who was that lady I saw you with last night?"

"That was no lady," Tucker said. "That was your secretary." The men laughed.

"But didn't I see you steering the professor-gal around?"

"Vivian? Sure. She had a big time. First election headquarters she ever saw."

"The tall brunette?" Ruggles winked at Tucker.

"Yeah. Vivian Reynolds."

"A professor," Pollock said. "Teaches over at State College for Women."

"My God! You mean *that* was a schoolteacher?"

"That's nothing," Cousin Hadley said. "You ought to see this teacher we got down in Jasper. Listen, this gal . . ."

It always starts, Tucker thought. Sooner or later. A bunch of men together, especially if none of them are spring roosters any more, and the stories begin. The shadier the better.

He hardly heard Hadley's yarn. He relaxed in the comfortable chair and thought of Vivian. I've been living with this damned election like it was my wife, he thought. Tonight I won't even think about it. Tonight with Vivian.

Like a vague, chill breeze, Martha Pollock's face floated suddenly in front of his eyes. Impatiently he swept the face from his mind. You ought not to even think about her and Vivian in the same day, he told himself. Bitch like that.

But Vivian. I could get serious with that girl. I could—

He chuckled. Funny how you change your ideas, he thought. Or how folks change them for you. First time I ever saw her, if anybody told me I'd ever be thinking like this—

Tucker was busy in the private office that day. Colonel Pollock was out shaking hands at a county rally in the south of the State.

Tucker punched viciously at the typewriter keyboard. He was a fast but not too accurate hunt-and-pecker, and he often turned out his own correspondence, especially when it was of a more or less private nature. At the moment he was busy on a letter to a key man in one of the on-the-fence counties, and some of the instructions imparted were not for shorthand books or carbon copies.

The door opened and a tall man stuck his head into the room.

"Lady to see you, Bill."

Tucker looked up in annoyance. Another goddam clubwoman looking for a speaker. The Corset Corps.

"A looker." The tall man winked. He was one of the volunteer workers who came in every Saturday.

Junior League then, Tucker thought. The worst kind. Absolutely the worst. Sex and good works mixed. They make me want to puke.

"Okay," he said. "Send her in. Come back and knock in a minute or two, will you?"

"Sure." The door closed.

Tucker pushed away from the typewriter and straightened his tie. You had to impress the bitches. You couldn't win without the women any more.

A soft knock on the door caused the annoyed frown to disappear. A cheerful grin dropped across his face like a theater curtain.

"Come in."

The door opened and a tall girl entered. She glanced quickly at Tucker, closed the door behind her, and stepped forward, holding out her hand like a man. She was smiling slightly. Tucker rose.

"I'm Vivian Reynolds."

"Won't you sit down? I'm Tucker." He shook hands and waved at a comfortable chair across the desk, waited for her to seat herself and cross her legs, then sat down himself and leaned forward.

Junior League to the damn core, he thought. Expensive but plain. Sexy in that quick I'm-married-and-I-know-all-about-it way. Assured but not too snotty. Perfect young matron looking for somebody to tell the girls what good citizens they are.

"Won't you have a cigarette?" He held out his pack.

"Thanks, I have my own."

Tucker watched her open an alligator bag which matched her shoes. She bent her head to light the cigarette and he took the opportunity to study her legs. They were long and slender and she had good, slim ankles.

She wore a rather severely tailored gray suit and a single strand of pearls. A small black hat was attached mysteriously to her head and her dark, almost black, hair was long and gathered to the back of her neck.

And then Tucker saw that he was wrong on the matron business. She wore no rings at all.

"I hope I'm not taking too much of your time, Mr. Tucker."

"Not atall, not atall."

She relaxed in her chair.

"I teach at the State College for Women. Political science."

I've had it, Tucker thought. I've either got to give a lecture or listen to one.

"Is that so? Mighty good school."

She nodded.

"I'm working on a Ph.D. and my thesis is to be on the effects of women's suffrage in a specific election."

"The ladies' vote," Tucker said, "is mighty important."

A goddamned scholar, he thought. How wrong can you get?

Suddenly he saw how blue her eyes were. With that dark hair, he thought. Some scholar.

"I'd like to find out just how important it is, Mr. Tucker."

"Well, I'll be glad to tell you all I know, Miss Reynolds, I—"

"That's very nice, but I'm afraid if you told me everything I need to know it would take you all summer."

Tucker decided he liked her smile. It was not a simper, nor was it a mannish grin, just a nice smile that turned the corners of her mouth up and showed white teeth, not too even, and put a friendly look in her eyes.

Tucker smiled back. I should have had college teachers like this, he thought.

"Well, then, how can I help you, Miss Reynolds?"

She hesitated.

"Well—the school has given me leave until after the election. I thought if I could actually make myself a part of the campaign I could learn more than I ever could from books or statistics."

I haven't got enough troubles already, Tucker thought. If this babe thinks I—

"You mean you want to work in our campaign, ma'am?"

A hint of edginess had crept into his voice, although he still had the cheery smile attached to his face. She looked at him a moment.

"I'd have to be neutral, of course."

"Neutral," Tucker said. "Nobody's neutral."

She smiled.

"Teachers have to be."

He grunted, not unpleasantly.

"Just what would you like to do, Miss Reynolds?"

"I want to sort of come and go around your headquarters here and see how things are run. Maybe go out in the counties with a speaker. Talk to some of the people who come in. I want to see the campaign from the inside."

Tucker was cursing inwardly. It's worse than I thought. Poking into everything and not even doing any work. We haven't got time to waste on her.

"I suppose," she said, "what I'm really asking is to be allowed to make a nuisance of myself."

You're damn right, Tucker thought.

"I've already seen Mr. Kirby. He said he thought it would be a fine idea."

He would. If he paid attention to his business, he'd be a lot better off. Of all the people Anson could have got to run things for him—

"Frankly, Miss Reynolds, I don't know. I just don't—glad to have you around of course. Fine project you have. But I don't know if we'd be able to help you very much. You see—"

Tucker was good at reading people and he saw her face change almost before it actually did. A flush tinged her cheeks and she leaned slightly forward.

"You could help me a lot," she said. "I know you could—"

"Well—" Tucker fought against a frown. It was one of those things you couldn't come right out and refuse. Still—well, dammit, this wasn't the kind of campaign you could afford to have a busybody schoolteacher taking notes on.

She rose quickly.

"I'm afraid it's too much to ask of you," she said. Tucker automatically started to protest. She shook her head.

"I expect I'd better drop the whole idea," she said. "I'll tell the dean it was too much of an imposition on you. After all, it *was* his idea, not mine."

I will be goddamned, Tucker thought.

She looked at him steadily and he saw the cool amusement in her face. He felt a grudging admiration for her. She knew they couldn't afford to have her saying things like that. It was just such little stories that cost you votes.

"Well, now," he said. "I expect we can manage it all right."

"Oh, no, I—"

Tucker stood up too.

"Sit down, Miss Reynolds. Now that I think of it, Colonel Pollock will be delighted. He's very interested in anything concerning education."

"Well—" She smiled again, openly this time, the way she had when she first entered the room. "I'll try not to be too much trouble."

"We'll be glad to have you."

Tucker watched her sit down and cross her legs again. He perched on the edge of the desk. I'll just have to make the best of it, he thought. I'll have to find somebody to keep her nose out of the wrong places.

"You come in about ten tomorrow," he said. "Colonel Pollock will be back then and we'll make some plans for you."

"Fine. I'm anxious to meet him."

Tucker was smiling again and, with an ease perfected through long practice, was looking her over more closely. He saw the slim, strong fingers, the red lips, the smooth curve of her breast.

This might not be too bad at that, he thought. I've seen 'em prettier, but she's okay. All the standard equipment and a bit to boot.

"Colonel Pollock will want to meet you too." He lifted an eyebrow. "Of course you're going to vote for him, aren't you?"

She laughed. The sound of it was frank and unaffected.

"I told you. Teachers have to be neutral."

"And I told you—"

"Nobody's neutral? Well, I am, Mr. Tucker. By law. I'm a legal resident of the State of Maryland and I'm not registered in this State."

Tucker frowned.

"Haven't you lived here for a year?"

"Oh yes, nearly two. I just haven't changed my registration."

"You ought to do that, Miss Reynolds."

She stood up, holding out her hand, still smiling.

"Maybe I will," she said. "Someday. Thank you so much, Mr. Tucker. I'll be here tomorrow at ten."

He took her hand. It was soft and warm. A hand for a dark night, Tucker thought. To feel touching your cheek. A hand for —lots of things—

"Fine." He walked with her to the door and opened it.

"You really should change your registration."

She laughed again.

"You certainly are interested in my vote, Mr. Tucker. What difference would it make all by itself?" She was standing in the hall looking back at him. He leaned easily against the doorjamb.

"Everybody's vote makes a difference," he said. "To me, it does."

"I guess it does at that. Well, thank you again, Mr. Tucker."

❧

Not at all, Tucker thought. The pleasure was all mine.

That's been the best part of this whole thing, he thought. Having Vivian around. Not a bit like I was afraid it would be. Never in anybody's way, never prying into places she wasn't wanted. Not always worrying you to death with questions.

He thought back over the dinner dates they had already had. She had a lot of sense too. She'd shown that the first day there in the office. And always in good spirits. That was quite a trick nowadays.

· 68 ·

He heard the other men laughing, probably at Hadley's school-teacher story. But Vivian lingered in his mind.

Yessir, Tucker thought. A man could do worse for himself. Wonder some guy hasn't already snapped that up. Asset to anybody. And in bed . . .

He tried to think of Vivian in bed. But somehow, the face he visualized, the long smooth body he set his mind upon, belonged to Martha Pollock. He cursed himself. Thinking about Vivian you could get all warm inside. Thinking about Martha was like getting an ice pick in the belly. You could feel your guts curl up.

He heard someone ask if he were ready for another drink. He shook his head, still annoyed at himself. Damn Martha Pollock. The bitch didn't have any business popping into his mind like that.

"Tuck, I suppose you still think we should hold off the announcement that we want a second primary?"

"What? Oh—sure, we'll have it on the air ten minutes after we get the Hartsville decision. It's a natural."

"In about a week, maybe?"

"Oh—ten days."

"Will that leave time?" Gary asked. "Seems to me that cuts it mighty fine."

"It'll leave over three weeks," Ruggles said. "This thing will either go over or it won't. Three weeks, six weeks, it wouldn't make a hell of a lot of difference."

"It's better," Tucker said. "The whole thing will be fresh in their minds. It'll be like a bombshell."

"Lissen at that," Cousin Hadley said. "That man don't even have any doubts."

"That's what you think. But I admit I think we're going to pull this thing off. Damn if I don't."

"Puts me in mind of one of my cousins down in Jasper," Hadley said. "Couldn't call up his hogs. Had to get a neighbor to round 'em up of an evenin. Know why he couldn't get 'em up?"

"Tell us more," Ruggles said. "We might all need to know how to call a hog or two someday."

"Well, this felluh he just didn't put no stock in hog callin to begin with. Knew they weren't comin fore he ever let out a whoop. And he was right, cause them hogs knew he didn't really expect nothin to happen. They just didn't see no reason to come."

He puffed a lazy cloud of smoke toward Tucker.

"But this neighbor, hell, he'd been callin up hogs all his life.

"He'd step out there and crank him up a yell and here'd come them hogs lickety-split through the woods faster'n you could count. Goes to show you. Give me a confident man evry time."

Tucker laughed with the rest, but his face was thoughtful as he studied Hadley. That bastard doesn't forgive and forget, he thought. He'll remember today a long time, funny stories or no funny stories. I better keep an eye on that district of his.

The meeting broke up in the comfortable laughter which followed Cousin's story. The men shook hands all around and moved into the hall to collect their hats.

The Colonel and Martha stood at the door as they left, his arm companionably around her slim waist. Tucker watched the intimate little smile she had for each of the men, the lingering touch of her fingers on their hands.

She's crawling with it, he thought. I wonder if the Colonel really keeps all that woman satisfied. I wonder if anybody could.

Cousin Hadley left first, then Gary, then Tucker and Ruggles together.

"I'll see you long about Saturday, Tuck," Pollock said. "I don't think I ought to leave now, but if you say—"

"Sure," Tucker said. "Just the ticket. We'll play it just right in the papers. You know—down at your humble beach cottage, Martha doing the cooking, deciding whether you owe it to the people to run again—"

Ruggles chuckled.

"Colonel," he said, "long as Tucker's here, we can all go to the beach."

Tucker put out his hand to Martha.

"Be a good thing for you to go along, Martha. You're looking a little peaked." He smiled at her.

She smiled back and there was something near amusement in her eyes.

"Never tell a woman that, Bill. But I think I'll go anyway."

"And try not to worry," Tucker said, working hard to keep mockery out of his eyes. "About the Colonel, I mean."

"I'll try to, Bill. I really will." What might have been amusement turned sardonic and he squeezed her hand, harder than necessary, and followed Ruggles out, still smiling.

"You know, Tuck, I got a wife of my own and I ought not to talk about our new Senator's lady. But confidentially, how would you like to—"

"Don't say it. Don't even think about it. Zeb, how old is that woman, anyway?"

"Bout like my wife. Fortyish." Ruggles stopped by his car. "Resemblance ends right there."

"The Colonel must have something not visible to the naked eye. How could one man keep all of that home by the fire?"

"I am of the opinion that he doesn't keep it home by the fire, my friend. Let's just pray he'll manage to till after election."

They chuckled.

"Preciate your help in there," Tucker said. "Steve and Cousin got a little off the reservation."

"Forget it. You handled those two just right."

Ruggles climbed into his car and seemed to unjoint himself behind the wheel.

"Mind some advice, Tuck?"

"Not from you."

"Give the Colonel a little more rope. Don't order him around too much."

Tucker laughed.

"Somebody's got to."

"Don't underestimate him, Tuck."

"I never underestimate anybody."

Ruggles lit a cigarette.

"You've been right so far," he said. "I should argue with you, I guess, but maybe you're still right."

"Anyway, thanks for the tip."

They shook hands and Ruggles drove off. Now there's a guy I'm going to make Governor some day, Tucker thought. When he decides he wants it.

He went to his own car. That goddam Harrison was waiting. There was that to do and then there would be the night and Vivian, and for just this once the hell with all the rest of it.

Chapter Five

The Ranch House was the favorite restaurant of Capital City. The food was the best in town and so was the "atmosphere"; the waitresses were the prettiest, the service the best, the Hammond organ the softest.

The Ranch House was the place to go, no doubt of it. Acres of parking for one thing. The modern décor for another: wide fieldstones formed the walls and the entire front of the building was a panel of glass. Between the glass and the parking lot a flower garden bloomed brightly, lending to patrons the illusion of dining in a garden.

What woodwork there was was done in Williamsburg green. Lights were dim enough for intimacy, bright enough for reading the menu. Soundproof walls shut out kitchen clatter and the hum of conversation was hardly audible above the organ.

"An oasis," Tucker said. "Not frequented by politicians. What more could you ask?"

"Politicians interest me," Vivian said. "That's why I like the Coffee Shop."

"You can have the Coffee Shop. Politics on rye. Fat men with cigars. Deals being made. I'll take the Ranch House."

"You're just discouraged. Just because you got licked yesterday."

Tucker chuckled.

"Maybe I am at that. Awful, wasn't it?"

A blond waitress appeared with two glasses of ice, filled them with water and waited for their order.

"How're the hip steaks?" Tucker said.

"Very nice tonight, sir."

He cocked an eye at Vivian and she nodded, smiling.

"Two," Tucker said. "With coffee. All the trimmings. And two of those good salads."

The waitress moved away.

Tucker relaxed in the soft leather. They were near the big picture window and the garden was colorful and cheerful. The organ was playing *Over the Rainbow* and Vivian was looking like a million dollars, cold cash, in a blue dress that matched her eyes and buttoned decorously at the neck.

Peace, Tucker thought, it's wonderful. Vivian is wonderful. And I'm not so damn bad myself. This shapes up as a night. An honest-to-God night. Even a moon out there somewhere.

"Wait till you taste that salad," he said. "The things that chef does to a head of lettuce."

"Ummm. I'm a salad fan."

He laughed but not at her answer. He took a pack of cigarettes from his pocket, offered her one, lit both.

"People change," he said. "It's funny. Take me now. I used to knock myself out in a place like this."

"How?" Vivian had a way of seemingly devoting her entire attention to you. Nice, Tucker thought. Nice to be really listened to for once.

"Sure. New rich. Twenty-five bucks was rich to me. I guess your family's loaded, isn't it?"

"Loaded."

He nodded. Nice, direct answer, he thought. None of the "I don't really know" crap.

"I can always tell. I've thought about rich folks enough. Say, you know what I did once in a restaurant uptown?"

She leaned forward, conspiratorially.

"Did you walk out on the check?"

"Oh no, nothing like that. I—"

"I always wanted to walk out on the check. See if I could get away with it."

"You could. You look so much like Mrs. Gotbucks. Nobody would ever think of you as anything but Chase National Bank."

She frowned.

"Is that a compliment?"

"Finest one I know. What I was going to tell you—it was

when I was with the Highway Department. Bucking for Chief Statistician. I got a date with the Commissioner's daughter. Polishing the old apple, you know."

Vivian lifted her eyebrows.

"Some apple, I'll bet."

"Not bad. Not bad atall. Anyway, we went to this place and I really did it up brown. Ordered the best in the house. When they brought on the salad, I really did my stuff. Whipped out my own salad dressing—ordered it from New York. Made the salad right there in front of everybody. It must of been a howl."

"What in the world for?"

He grinned, almost sheepishly.

"Hell, I wasn't far out of college. In those days I could still hear that damn cotton mill I grew up with. I had to be a real wheel. I thought that would knock this girl out. Probably did, at that. Anyway I got the job. Two years later."

They laughed.

"I used to do a lot of things like that till I got wise."

Vivian snubbed her cigarette in the ash tray.

"You *have* changed," she said. "I don't think I ever met a man with more—assurance, I guess. I guess that's the word."

"Good as any. I told you I finally got wise. Things like that don't bother me any more."

She smiled. "Like me being loaded?"

"Hell, I'm loaded too. Want to see my checkbook?"

Vivian assumed an air of mock boredom.

"I detest men who display their vulgar wealth."

"Me too. Especially if it's more vulgar than mine."

They laughed together and comfortable silence dropped over them. This is the kind of woman I go for, Tucker thought. I feel like I had my carpet slippers on. No airs. All that . . .

"Now there's a word I hate," he said.

"What word?"

"Class. I was just thinking about you. Hate the word, but I guess it's the best one. You've got class."

"For the second time. Is that a compliment?"

He nodded. "Take me, now. I've got assurance. Plenty of it. Also brains, energy, determination, money, and twenty-twenty

· 75 ·

vision. But no class. Whatever class is. You're lousy with it. Me—none."

"Bill! That's not so! You're—"

"Nope. No class. Have to be born with class and I wasn't. I don't mind. Not any more. Plenty of other fish in the sea."

"Well, I still think you've got lots of class. You know, I believe I dislike that word too, come to think of it."

"Let's take it out of the language." He raised his water glass in a toast. "To all the things a guy can have besides class."

They drank water, solemnly. Vivian put her glass down and touched her dark hair with light fingers. Tucker liked the gesture. Men, he thought. The hell with men.

Just to see a woman move. Just to watch the way they do things. All men can do is sign checks and flex muscles.

"All right," Vivian said. "You have no class. Now what have you got instead? Those other fish in the sea."

"That's a deep question, Miss Reynolds. Mighty deep."

"No. Seriously."

"Seriously? You mean you want to hear my philosophy of life?"

"God forbid. I just wondered what you meant."

"Well—" He fumbled again for cigarettes. Sure as I get one lit, they'll bring the food, he thought. "I tell you. I had a dream one time, just once. Never forgotten it."

She shook her head at the extended pack. He took one out and lit it.

"There was this big saloon, like you see in horse oprys. Full of people. I was there, having a hell of a time. Well, somehow this fight got started. Still just like the movies."

He blew three smoke rings in quick succession. Vivian poked her finger through each of them and waved the smoke away.

"Well, there everybody was, knocking the hell out of everybody else. Except old Tucker. When the fight started, something took hold of me and pulled me right up in the air. Just high enough nobody could reach me. And every now and then whatever it was would let me down a little and I'd kick somebody right in the snoot and then I'd get yanked up again."

"That was never in the movies."

"Hell, no. I've left the screen now, honey. Well, pretty soon everybody stopped fighting everybody else and tried to get at me. But they couldn't reach me. I was just a little too high. There I was, hanging up there in the air. Down below me all those folks growling and yelling like a pack of dogs. They'd keep reaching for me and not being able to get me. Every now and then I'd drop, real quick, and kick somebody else in the face. Then I'd get yanked up, and they'd be madder than ever and still couldn't get at me. And you know what I was doing?"

"What?"

"I was laughing. Sitting up there in the middle of the air, laughing fit to kill. Because nobody could get to me."

"It sounds horrible," Vivian said. "I hate nightmares."

"Horrible? Hell, that was the finest dream I ever had, Vivian. And you know what the finest part of all was? The very best part?"

"I don't know," Vivian said. "It's too crazy."

"The finest part of the whole thing was pretty soon I twisted my head around and found out what was holding me up. What it was, I had hold of the seat of my own britches, holding myself right up there in the air."

"You never dreamed all that."

"I swear it. Imagine it, Vivian! Holding yourself up there above everybody, laughing yourself to death. Lady, they can have the class, every damn bit of it. I'll take that dream."

"You don't mean that, Bill."

"Hell I don't."

"But nobody ever gets like that. You never get to the point where nobody can—reach you. Not till you die."

"Well, I'd like to try. I am trying."

"Trying what?" a man's voice said over his shoulder. "I thought you'd tried everything already."

"My God," Tucker said. "I came out here to get away from cigars."

"Can't evade the facts of life," Ben Kirby said. "Hello, Vivian. Don't get up, Tuck."

"I wasn't going to."

"Didn't think you were. Burdened down with defeat and all. Mighty nice of you to console the loser, Vivian."

She laughed. "I'm a good Samaritan, Ben. Why don't you sit down?"

"Watch out there," Tucker said. "He might take you up on that."

"Nope. Can't stand a bad loser."

"You're mighty pleased with yourself," Vivian said. "You must think the battle's over."

"If it's not it should be."

"Ah-ha," Tucker said. "Trying to pump me. Just because I knew you at college."

"Name-dropper."

"You two," Vivian said. "Why don't you kiss and make up?"

"Because he smokes cigars," Tucker said. "You should get a whiff of the breath on this guy."

Kirby was unperturbed. He was a big man, rapidly growing bald, solid and muscular in an inexpensive suit, slightly in need of pressing.

"I just came over to rub it in," he said. "My welcome being what it is, guess I'll leave. Better luck next time, Tuck. Unless it's a second primary."

"Are you crazy? A second primary after the licking we took?"

"I hear tell the Colonel is thinking it over," Kirby said. "Going to the beach, in fact, to think it over."

"He's an optimist."

"Among other things. When will you make up his mind?"

"I'm just a hired hand, Ben. Like you."

The waitress arrived with the two hip steaks. Kirby patted Vivian's shoulder and moved out of the way.

"Got to go, folks. Count all the votes again. Makes me feel so good."

"I'll bet," Tucker said. "Take it easy, Ben."

"'By, Ben."

Kirby moved away, then stopped. His eyes suddenly hardened, became flat and impelling. The bantering tone dropped from his voice. "When you do make up his mind, Tuck, better remember one thing."

"I'll remember a lot of things, Ben."

Tucker's voice had changed too. Vivian's brows moved together in a faint frown.

"Well, include this. There's a lot more at stake than the Colonel's vanity. Or yours."

"I haven't got any. In my business, I can't afford it."

Kirby's face split into a cheerful grin. It was a friendly, open face, homely as sin but somehow likable and strong.

"Have a nice dinner," he said. He nodded again and moved away.

They watched his broad form move among the tables toward the door.

"That guy," Tucker said. He took a bite of steak.

"Was I imagining things? Or were those barbed words you two were pitching at each other."

"Barbed is right." Tucker grinned. "Ben and I are old buddies, in a funny sort of way. He thinks I'm a louse and I think he's an idiot, but we get along."

"Sounds like a beautiful friendship. Why does he think you're a louse? May I have some salt?"

"Usually or recently?" He handed her the silver salt shaker. "No, seriously, Ben thinks Ralph Anson and God are at least first cousins. He thinks we played dirty pool, running against God's first cousin."

Vivian nodded. "For a political science teacher," she said, "I know mighty little about politics. But even I could see there weren't any punches pulled in this election."

"There never are, honey. You play to win or you don't play. You have to make do with what you have."

"I know. All's fair in love, war, politics, and paying taxes." She leaned forward and placed a hand on the table, looking Tucker in the eye. "But do you really believe all those things Colonel Pollock says about Senator Anson?"

"I don't have to believe them or not believe them. I *know* who I want to vote for to begin with."

"But just between you and me, I mean."

"Just between you and me"—he took her hand—"you're beginning to sound a lot like an Anson voter."

"Don't start that again. You know I'm neutral, no matter what you say."

He took his hand away and picked up his fork again. "Damn good steak," he said.

"Excellent. My vote wouldn't mean a thing," she said. "Quit worrying about how I would have voted if I could have voted and stop changing the subject."

"Did anyone ever tell you that you are one hell of a good-looking woman?"

"Regularly. And thank you. Now answer my question."

"What question?"

"Do you really think Ralph Anson is all those things you—yes, you, Bill Tucker—accused him of being?"

"What difference does it make? You're not going to vote. Your vote wouldn't count for anything if you did."

"I'm going to throw this glass of water at you."

"Well, you said so yourself."

Suddenly they both laughed. I'll bet we look like we're married, Tucker thought. Having a night out while Grandma sits with the kids. Young executive and wife.

"Let's forget the damned election," he said. "Do you realize how little I know about you?"

"Standard opening, Tucker. You go to the movies too much."

"No, I'm serious. You're sort of a mystery. Obviously a wealthy woman and a beautiful one, yet you're a schoolteacher."

"I have a classroom in lieu of a home and family, Mr. Tucker. I have failed to place in the matrimonial stakes, so far, and teaching relieves my frustrations."

"Are you frustrated too?"

"Not the way you mean. Stop leering at me."

"Ah. Cold-hearted woman."

Cold-hearted, my fanny, he thought. The way she dresses, sort of quiet and plain, you don't notice that body much. But when you do . . .

"My mother is great for society doings. I tried it for a while myself, but it's not for me. I guess I'm Plain Jane at heart. So I got an M.A. in the same course I'd studied at college. It was interesting anyway. Then down here to get my Ph.D. and teaching on the side. There you are. Story of my life."

"Not quite. No romantic interest included."

"My share, I guess. I'm not a teen-ager any more, Bill. But —none of it took. Not permanently."

"Fine," Tucker said. "Couldn't be better. No man back home or any of that stuff?"

She smiled and shook her head. Tucker took her hand again. His face became dead serious.

"Let me take you out of all this, Vivian. I happen to know the Mayor of Hollywood. Did him a favor once. Greasy little bastard, but influential. Now if you'd care to come up to my apartment while I phone him, I think—"

She laughed. "No, thanks. I'll stick to teaching, if you don't mind."

"Well, if you don't mind my saying so, you are one hell of a political science teacher."

"I never saw one that wasn't. That's why this is so good for me, observing this election. Find out what the textbooks don't mention."

"I don't mean that. I mean all that stuff you talk about." His voice rose into high-pitched mimicry. " 'My vote wouldn't mean a thing.' "

She laughed.

"No laughing matter. Stuffing the heads of the mothers of the nation's future with that sort of mess."

Her face became serious.

"I suppose you're right. But I just can't help feeling that way. There are so many people, Bill! I read one time where every day people disappear, just get swallowed up into thin air, no trace at all. Well, the world goes right on, doesn't it?"

"Sure, but—"

"I get to thinking about myself. Suppose I disappeared. Some people would care, of course. But nothing would change, not really. Not a thing. The school would get a new teacher and things would go right on. It's a horrible thought."

"It sure is. It's a lot of bull, too."

"I don't know. One time when I was in the Waves I worked

in the Central File Room of a big base in Florida. I was really an eager beaver, helping to win the war. My job was the most important thing in the world. You know how it was during the war."

"I know."

"Well, I got appendicitis. I was out nearly a month. I worried the whole time for fear something would go wrong in the file room. That I wouldn't be there when I was needed. Well, when I finally got back on the job, I found I'd hardly been missed. They'd moved another girl in and everything went right on. No fuss, no bother. I needn't even have come back. Brother, that took me down a peg or two. The whole damn thing didn't seem to matter after that. Just another job."

"Yeah," Tucker said. "I can imagine."

I can imagine, all right. I can imagine you in the slick blue uniform and the cute hat and the sensible shoes. I can imagine you doing your job, the most important thing in the world.

Sometimes I think they took everybody but me.

Every goddam body but me. The long and the short and the tall, doctor lawyer Indian chief, butcher baker beggarman thief. Every damn body in the world but me.

I used to hear Ma talk about it. The "high blood." Something she had, whatever the hell it was, that made her not eat salt even on rice, or anything fried, even when something fried was all there was in that stinking house.

I used to hear her talk about it and then, by God, they told me I had it too. When I went down to enlist. What a goddam laugh that was. Full of red-white-and-blue. Marching down to enlist to save the goddam world.

All that crap they told me. And I tried it all. How many times did I try it?

Lying flat on my back on the bed for days before I'd go for the exam, not moving, scared even to breathe for Christ sake, trying to get it down. Not even thinking about anything that might excite me, not even eating any goddam thing worth eat-

· 82 ·

ing, watching myself like an old man, trying to get it down. Trying to get it down.

I tried it till I was as careful as a man can be and still go on breathing. I tried it in the summer and in the fall and the spring and the winter, and I even went to Florida and didn't turn my hand over for a solid month and I tried it there too. Tried to get it down.

Only I never did. Not after all that. Not after all the times I tried. It never came down.

But I went on trying. They have to give me that. I kept on trying until there wasn't any use any more, until there wasn't anything left to try.

And then I gave up and told myself I was a 4-F.

A 4-F. A goddam stinking 4-F.

The way they'd look at you. The way you could see their eyes under the white hats or the overseas caps or those silly lids with the bill the Marines were so proud of—the way you could see their eyes, looking at you.

The hearty voices—"man, you're lucky!"—false as a three-dollar bill. The contempt in the faces of the girls, clinging to the men in uniform. The men in uniform.

And you a lousy no-good 4-F.

The way you felt. Inside of you. The greatest leveler in history, the greatest measuring rod. Where what counted was whether you had it inside and whether you could stay alive, not where you came from or what your lousy name was. The way you felt to be cut off even from that.

The way you started praying to let It end, let It be over, God, let It stop so I can stop too, so I won't have to breathe It in my nostrils and drink It with my coffee in the morning and my ration-stamp gin at night. Let the war be over, God, for them and, please God, for me. Most of all for me.

Just let It be over.

Only when It was—how amazed you were to have It over, something that had no end, only a beginning and a middle but no end—It was still with you, fading a little every day maybe, but not all the way, still a little bit of It there and not ever going to fade all the way either. Not ever.

You were a 4-F in the war and you were a 4-F in the peace. A goddamned 4-F now, henceforthandforevermoreamen.

You read *The Naked and the Dead* and *The Young Lions* and *The Crusaders*, you even went back to *The Red Badge of Courage* and *Three Soldiers*. You saw *The Sands of Iwo Jima* and *Battleground* and *Fighting Lady*. If you had any illusions left about war, they were mighty damn scarce. You saw the armless and the legless and the blind and the burned and the crazed. You weren't any romantic fool, dreaming of a yellow sash and a sword of burnished steel.

It was hell, all right. Sherman didn't know the half of it. You knew that. The veterans were right. You never had it so good, Jack. Everybody couldn't go. Keep the home fires burning. There was no shame and no disgrace for you, and there damn well wouldn't have been any glory if you had gone, nothing but mud and blood and stink and ache and cuss and die and crap in your pants when the guns went off.

But the thing was, you had missed it and everybody else had been in it. You were never going to forget that you were the lucky stiff and not the dog-face. You were never going to know whether you would have had the guts or not. You were never going to know whether you had what it took when you either did or you died, and you were never going to know whether you had what it took when it didn't even matter whether you had it or not because having it or not, one way or the other, didn't make a goddam bit of difference to what was coming.

No. If the war set the veterans apart forever, made them all something they might never have been otherwise, it did the same for the 4-F's. Us 4-F's. And nobody could help it, nobody asked for his portion, everybody just had it handed out to him and took it and tried to get along somehow, some way.

Only there was a difference. Because the veterans had company. Plenty of company. Practically every damn body alive.

But you never heard a bunch of lousy 4-F's telling about *their* war experiences, did you?

The lucky stiffs.

Chapter Six

Harvey Pollock sat in the library of his home, well-pleased with the day and himself.

There was a highball at his elbow and the Sunday *New York Times* lay scattered at his feet. Through the open window at his back, a faint breeze stirred away the heat of the day. Insects made night noises and far away the faint hum of traffic bore the comforting knowledge of other people, of movement, of life there for the taking.

But not tonight, Pollock thought. Tonight is for rest and getting things straight and just sitting here taking it easy.

He heard the front door close. Martha, he thought. Tonight I even feel good toward her.

Funny. I ought not to be feeling so well, the way it turned out yesterday. I ought to be worrying myself sick.

Yet, here I am, carefree as hell. Because I'm going to be a Senator. Because—

It's Tucker, he thought. The bastard is catching. He said we were going to win. He's always said we were going to win, ever since that first day he came to my office.

Pollock had welcomed having a visitor. Breaks the monotony, he thought. There are certainly busier jobs than being vice-president of a bank that runs so well and that you know so little about all you ever have to do is sign your name where they tell you.

He watched the man coming across the deep carpet of his office floor. The man was young, thirty-five or so, Pollock judged, and well-dressed. He carried an efficient-looking brief case in an efficient-looking hand.

"Colonel," he said, "I'm Bill Tucker."

Pollock put out his hand. It was taken in a hard, peremptory clasp, short, meaningless.

"What can I do for you, Mr. Tucker? Sit down please."

He waved at a chair. Tucker glanced once about the office and sat down. Pollock relaxed into his own chair and began to tamp tobacco into a well-smoked pipe.

"Now, let's see," he said. "I believe you're—"

He let the sentence hang in the air.

"Chief Statistician for the State Highway Department," Tucker said. "Right now I am."

"Oh yes." Pollock put a match to his pipe. "Well, I'm not up on statistics, or highways either. But maybe this is a good time to put in a plug to get the road paved out to my Hereford farm in Cullman County."

"That's a county road, Colonel. But we put up most of the money for county road paving. I can fix it for you."

It was a matter-of-fact remark. It was so matter-of-fact, Pollock thought, that it left no room for doubt. I believe he could, he thought. He could get that road paved for me. If he wanted to.

"Do you keep a road map in your head, Mr. Tucker? That's pretty out-of-the-way country."

"I have to keep up pretty well, Colonel. That's my job."

Pollock chuckled. "Well, well," he said. "What did you want to see me about? Besides getting my road paved."

Tucker reached for his own cigarettes.

"Well, Colonel, you've only been back in the States a couple of months now. You're all set up here with the oldest bank in the State. And I've got the gall to come in here and ask you if you wouldn't like to make a change already."

Pollock took his pipe out of his mouth. What the hell, he thought. I never saw this character before in my life. Is *he* offering *me* some kind of a job?

"Well, now, that's an odd thing to say."

Tucker laughed. There was mirth in the short, sharp sound,

and Pollock had an uncomfortable feeling that it might be directed at him.

"I don't believe in beating about the bush, Colonel."

"I see that. Just what did you have in mind?"

Tucker leaned forward and the smile faded from his face.

"I was wondering," he said, "if you would like to be a United States Senator."

Pollock started violently. He felt his eyes bulge in their sockets.

A Senator! He said a Senator. The words echoed in his mind and he felt his mouth open slightly. He tried to find words to fill it.

"Mr. Tucker . . . that's . . . the most absurd thing I ever heard!"

Tucker nodded.

"That's what anybody would say. Most likely."

"I've never run for office . . . I—"

"Neither has Ralph Anson."

"But I don't know anything about politics. I don't even—"

"I do."

"Well—" Pollock began to get hold of himself. Just a nut with a proposition, he thought. "You've certainly taken me by surprise. You certainly have."

"You'll have to get over that. In politics, it doesn't pay to get yourself surprised."

Pollock put his pipe in the ash tray.

"I don't think I like that remark." I don't like it a goddam bit, he thought. Talking to me like that.

"A lot of people wouldn't. But then I'm not running for anything."

Pollock stood up. That did it, brother. You don't know who you're talking to.

"Mr. Tucker, I'm a busy man. I'm sorry but—"

"You mean you're not interested? You don't want to be a Senator?"

Pollock stared at him. Tucker's unemotional blue eyes held the stare. They were not the eyes of a harebrain. Pollock was suddenly sure of that.

A Senator. A United States Senator. Washington. Damn this

man, he thought. If he's making fun of me . . . a Senator . . . me a Senator . . .

"All right. It sounds silly to me and I must say I don't like your manner at all. But I'd be a fool not to listen, I guess."

He sat down slowly and stiffly, his eyes cautious, still fastened on Tucker. A Senator, he thought.

Tucker rubbed at his broad, somewhat sunburned nose with his forefinger. Then he leaned over and picked up his brief case. He held it loosely across his knees.

"Ralph Anson can be beaten, Colonel."

"That's not what the papers say."

"The hell with them. I expect I'm the only man in the State who believes he can be beaten—now—but he can be. You can beat him. If I help you."

"Sure of yourself, aren't you?" Pollock's eyes had become fixed at a point about two feet above Tucker's blond head. He's right, he thought. It doesn't pay to get surprised.

"I've worked hard and waited a long time so I could be sure of myself, Colonel. I'm sorry if I seem disrespectful. But if we don't go into this thing, it won't matter. If we do, I'm going to have to be blunt about a lot of things, because that's the only way I can help you win. And I don't see any use in playing if you don't win."

"Fair enough," Pollock said. But not too goddam blunt, he thought. "And if I seem a little fuddled it's because this is a bolt out of the blue to me, you know. I've thought of politics, I'll admit. But so soon—and the Senate!"

"All right. Now I'll tell you how we're going to do it."

Pollock smiled. "I haven't said we were yet."

Tucker waved an impatient hand. "You haven't heard anything about it yet either, Colonel."

Pollock settled more comfortably in his chair. Let the man talk, he thought. No use saying anything till I hear what he has to say.

"When old Senator Johnston died, every politician in the State was after his job. The pressure was terrific. But the Governor named Anson—a guy who has stayed out of everyday politics as hard as he can for as long as I can remember. You can imagine, that went over like a ton of bricks with the courthouse boys. Colonel, have you got any idea why the Governor cooked his own political goose like that?"

Pollock shook his head. He looks like a football player, he thought. He looks powerful, completely unsubtle. But I don't think he is unsubtle. I don't think he is at all.

"When the Governor goes out of office two years from now, he's going to get a nice, soft, cushy Federal judge's bench for the rest of his life and the fat salary that goes with it. And nobody can get him off it until he wants to retire. That's the price Washington paid to get Ralph Anson in the Senate. They wanted him and they shelled out what they had to so they could get him."

"I've always heard," Pollock said, "that politics is a dirty business."

"All politics is dirty, Colonel. It's dirty if you get anywhere in it. The primary to elect somebody to take that Senate seat permanently won't be a bit different. That's the one I'm talking about."

"Just where do I fit in, Mr. Tucker?" And where do you fit in? Pollock thought.

Tucker leaned forward, hands clasped, elbows on his knees. "There's not a politician in the State who wouldn't give his cigar to get Anson out of there. But they've figured it wrong. They think he's too popular, that he can win in a walk this year. None of them want to stick out their necks against him. They figure to wait four more years, when he'll be up for election again.

"They think by that time there'll have been enough civil rights votes and foreign aid bills and labor laws and so on to give everybody a good look at the kind of guy Anson really is. Then—" Tucker drew his finger across his throat, quickly, and Pollock jumped slightly at the gesture.

He smiled, rather faintly. "Maybe I don't have a politician's perception," he said. "I'm afraid that sounds like good sense to me. Assuming you want Anson out of there."

Give him lots of rope, he thought. Let him do all the talking.

He gazed, smiling, at Tucker. Tucker's lips twitched in exasperation.

"Sure it is. Only it means that for four years they'll have to twiddle their thumbs. I don't aim to twiddle mine, Colonel. He can not only be licked now"—Pollock saw the fire begin in his eyes, saw the slight tremor of his hand—"but the man who does it, the guy with the guts to stick out his neck and run against him now, can take over the party organization. He can run things pretty much the way he wants them run." He leaned back suddenly in his chair.

"That's opportunity, Colonel. You ought to know it when you see it."

Pollock shook pipe dottle into his ash tray and methodically began to run a cleaner through the stem. Mr. Tucker, he thought, maybe you and I are going to do some business after all. Maybe.

"Go on," he said. "I admit I'm interested so far."

"You've got one of the oldest names in the State," Tucker said. "That's blue blood. The South doesn't always vote for blue blood and most of the time it hates it. But it always respects it."

He held up the fingers of his right hand and bent one down. He went on, talking almost to himself. Street noises floated in the window behind him.

"You've got a war record. That means courage. The South loves courage. Courage is all it's had to be proud of for so long."

He bent another finger. "You're a Baptist. Throw a stick in this State and you hit a Baptist in the fanny. And they stick together like molasses."

Another finger went down.

"You're a businessman and you've got connections. Money connections. People who like Anson the way they like a rattlesnake. People who think politics and business go together like ham and eggs. People who are used to shelling out for what they want."

A fourth finger bent.

"You've got me. I know how to put it all together for you and make it stick."

His fist closed into a tight ball.

"And you've got plenty of stuff to hit him in the face with."

He makes it sound like a jigsaw puzzle, Pollock thought. Just find all the right pieces and then put them together. Could it possibly be as simple as he makes it sound?

Tucker had relaxed into his chair. Waiting for me to say something, Pollock thought. Only I haven't anything to say. Not yet.

He gazed solemnly at Tucker.

"Well, Colonel, I'd be here all day if I went into details. But everything, all my plans, are in here." He took a thick sheaf of papers from his brief case and placed them on the desk. "And a lot of research work, too," he said. His hand lingered briefly on the papers, touching them softly.

His eyes probed directly at Pollock. You'd have a hard time fooling this man, Pollock thought. You couldn't look him in the eye and get away with lying.

"You said politics is a dirty business, Colonel. And it is. It's a lot like murder. You need motive, opportunity, and method. And luck."

"Luck," Pollock said, "is something I have always been blessed with."

Tucker grinned.

"Good. I've given you opportunity. Now here's the method:

"We attack. No holds barred. We almost call him a Communist—not quite. We almost call him a Socialist—not quite. We imply he's selling American freedom and initiative down the river. We link him with the civil rights boys. We dig up every one-horse outfit he ever contributed to and you'd be surprised how many of them have had a Red or two on the Board of Directors.

"We let it be known that the CIO is paying his expenses. Whether they are or not. We say Yankee agitators are running his campaign. I've got a lot of dope on some of his activities in that—" he indicated the papers—"and it'll give you a good idea of the case we can make out of what's actually harmless stuff. Colonel, by the time the first primary is over, we can make Senator Ralph Anson look like Joe Stalin's brother."

Pollock stood up and moved to one of the windows that looked out on the busy street. Scruples, he thought, not even any pretense of scruples. I would rather have my share served up more delicately. But—

He felt Tucker standing beside him at the window. Pollock looked at him.

"The motive, Tucker. That's the only one left. What makes you think I want to be a Senator?"

Tucker pointed to the street. He seemed to have an ear cocked to the sound of horns and the rumble of motors and the quick swish of tires.

"Look down there. Just look. All those people hurrying along and all those cars. Every damn one of them stops when the light turns red and goes when it turns green. That's people for you, Colonel. They stop and go. And who the hell makes them do that? The law, that's who. The law put that light there. The law those same people elected so they could put it there."

He looked Pollock full in the eye again and his voice dropped almost to a whisper. There was a fervor in it and a zeal, Pollock thought. As he spoke the light on the corner turned red and cars slowed and stopped and waited.

"You want to make the lights turn red, Colonel. So do I."

I don't like him, Pollock thought. I don't like him, but he's got something. He's got plenty.

He spoke slowly. "What sort of a man are you, Tucker? To say a thing like that to me?"

Tucker smiled and a derisive shadow dropped over the fervent light in his eyes.

"A young man," he said. "Just a young man trying to get ahead."

⚓

Coming out of the blue like that, Pollock thought. Just walking in and laying it on the line.

The memory of that day fascinated him, left him with a feeling of awe deep within his belly.

Not Tucker so much, he told himself. There are other men who get ideas, who aren't afraid to push things the way they want them to go.

But it was so unexpected. All of a sudden there it was. Just when I was realizing I didn't know and didn't care anything about that damn bank, even if Martha does own most of its stock.

He was very conscious now of the fascination and of the awe, sitting comfortably in the den, the cool of the glass moist in his hand, the breeze still tickling through the room.

Because it was an embodiment, he thought. A living goddamned embodiment. The opportunity—the one I've always looked for, hoped for, the big one I knew was coming, the big one that had to follow all the little ones. The big one that had to be, that had to tread my path, come my way, knock, as they say it does but once, at my door.

My door.

And there it was, he thought. So clear a child couldn't have missed it. And I took it. The way I always knew I would have the guts to do when it came.

I took it and I'm going to keep it. Nothing is going to stop me. Not that putrid Anson, not anybody. I am going to be a United States Senator.

Because everything is stacked my way, just like Tucker said that day. Because everything is going, will keep on going, just the way Tucker said it would go.

Tucker.

Yes, he thought. Tucker. That.

There is always that. There is always Tucker.

He lifted the glass and drank. The cool liquid soothed his throat, trickled gently through him.

Maybe I should take care of that too, he thought.

Just in case.

Chapter Seven

Tucker reached around the doorjamb, fumbled for the switch, and turned on the lights. Vivian walked ahead of him into the room.

"What a perfect setting for a seduction," she said.

"I bring all my victims here." He leered elaborately.

The wall switch had turned on two lamps placed on end tables flanking a large sofa. They were dim and shaded and left much of the rest of the room in shadow. Vivian saw a bookcase against the far wall and a picture window to the right of the door. Magazines were neatly displayed across a severe blond coffee table in front of the sofa. She felt soft carpet under her feet.

"But your virtue is safe with me," Tucker said. "I'm afraid of girls over sixteen. Even in my own lair."

"Some lair." She moved on into the room. Behind her Tucker switched on a large floor lamp which lit up the whole room. It's too neat, she thought. I'll bet he picked up all the old newspapers before he left tonight. And arranged these magazines.

"All this and television too," she said. "You do yourself pretty proud, Mr. Tucker."

"Like my taste?"

I believe he really wants to know, she thought. She looked carefully around her. A faint scent of tobacco was in the air.

"It's a lot like you. The furniture is all so plain. Not severe exactly, except that coffee table. Just plain. And you can tell what the pictures are."

Tucker put his hands in his pockets and looked at his pictures. "I'm damned if I'll put any hen-scratches on walls that cost what these do every month. Sit down, Vivian, and I'll fix us drinks."

"I get tight on two drinks," she said. "Blight of my life."

"Good. I like inexpensive women."

"But I do like a weak Scotch and soda."

"Yankees," Tucker said, shaking his head. "Good bourbon in the house and the lady wants Scotch."

"Yankee! If my old mammy could hear that!"

"I'll bet she drinks Scotch too. Oh, well." He went through a door into what she supposed was the kitchen. Other doors led to the bedroom and either a closet or a bath.

Vivian relaxed on the sofa. The place *is* like him, she thought. But it's not comfortable. It's too—self-sufficient.

Was Bill Tucker like that too? Was he sufficient unto himself?

Maybe that's what it is about him, she thought. The off-beat something. Maybe it's the feeling you get that he doesn't need you or anybody or anything.

Only that can't be, she told herself. Nobody is like that. Everybody needs something, everybody I've ever known anyway.

She crossed her legs and looked at her face in the mirror of her compact. Ice rattled against glass in the kitchen.

Like me, she thought. God knows I need a lot of things. Too many things. Or maybe I've got too many things. Maybe I need to get rid of a few.

Tucker's sofa was hard, but she began to feel luxurious. It had been a long hot day and it was good to feel her skin cool and clean again. A good dinner and good talk. Rare combination for me.

And what comes next? She remembered the half-serious bantering about seduction. And I started it, she thought. Which shows the way my innocent mind is roaming.

Well, I might not mind a pass being made at me tonight. A mild one. I don't think I'd mind at all tonight.

The conceit of the thought amused her and she laughed out loud. I *must* be frustrated, she thought. The sound of her laughter lingered in the night quiet of the apartment, coming back at her a little hollowly. There was an edge to it, she thought, an overtone perhaps of desperation.

"You say something?" Tucker called.

"Nothing. Just laughing to myself."

He came through the door, a napkin-wrapped glass in each hand.

"I got a tray somewhere," he said. "Didn't know where to look for it though."

He handed her one of the glasses and went over to the television set. It was a console model and she saw now that the cabinet also contained a radio and a record player.

She sipped at her drink. "Good," she said. Strong as hell, she thought.

He was bending over a stack of records in the bottom section of the television set. Vivian liked the way his clothes fit him. Most men look like laundry bags from the rear, she thought. All rumpled in the seat and wrinkled across the shoulders.

But he knows how to dress. He doesn't miss on the little things like that. And he says he has no class.

He must have had lots of women. That—force you feel coming out of him. All that assurance. Cave man mixed with Phi Beta Kappa.

Tucker pulled a record from the stack and put it on the turntable. "You'll like this one, I'll bet."

"Ummm." Well, a man like that is not the ticket for me. I want to mother my man a little bit, if I ever get one. I want to match his socks and his ties for him and keep his shirts laundered. I can't imagine Bill Tucker ever having dirty shirts.

It was Beethoven's *Third* playing. *The Eroica*, she thought. Hardly seduction music. Well, what was I expecting? *Body and Soul?*

Tucker sat on the sofa beside her.

"My favorite," he said.

"What do you like about it?" Everybody likes *The Eroica*, she thought. Everybody I know.

"How should I know? Just like to listen to it, I guess."

"That's a good reason."

"Only one I have. I don't know an étude from a concerto, tell you the truth."

"No class. No class at all, Mr. Tucker."

"Nope. Books, music, they're mostly Greek to me. I used to buy some of the damnedest things. What I'd do, I'd read *The*

New York Times and *The New Yorker* and rush right out and get anything they said was good. You know I even bought *Ulysses?* I never read such crap."

She shook her head in mock bewilderment.

"Just like fixing that salad. What were you trying to do?"

"I was on the make for culture."

"Like it was a commodity." And if it was, you'd have cornered the market, she thought.

"Yep. Man, the money I spent! But I never did find a store that sold it."

"Stop telling me about your ugly past. You're fine the way you are."

"Well, like the fellow said, I used to be an awful heel, but now I'm a swell guy."

There was a sudden clatter from the back of the house and Vivian jumped. The sibilant violence of cats spitting at each other followed what might have been shattering glass.

"There go the milk bottles," Tucker said. "Grace Coolidge and the Visiting Cat. At it again."

"Who?"

"My cats. Or one of 'em is mine. Grace Coolidge."

They listened again to the piercing brawl. Tucker's apartment was on the ground floor in a large development of four-apartment buildings. The noise seemed to be just outside the back door.

"In my youth," Tucker said, "and I still remember it, Grace Coolidge—the real one—was the very epitome of dignity. This cat puts her to shame. I started to name her Emily Post, but I finally decided Grace Coolidge was more appropriate. Of course, every now and then Grace gets mixed up with degenerate characters like the Visiting Cat."

"The Visiting Cat?"

"Took up here about two years ago. Don't know if it was because of Grace or my cat food. Been here ever since. Very bad influence on Grace. She's had kittens twice."

"Why don't you name him?"

"He doesn't belong to me. I just feed him and provide him with female companionship. Ugly old devil hates me anyway."

There was real affection in his tone. He would be a cat-lover,

· 97 ·

Vivian thought. You can love a cat without having to get involved with it. Cats are so superior and reserved. All they ask is food and warmth and no baths.

"That's mean," she said. "You'll give him a complex or something, not naming him."

"Cats don't get complexes," Tucker said. "They've got too much sense. They're not like people."

A final infuriated yowl split the night.

"Hadn't you better rescue Grace?"

"Listen, if Grace doesn't want to co-operate, she'll tear that old alley cat to shreds."

"He must be hen-pecked. I don't think I like Grace Coolidge at all."

Beethoven thundered majestically through the room. Vivian let the music roll over her, surround her, while her thoughts moved slowly, almost languorously, within her.

Relaxed. To be relaxed. Out of all the hurrying, all the going on, all the keeping up, to be able to let it all go. Why am I relaxed now? With all the things on my mind . . .

Going back to school tomorrow . . . getting my notes together . . . thesis . . . classes . . . faculty tea on Friday . . . and Mr. Howard . . . dusty jokes of his, math-teacher jokes . . . classes . . . nights . . . long, lonely nights . . . hearing all the beautiful girls and all the beautiful boys coming and going and laughing and talking . . . nights . . .

Not now, she thought. Time enough for all that tomorrow and the next day and the day after. Time enough for the loneliness then.

She felt Tucker's hand close over hers.

Hard, she thought. Hard and practical. A hand to drive a nail. To hold an ax. Slap a man's face with. How did his hand get so hard?

Holding girls' hands maybe. All the hands that hold yours. Why doesn't a girl's hand get hard and worn smooth like a piece of polished wood? Squeezed, caressed, stroked, tickled, grasped, even slapped. The things a girl's hand has to put up with.

Tucker shifted closer on the sofa. Vivian sipped again. The Scotch tingled dryly in her throat.

Let it all go for now. Let it all be tomorrow and not tonight, tomorrow and the next day and the day after.

A breeze moved through the open window behind her, stirring softly in her hair. Somewhere a cricket chirped and a bullbat argued raucously with the quiet. A man passed on the street, whistling.

"Quiet out here, isn't it?" Tucker said. "Just people and animal noises."

"Nice noises. Even the Visiting Cat."

"Lots of cars going by in the daytime, but I'm not here much except at night. Want another drink?"

"Not yet."

Beethoven fell into silence and Tucker got up to turn over the record. Her hand felt cool when he released it. She sipped her drink and saw that the glass was nearly empty. Too fast, she thought.

I feel funny. I feel suddenly—sad. Maybe because I'm leaving tomorrow, because this particular part of my life is finished, over and done with. Even if I come back, this part is finished.

She looked moodily at her glass.

Yesterday and today and tonight will never come again, she thought. How horrible! None of us will ever be the same again, even in another hour, even in ten minutes. Because we will be going on.

Maybe that's it, she thought. Maybe I just don't want to let something go and I don't even know what the something is. Maybe something besides time is passing.

I've never felt quite like this before, she thought. Have I stumbled on some great truth?

She looked at her glass, empty now, and thought sadly that she was probably only getting a little buzz on.

Me and Ralph Waldo Emerson, she thought. A fine time to get philosophical.

Suddenly she saw that Tucker stood over her, looking at her. She was sitting low on the sofa and from her point of view he seemed to loom immeasurably high, his head seemed to be far above where legs and body and neck should project it, his eyes seemed to burn and gleam from distance as illimitable as night.

One exquisite thrill of animal terror pierced her and she had time only to think, He is so tall. So strong and so hard.

"Stand up, Vivian."

The terror was gone then, exorcised in the human voice of this apparition, and she put her glass on the end table, carefully. She noticed faint dust on the lamp shade and she stood up and felt his hands at her waist.

I didn't make her stand up, Tucker thought. She didn't have to.

He felt the soft aliveness of her and the gentle pressure of her forehead against his shoulder, the clean scent of her hair, and the hair itself tickling softly at his jawline.

He became immensely powerful. His whole body became a tremendous repository of strength, strength flowing smoothly along bone and muscle, through veins and arteries. He wanted to crush her against his massiveness.

"Vivian," he said.

He is not so tall after all, she thought. But he is so strong. She felt the whole length of his body against hers, his arms close around her; she felt the tremor of a muscle in his neck.

How odd, she thought.

How strange it is. To stand tightly against this man of whom I know only that he is strong, that he is unbelievably strong, and to want to give myself to him.

How odd. Because what can I give to him except a body? And what is my body except another body? What can I give to him, the way I want to give something to him, that he needs? Needs from me alone?

She felt her hand slide along his arm, past his elbow, touch the rigidity of his biceps.

It has been so long, she thought. So long since my body touched a man, since I have felt my blood race like old wine to my head.

She felt his lips against her ear, his breath idle in her hair, his hands move upon her back.

Her head moved from his shoulder, her face turned upward to his, and he saw lashes long and delicate sweep down over blue eyes. Her lips parted slightly and her teeth were white and strong, and the scent of her came to him like faint music at midnight.

Your mouth is so soft, Tucker thought. All over you are so soft. With my two arms I could squeeze the life from you.

Mine. All of you mine.

Now and forever mine.

He felt the movement of her lips, the sudden unendurable heat of her long body.

Why not? Vivian thought.

If it can never come again, this night, this time. Why not let the old wine have me?

A strange thing happened to Tucker.

Katherine, he thought.

Katherine.

No, he thought. Not again. Not ever again.

His arms loosened. He jerked his mouth from Vivian's lips. Her eyes opened. He saw the question in them, the quick hurt.

And, in despair, he knew he had been wrong. It was Vivian in his arms, not Katherine.

He felt her pushing away from him, her hands on his chest now. He tried to hold her, find her lips again.

"Let me go," she said. She looked away, avoiding his kiss.

She knows, Tucker thought. She feels it. She knows how suddenly all the strength has run out of me to the floor.

"Please let me go," she said.

His arms fell to his sides and he turned slightly away from her and stepped to the window.

"I'm sorry," he said.

"It's all right. I'm glad you stopped."

"I don't know what happened to me." But I do, he thought. I know.

"You swept me off my feet," she said. "And then you put me down again, and my mother thanks you and my father thanks you and I thank you."

We really do, she thought. We thank you for reminding me that I'm just another woman, just another body, and you're just another man who takes what he can get when he can get it. Whatever it was that made you stop gave me time to remember, we thank you for it.

"I think you'd better take me home now," she said.

"No, listen, I—"

"Oh, Bill, don't be silly. It hasn't anything to do with what happened. It's just that I have to leave so early in the morning I think I'd better get some sleep."

"Sure. Sure, I guess so."

Leaving, he thought. She'll be leaving in the morning.

"Listen, will you be coming back if there's another primary?"

"I expect so. Is there going to be?"

For a moment he wanted to tell her, wanted to make sure that she would return. And then his old caution descended on him.

Not even her, he thought. You never can tell.

"Maybe," he said. "I hope so."

"Would you like me to come back?"

She was standing close behind him now, and Tucker thought of taking her in his arms again, remembered the warm, soft length of her, the sweet taste of her lips. He half-turned, uncertain.

She looked at him quickly and reached for her pocketbook, backing away.

"Sure," he said. "You're nice to have around."

She opened the pocketbook.

"You say the nicest things," she said. "Now let me go powder my nose and then take me home."

On the way to the motel Vivian chattered feverishly. She did not want to talk. She wanted to sit quietly in the dark, listening to the even hum of the motor, watching the lights slide past, and call back the early part of the evening, the gaiety and the ease of it.

She wanted to think about that, but she knew that if she allowed herself to think at all she would have to think about why he had stopped when she had given herself up to him. She would have to think about that.

So she talked and talked about nothing, stuffing thought, each time it escaped, back into the overflowing bag of her brain.

Tucker was grateful for this. She's trying to cover up for me, he thought.

She's trying to make me believe I didn't fail somehow. She is even trying to make herself believe that.

The motor court was dark, except for the gaudy neon sign. Lines of cars were drawn up neatly before impersonal numbered doors. The grotesque flickering of the neon cast yellow half-light about the three-sided square.

Vivian gave him her key and he unlocked the door for her. He stood aside and she looked up at him. He imagined he could see her eyes glowing through the dark.

"I hate leaving a place," she said. "Seems so final or something."

"Don't let it be this time."

"Jamestown's not so far away."

"I might come over some time. How would that be?"

"Fine. It really would."

"Vivian, I—"

Hell, he thought, what's the use? What's the damned use until I get it all straightened out for myself?

"I'm going to miss you, Vivian." He took her hand.

"Then come to see me."

They stood there in the doorway of Number Fifteen, holding hands and looking at one another. This is silly, Tucker thought. Like a couple of damned kids.

He pulled her to him roughly and kissed her. His right hand moved harshly along her back and he squeezed her viciously, felt the bony structure of her hip against him.

Abruptly he let her go, her gasp tickling against his cheek. He turned and walked quickly toward his car.

Later he lay in his shorts on the long sofa in his living room.

"You sniveling bastard," he said to no one, to the empty room.

You find in a woman all the things you have never found in anyone and you think of Katherine.

You know this is one you can go all the way for, one you can want forever and ever amen, and still you think of Katherine.

You think of Katherine and knowing better all the time, it comes to you that maybe this one too will take you for a long, sweet ride, get you by the short hair, and yank till you scream.

It comes to you that maybe this one too is like Katherine . . .
He almost cried aloud in shame.

He put his arm across his eyes. Seeing Katherine yesterday
should have cut her out of me, he thought. Her and all she did
to me. Cut her out of me like a surgeon does a tumor.

If it hadn't meant so much. Once. A long time ago.

If Katherine had been just a pair of hot pants on the make.
If she hadn't got into me so long ago—like a tapeworm, a tapeworm in my guts . . .

1937

The sound of the waves breaking against the white beach comes
steadily up through the cool salt air to the cottage. The couples
sitting on the veranda hear it, feel it, a relentless bass pounding
and pounding and pounding against their talk and laughter,
against the tinny blare of their radio.

The cottage is almost in darkness. One by one the couples have
slipped away, laughing and whispering in the dark, strolling toward the white beach and the waves foaming white in the glow
of a half-full moon. Now there are only six people on the broad
porch.

Two boys in bathing trunks and tee shirts sit with their feet
on the porch rail. A blond girl sits in the lap of one of them.
She also wears a bathing suit. She has a white, short jacket over
her shoulders, and she lies passively back against the boy.

Another girl, a nondescript brunette, leans on the back of the
chair in which the second boy is sitting. She too wears a bathing
suit, cut so low it barely covers her young breasts. She is holding
a brown bottle.

"Come on," she says, patting the boy's cheek. "You can't get
up if you drink any more."

"Fa Chrisake," the boy says. "Fa Chrisake you eager or something?"

"Give her what she wants," a third girl says. "Make her give
me the bottle and you go give her what she wants."

"Oh, *you!*" the girl in the low-cut bathing suit cries, stamping
her bare foot. "You talk so *awful!*"

The third girl laughs. The sound is moist, taunting. She is sitting with her feet on the rail like the boys, a little apart from them. She draws deeply on a cigarette and the yellow gleam of it lights her face for a moment, making the painted mouth a black slash against the white skin. Even in the dark there is about her something of contempt, some certainty rising from her in waves more tangible than the cigarette smoke.

"Give me the bottle," she says.

"Oh, *you!*" The young breasts move under the low-cut bathing suit, jerkily, as the girl stamps her foot again.

"Fa Chrisake," the boy says. "Give Kathrin the bottle, willya, Becky?"

Becky stamps her foot a third time, an angry little cry welling up out of the low-cut bathing suit. She thrusts the bottle into the darkness, toward the cigarette glow. She runs off the porch.

The boy stands up and looks after her.

"Go give her what she wants," the girl says, the cigarette momentarily lighting her face again, the black mouth across it like a stripe. "Don't just stand there."

"Fa Chrisake," the boy says. He walks unsteadily off the porch, toward the white beach.

Again the moist, taunting laugh.

"I never said *what* she wants. Did I?" The voice is tinged with arrogance.

"You made it plain," the second boy says. He puts his hand against the back of the blond girl on his lap and pushes her to her feet. She pulls the white jacket about her and looks up at him as he stands.

"Where we goin, Ben?"

"Get a little fresh air."

"Oh." She sways close to him. "Got a bottle, honey?"

"Yes." He holds it up. There is something overpatient in his voice, something tired. "Everybody's got a bottle."

"It gets cold on that ol beach sometimes."

"You ought to know." The third girl is still sitting with her feet on the porch railing, the arrogance and the contempt plain in her words.

The blond girl laughs, sways closer to the boy called Ben, putting both hands on his arm.

"But you'll never know, honey. Not sittin there you won't."

"Oh, hell," Ben says. He picks up a folded blanket from the floor by his chair. "Let's go be young and modern." He almost drags the blond girl with him off the porch.

"Give me the bottle," she squeals. "Let me carry the bottle, Ben!"

"Take it," Ben says. "Take it and shut up." Then they are gone into the night, the rhythmic pound of the waves.

For a long time the girl on the porch remains motionless, her long legs extended to the rail, the glow of the cigarette coal moving occasionally in a long, slow arc to or from her face. Behind her, in the vacant interior of the cottage, the radio bounces tinny music into the darkness.

She snaps the cigarette butt over the rail.

"What rotten luck," she says.

A figure sits up, slowly, reluctantly, from a cot at the other end of the porch. She sees the movement from the corner of her eye, not turning her head.

"Oh, don't get up, Tucker. Don't bother."

He stands up from the cot and walks toward her until he is behind her chair, looking down on her. He wears slacks and a sport shirt. He is barefoot.

"You still think I smell bad?"

The moist laugh is almost lost in the shrieking music, the booming fall of a breaker on the beach.

"I haven't smelled you lately."

He turns and goes into the cottage and shuts off the radio. The sudden cessation of the music doubles the pounding crash of the surf. He comes back, still moving slowly, until he stands over her again.

"You don't think I'd have come, do you? If I'd known you were the girl?"

She lights another cigarette. In the bright flare of the match he sees the deep, shadowed cleft between her heavy breasts. She holds the match a long time after the cigarette is lit, letting it burn almost down to her fingers. He stands looking down at her breasts and the cleft between them, at the long whiteness of her legs stretched to the porch rail.

She flips the match away.

"You can go," she says. "Nobody's stopping you."

"I might. You can always get a replacement for me."

She nods, drawing at the cigarette.

"I shouldn't have come anyway. I should have known my luck better. But Ben talked me into it."

"So he's to blame," she said.

"It's almost funny. After all these years you and me on a blind date."

She stands up and turns. She leans back against the porch rail, her arms behind her, supporting her. He looks at the shadow the moon drops across her thrust-out breasts.

"Relax," he says. "I can see them all right."

"I've grown up, haven't I?" She does not move.

"Not much. But I have."

"Oh, you're a big strong man. You always were."

"Even when I was a smelly mill hand's son? Even when you used to laugh at me in high school?"

"Just like your damn father," she says. "Just like him."

For the first time he laughs. He laughs loudly and clearly, and then he stops abruptly.

"I was just thinking," he says, "the exact same thing about you."

"I hate your father, Tucker. You know that?" The voice is almost a whisper now, a whisper stabbing fiercely at him across the empty chair, above the sullen boom of the waves.

He does not answer. He grips the back of the chair, feeling the soft wood smooth under his palms.

"I was there looking out the window that night when he wanted to blow us up during the strike. I saw Daddy give in to him."

"Yes," he says. "I was there too."

"That lint head," she says, a tremor in the whisper now. "Good God! My Daddy giving in to that lint head—"

"Aren't you lovely?" he says. "Aren't you a lovely girl?"

And the whisper again, so fierce now he feels the hot rush of it on his cheek.

"You lint-head bastard—"

He steps around the chair and slaps her. He stands looking down at her, at her heavy breasts. His fingers flex, convulse, flex again.

"But you'll never beat me," she whispers, as if she has not been struck. "You never will."

"I'm leaving," he says. "So you won't have to smell me."

She does not answer. He slaps her again, harder. He turns and goes into the cottage. He goes to the small room where he shares a single bed with Ben. He begins to put his clothes into a suitcase.

Five minutes later he comes out on the porch again, carrying the suitcase. He does not look for her but goes straight across the porch to the steps.

"Tucker."

He stops, turning his head slowly until he sees the glow of her cigarette.

"I'm game if you are, Tucker."

He puts the suitcase down. She is leaning against the wall of the cottage by the door. In the shadowed darkness he sees only the darker darkness where she stands.

"I deserved to be slapped," she says.

Tucker goes slowly across the wide planks of the porch. He can see the whiteness of her face now.

"Have a drink with me," she says. "And stay."

She pushes the bottle at him. He feels it against his chest. He takes it in his hand.

"Don't tell me you don't drink," she says. "I heard you say that before."

"I don't."

"You do now."

He drinks. The unfamiliar fire of the liquor scalds his stomach. He chokes, hears the moist laugh, feels the bottle taken from his hand.

He watches her drink, put the bottle on the arm of a chair. His eyes are accustomed to the dark now and he can see all of her face, the swelling outlines of her body.

And there is within him, instantaneously, inexplicably, a great longing. He has felt it before but he has never known what it is. Now, in the white upturned face, in the heavy breasts, in that air of confidence, of certainty, of blooded arrogance, that aura rising from her like gray, lazy curls of cigarette smoke, he discovers what it is he has longed for so often.

"Katherine," he says. "Katherine—"

He puts his hands on her hips. He sees her arms rise, sees her hands go by his face, feels them cool and strong on the back of his neck. She is pulling at him then, eagerly, and his muscles surrender. He bends to her pull.

He feels his face crush against the softness of her breasts, smells the clinging, female scent of her flesh even above the smell of her damp bathing suit.

God, he thinks. God.

This is all I ever wanted.

After a while she pushes his head away. He stands upright again and she is smiling at him, her hands still cool and moving on the back of his neck.

"Now will you stay?"

He nods. His voice is thick, hoarse.

"I'll stay."

She laughs, the moistness of it almost liquid now.

"For old times' sake?"

"Damn old times," he says. He pulls her to him, his hands moving over her, his head bending toward the black scar of her mouth.

She slips deftly from his arms.

"Time enough," she says. She picks up the bottle from the chair-arm, takes a folded blanket from the same chair.

"Come on." She goes swiftly down the steps. He hears the laugh float behind her, mocking, arrogant, liquid.

He runs after her, toward the sound of the waves pounding and pounding and pounding against the white beach, the oblivious shore.

⋈

Tucker shook himself like a drenched dog and sat up. He reached for his cigarettes.

How she must have laughed, he thought. She must have been

laughing at me even that night, even as she ran from me toward the beach. She must have been laughing at me even then. The first night she beat me.

Long enough, he thought. Too goddam long.

She won't beat me this time. Not ever again. No matter what. If I have to lie and cheat and steal. I'm going to have what I want and Vivian is part of it. No matter what. Katherine won't beat me again.

He drew deeply on the cigarette.

You're dead, Katherine.

As of now.

Worms are crawling in your beautiful body. Worms are looking at me through your beautiful eyes.

A chill passed through him. It was almost like fear. He stood up abruptly and went to the window.

Sitting on the sill, its disdainful face pressed to the screen, its jaunty whiskers contemptuously askew, was the Visiting Cat.

The son of a bitch is laughing at me too, Tucker thought. Sitting there and laughing at me.

He raked his nails sharply across the screen.

There was almost invisible movement and the Visiting Cat was gone, a single, sibilant, dying hiss of scorn and mockery remaining behind him.

Laughing at me, Tucker thought.

Sitting there and laughing at me.

Chapter Eight

To the men who regarded the ballot box as a means to an end rather than an end in itself, it was all too plain that politics, as it had been known in the State, stood at Armageddon.

Three men had created this situation: the Governor, Ralph Anson, and Tucker.

The Governor:

Who had been awakened one midnight with the news that Senator Johnston was dead, the first Senator from the State to die in office in nearly fifty years. The Governor suddenly became the most powerful chief executive in nearly fifty years.

By the constitution, he, a party hack who chewed Brown's Mule and stayed out of trouble, had the sole power and right to appoint a Senator, subject not even to the confirmation of public opinion. The Governor was not so much of a hack as to drop such a delectable fly ball.

The machine, which could not rightfully be called the Jones Machine or the Honest John Doe Machine, was not an organization in the sense of the Hague or Crump or Kelly organizations; it was merely a loosely knit collection of politically astute lawyers, farmers, businessmen, and county and State officials. (For all that, the machine had power; it had discipline, unspoken but effective; it had learned to work in harmony with its various cogs; it firmly believed in one for all and all for one, and if you keep the graft down and the people happy, the hell with the college professors. Because who the hell cared how the tax laws were padded or how State contracts were awarded or where highways were built or if the State had such new-fangled crap as stream pollution laws? Who the hell cared as long as you could keep them interested in other things, like prohibition and the highway death toll?

Whose business was it anyway?) The machine found itself, for once, powerless. What it could do to the Governor was not half so potent as what a hard-pressed Washington Administration could do for him.

Ralph Anson:

Who, to the absolute consternation of the machine (it was almost one man—the various members of the tribe were as like as fluffs of popcorn), thus became, because the Administration wanted him in Washington, the first threat in nearly fifty years to party harmony and control.

Tall, gaunt, his ears wide and red, his bony face topped by a drifting shock of white hair, he had captured the imagination of the State and had held it for years.

He had never finished the fourth grade, going to work in a print shop to support his widowed mother. At the age of twenty he was editor and publisher of the Florence *Herald*, self-educated in the best Abe Lincoln manner. At the age of thirty he published an unpolished but penetrating book on textile labor relations and became a nationally quoted authority on the subject.

His national publicity had trebled due to a peace-making role in the bloody Florence strike of 1928. Then President Roosevelt began to send him about the country as a mediator. By World War II, he was a top trouble-shooter for the War Labor Board.

Assignments to the U.N., among other things, followed. With the Governor's thunderclap appointment, the machine exploded like a pin wheel. In thirty years of trying they had never succeeded in making Ralph Anson one of them. They did not underestimate him; most of all, they did not underestimate the power of a Senator:

Who could hand-pick postmasters, tax collectors, Federal attorneys and judges, who could make or break an appropriation for a bridge or a highway or a post office, who could stop or greatly slow up the machine's life blood—the favors it could do and receive and withhold. Especially a maverick Senator with a White House calling card.

The third man, Tucker, knew these things also. But he had not come up through the ranks of the machine for nothing. He had not committed innumerable names and faces to memory as an exercise, and he had not done and received uncounted favors as good, clean fun; he had not schemed and studied and bided his time in vain.

Tucker, better than any other member of the machine, knew Ralph Anson. No one underestimated the Senator; Tucker alone did not overestimate him.

He knew that popularity is a fleeting thing which will not always withstand attack; he knew that a captured imagination is a prisoner, not a convert; that an honest man is a vulnerable man because he has not troubled to make himself invulnerable.

Above all, Tucker understood the things of which people were afraid.

It was, as he immediately saw, a time to strike, to take command, to stick out his neck, and Harvey Pollock was the best-looking front man in sight.

A Baptist businessman and banker; a decorated veteran who had held a post in the Japanese Occupation Forces and achieved no little publicity in the process; a member of an old State family; irreproachably American; undeniably Southern; financially well-heeled; and, judged by his past record, not brilliant enough to make anyone much trouble—tailor-made for a candidate.

He had one drawback. He was not well-known in the State. But only time was needed, Tucker knew, to remedy this.

Tucker and Pollock, with the task force of Ruggles, Gary, and Hadley, long ago selected by Tucker for just such an opportunity, and, to be fair, some added momentum from Joe Harrison, moved quickly. They had the tacit consent of the machine. They had the promise of extra time by Rooster Ed McDowell's entrance into the fray. The rest they supplied themselves.

They attacked: Anson's publicized liberal stand on labor, his known belief in social welfare, his alleged connection with the CIO, his fictitious preference for socialism (reasoned Tucker: if we attack something that doesn't exist, it automatically does exist; how else could you attack it?).

They said, not untruthfully, that Ralph Anson did not walk in step with other Southern Senators and produced chapter and verse from the *Congressional Record* to back the statement. They said that he favored socialized medicine (which he did not) and

Federal Aid to Education (which he did). They said he was for high taxes and a labor draft (soon after claiming he was a tool of the CIO). They made much of his friendship with Wilson Holloway, the famous apologist for communism (the two men had once exchanged letters).

They mentioned organizations to which Anson had belonged, or upon whose stationery his name had appeared. There were seventeen of these: ten no longer existed; three of them never had; four had been placed on the subversive list only in the last three years—in each case, more than eight years had elapsed since Anson had quit them or forbade them the use of his name.

Most of these organizations, however, were footsy with the Reds, they said, and where there was that much smoke, any red-blooded American knew there was bound to be some fire.

They did not say so much about Harvey Pollock. They said only that he was a true-blue American; that he had never belonged to any organizations but Kiwanis and the American Legion; that he was a man of the soil (his wife did own one farm and he occasionally spent a week end there); that he had a war record; that he wouldn't know Wilson Holloway if he saw him (neither would Ralph Anson, but both would have recognized his picture); that he would fit right in with the great statesmen of the South; that he thought the Government was mighty big for its britches these days; that he hated a Socialist almost as badly as a Communist, if you could tell the difference.

"I am," said Colonel Pollock (the military title was an asset, Tucker finally decided, if soft-pedaled in urban districts), "a middle-of-the-roader. I believe in Southern Democracy."

"Southern Democracy" became his watchword. He never said what it was (when the band played *Dixie*, who cared? You could almost see Jeb Stuart riding into the sunset), but it sounded safe and familiar.

"In working to develop new ideas freely," Ralph Anson said, "a man has to take positions. That is a risk and a duty no man, if he has an open mind, can avoid. Else there would be no new ideas."

This was as strong a defense as the Senator, who had served most of one session before having to come home to campaign, ever made for himself. He did not seem to be interested in what was said about him and in nearly three hundred speeches—some short, some long—he did not once mention "Pollock" or "my opponent."

To the despair of his executive assistant, Ben Kirby, who was also his campaign manager, he insisted on basing his campaign on foreign policy, with which he had occupied himself in late years. He spoke earnestly for the Marshall Plan, the Atlantic Pact, Point Four, for a new evaluation of policy in the Middle East (how in the name of God, Ben Kirby thought, does he expect a peanut farmer to know what even the old policy is?).

Without embarrassment, the Senator put forth a world peace plan based on "the brotherhood of man and the fatherhood of God." In his few excursions into domestic affairs, he spoke briefly in favor of Social Security for broader groups of working people, a strengthened Army and Navy, peaceful development of atomic energy, and more "responsibility" on the part of both labor and management.

His popularity, so it seemed, held strong. He won by 40,000 votes. But he did not win by 100,000 as the *Capital Times* had predicted. He did not achieve a majority of the total votes. He was not, in the closing days of the campaign, being cheered wildly.

Tucker saw this happen, in fact presided over it, with the detachment of a sidewalk superintendent. It was no more than he had expected; no less, indeed, than he had planned.

If the words were Joe Harrison's, and the voice Harvey Pollock's, the idea was his. The organization was his. The control was his. He was the power behind the throne, the man behind the man behind the gun.

For Tucker had long ago decided that the popularity of Ralph Anson was based on two factors: that he was known to be a self-made man, coming from nothing, coming from less than most of the people who looked up to him; that in twenty years of public life his reputation for integrity had never been questioned because it had been thought unquestionable.

The first fact could not be taken from him. The second, Tucker

knew, could be destroyed as simply and efficiently as a huge swinging iron ball knocks down a building and grinds it into rubble.
Not just Senator Ralph Anson's reputation for integrity.

Anybody's.

By Tuesday morning after Saturday's primary election significant
things began to happen around the State.

In Bledsoe County the Minute Men passed a resolution urging
Harvey Pollock to seek a second primary.

The Minute Men, of which there was a chapter in each county,
were all boys and girls under eighteen. The emblem of the group
was the Confederate flag and all good Minute Men possessed
floppy gray hats supposedly like that of General Lee. Their meet-
ings were enlivened with more or less accurate versions of the
rebel yell.

Similar resolutions followed from chapters all over the State.

In Fentress County Pollock Headquarters reopened with great
fanfare. Other county headquarters followed suit. None of the
managers knew, of course, whether the Colonel would run and
said as much. But they all left the impression that a real American could not do otherwise.

In Marlborough County, where the population was fifty-seven
per cent Negro, many colored people received post cards from a
Negro organization in New York (the National Society for the
Advance of Colored People, according to the signature), urging
the election of Senator Ralph Anson—although only twenty-two
per cent of the Negroes in the county could read and were eligible
to vote.

Many whites were quite indignant when some of these cards
fell by mistake into their hands.

In Hancock County the Director of Public Welfare gave his
brother, who was chairman of the board of county commissioners, a list of those who were receiving Old Age Assistance and Aid
to Dependent Children grants. The list, by Federal and State
law, was confidential.

But it won't hurt these goddam parasites to know where their
money comes from, will it? the chairman of the board of com-

missioners demanded of the Welfare Director, who had never been able to hold a job before getting his present office. The least they can do, the chairman of the board continued, winking at the director, is show a little gratitude after all the help we give them.

In Sequatchie County Zeb Ruggles made out a personal check for $10,000 to the State Development Corporation and mailed it, with several other large checks similarly made out by business associates and friends, to an address in Capital City.

There were, in every county, conferences of Pollock forces. Veteran reporters wrote many pieces in the State press, predicting that Pollock would run. So much activity so well co-ordinated, they said, could have but one meaning. When the signal had been given, or what it had been, they did not know. But it had been given, they were sure.

The Anson organization, which had been set up hastily and with a good deal of confidence but with little thought to permanence, was also sure of this. Members of the organization, mostly amateur politicians, schoolteachers, a few editors, preachers, even a merchant or two, were not worried too much, however. A lead like theirs couldn't be overcome in the short time the Pollock men had.

Of course it couldn't, they agreed, not even if the last circular letter from Ben Kirby had cautioned against overconfidence and urged a redoubled effort for the second primary Kirby seemed to be sure was coming.

There was also the question of money. There had never been too much of it; Pollock naturally had most of the big contributors in his pocket. And now, when there might not even be another vote, when Anson had such a huge lead, on what could you base an appeal for campaign funds?

There was, of course, no sense in taking chances. Senator Anson's return to Washington and his duties there while he awaited Pollock's decision were duly publicized; Anson voters were reminded that, to make their first vote count, they might have to vote again and were urged not to fail in this duty.

There was little, if any, effort to attract new support. Why should there be? All they had to do was hold what they had and Anson was in.

There was much indignation over the Pollock campaign in the first primary. If this indignation often sounded merely defensive, how the hell else could it sound? You couldn't let a man get away scot free with Pollock's kind of lying and mudslinging, could you? And if you had orders to keep your own hands clean, then all you could do was deny what the son of a bitch was saying, wasn't it?

The appeal to regional conceit and youthful passion which made a success of the Minute Men was decried—but, at the same time, you had to be careful to compliment the brats on their public spirit and their civic interest.

The reopening of Pollock Headquarters throughout the State was greeted with derision—but it was almost impossible to say anything at all in that line and not disclose that you wished the bastard would go on and announce and let you get your tail off the fence.

In Marlborough County, after the post card incident, the Anson manager, a school principal, denied emphatically the legitimacy of the cards, pointing out that the National Association for the Advancement of Colored People also denied it and that there was no such group as the National Society for the Advance of Colored People.

He knew as he spoke that the harm was done: those who had believed the cards to begin with had the seed in their minds now; those who had not needed no denials. And even some of these might have fallen victim to at least a twinge of wonder.

In Hancock, when the Anson manager learned that many people on the welfare lists were being threatened with loss of their grants unless they voted for Pollock—the old fellow who reported this said he'd be durned if he was gonna take the roof offen his head for any danged politicians; he was too durn old to git on his high horse—he found it quite impossible to prove it. He also found it impossible—as well as illegal—to get such lists for himself in order to reassure the old folks and the poverty-stricken young mothers that their politics, if any, had nothing to do with their grants.

In the end he said and did nothing. What else could he say? Or do?

An auditor hired to investigate the State Development Corporation found that it was legitimately certified by the Corporation Commission, and that its officers and directors were five bona fide residents of Capital City of whom no one but their neighbors had ever heard. The five said that their future plans called for the building of tourist courts over the State, and they indignantly refused to disclose their financial statement or their list of stockholders.

But there was no apparent loss of confidence among men who believed in Ralph Anson. There was not even any assurance that there would be another election.

Ben Kirby needed no such assurance.

Tucker, he thought. His hand is in all of this.

Like a dirty footprint on a clean, white sheet. You rarely see him, you never hear him. You just feel him looking over your shoulder. You just feel his fingers reaching for your wallet.

And you turn suddenly and he is gone. Your wallet too, like as not.

Ben worked long hours at the office, wrote hundreds of letters, made so many phone calls he began to dread the coming of the bill, traveled many miles consulting with field workers, conferred endlessly with visitors and backers and reporters and casual callers.

That much I can do, he thought. My goddamned dead level best.

And even as he thought it, he thought also that it was not enough. His best was not good enough against Tucker. Because Tucker would do what he had to do to win. Whatever he had to do.

And I won't, Ben thought. Neither will the Senator.

But how can it be?

How can such a man defeat the Senator?

How can such lies, such deceit, such deliberate dishonesty be rewarded?

How can any man believe as I believe, as the Senator believes, and admit this thing is happening, admit that it can happen?

It can't happen, he told himself. That's the only answer. It can't happen.

✁

Joe Harrison moved his black onyx desk set to the exact center of his blotter pad. His name was engraved on a gold plate on the base and it was one of his proudest possessions. It had been awarded him by a civic club which had judged him "Young Man of the Year" in the State.

He leaned back heavily in the swivel chair and passed a hand tiredly across his eyes. The gesture expressed the volume of his fatigue, engendered in faith and loyalty to the cause, but he watched closely to make sure Fred would notice the desk set.

"So you're coming to work for us?" He sighed between each word.

Fred flicked cigarette ashes on the rug.

"It's not my idea," he said. The bored elegance of his knit tie, the casual drape of his gray suit, the careless wave of his dark hair, all were out of place in the room. There was an insolence about him that seemed an affront to the huge portrait of his father, beaming gallantly from the wall behind him.

"We need every man," Joe said. "Everybody's got to pull his weight. Do his share."

Fred looked at him blankly. This eight-ball never gets off the radio, he thought.

"You've come up in the world, haven't you, Mr. Harrison. Last time I was up here they had you out in the bull pen with the hoi polloi."

Joe stiffened.

"I'm in charge"—crisply, fingers drumming on the desk—"while Colonel Pollock and Mr. Tucker are away."

"Well, well. Three cheers."

"What?"

"Three cheers. You said you were in charge and I said three cheers."

"Oh." Joe looked doubtful.

He cleared his throat and the strong, peremptory sound he achieved reassured him. After all, he was in charge here.

"What can you do, Fred? Type, anything like that?"

Fred shuddered visibly. This is a hell of a way to start a summer vacation, he thought. I'm not even getting *paid*, for Christ sake.

"No typing. I got a liberal education."

"Mr. Tucker suggested before he left that we put you with the mimeograph crew."

"That bastard. He would."

"Now, listen," Joe said. "You might as well get that chip off your shoulder." Don't be too rough on him, he thought, you don't know how much weight he swings with the Colonel. "You know your father thinks your working here a good thing. He thinks—"

"I know, I know. The experience will be good for me." It might also pick up a vote or two. Family solidarity. My aching ass.

Joe grinned slyly. Make it attractive, he thought. That's the way to handle it.

"There's a couple of cute chicks on the mimeograph crew, Fred. Best spot in the office." He winked elaborately.

"Hell, I might as well try that as anything else."

"I can fix you up with one of them. She—"

"No, thanks. I don't get along much with girls." Not your kind anyway, Fred thought. I can imagine the kind of cute chicks would interest a tool like you.

"Wait till you see this one." Joe rolled his eyes ceilingward. Fred had the feeling that he was about to launch into description. He spoke hastily to avoid the possibility.

"When will Tucker be back?"

Joe returned to earth. Everybody wants to know when Tucker will be back, he thought.

"I don't know exactly. Lot of things to attend to, you know."

"Sure. Throats to cut and all."

Joe frowned slightly. He ought to watch that kind of talk. You never can tell.

"You don't like Tucker?"

"It's not that. I don't like anybody. He's just another snake in the grass, far as I can see."

Joe's frown increased. The interview was not going the way it should, the way the Colonel would have wanted it. The boy obviously just didn't give a damn and that was bad.

"We've all got to work together here, Fred. We can't afford petty jealousies. What we're working for is pretty important and we've got to be one big happy family. You're your father's son, Fred. I know you've got the same stuff in you."

My God, Fred thought. I hope I'm not as full of it as he is.

He stood up and snuffed out his cigarette. I am not going to be sick, he told himself. I refuse to be sick. I absolutely refuse.

"I think I'll go—pitch right in, Mr. Harrison."

"Good! That's the way to talk! Know where to go?"

"I guess I can find a mimeograph machine somewhere."

He went to the door and turned, looking at the portrait of Colonel Pollock. The portrait looked back benignly and Fred glanced away.

"After all," he said, his voice almost a whisper. "I am my father's son. Just like you said."

He closed the door gently behind him.

Now what in hell did he mean by that? Joe thought. You can't figure these kids out. Not a brain in their heads.

This Fred now. I do my best to help him out, help him see the way life is, the way to get something out of it. And he doesn't even have a word to say. Even offered to fix him up with Ellen.

There's one thing I can agree with Fred on. I bet that superior son of a bitch Tucker would be surprised to know what a lot of people think about him. The way he walks over you like you were a piece of rug.

He picked up a report from one of the mountain counties, then suddenly put it down again and leaned back in the chair, his hands clasping the padded arms.

Now by God, he thought. Maybe I've come up with something. So Fred hates him too?

He stared, unseeing, at the portrait of Colonel Pollock. On the desk an electric clock whirred softly, and somewhere on the street beneath the open windows a newsboy howled the afternoon headlines.

Fred, Joe thought. Tucker. Me.

Suddenly he became poignantly aware of the portrait. The late afternoon sun slanted through the Venetian blinds and latticed the Colonel's face with shadow. It seemed to Joe that the eyes looking down at him were deep and sorrowful and somehow trusting.

I've got to find a way, he thought. I've got to fix Tucker before he takes the Colonel for a ride. And me with him. I've got to find some way to fix him.

His head began to ache sharply. There was so much going on inside of it. There were so many little parts of a puzzle floating around in it. Only something was missing. Something threw the whole thing out of kilter.

God damn it, Joe thought.

He's not that smart. Nobody is.

There must be a way. He must have left himself open somewhere.

Everybody makes mistakes. Even Tucker.

Chapter Nine

The old man spat tobacco juice over the porch railing. Before him, clasped about the knobby head of a rough-cut walking stick, his ancient, long fingers curled like bird claws. He did not look at Tucker.

In the clear, country silence, Tucker heard a hen cluck. He paused, one foot on the faded white step. He pushed his hat back on his head and waited for the old man to speak. A fat yellow cat lazed from under the step and pushed selfishly against his leg.

The old man's head twitched on his thin shoulders.

"I showd 'em, I reckon. Eh?" His eyes, faded and blue and unfocused, blobbed toward Tucker.

Tucker came up on the porch.

"I reckon you did, Mr. Ed."

"I showd 'em, right enough."

Tucker sat on the porch railing and turned his head to look out over the country. The old boy's got himself a view, he thought. Mountains open up a man inside some way.

The old man thumped his stick against the floor.

"I sure-God did." He cackled thinly, the sound like an ungreased axle. "Woulda won if I coulda got out an talk to folks."

Tucker nodded but the old man was no longer looking at him. His undirected eyes had flopped back toward the hills.

The yard, dusty, almost grassless, sloped away from the porch to a snag-toothed picket fence beside a modern black-top highway. Beyond the highway open country climbed into mountains.

These were green mountains, etched bulkily against a higher ridge beyond, less green than blue, and an even higher one beyond that, only a faint blue haze against the lighter blue of the sky.

The house itself was on the down slope of a smaller hill. To its right a gap opened, through which the highway came curving from the east and the lowlands. To its left the gap also opened, but only to another range, to another valley like this one, imprisoned by the splendor of mountains. The paved highway ended a few feet beyond the picket fence, trickling off into yellow, washboard clay.

What must it be? Tucker thought. To live among mountains? To wake to them in the morning and work by them in the day, to sleep with them at night?

They are so—immovable.

He heard breath whine and looked around. A thin slime of tobacco juice lingered in the corner of the old man's mouth and his frail shoulders shook slightly.

The mountains have seen you come, Tucker thought, and they damn sure are going to see you go. Before too long.

"Kinda risky, ain't it?" the old man squeaked. "You comin up here?"

"Not now. I'm just trying to get you to support Colonel Pollock, if anybody asks."

Again creaky laughter spat out of the old man. He thumped his stick.

"My support. That's good, that is. My support."

He wiped his mouth with his hand, darting it to his lips. That hand, Tucker thought. That very one, that collection of dry bones and frail, decaying flesh—that hand he could hurl like a spear toward the sky and the rooster, that hand with which, by the mere flick of a finger, imperious and arrogant beyond even the rooster, he could arouse the anger in a thousand bellies.

That hand, returning now, even with the watered old blood still trickling through it, returning now to the dust of its creation.

"My support," the old man sneezed. "Old folks. They wouldn't vote for nobody but me. Never have. They remember, I reckon."

"Sure. They're your folks, Mr. Ed."

The old man did not answer. And you can have them, Tucker thought.

"You come a long way, boy."

"Lot to do, Mr. Ed. You know what a second primary is."

The old man snorted. The sound was like a child's cough.

"Never had but one. First time I run. Never let 'em get that fur, any more."

"I reckon not."

"Never let 'em get that fur with ol Ed."

A sound from behind broke the stillness. Tucker turned and saw a young girl in the door of the little house. Her face was vacant, ugly, and he saw that she was barefoot. Her mouth was slightly open as she stared at him.

"You, Cartie," the old man said, not moving. "Get along from there."

The girl moved back into the house, still watching Tucker. The cat came arrogantly up on the porch. It sat down by the screen door and began to lick its leg.

"Grandawter," the old man said. He snickered. "I got to be tuck care of these days, seem like."

He looks like one of these mountain breezes would blow him right out of the valley, Tucker thought. I guess that kid has to do for him. Some life.

He felt the old man, who had not taken his eyes from the hills in five minutes, jerk violently toward him.

"Boy got kilt in the war," he said. "Know that?"

"I heard tell, Mr. Ed. That was tough."

"Her pappy." The old man sniggered again. "Hated my guts. Got kilt in the war though."

I'm going to get this over with, Tucker thought. The morbid old coot will have me in the nuthouse. To think what he's come to.

"Kilt in the war. Shot spang in the head. Feller wrote me all about it."

"They do that sometimes."

"Spang in the head. Feller wrote me."

"Listen," Tucker said, "I brought you your money."

The old man did not seem to hear. Tucker reached to his inside coat pocket. He took out the neat stack of new bills and leaned forward to put them in the old man's lap.

"It's all there, Mr. Ed."

He felt the cat rub against his leg again. Why do cats always pick out my legs? he thought.

"Well, I been me some places," the old man said. "Seen me some things."

"Sure—listen, I have to go. You want to count the money?"

The old man thumped his cane on the floor.

"Seen me some things," he said.

"I have to go now, Mr. Ed, I—"

"Use to look at them hills over ther. When I was a strutter like you. Use to look at them hills and think they want nair one I couldn't climb up."

Jesus Christ, Tucker thought. I put enough money in his lap to take care of him the rest of his days and he talks about mountains.

The poor old bastard.

"Not nair one I couldn't climb up to the top and piss on."

Tucker stood up and the cat shied at the sudden movement.

"You take care of yourself, Mr. Ed."

The old man's bulbous eyes wobbled toward him. Suddenly they cleared, for a moment became the pale, piercing blue that had impaled Tucker one long-ago day in a ball park.

Tucker stopped.

"I ain't counted my money yet."

"Go ahead then. I don't care."

The thin, clawing fingers shuffled slowly at the bills. He's not that old, Tucker thought. He won't ever be that old.

He looked again at the mountains. The green trees on the near slope might have been one enormous matted growth, covering the hillside to the summit. Little slashes and scars occasionally broke this surface and these were rutted roads and cornfields. To his left a feather of blue smoke hazed out of the green toward the sky. It could have been a house or a still. There were plenty of both up there, but you couldn't see either.

He began to feel trapped. There was too much of them, he thought. They loomed all around you and didn't even bother to laugh at how small you were. A mountain wouldn't even know a man existed.

I wouldn't like it, he thought. I wouldn't want any mountains around me all the time.

He heard the raspy snigger file against the old man's throat. He saw the old man stuff the bills clumsily in his pants pocket.

"That ought to buy you a lot of corn liquor," Tucker said, smiling.

The old man did not answer. And then Tucker saw the eyes unfocus and wander again toward the hills.

"Reckon this is the bottom of the well," the old man wheezed. "Reckon I plumb hit bottom."

Fine time to develop a conscience, Tucker thought.

"Don't feel like that," he said. "It was just a business deal. What the voters don't know is none of their business."

"Voters!"

Contempt smoked the word. It had almost been the voice, Tucker thought, which once could cast the word "nigger" at you like a blob of spittle.

"I mean me," the old man said. "I don't give a shit for no voters."

"Well," Tucker said, "I have to be getting on—"

"Some day"—an incredibly thin finger shook toward the hills —"I'm a-goin to walk over to that ther mountain. I'm a-goin to dig me a hole under it an I'm a-goin to lay down an stick my head in it."

"Now, Mr. Ed, you ought not to—"

"Let that mountain sit on me."

Tucker managed a laugh. "Take more than a mountain to hold you down, Mr. Ed."

"Use to think I could piss on ever one. When I was a strutter like you. Piss on 'em all."

Tucker stumbled over the cat. Get out of the goddam way, he thought.

"I'll be seeing you, Mr. Ed." He stepped down from the porch and moved toward his car. He felt the silence of the oblivious mountains packed tight against his ears.

In a pig's ass, I will, he thought. I'll be goddamned if I can listen to crap like this. I got too much to do to listen to—

The poor old bastard.

"Well, I been me some places," he heard the old man say. "I seen me some things."

The hen was clucking again and Tucker felt the girl in the doorway again, felt her eyes on his spine, felt her looking after him. The dry rustle of the old man's voice echoed from the silent mountains.

He slammed the car door and drove quickly away. In the high, still air, the engine noise was smooth and powerful.

The poor old bastard, he thought. Alone with that girl and the mountains.

The poor old bastard.

No matter what. The poor old crazy dead bastard.

John Briggs settled his bulk more comfortably in the cane-bottom rocker and extended his legs in front of him to the porch rail.

From under the brim of his hat he could see the nervous feet in the bright tan shoes on the floor beside him. Looks like he could of come some decent hour, he thought. Reckon I can't pick and choose any more, but I sure could use a little peace right now.

For twenty years he had topped off his midday meal with this hour of relaxation, his hat tipped low over his eyes so that casual passers-by would think him asleep and not bother him with greetings.

Being Sheriff John Briggs now made no difference, he thought. A nap was still good for his digestion.

He contrasted the shining leather of the tan shoes with his own plain black brogans. Goes to show you, he thought.

"What's this all about, Sheriff?" The voice irritated him. No sense a man whining like that, he thought.

"Now you ain't no fool, Odell," he said.

"Try not to be, I reckon."

"Ought to know what it's about, then."

"You don't mean all that lection talk, do you, Sheriff? Hell, I figgered you was only politickin."

"Politickin is a right big word," the sheriff said, swatting at a fly on his jowly cheek. "Means one thing to some folks, somethin else to others."

"Yeah," Odell said. "Reckon it does." The tan shoes slid uneasily on the wide porch planking.

"Now you take me. I take politickin to mean sayin what you aim to do oncet you git in office."

"Listen, Sheriff—"

"Odell, you got a nice little place out there. Lots of folks like to git a good meal, dance a little. They like your place."

"I run a clean club, Sheriff. I swear—"

"Them women clean?" The sheriff's voice eased gently along on the same pitch. "That likker you sellin legal?"

"You can't prove none of that, Sheriff, you . . ."

The sheriff sighed gustily, scarcely listening. A car zipped by on the street, its tires sucking noisily at the tar strips linking the concrete. Could use a little breeze, the sheriff thought. Gets mighty hot on toward this time of day.

"Don't you b'lieve nothin like that, Odell," he said. "You ought to know ol John better. You lible to wind up on the roads thinkin that-away."

He watched the feet cross and uncross. A pointed toe nudged at a thin ankle. Glad I ain't nervous, he thought. Hard on a body's digestion.

"Yeah," Odell said. "Mebbe so."

"I ain't been swore in yet, Odell. Won't be till December."

"Yeah."

The sheriff belched moistly.

"Scuse me," he said. "Them field peas, I reckon. Give me gas evry time. Well, Odell, you just git that place of yours cleaned up come December and you'll be all right. Shine it up pretty on account I aim to be out to look it over, first day I git in office."

"Sheriff—listen, I could—I been doing okay lately. I might see my way clear, you say the word, to . . ."

The sheriff tipped his hat back. Odell's voice faded away.

Next door, a young girl came out of a plain white house and started up the street.

"Hi, Sheriff!"

He waved a shirt-sleeved arm at her. Gittin prettier evry day, he thought. Young folks are mighty nice to have around. It would of been fine if me and Lucy could of had some. Mighty fine.

He sighed. Praise be for what I got, he thought.

"What was that you was sayin, Odell?"

Odell closely inspected his yellow satin tie.

"Nothin. Just talkin."

"I thought for a minute there you was tryin to bribe ol John. That wouldn't set well to my stomick."

Odell's narrow face, above his bright blue suit, pinched in around the eyes.

"You ain't givin me a chancet," he said. "It ain't fair, Sheriff, it—"

"Why, Odell! Ol John's givin you nigh on six months. What more you want?"

Odell's scanty lips almost pouted.

"I'm a businessman," he said. "All I want is to do business." The reedy words sounded posed and unreal.

Sheriff Briggs tipped his hat back down over his eyes. He folded large red hands over a protruding belly, wishing it were the part of dignity for a sheriff to loosen his belt.

"They ain't but three things you can't do no business with in this county, Odell. Likker an cheap women an ol John."

Odell remained silent.

"You ain't a bad feller, Odell. Got a nice place, like I say. Work hard. Only thing is, you ain't honest."

The crafty feet toed nervously at the floor.

"Dishonest folks is hard on my digestion, Odell. I got a awful digestion."

"Yeah. I heard tell."

A car pulled to a halt in front of the house. The sheriff decided against lifting his hat to see who it was. Maybe it ain't for me, he thought. Then he heard steps coming up the walk.

"Git, Odell. I got more compny."

"Look, Sheriff, can't—" The nervous feet tensed.

"Git," the sheriff said. Puny man, he thought. More'n my in-nards can stand sometimes.

The tan shoes left the porch swiftly. The sheriff watched them tip down the steps, then watched more shoes, less bright, less pointed, come up the same steps.

"Sheriff Briggs?" It was a cheerful voice, full of good humor and courtesy and, the sheriff thought, good digestion.

The sheriff tipped his hat back and looked at his second visitor. The man was young, thirty-five or so, dressed in a suit not nearly so blue as Odell's, with a face not quite so narrow as Odell's.

There was something familiar about the wide shoulders, the short blond hair, the broad, slightly upturned nose. Seen him before, the sheriff thought. Stranger here, though.

The man held out his hand. The sheriff sighed and leaned forward to take it.

"Set down," he said. "Scuse my not gittin up. Been havin a turble time with my stomick."

The man sat down. He too leaned back in his chair and put a foot on the porch railing.

"Sorry to hear that, Sheriff. Not ulcers, I hope."

"Naw. Just my dang digestion."

The man nodded. "I'm Bill Tucker," he said.

"Tucker." The sheriff scratched under one arm. "You kin to Tuckers live down by One-Mile Crick?"

"Could be. Don't know them, though."

"Nice folks. Gotta nice farm."

"Good farm country all around here, isn't it?"

"Best in the State." There was more than a little pride in the sheriff's voice. A farmer himself—or he had been—he took pleasure in a field of corn, in green tobacco growing tall in the row.

Sometimes, sitting here on his porch, looking across the street to the big old Lowry place, or at his own small lawn and scanty shrubbery, or next door at the Kinlaw kids playing in the side-yard, hearing the cars going purposefully by on the cement street —they'd have gutters before long—feeling the cool shadow of the water oak falling across his porch, he would wish suddenly for the quiet of the old home place again, for the fussing of chickens in the yard, the sweetness of well-water at noon and the smell of mules standing aimless in the barn.

Well, that was all a long time ago. And a man could always go somewhere and smell a mule if he had a mind to.

"Best in the State," he said again. "What can ol John do for you, son?"

"I reckon you didn't call to mind anything when I said my name. I'm representing Harvey Pollock."

The sheriff grunted. Seen him in the *Times*, he thought. That's where it was. Knowed he looked familiar.

"Feller runnin for Senator?"

"That's him."

"You shore got a turble lickin."

Tucker nodded.

"Sure did. I hear you came out pretty well, though."

"Reckon so." What's he want out of me? the sheriff thought. I got no truck with his kind of politics.

"No second primary for you, eh, Sheriff?"

Might's well be honest now as later, Briggs thought.

"You neither, son, you got any sense."

Tucker looked at him gravely.

"You really think so?"

"You can't drive no railroad spike with a tack hammer, boy."

"That's right, Sheriff. You need a big sledge. Biggest you can get."

The sheriff felt another belch rising in his chest. But this man was not Odell. He grumpily swallowed the belch.

"Dang field peas burnin my shirt collar off," he said. "You got somethin on your mind, son?"

Tucker took out a pack of cigarettes and offered them to the sheriff. Briggs shook his head and Tucker lit one for himself, flipping the match over the railing into the spiraea bush.

"Tell you the truth, Sheriff, we got it in mind to give it another try. Think we might do a little better."

The sheriff nodded slowly. They don't never give up, he thought. If they got the least little tad of a chancet, no matter

· 133 ·

how bad they got licked the first time out, they got to try it again. I reckon there ain't no such thing as no hope at all.

"Can't get beat no worse'n before, I reckon."

"Maybe not at all. We've already picked up some ground. We just need the right kind of support."

That's it, eh, Briggs thought. Might of knowed.

"Like a fellow was telling me downtown." Tucker waved a hand in the direction of the business district. "He said you were about the most respected man in this county. Said everybody knew they had elected an honest sheriff at last when they got you."

"I ain't never robbed no widows, I reckon." They say that, do they? the sheriff thought.

"Folks put a lot of confidence in a man like you, Sheriff. Small town like this, they all know you, know the kind of man you are. They listen to you."

Briggs sighed. He ain't got much more sense than Odell, he thought. Even if he is prettier. They's all kinds of bribery.

"I ain't goin to support your man, son," he said. "Mighty kind of you to ask it. Pears to me though, this here Anson you runnin against is a right good man. Can't see no gain in swappin him in on your man."

"Sorry to hear that, Sheriff." Tucker leaned confidentially over the arm of his chair. "You could swing a lot of votes our way. We wouldn't forget a thing like that."

The sheriff shook his head. My belly ain't enough, he thought. I got this kind of mess to put up with too.

"I ain't got much, son. Little house here, two-bit feed store downtown. Reckon it's bout all I need though."

Tucker laughed and shook his head regretfully.

"And now you're sheriff too."

"Yep."

One of them talkers, the sheriff thought. Reckon I got him for the afternoon. Him and my innards.

He watched Tucker's cigarette sail out onto the lawn.

"You were constable before you ran for sheriff, weren't you?"

"Still am. Don't go in as sheriff till December."

"How long you been constable, don't mind my askin?"

Might's well listen to him as anybody, the sheriff thought. That boy can hold down the store awhile iffen he don't git to listnin to the radio.

He tipped his hat down over his eyes again, wondering if a good loud belch might not drive his visitor away.

"Sixteen years. Near bout. Had to wait for the sheriff to retire fore I could run. Folks don't never turn a sheriff out round here, oncet he gits in."

"Sixteen years. That's a long time."

"Yep." It passed fast enough, he thought. It wasn't so long.

"Guess you still remember that chain vote you worked, though?"

I ain't hearin right, the sheriff thought. He pushed his hat back.

"Man wouldn't forget a thing like that," Tucker said.

"I reckon I heard wrong, son."

"I mean when you first got elected constable."

Sheriff Briggs stared at Tucker. He saw, for the first time, the dark glint in the clear blue eyes, the fine cobweb of wrinkles at their corners. Odell's got them same wrinkles, he thought.

"Why, Sheriff, I believe you had forgotten!"

I wouldn't say forgotten, the sheriff thought. I'd just sort of say I learned to keep it on my stomick.

"You got a nasty mouth, boy."

Tucker laughed easily.

"Nasty mind, nasty mouth. It follows."

Sheriff Briggs took his feet from the railing and sat up.

"Like to know how I found out, Sheriff?"

"A man like you has always got ways to find out things."

"Always. Couldn't stay in business if I couldn't find out things."

"You see this house, boy?"

Tucker nodded.

"I told you it's bout all I got. Sixteen years ago it *was* all I had."

"Depression," Tucker said. "Bad time for everybody."

"I wasn't aimin to lose it."

"Didn't say I blamed you, did I? I only—"

"Only job I could find was open was that constable job."

"So you got hold of some ballots. Only needed one or two.

And you marked them the way you wanted them, the old X right by your name. Then you got hold of plenty of white folks who couldn't read or write, who could just vote. You told them you'd help them out, fix up the ballot the way they wanted it."

The sheriff closed his eyes.

"You ain't got to run off at the mouth, son."

"But it was such a slick little scheme, Sheriff! The kind I like. You'd give them a ballot you had marked and tell them to bring the one they got at the polls back to you. Then you'd mark that one right and pass it on to some other illiterate sucker."

Red flashes plucked at the dark insides of the sheriff's eyelids. I ain't scared of it any more, he thought. A man's got things to remember he don't want to. After a while you get so's you can sleep all right.

"Well, we all have to get a start somewhere," Tucker said.

The sheriff felt the dull ache in his stomach. Your own sins, he thought, black as they are, don't never look as bad as anybody else's. I'm glad I ain't this feller.

"Son, if you're figgerin on blackmailin ol John into comin out for your man you ain't very bright."

The smile dropped from Tucker's face, the friendliness from his voice.

"And you're dumb, Sheriff. Just plain dumb."

Callin names, the sheriff thought. He should have my stomick and learn him some patience.

"Boy, I learnt a long time ago we're all sinners. I ain't grievin too much over something I wouldn't do now even if I did it sixteen years ago. I had an empty belly sixteen years ago and I figure the one I got now is price enough for fillin it."

"You and your belly," Tucker said. Impatience sharpened his voice.

"Besides I never broke no law. Sixteen years ago ballot-markin was legal."

"If you marked it the way you were told to."

"I coulda made mistakes."

Tucker laughed. There was good humor in his voice again.

"Maybe so," he said. "Thing is, I don't care how you feel about it. Folks sure do think a lot of you, Sheriff."

Briggs blinked. These younguns, he thought. You can't figure 'em out.

"They'd hate to hear rumors about their new sheriff, I bet."

A sharp stab from his stomach struck Sheriff Briggs, then subsided slowly to a dull ache. The ache was beginning in his head too.

Sixteen years ago, he thought. He was just a youngster then.

He saw what Tucker was driving at now, too clearly. He could live with it himself—had been living with it these sixteen years. It could be made a thing between himself and his Maker, and the sheriff had always considered his Maker to be a reasonable man.

But could he live with it if everybody else knew about it too?

They set a lot of store by me, he thought. Makes a man feel proud.

"I don't think you've got the guts," Tucker said. "You're too much old John, the honest sheriff, the most respected man in the county. Sheriff, I don't think you've got the guts to go back sixteen years and start all over."

Makes a man feel proud, the sheriff thought. Knowin the way they look up to you. Knowin you can talk an have folks listen. Sets you up inside.

"I don't think anybody would have the guts," Tucker said.

Sometimes you got to look at a thing from the outside in, the sheriff thought. You got to do what it seems like is the only thing to do, no matter what.

You got to have somethin in this world. If it ain't one thing it's another. You still got to have somethin even if when you got it it ain't worth what it cost you.

"You right. Most folks ain't got the guts they ought to have."

Tucker stood up, slowly, and touched the sheriff's shoulder.

"You're okay, Sheriff. I'm sorry I got snotty with you."

"Why, that's all right, son. You young yet."

They looked at each other. Mighty young, the sheriff thought. Mighty prideful.

"Well, Sheriff, I guess we understand each other."

"Not exactly, son. I bet you don't even own no house."

The hard glint flared briefly, then died, in Tucker's eyes. His voice was still friendly.

"I've got some people to see. Guess I'll run along. It'd be a good idea for you to get your statement supporting Pollock ready. We'll let you know when to use it."

"I'll do that," the sheriff said. He tipped his hat once again over his eyes.

"Take care of your stomach," Tucker said.

The sheriff watched the brown leather shoes, the fine pebbled leather of them, move away, heard the feet on the steps, the powerful whir of the car engine.

Suddenly the dull ache beneath his belt burned to white heat. The sheriff clenched his teeth until the pain went away.

Across the street a lawn mower began to clatter. That'd be young Tom Lowry. Nobody else big enough damn-fool to mow a lawn this early in the day. Hot as that sun is.

You sure would think a man could outrun his foolishness.

Only, maybe he can. Maybe I did.

Come to think of it, I reckon maybe after all that ain't the thing I got up behind me breathin down my neck now.

I reckon that ain't it at all, what I did sixteen years ago.

Well, a man has got to have somethin but he can't have everything. He purely can't. I got my house here. I got my business and I got my badge. Folks set a lot of store by me.

Another spasm gripped him. I got my dang digestion too, he thought. I sure-God have. In place of any guts.

❧

"You sure it's all fixed now? You ain't just tellin me?"

"It's all fixed," Tucker said. "You know I shoot square, Harry."

"I ain't sayin you don't shoot square." The voice was a motorized whine, like that of a turning lathe. "All I said is are you sure?"

"Quit worrying. I told you everything was okay."

Tucker was tired. It had been a long drive and a flat tire hadn't helped anything. He'd hoped to get here earlier in the day, get this over with and get on to somewhere with a decent hotel.

Now look at me, he thought, stuck here for the night because of that damn tire.

"Show me the stuff," Tucker said. He tipped back a little in the straight-backed chair and thrust his hands into his pants pockets. The single light bulb dropped a circle of yellow on the dirty concrete floor. Within the circle was his chair, another heaped high with newspapers, old envelopes, a magazine or two and a cardboard box filled with what looked like dusty letterheads, Harry Wilson's stained and cluttered desk, and Wilson himself, fidgeting in an ungreased swivel chair.

"I ain't run it off yet," Harry said. "Only the proofs."

"Let me see those, then. You'll have to get busy on them pretty soon, won't you?"

Harry jerked to his feet. His Adam's apple bobbed like a steam gauge and his jaws pounded rapidly at a wad of gum.

"Time enough. Only thing is, I got to git it done nights. Couldn't start fore you checked the proofs."

He stepped to a wooden filing cabinet just beyond the circle of light and pulled out the top drawer. Its metal runners grated shrilly in the silence of the little office.

Through an open door beyond Harry's desk, Tucker saw idle machinery looming in the dimness of the print shop. There were faint smells of ink and of grease, almost drowned in the tang of molten lead. Some small machine thumped steadily in the darkness.

"I got 'em in here somewheres," Harry said. "I only pulled them proofs last night."

Tucker settled more comfortably in the stiff chair. The things I have to do, he thought. The people I have to mess with.

Vivian. Now if Vivian were here. Now if we were sitting somewhere together—at the beach maybe, the beach is always good—and if my arms were about her and if her lips opened as her head tipped back slowly, and if I kissed them and my hand touched gently her soft breasts . . .

He grunted. It was never comfortable to remember the last time he had been with Vivian. It was never comfortable, in fact, to remember Vivian.

"What?" Harry said.

"Nothing. Just making noises."

"Oh." Harry's ratchety fingers fumbled again among the papers in the file drawer.

That girl put the hooks in me, Tucker thought. Deep.

Maybe I ought to try to knock off a piece of that and get her off my mind. A week end at the beach, maybe. When this damned election is over.

"Here they are, Mr. Tucker."

Only I don't think it would do any good, Tucker thought. Assuming she would go to the beach for a week end with me, I don't think it would do any good. I don't think it would get her off my mind. The warmth of her. The clear, uncomplicated blue of her eyes and the easy understanding, the not asking you to be anything but what you already are . . .

He held out his hand for the proofs. Harry gave them to him and leaned the thin bumpers of his buttocks against the edge of the desk.

"Pretty thin paper, isn't it?"

Harry's arms, like levers enmeshing gears, folded across his chest.

"That's a good stock there, Mr. Tucker. It ain't expensive, but it's a good stock, all right."

"It looks pretty thin to me." Tucker held one of the sheets up to the light.

"What I always say is ain't no use wastin a customer's money when you ain't got to." Harry's whine was as automatic, as unexcited, as the clack of a linotype machine. "Now you take that stock, it only—"

"I guess it's all right," Tucker said. "I just thought it felt kind of flimsy."

He studied the proofs. This was a touchy business. You had to be careful not to overplay your hand, using stuff like this. You could get away with it in the sticks, do yourself some good, but it wasn't smart at all to turn it loose where they had running water.

All the same, these were pretty damn good. Pretty damn good.

The guy who'd made the plates knew his business, all right. It had taken some doing to find a guy who could do the job right and keep his mouth shut, but it had been worth it. The stuff was pretty damn good.

Tucker chuckled. Wait till Ben Kirby gets a load of these, he thought.

"What?" Harry said.

"I was just thinking of a—friend of mine. He'll have a hemorrhage when he sees these items."

Harry nodded. His eyes poked out like rivets from his thin cheeks. His jaws still worked at the gum.

There were five proofs. Each was of a line drawing in much the same style as editorial page cartoons. The proofs were smeared and dim, but the cartoons were plain enough.

The one which Tucker liked least showed Joe Stalin as a genial puppet-master, beaming through a bushy mustache. Dancing merrily at the end of the puppet-strings was a tall, lean, flap-eared caricature of Senator Ralph Anson. The captain read, GUESS WHO RUNS THIS SHOW? Much better, Tucker thought, was the one of the same caricatured figure eating with three ragged Negroes, splayed feet bare, thick lips slack, broad faces beaming with vacant delight as they slobbered over their food. MAYBE ANSON WANTS THIS BUT DO YOU? read the caption.

Another good one did not show Anson and had no caption. A line of dejected white men were being turned away from a window by an imperious Negro, who wore a king's crown. A sign above the window read *Employment*. Beneath it was a larger sign: *FEPC in Force Here*.

Senator Anson reappeared on the next proof. The familiar, gaunt face leered knowingly at a voluptuous Negro girl who sat upon his lap, her skirt far above her knees, her bosom thrusting out of a half-open blouse. Tucker grinned at the caption: WHY DOES HE LOVE THE DARKIES SO MUCH?

But best of all was the last. Now that is art, Tucker thought. That is truly art.

Senator Anson was, with one hand, pushing open barroom swinging doors, beneath a sign: *Civil Rights Social Club*. Beyond the doors, Negro men licked thick lips in anticipation. Clinging hesitantly to the Senator's other hand was a fresh young white girl, as demure as a Sunday school teacher. Read the caption: WILL YOUR DAUGHTER BE INVITED TO THIS PARTY?

"You want a drink?" Harry said. "I got a bottle in the desk."

"No thanks. You go ahead, though."

Harry went around the desk and sat down in the swivel chair. He pulled open one of the desk drawers.

"I think I'll change this caption a little bit," Tucker said. He took a fountain pen from his pocket and scratched out the line of print beneath the last cartoon. He printed in above it: WILL ANSON INVITE YOUR DAUGHTER TO THIS PARTY?

"How long will it take to get these out, Harry?"

Harry took a pint bottle of whisky from the desk drawer. He slowly unscrewed the top.

"Not long. I ought to have 'em the first of the week."

He tipped the bottle to metal-gray lips, took a long pull, and shuddered. He put the bottle down and wiped his mouth with the back of his hand.

"What about my money?" Harry's hand pushed the bottle a little further away.

"Give it to you now." Tucker took out his wallet, counted out a stack of bills.

Harry's hand darted like a loom shuttle across the desk. His fingers moved swiftly through the bills.

"I suppose your help can be trusted," Tucker said. The son of a bitch could eat that money, he thought. Like it was strawberry shortcake.

Harry nodded, still flicking at the bills.

"I got a nigger boy goin to help me nights. I'll see he don't say nothin."

"Good. You get them ready by Monday, then. Have them in packages of five hundred, one hundred of each cartoon. There'll be a truck here to pick them up."

Harry clutched the bills lovingly to his stomach.

"Better make it Tuesday, Mr. Tucker. Be on the safe side."

"All right, if you think so. No later, though."

Tucker stood up and stretched. His back ached from the long

day's driving and his hands still felt grimy from changing the tire. The thought of the dingy hotel room awaiting him made him wince.

Vivian.

If you were here now. If you were waiting for me—

"What's on at the movies, Harry?"

Harry looked up from his money.

"I ain't been inside a movie in ten years. Waste of money, you ask me."

"Got something there all right. Kills time, though."

"Time's money," Harry said. His fingers edged toward the bottle. "It ain't but a block up the street," he added, grudgingly.

Tucker nodded. He fingered the proofs lying on the desk. This will be a real low blow, he thought. Right down there in the kidney.

"Last time I went it was this here Betty Gable. Runnin round near bout—"

"Grable, you mean."

"Yeah. The blond one. Runnin round near bout nekkid." Harry's gray tongue licked at his lips and his eyes brightened. His shaking head pronounced regretful judgment on the movies.

He picked up the bottle and took a quick, determined drink.

"I'll be seeing you," Tucker said. "Have things ready Tuesday."

Harry put the bottle down and wiped his mouth again. Tucker stepped toward the door.

"When'll my boy be home?" An aggrieved note had crept into the whine.

Tucker stopped. My God, he thought. I should have drawn him a picture.

"I told you. The parole board meets next month."

"Alton ain't no bad boy." Harry shook his head vigorously.

"Sure, I know. His case comes up next month."

"Alton didn't go to cut that nigger." Harry stood up, still clutching his money.

Tucker shrugged. "I don't know anything about it. But he ought to be home in six, seven weeks. I promise you."

"Lissen," Harry said. "That nigger pushed him. He didn't have no call to push my boy. How come they can lock up a good boy like Alton what always helped out his pa and ma for pertecktin hisself against a nigger?"

"Listen, Harry. Your boy's getting a parole. I told you that. I don't know anything about the rest of it."

Fine lines, radiating like screw threads from Harry's lips, tightened, grime caked in them forever.

"Well, he better. A man's got a right to pertect hisself, ain't he?"

"That's right."

"Speshly against a nigger." Harry's lips moved silently. "He better git that parole."

"For Christ sake, Harry, I told you a hundred times everything is fixed. Quit worrying, will you?"

"Well, they better give it to 'im, that's all. Alton ought not to be in no prison."

Tucker sighed. The hell with it. I'm going to the movies. The hell with you, Harry. The hell with Alton, too.

"Take it easy, Harry." He stepped through the door to the still-warm sidewalk. The automatic whine of Harry's voice followed him out on the street.

Jesus Christ, Tucker thought. The *crap* I have to put up with.

Sure, Alton's a good boy. What the hell, he just cut a man's liver out. You can hardly call a little harmless fun like that a crime.

All the same, he thought, I hope to hell nothing goes wrong with that parole. That crazy old liquor-head back there could make us some trouble.

His footsteps clicked back at him from the silent street. Another day, another dollar, he thought. And another night.

Ahead were the bare bulbs of the theater marquee. The stores were dark and silent and only a few cars waited at the curb. A pickup truck clattered along the street, and from the back three Negro children peered owl-eyed at him.

There was a sweet touch of magnolia in the air, cloying in his nostrils, and somewhere down the street he heard a boy's thin high laugh. Above his head the neon sign of a furniture store buzzed busily. As he walked on he saw the lights in a drugstore go out.

He paused under the marquee, glanced at the billboards and made a face. He stepped up to the ticket window, took out some change, picked up his ticket, and went without eagerness into the theater.

Chapter Ten

T ucker pushed open the swinging doors; a smell of disinfectant awaited him in the hotel hallway. His room was on the first floor, one of the few in the place with a connecting bath.

He unlocked his door, snapped on the overhead light and threw himself across the bed. The springs squawked loudly and the mattress seemed to have a spine and vertebrae.

The ceiling paper was streaked and in one corner hung down in a long, thin stalactite; the brown shade over the window shut out the view and the walls were as cheerless as those of a cell. A lavatory in the corner dripped vindictively.

That lousy movie, Tucker thought. I should have driven home tonight. No matter how tired I was.

He sat up, pulled up a leg, and yanked viciously at a shoestring. He untied the shoe, dropped it to the floor, and pulled up his other leg. He felt a trickle of sweat under his arm, felt himself sinking in the hot, stale air of the room. The disinfectant smell was stronger than ever.

He got up and padded in stocking feet across the bare floor, raised the shade, and wrestled the window up about a foot.

A lot of breeze I'll get from that, he thought. This crummy fleabag.

Later he lay naked and perspiring on the bed, staring into the dark, hearing the steady *drip-drop* of the lavatory. I wish I had a book or something. Even a damned comic book. Anything to get myself to sleep. Even *Ulysses*.

He had been increasingly troubled with sleeplessness lately. He did not think conscience was at fault, because he believed he had trained conscience out of himself. Nor did he blame the heat.

It was more a vague, disembodied sense of sadness, becoming less vague, less disembodied, every night. It was beginning to take a definite shape and on this night as he sweltered on the cheap sheets beneath the streaked and cheerless wallpaper, Tucker admitted finally, almost with relief, that the shape was the tall, gaunt one of Senator Ralph Anson.

Tucker had not seen the Senator to speak to him in nearly three years, not even in the busiest days of the first campaign, when both Pollock Headquarters in the Bright Leaf Room and those of Senator Anson a few floors above were frenzied with activity. It was not that Tucker had avoided the Senator; it was simply that he believed Ralph Anson to be the one man in the world to whom he need never explain anything. He did not seek him out, therefore, and luck or fate had it that they did not meet by accident.

Tucker tossed over on his side, feeling the warm, wet pillow under his cheek.

He knows why I'm doing it, he thought. Or figures I've got reason. Either way, he understands.

Only I wish it didn't have to be him. I wish it didn't. Why couldn't it have been some stuffed shirt like Pollock? Why did it have to be Mr. Anson?

But he knew as he thought it that it was the special quality of Ralph Anson which had created the opportunity. If there had only been some stuffed shirt, there would have been no opportunity.

So it had to be, he told himself, sweating freely now, feeling the driplets on his forehead, in the hair on his chest, under his arms, between his legs. It had to be this way. I didn't have any choice.

I couldn't have had it different if I'd tried. You play your cards the way they fall or you get mashed. I ought to know.

And there passed through him, in one stiffening hurtling bolt, the old anger and hurt and outrage, the old defiance, the old certainty.

He has to take his chances with the rest, he thought. He came down out of his ivory tower and asked for it, and he has to take it the way it comes. Nobody ever wiped my nose for me.

Not by a damn sight, they didn't. They threw me in over my head the day I was born and told me to swim or else.

Well, by God, I swam. I swam all right. Nobody ever tried to teach me how, either, nobody ever gave *me* a break, did they?

Not even my own father, not even Anson when you get right down to it. And certainly not Katherine.

Katherine.

His mind lurched, tried desperately to regain its balance. But he had opened, with her name, a box full of wiggling things, trying to escape, squirming past the lid he quickly clamped back into place.

I won't think about her, he told himself, feeling something pull into rigidity along his jawline. I'm not going to think about her any more. I'm not.

It was no use. The pressure under the lid was irresistible.

There had been too much of her. There had been too much of her and it was never any use, not even when he called upon that iron discipline of mind he had slowly, painfully, through the years of nonentity, the years of struggle and scheme, developed for himself.

There had always been too much of Katherine.

There had been the pink little girl, trotting chubbily by her father's side; there had been the long-legged high-school girl, no longer chubby but still pink, in her eyes the beginnings of that faint scorn, that sure arrogance; there had been the heavy-breasted woman in the bathing suit, not pink at all, the black mouth across her face like a wound.

There had always been Katherine. There had always been too much of her too far above, too far beyond.

He rolled over and buried his face, feeling against his skin the clamminess of his own sweat damp upon the pillow. The box was open now, the lid pushed aside, and the wiggling things swarmed from it in slimy masses.

All those thoughts and all those dreams. Those weeks, those months stretching into years. Those years of work, of struggle, of hope, those years made endurable only by the week ends. The long lonely drives for the long agonized week ends with Katherine.

I've got to beat this, he thought. I've got to stop thinking about her. I've got to.

But he could not. He tried and could not and gave himself up to the wiggling things.

The money. The clothes. The places to go, the things to do, the people to see.

Never enough of any of them. Never enough for her.

The parties and the whisky and the football tickets and the dancing and the teasing tantalizing touch of the lips, the hands, the heavy breasts.

Always too much of all of them. Too much with her.

Chasing her, trying to keep up, seeing and hearing and fearing the others chasing her too, trying to keep up too. The arms stretched out to her, stretched until they grew numb with reaching, reaching for Katherine.

And wondering. God, the wondering! Forever wondering where you were going to get the money and the courage and the luck and the hope to keep it up.

Then suddenly. Without warning. That night.

That cool dark night on the creaking old glider on the creaking old porch, while the moon looked whitely down on that green lawn where my father once stood, where for her it all began. Those teasing tantalizing lips and hands and breasts no longer vanishing, that sinuous demanding body beneath mine, that mouth again black across her face like a wound, a scar, the fingernails at my neck, at my numb uncaring neck, and the voice whispering loud as doom in my ear, whispering give it to me you lint-head bastard, give it to me dirty you ape you greasy lint-head ape . . .

And then in the warm afterglow, in the dim leisure of the afterglow, the sure, proud afterglow, the words not whispered, hardly even spoken, the voice as calm, as even, as cold and impersonal as a death sentence:

You think you beat me, don't you?

Over the patient years, as if it were yesterday, I hear the voice. I hear the words. I remember the first faint stir of understanding.

Tucker pushed himself away from the pillow. He rolled, sat

up, slumped heavily on the edge of the bed, the sweat streaming from his body, the smell of his own flesh sour in his nostrils.

Won't I ever forget that?

Won't I ever forget the day, not a week later, when the Florence paper, Mr. Anson's paper, announced her engagement to Harry Watts?

The doctor's son. Who had tried to keep up too. Who had more money and clothes and whisky and football tickets than all of us. And cotton mill stock, not cotton mill wages.

Tucker stood up, moving with great effort, feeling the heat heavy in the air about him. He moved to the window, trying to find some hope of a breeze.

There was none. There was no hope for anything.

He shook his head at the melodrama of the thought. There is nothing, he thought, quite so exquisite as self-pity.

It was funny how he could never seem to get away from two people. Anson and Katherine. It was as if some invisible cord bound him to both, some cord of a strength not even to be conceived.

Since the strike, he thought.

That's when it began for her.

Maybe that's when it began for me and for all I know for him too.

1928

"It's now or never," the tall man says, his lean fingers knotting together, the joints popping like old and brittle bones.

The boy hears the cracking knuckles punctuate the slow words.

"They're all up there," the bald man says. "All up there at Dan Sprague's." He spits and saliva sizzles viciously against the little stove.

"It's now or never," the tall man says again, not looking away from the floor.

Outside the silence of winter is on the land. But the silence is more than that of winter. It is the silence of death too, hanging over the street of nine houses, over the mill, over the village, over the human cogs of the mill.

It is the third month of the strike. It is the third month of no work, the third month of no paycheck. It is the third month of picketing, of masses of men coming together in anger, of blood stains on the gray, frozen earth.

And of hot and puzzled eyes watching the slow dwindling of nickels hoarded in the lard can. Of children crying. Of women weeping. Of men cursing, quietly, venomously.

It is the third month of silence. It is for many the first time in their lives when they have not, waking and sleeping, man and boy, heard the constant hum of the mill, above even the sound of their own voices.

"The men er with us, Sam."

"They're hungry. They got no choice."

The bald man nods.

"We tried it evry way, Sam. We tried it evry way we knowed. We sure-God did."

Sam Tucker stands up.

"I'm done," he says. "I ain't waitin no more."

The bald man blinks at him, his head thrusting jerkily forward with the down-move of his eyelids.

"What you want me to do, Sam? You the boss."

"All right. I got to think a minute."

The boy stands up. The two men are near the stove, the bald man seated backward in a straight chair, chin resting on hands. Sam Tucker stands, his thin shoulder blades like edges of planks, his neck bursting, lean, stiff, from stooped and pointed shoulders.

Through the door to the kitchen the boy hears the quick clatter of dishes. No use her washin dishes, he thinks. Nothin to put on 'em anyway.

He feels the sharp thought of hunger in his belly. He has eaten; he is not starving—but for three months now his meals have grown scarcer, smaller. Meat is a thing to be remembered, coffee an old delight. He tastes the sour grease of greens, the stale bloat of bread.

Now even the greens are gone, even the bread. Hunger is no longer a thing feared, a ghost, a threat, half-defeated each day. Hunger is tomorrow. Hunger is from now on.

"Ceph," Sam Tucker says. "You know where the dynimite is hid at."

"Yeah. Down by—"

"You go tell Jim Shore I said have the men over to the church in twenny minutes. Then you git Bud Hitt an Bob Patterson an git the dynimite."

"All of it?"

"All of it. Then come on down to the church."

"Sam?"

The voice is quiet, so quiet the boy almost fails to hear it. He looks toward the kitchen door. His father half-wheels. The bald man looks up from the stove.

"What you fixin to do, Sam?"

"You go on," Sam says. "Git them dishes washt an git in bed."

The woman takes a step into the room. A sleazy dish towel is still in her hand. Her eyes dim and water in the light.

"You gittin that dynimite. Ain't you, Sam?"

"It ain't none of your worry. It ain't—"

"None of my worry," she said. "Iffen you git yourself kilt it ain't none of my worry? Or hissen?" She nods at the boy.

"I ain't a-gonna—"

"You don't know who's a-gonna git kilt you go to messin with dynimite."

Sam's hands move in quick exasperation.

"You got no call to butt in, woman."

"It ain't Christian, Sam. It ain't hardly like you."

Almost a pleading note is in Sam's voice now. He ought to tell her to git on back in the kitchen, the boy thinks.

"A man ain't gonna be pushed but so far, Mary. We done tried. Evrything we knowed to try we done tried, an it ain't done no good! He ain't even talked to us. He ain't—"

"You ain't tried goin back to work."

"Mary!" There is horror, disbelief in the word.

"You ain't tried puttin food on your boy's table."

Sam's hand rises as if to strike at her. She does not move. He stands before her, his hand raised, his face contorted, his body

· 152 ·

for once straight and tall, his breath gasping out of his thin chest, his whole being stretched to the breaking point.

"I never thought to hear it," he cries. "Not in my own house. I never did!"

He ought to shut her mouth for her, the boy thinks. Talkin like that.

"Ceph," Sam says. "Do like I tolt you." Slowly his hand falls and he turns away. Ceph stands up.

"Sam! You ain't a-gonna do it! I ain't a-gonna let you—"

Mealy-mouth ol woman, the boy thinks.

"Ain't nobody gonna stop me, Mary. Not even you."

Sam does not look at her. Ceph moves slowly toward the door. He glances back once, then goes out, his steps falling softly across the porch into the night.

"Well, it's done," the woman says. "You done it anyway."

"I got no choice. It's now or never."

"You could let it be never. We got along up to now."

"Got along is all." He laughs, the sound of it harsh and ringing.

"It wan't so bad, Sam. We had food to the table." Her eyes wander around the room, peering weakly for the boy.

"You got to have more than food, Mary!" Clenched fists pound at his thighs. "A man has got to have more than that."

"A man has got to have a lot of things, Sam. But not nothin you got to use dynimite to git."

"It ain't no use," Sam says. "I got no choice, I tell you."

The woman's hands twist at her skirt, her head bowing briefly.

"I know it," she says. "It wan't no use to ask." She comes to his side and puts her hand on his arm. "I know you got no choice, Sam. Not an you bein a man."

He looks down at her. The boy sees the back of his neck, the hair growing lank along it, the mole below his ear. It ain't like Pa, he thinks. It ain't like him to talk so much.

"I didn't go to lift my hand to you," Sam says. "Seem like I go crazy sometimes. Seem like I get to thinkin and like to go plumb crazy."

"Sam. You take care."

The boy slips out the door, goes silently down the steps. You can't figure ol folks out, he thinks. They got to talk, talk, talk.

He breaks into a run up the street, feels the cold touch of the night on his cheek. He runs into the bare yard of the house with the rubber-tire swing, gives the tire a push with his hand, and steps softly around to the side of the house, feeling underfoot the dead, dry pebbles of old chinaberries.

"George!" he calls softly, his voice like wind whispering around a corner.

Beyond the rear of the house, a white moon and chill stars hang low in the winter sky. A dog barks frostily in the distance. The boy feels the cold of earth through thin shoe soles.

"George!"

The window slides open a few inches.

"That you, Bill?"

"Come on, George! They're a-gittin ready."

"What?" The window opens further.

"Come on! We ain't got much time."

"It's too durn cold," George says. "I ain't a-goin out—"

"Dad-blast it," the boy says. "They're a-fixin to blow up Dan Sprague!" And her, too, he thinks. Maybe they'll blow her up too.

"Huh?" George's voice is awake now. The white moon catches red glints from his outthrust head, flings shadow across his open mouth.

"Come *on*, George!"

George's head disappears. If he ain't the slowest thing, the boy thinks.

He stamps his feet and feels needles of fire shoot into his ankles. He flaps his arms rapidly across his thin sweater.

"Hurry!" His whisper is urgent. I don't want to miss it, he thinks. I ain't never seen no dynimite go off.

Sudden footsteps sound on the porch of the house. The boy slinks quickly against the siding, flattening into the shadows. He hears the knock at the door, the silence, the faint creak of a hinge.

Then voices, speaking softly but with the urgency of his own whispers. One of the voices is Sam Tucker's.

A leg swings out the window by his head, kicking against the house. The boy seizes it and feels George grow rigid.

"Be quiet. Pa's out there!"

He lets go of the leg and George slides easily to the ground. The boy pushes him toward the rear of the house and they trot off, bent low, keeping to the shadows.

Then they are away from the house, into the back yard of another, past this house and into another street, running easily and silently, breath clouding from their open mouths, sharp night cold slapping through their clothes.

George catches the boy's arm. George is the taller and the stronger; his shoulders bulk like a man's under his overall jacket. He easily swings the boy to a halt.

"Where we goin, Bill?"

The boy jerks away his arm.

"I tolt you. They aimin to blow up Mister Sprague."

"*Who* is?"

"Ain't you got *any* sense? The *men*, that's who. Pa and your pa an the rest of 'em."

"How?" George says. "What they gonna blow 'em up with?"

"Goddammit," the boy says, "with dynimite, that's what with." I ought not to brung him, he thinks, he ain't got no sense atall sometimes.

George shakes his head.

"Yo pa'd whale the tar outen you," he says. "Talkin nasty like that."

The boy grabs his arm, pulls him along.

"We got to *go*, George! We ain't got much time."

"Well, I just wanted—"

"You just ain't got no sense."

The boy breaks into a run. George shakes his head again and follows.

They turn into another street, run between quiet rows of dark houses. Behind them, as if their passing has ignited a giant wick, windows begin to glow with light; soft knocks sound on locked doors; sleepy men, hard-eyed now, struggle into trousers and shirts; women watch over the frayed edges of patchwork quilts and cheap blankets. The hard-eyed men do not look at them.

The boys run on. They turn another corner and the boy slows

to a trot. George looks back at him and slows too and they stop, breath coming hard now, vapor before it leaves their chests, throats raw and raspy in the cold, eyes tear-stung from the running, blood racing free and hot in their feet and legs.

"We got to take care," the boy says. "Them scabs."

"You mean they up at Sprague's?"

"Course they up there. Where you think they'd be at?"

"I don't like this," George says. "You didn't say nothin bout them bein there."

"You ain't a-goin to back out on me?"

"I sure-God am. I ain't got but one head."

"Don't you want to see that dynimite go off?"

"Well, I—"

"Blow the hell outen 'em all," the boy says. "Scabs an evrybody." His arms wave about his head.

"Where we gonna git? Sposen them scabs ketch us?"

"They ain't a-goin to. You just follow me."

He moves into thick shrubbery bordering the sidewalk. George looks after him for a moment, then follows. They crawl silently through the shrubs, dash quickly across a lawn and behind a brick house. A garage looms out of the darkness. The boy signals over his shoulder and moves around it, close in its shadow.

At the back of the garage are more shrubs. The boys move silently into them and hunker down to the soft, loam-smelling earth. Silently they part the greenery before them and look across a stretch of grass to the Sprague home.

It is of white clapboard, three stories high, fronted by a gracious, pillared gallery. Before it, the lawn slopes away to the street. On the corner nearest the boys a room is brilliantly lit. The rest of the house is dark.

"We can see good here."

George grunts.

"How you find this place, Bill?"

"I come up here oncet." The boy remembers:

The fine, clean sun of that day, the smell of new-cut grass, the feel of the lawn mower beneath his hands, the good sting of the sweat in his eyes, the salt taste of it on his lips. The smiling man, holding in one hand a fifty-cent piece, in the other the pink and chubby fingers of a little girl. The blue eyes, beneath the frilly bonnet, staring at him, shaded a little, not open like a child's eyes.

Him and his fifty-centses, the boy thinks now. I hope they blow 'im clean up in the sky. And her too. Her most of all.

I may of smelt bad but she didn't have to say so. I hope they blow her higher than anybody. In little bitty pieces.

Then I won't have to sneak into these ol bushes no more, he thinks. I won't have to watch her playin in that big yard no more with that nigger woman.

Rage fills his mouth, his throat, with sourness. Little bitty pieces, he thinks again. Blow her all to pieces.

So I won't ever have to watch her no more.

A shadow slips between them and the light.

"There's one, George!"

"What? Where?"

"Scab."

"I'm gettin out of here," George says. "I seen them billy clubs they got."

The boy catches his jacket.

"You better not. Sposen they was one back out there was to ketch you all alone."

"They wan't none out there when we come in," George says.

"You better stay put. Best place to hide is right here."

"Well, I wisht they'd come on an do it. My pa find out I snuck out he'll tan my hide. Sides, I'm gittin cold."

"You always got something wrong with you. I wisht I'd left you home."

"Me too," George says. "I sure-God do."

"Listen!" The boy's fingers clutch hard at George's arm.

"Let go of me," George says. "I ain't deef. I hear 'em."

At first it is only a beat in the air, a faint bass rhythm. And then it is a hum too, flesh on the bones of the beat, and then a deep and ominous rumble, growling across the cold clearness of the night, falling over the wide lawn like a canvas, a creeping, irrepressible, doom-bearing fog.

"On-ward CHRIS-*chun sol-ol-*JERS
Mar-chin as to-o war
With the CROSS *of Je-*SUS
Go-in on be-fore . . ."

"What they got to sing for?" the boy mutters. "They ought to of snuck up like we did."

"Look!" George whispers in his ear.

A shadow darts from shrubbery nearby, flits across the lawn toward the house, takes on in the white light of the winter moon the looming, dark-filled shape of a man, running hard toward the house.

"One of them stinkin scabs," the boy says. A cold finger tickles lightly at his spine.

"Christ the roy-al Ma-as-ter
*Leads a-*GAINST *the foe . . ."*

The rumble is louder now, the words more plain, here and there a voice standing out above the rest, high and sharp and clear. A faint red glow moves along the street behind the boys, its weak and flickering light like reflection from the banked coals of a furnace.

I wonder is Pa singin? the boy thinks. I ain't never heard Pa sing.

The running figure has reached the house now, jumping heavily to the porch, disappearing through the wide, glass-paneled doors. The yard is again still and lonely and shadowed, silent but for the growing rumble, near now.

*"For-ward in-to ba-a-*TULL
See his BAN-*ners go . . ."*

And now the torches can be seen. Now they appear, singly, now in twos, now in great masses of flaming orange and red, now coming on up the lawn, beneath them the faceless, nameless men, still sending across the cool night the rumble of their voices, deep and hot and ancient.

And now the mass becomes men. Now a face can be seen, here, there, now a hat, now an overall jumper, now the flash of a button reflecting the torches, now a mouth, open, singing.

· 158 ·

And a tall man, robbed of his rightful height but still tall, his head poised, unyielding, on a lean and outthrust neck, his long arms swinging like scythe blades, his bony knees coming on, never pausing, never faltering, his bony knees coming on and his head thrust forward and the arms swinging, proud and unafraid and indomitable.

"With the CROSS *of Je-sus*
Go-in on be-fore. . . ."

The boy hears George's breath coming hard, feels the sudden clutch of his fingers.

From the bushes, from behind the house, from beyond its corners, the shadows arise. The shadows move, slow, unhurried, toward the torches and the men and the singing. The shadows move together, the long clubs dangling at their belts, the shadows of these in turn athwart the moving shadows of men, the rifles and the shotguns loose and free in the crooks of their arms. The shadows move into a thin long line of shadow, cast like a chain across the front of the house.

"They ought to of snuck up!" the boy whispers fiercely, pounding at a knee. "They ought not to of been singin like that."

"Somebody's gonna get kilt, Bill! I feel it . . . I . . . feel it in my belly!" George's fingers bite deeply into his arm.

"You damn right," the boy whispers, feeling his teeth clench hard. "You damn right they are."

Now his eyes do not leave the tall man, the stooped man, the man coming on, slower now, but coming on, the singing dying now in the throats around him, the words falling more faintly now, but the mass behind him still coming on too, the torches still glaring redly across the lawn to the shadows now no longer shadows.

The boy's eyes rivet on the tall man and fear claws wildly along his back. Pa! he thinks. Pa! I never thought . . . I never thought . . .

And now the singing is done, the voices gone, the silence falling again, white and still and waiting, the silence broken only by the slowing tramp of feet, the movement of leather on grass, and now that gone too, gone in the night, the silence in command now, the men under the flaring torches motionless and massed and waiting, the thin line of shadow-men rooted and taut and waiting, the house behind them brooding and dark and waiting, the night cold and hushed and waiting and over them all the moon and the stars and the sky, waiting too.

And then the boy hears a voice, low, even, and thinks, I have heard that voice before. And knows it for his father's voice, changed, softened, eased, but somehow deadly, somehow terrifying, more terrifying than the quiet and the waiting, more vast and awesome and ruthless than all the vast, awesome ruthlessness of Heaven.

"You best git outen the way."

Again the silence.

Terror is all through the boy now, replacing the blood in his veins, the marrow in his bones. He feels his arm shake in George's grip. Maybe they won't do it, he thinks. Maybe Pa won't do it.

"Somebody's sure-God gonna git kilt," George whispers again.

The boy hears the tremor in the voice. It's so quiet, he thinks. If only they would yell or sing some more or something so it wouldn't be so quiet. If only—

Sudden light jumps across the lawn from the porch and a mutter ripples over the massed men. The front of the house is whitely brilliant from the porch lights and the line of defenders is sharply lit. The front rows of the mass of men are also caught in the glare of the lights. The men blink and shift and mutter, behind them in the darkness the hindmost torches glaring less redly now.

The door opens and two men come out on the porch. A third lounges slowly behind them.

"That's him!" the boy hisses. "That's ol Sprague."

"I don't care who it is," George says. "He's just as lible to get kilt as anybody."

"Who's them other ones?"

"I don't know. They ain't got no sense, though, I know that."

"One of 'em's Mr. Anson! That's who it is, George!"

"He wouldn't be here if he had any sense," George says. "An neither would I."

The first two men move forward to the steps of the porch.

The shorter of them, in his shirt sleeves, stands with hands on hips, looking out over the crowd. His voice, deep and confident and commanding, carries easily to the boys.

"I want you men off my grass. I want you off now."

Again the quiet voice, the voice from the gaunt, stooped man.

"We ain't a-goin. Not till we talk."

Fierce pride tingles in the boy. His father's voice carries as far, is as commanding as Dan Sprague's.

Sprague speaks again now and terror returns to the boy, clamping like a giant forceps across his belly.

"I won't be forced to anything, Sam. Get your men out of here."

"They ain't my men. They ain't anybody's men."

"Well, get them off my grass. Get them off now!"

The muttering begins behind Sam Tucker. No voice can be distinguished, but the boy hears the animal in the sound. He can't talk to them like that no more, he thinks. They ain't a-gonna take it no more.

"We aim to talk to you. We aim to talk now."

"That's Pa," the boy whispers. "That's Pa talkin."

"He's gonna get kilt," George says. "They all are."

"You shut up, you—"

"McBride!" Dan Sprague's voice roars in sudden anger. "Get these men away from here!"

The third man lounges away from the porch siding where he has been leaning. A hand touches his forehead and he moves toward the steps, a tall, slouching figure.

"McBride," the quiet voice says, "you set foot on them steps you're a dead man. We got dynimite."

The boy wants to cower into the ground, to dig his head down between his knees into the cold, damp earth. I never thought . . . I never thought . . . it would be like this.

The tall, slouchy man stops and looks at Dan Sprague.

"You heard me!" Sprague roars. "Get them away from my house!"

"All right," the other man on the porch says, "keep your shirt on, Dan."

"You keep out of this, Ralph! By *God*, I won't—"

"Let him come on," the quiet voice says. "Let McBride come on down an put us off the grass."

The third man looks out over the lawn.

"Now that's about enough, Sam. Neither of you is goin to get anywhere threatenin people."

"We just want to talk, Mr. Anson. Ain't no law agin his talkin to us, is they?"

"I'll talk to you when I'm ready! You can't—"

"Take it easy," Anson says. "You already agreed to talk to them."

"Not now, I haven't!"

"He ain't never agreed to anything," the quiet voice says. "Not lessen it was somethin to make hisself a dollar."

"He agreed to talk to you," Anson said. "He decided tonight."

"That was before these men came here and tried—"

"I don't believe it," Sam says. "Not him."

"Well, you believe me, don't you?"

Let it be true, the boy prayed. Don't let Pa get blowed up.

"I never thought to find you in his house," Sam said.

"I never thought to see you men standing out there ready to break the law, either. That wasn't any part of what you set out to do."

"No, by God!" Sprague roars. "McBride! You—"

"Now, listen," Anson says, his calm voice cutting the shouting one off in midsentence. "You send that man down there to start a fight an—"

"*They* started it, by God, they—"

"You send him down there and somebody is goin to get hurt. Maybe Sam Tucker out there or Jim Shore or Ceph Gathins. Maybe Mr. McBride here. Maybe even that pretty little girl upstairs when they blow the house up."

The boy is listening now, the prayer ended, listening for the solemn calm words Ralph Anson speaks. The boy feels the new silence, the silence still waiting and taut, but the edge gone out of it now, the fuse still sputtering but not so brightly, not so fiercely, even the glow of the torches no longer fierce.

"What good will any of that do? Will that get your mill in production, Dan? Will it put food on your table, Sam?"

The tall figure swings toward McBride.

"Will it help your family if you get blown up? Or kill one of these men—" a long arm sweeps toward the massed men— "what good will it do anybody?"

His head shakes slowly, infinite sadness in the movement.

"This strike's been goin on three months," he says. "Two plant guards and a worker already killed. More hurt. My God in Heaven, isn't that enough blood? Have you got to shed more? Have all of you got to be blown up before this thing ends?"

The long arms sweep out and up, seeming to claw in futility at the very air around him.

"Can't you sit down and talk like human beings instead of killing like animals?"

"We always been willin to talk," Sam Tucker says. "Right from the first. It was him that—"

"He's willin to now. Aren't you, Dan?"

"Not with those men in my yard, I'm not!"

"All right," Sam says. "It's on your hands. We aim to stay."

McBride moves again toward the steps.

"You move another inch," Ralph Anson says, "an I'll have you and Dan Sprague indicted for murder."

The man stops, looks at Sprague. Sprague is staring incredulously at the gaunt figure now facing the men on the lawn.

"And if any of you men do anything to start a fight—including you, Sam—I'll do the same. I'll have every one of you I can identify indicted. I don't aim to see any more killin."

He's all alone, the boy thinks. Standin there all alone, talkin like that to them.

Gone now is his fear for his father. Suddenly he knows that it will be all right. Mr. Anson will make it be all right, he thinks. Mr. Anson won't let anything happen to anybody.

And to him the whole unbelievable scene—the mass of angry men stolidly planted before the house, the thin line of men facing them, the two tall men and the stout one on the porch, the dimming flare of the torches and the harsh brilliance of the porch lights, the house standing huge and white and mellow in the moonlight, the sharp touch of winter and the vast quiet of the night over all—seems to be a giant canvas, a huge, static painting out of some legendary book, a setting of medieval dash and color and fire, a portrait of chivalric glory, the long figure on the porch rising mighty and resplendent like some ancient knight of arms, brave and strong and shining.

"Dan here told me tonight he would talk to you, Sam, you bein the leader. That was before you men decided to take the law in your own hands. Well, it's not too late—"

He looks sharply at Sprague.

"If these men go home will you sit down with Sam, here and now, an try to work this thing out?"

"Well, I . . . if they—"

Anson steps to the edge of the porch.

"Tell them to go home, Sam, and get rid of those sticks of dynamite. Tell them it's all over and then come up here and settle your business."

Sam Tucker does not move. The men behind him shift uneasily, their murmurs subdued now. The guards facing them watch closely. Somewhere, far away, a train whistles lonesomely at the moon.

"How do I know he'll listen to me?" Sam says.

The boy feels anger rise in him. Always spicious, he thinks. Can't he never trust anybody?

"He'll listen. He wants the mill open bad as you want to get back to work."

"All right," Sam says. "I reckon talkin's what we come for."

The boy feels a sickening sense of shame in his belly. He knows his father's voice as well as he knows the bare, clean boards of the little house in which he lives. He knows every mood and tone and inflection of this harsh, flat voice.

And he knows now, knows surely and without anger, with only shock and shame, that there is disappointment in the voice, that his father is, within himself, disappointed and bitter at the very moment of his life when he should speak in triumph and relief and exultation.

"All right," his father's voice says, rising now. "You men go on along."

The men leave quietly. The shadows fade quietly into deeper shadow. The red glare of the torches is gone and the deep anger of the voices stilled. A stooped man moves slowly, unsurely, up unfamiliar steps. A shorter man waits and a tall, slouchy figure brushes contemptuously past and disappears in the shadow.

The stooped man and the shorter man enter the white house. Behind them, the tallest man of all stands silently a long moment, looking, perhaps, at the sky.

I want to be like him, the boy thinks. I want to be like him evry way I can. I want to be a man. Like he is.

And then this last figure too turns and enters the house. After a moment the porch lights click out and the night again drops darkness across the lawn.

"I got to git home," George says. "Pa'll whale me anyhow, but I got to git home."

They slip back from the bushes, move around the garage, and walk silently toward the street.

"You know, Bill, I'm glad nobody got blowed up. Danged if I ain't."

"Yeah," the boy says, hearing again his father's voice. "Me too." Even her, he thought. I'm glad they didn't blow her up.

"I reckon it'll all be over soon," George says. "Mill'll be open again an all."

"I reckon." But I ain't goin to watch her any more. I ain't ever goin to.

"Gosh. I sure thought somebody was a-gonna get kilt."

"Oh, shut up, George," the boy says. "You talk so dang much."

Chapter Eleven

Cracked ice swished pleasantly as Martha jerked the cocktail shaker back and forth. The cool metal in her palms sent easy little chills through her body. In the afternoon heat the shivers were welcome.

Not that it was hot in her house. In winter and summer the temperature of Martha Pollock's rooms was as near perfection as could be attained. And not only the temperature—no speck of dust ever grayed the glistening hardwood of her floors, no rip or tear defaced the good taste of rugs and upholstery, no picture hung awry on her beautifully plastered, papered, or paneled walls, no idle newspaper lay across a cluttered coffee table. Cobwebs had to be satisfied with the basement in Martha's house and a book or a lamp moved from its assigned location would have been as glaringly out of place as she herself on a bus full of sweaty commuters.

She settled back on the comfortable couch, the shaker still in her hands, and looked at what she had wrought. The house had been hers only a little over a year. Not a stick of furniture, not a single coat of paint remained from the former owners.

And already I'm bored with it, she thought. After all, there are only so many things you can do to a house or a room, so many improvements you can make. After that it's just moving furniture from one spot to another.

The gloomy face of Randolph Pollock looked down its nose at her from above the antique mantel. It was a face out of childhood, a face recalling always a voice, snarling and unpleasant, the voice in its turn recalling a sort of terror she had never outgrown.

The old bastard, she thought. (The words also invariably associated with the gold-edged face on the wall.) To think the little tenant girl he despised has a home like this, a room like this, sits here looking at his picture calling him an old bastard. And supports his son in a manner to which he was never accustomed when you, you old bastard, were footing the bills.

A Joan Crawford part, she thought. It's just like a Joan Crawford part.

She leaned forward to the glass expanse of the coffee table and poured from the shaker. I wish Tucker would come, she thought, I hate to be kept waiting like this.

She drank the cocktail in one quick swallow and poured again, feeling the quick slap of the liquor in her stomach. It was almost audible in the quietness of the house.

I might as well get crocked. I don't see any reason why not. Except Tucker and he doesn't count.

I hate to deal with the snake. But he's so damn greedy, it might work. There's just enough chance it'll work to make it worth while.

She laughed out loud, swinging her legs, in black lounging pajamas, to the sofa, letting her head fall back to the upholstered arm, feeling the cocktail glass cool and moist in her hand. The other hand lay idly across her stomach.

Mrs. Harvey Pollock, she thought. The social leader. The heiress. Mrs. Harvey Joan Crawford Pollock. Conniving with a dirty little politician because . . .

Because it will be fun to tear down the great Colonel Pollock. Because this is one time he's not going to get what he wants. Because I hate his fat guts.

A car door slammed on the street outside. Here we go, Martha thought.

She stood up swiftly and ran her hand efficiently through her hair. She quickly finished the second cocktail, glanced at herself in a mirror on the wall, and went into the hall.

She opened the door and waited for Tucker, feeling the warm air rise from the ground to her face, blinking once in the bright sunlight, the tickle of heat-stirred dust in her nostrils, hot sun burning suddenly at her bare arms.

He came up the steps, smiling at her, that hateful look in his eyes, the look that not only saw through the black pajamas (easy enough, she thought, in this bright sun) but also through what the pajamas could never conceal from eyes like his, saw through her to the tiny core of being she concealed so well beneath her careful exterior.

"It's good of you to come," she said, the mockery of the words almost a taste on her lips.

"Why, Martha," Tucker said, "you know I'm always at your service."

With the words she was at ease. After all, hadn't Tucker once said they understood each other?

That was one thing about him. You didn't have to treat a bastard like much of anything else, and you didn't expect a bastard to act like anything but what he was, just a plain old everyday bastard.

"Come on in," she said. "You probably need a drink as badly as I do."

"Now you're talking." He followed her into the perfect living room. She was completely aware of the movements of her body under the pajamas. But then, she thought, I always am.

She flung a careless hand toward the cocktail shaker. "Help yourself."

"Do you mind"—he looked around—"if I put a real drink together? I never learned to handle cocktails."

"Over there. The thing that looks like a radio. It has everything you need."

She arranged herself on the sofa and poured from the shaker as he made himself a highball. I might as well get drunk, she thought again. It's so much easier to be a bitch when I'm drunk.

"The Colonel will be back tomorrow, won't he?" Tucker came back to the sofa, a tall glass in his hand.

"I suppose. He'd better. He has the servants with him."

"I wish you had stayed with him longer. It had a lot of good publicity angles, your being there with him."

"The hell with it. I was bored stiff."

"I know. But it was only for—"

"Skip it. I'm back, so why go into it. I hate that damn beach place anyway. I hate bathing suits."

He sat down by her and reached for the shaker.

"Your glass is empty." She held it out and he poured for her, their eyes meeting a moment above the trickling fluid.

"Let's get crocked, Tucker. Let's get good and drunk."

You never know whether the son of a bitch is laughing with you or at you, she thought, hearing his chuckle. I never met a man quite like him.

She speculated briefly on his age. By all standards she could think of, he had to be at least five years younger than she. The unpleasant thought shuttled quickly out of her mind. (Martha did not make a fetish of remaining young. She worked at it, worked hard at it, but rarely let herself *think* of age at all.)

"I mean it," she said. "I feel like getting stinko."

"That's no way for a Senator's wife to talk."

"The hell with it. Let's drop the pose, Tucker."

She detected a faint lift of surprise around the corners of his mouth. "What pose?"

"I don't like you and I think you hate me. Let's own up."

He offered his glass in a mock toast.

"Done. But you overstate the case."

She shifted into a more comfortable position, feeling her bent knee touch his relaxed thigh. She sipped at the cocktail, noticing it was already half-gone, feeling a sudden quick lightness in her head.

"I suppose it's all set. The second primary, I mean."

His eyes pinched slightly and he lifted his glass to his lips.

"For God's sake," Martha said, "don't you think I have eyes?"

"All right. It's all set."

"That's what I wanted to see you 'bout. Why I called you." Why, my tongue's getting thick, she thought. I am getting a little drunk. I already am.

Tucker picked up the shaker.

"There ought to be one more in here," he said. He poured the last of the liquid in her glass, not quite filling it. Their eyes met again, and what she saw brought a flicker of satisfaction to Martha's stomach.

It's getting him, she thought. A woman in thin pajamas on a sofa in a big, empty house, right beside him, her leg touching him, getting herself drunk. A beautiful woman with big breasts and long legs and hot eyes. The most beautiful woman he ever saw. Me.

"Listen," she said, working hard at the word, not wanting blurred speech to disclose how nearly drunk she was. "Spose I don't want to be Mrs. Senator Pollock? Spose I told you that?"

"You just did."

"No, I didn't." She drank half the cocktail. "Don't twist my words. I only said spose. But it's true."

"Well, that's your tough luck, then. The Colonel's as good as in, you want to know the truth."

"Fat bastard."

"Agreed. But he's as good as in."

She leaned forward, spacing her words carefully. "What if he wasn't? What if you fixed him so he wasn't as good as in." She laughed. "So he was out on his ass."

Tucker finished his drink and placed the glass carefully on the coffee table. Break the goddam thing, she thought. See if I care.

"You fixed it so he was as good as in. You could fix it so he wasn't. Couldn't you?"

"I don't know. But I'm not going to, I know that."

"Course not. Not for nothing."

"Not for anything."

"Oh yes. Oh yes you would. Right price you would."

It was getting to be too much of an effort to speak clearly. Hell with it, she thought. Just so he understands.

Tucker picked up his glass and turned it in his hands.

"This is crazy, Martha. What have you got against being a Senator's wife?"

She finished the drink and let her arm fall to the floor, dropping the glass gently to the rug. She sat up, one leg on the floor, the other curled before her, touching easily against Tucker's leg.

"You know him," she said. "You know I hate him."

He nodded, his eyes moving over her.

"He brags," she said. "Throws my father in my face and my money. But he takes the money. Oh he takes that all right. An treats me like a fiel' hand, like I'm nothin, like he's the fines . . . finest thing ever walked."

"That's pretty strong," Tucker said. "He's not all that bad."

"Tha's not all."

She felt an old rage pounding in her.

"He lives off me. Like damn parsite. My money. My looks."

She shook her head solemnly, seeing his face blur with the movement.

"Not this time," she said. "This time he won't get what he wants."

She took Tucker's wrist in her hand and placed his hand on her thigh. His eyes widened, but she held firm to the suddenly tense wrist. Her voice was a whisper now.

"Feel how soft, Tucker. Feel how strong." She moved the hand gently along the smooth nylon. "What would you do, Tucker? If you had it? Soft an strong an white? What would you do?"

She could hardly keep from laughing. The look on his face, she thought. The way they get like little children. The way they all begin to sweat around the mouth like he is.

"Stop it," he said. "Stop this, Martha." But she clung to his wrist. He's not pulling away so hard, she thought. He's not pulling away nearly so hard. The bastard.

She leaned back to the arm of the sofa.

"Name your price," she said. "For seeing he never gets to be a Sentor."

"I've got my price," Tucker said. "But not for that."

She noticed he was not trying to take his hand from her thigh now. It moved, ever so slightly.

"You like to feel it," she said.

Tucker jerked his hand away from her as if the nylon were white hot. He stood up, his fists knotting at his sides.

"Get us a drink," she said, laughing up at him. "Get us a drink, Tucker, and maybe I'll let you play with my leg some more." I've got to quit laughing now, she thought. I've got to quit now or I never will.

"Don't push me, Martha. I'm not Colonel Pollock. Just don't push me around too much."

"Nobody pushes you around, Tucker. Jus get us a drink. Big drink."

He took his own glass to the portable bar and returned with two highballs. They sipped at the whisky.

It burns, she thought, it burns so nice all the way down to where I feel so warm and good and easy, all the way through the cold and the dark and the wet down to where I feel so warm and good and easy, and oh it burns so good and I feel so wonderful down where I am oh so warm and good and easy . . .

"You know," Tucker said. "I always wondered if the Colonel was man enough to take care of you."

Suddenly she despised him with a fury she had not known could exist side by side within her with the warm whisky. Like I was a brood mare, she thought. Like I was a cow to be serviced.

I want to punch a hole in his bloated hide. I want to watch the stink and corruption pour out of him. I want it now.

"How would you like twenny-five thousand a year, Tucker?" A note of fury seeped into the words, and Tucker drew a little away from her, as if expecting a blow.

"For what?"

"For being vice-president of a business I own. For not doing a damn thing but taking twenny-five thousan a year."

"And for fixing it so the Colonel takes a licking."

She nodded, waiting for his words, waiting for the stink and corruption.

"Stick it up your ass," he said. "In one-dollar bills."

Her eagerness was so great she hardly realized the crudity of the words. Now, she thought, now.

She stretched like a cat, feeling the outthrust of her breasts against the nylon, parting her lips, thrusting the warmth of her thigh hard against his leg, moving her hips luxuriously.

"Twenny-five thousan an me," she said. "Any way you want me."

And thought, Now. Now, you bastard, now it will come, all the bloat and stink and corruption within you. Now.

And for just one blessed, eternal moment, one moment in which her brain whirled and spun and danced in giddy triumph, she saw it in his face, saw all she wanted to see, and laughed.

Tucker slapped her. His hard, knotty hand came across her cheek and ear with clean, sharp force, a great hum began in

her ear and she felt her head rock over on her shoulder, felt
each finger drive separately into her soft flesh—and yet felt no
pain, no hurt, felt only shock and disbelief and terror that the
moment was gone, gone forever. If it had ever been.

"You goddamned slut," Tucker said, the words as even and
clean and sharp as his blow. "You can't buy me with your money,
and you can't buy me with your body. You slut."

The hum was louder now, louder than anything, and she listened to it avidly, trying to find in it a theme, trying to find
in it something in which she might lose herself, lose everything,
everything but the fading, dying memory of that one triumphant
moment.

"I take what I want," Tucker said, his voice faraway and
dimmed, hazing through the hum like a sound of aircraft on a
foggy night. "I take what I want when I want it."

She felt the glass ripped from her fingers, felt a small splash
of liquid on her stomach, felt his arms close about her, felt the
smell of him, felt the sound of his breath crashing through the
hum, felt herself clutch desperately, futilely, at the memory.

"You slut," he said again, as if through teeth clenched in
stone. "When I want something, I take it."

She felt his hands at the waist of her pajamas, felt the weight
of him crushing her breasts, felt her fists tiny against his massiveness, felt going from her, slipping and sliding and racing
away, the desperate remembrance, and thought, I have lost. I
have lost everything now.

She felt the rough texture of the sofa grating against her skin,
the harsh feel of his hands on her stomach and hips, the futility
of her fists against him again, and then nothing but the hum,
louder than ever, in both ears now, in all of her, and gave herself up to it, not remembering at all now, feeling only before the
hum devoured her the grain of his beard as her arms went about
his head.

Tucker stood at the window, his hands in his pockets. A cigarette projected loosely from his lips. He felt a tremor in his left
knee.

"You'd better go," Martha said. "Fred will be home soon."

"Damn Fred."

"Damn everybody. You know something, Tucker? I'm not even drunk any more."

"Listen," Tucker said, "I apologize." He did not turn around. "I shouldn't have done that and I know it."

Martha laughed. He heard the sound ring in his head, hollow, a little tinny.

"Stop worrying, Tucker. You big strong man. All you can think of is you're sorry you rolled the little woman because you don't know what she's going to do about it. All you know is you're scared to death."

Tucker took the cigarette out of his mouth, still not turning.

"You can't do anything about it," he said. "Because it wasn't rape and you know it. Not for long it wasn't."

"But it won't help you any if I tell about it."

He shook his head.

"Nor you. Quit bluffing, Martha."

"Get out, just get the hell out of here!"

He swung around.

"I tried to tell you," he said. "I'm sorry. Goddammit, what else you want me to say?"

She laughed harshly. She was lying back on the sofa, her hair only slightly disordered, the thin pajamas buttoned neatly around her. She was paler than usual and she had not put on fresh lipstick.

And, Tucker saw, she looked old.

Yes, he thought. Old. Now I see her the way she is, past all the beauty treatments, past the loving care, all the lavish expense, the lacquered perfection.

I see the foreboding wrinkles at the corners of her eyes. I see the yellow tinge seeping ever so stealthily into the flesh and the flesh itself beginning to sag, beginning to lose its sweetness, beginning to grow old and dry and tired.

It is as plain as the fear deep in her eyes. Age will be the last conqueror here, the last irresistible rapist. And age, having so long been cheated, will not be kind in victory.

"It never failed you before. Did it, Martha?"

In her eyes, in the fear, he read his answer. She knew then. She felt, as he saw, the sly advances of time.

"Please go," she said. "Just leave me alone."

"One more time, Martha. I really am sorry."

She half-rose from the couch, her voice nearly a snarl.

"You're so smug. You're so goddam wonderful, aren't you, Tucker?"

"No." He dropped his cigarette in an ash tray. He felt a great sadness that he could not altogether account for. "I'm about the same as you are. Only maybe a little more guts."

They looked at each other.

"We always did understand each other," Tucker said.

He turned and went out.

With no will to do so, he found himself thinking of Vivian. He felt shame, walking across the sunny lawn toward his car, to be thinking of her so soon after . . .

But I can't help it, he thought. Vivian is so fresh. So young and so clean.

I wish she were here. I wish she were here always, to make things fresh and young and clean. Even me.

✿

The decision was not unexpected.

At least it should not have been. The evidence was all there, conclusive and inescapable, reported in detail in the press. Yet, somehow, it had failed to register with the general public.

The word "bombshell," therefore, was not inaccurately used in a *Capital Times* headline which trumpeted the decision of Federal Judge Avery W. Benton that Hartsville, third largest municipality in the State, must immediately provide "equal" school facilities for Negroes or admit them to the city's white schools (which were, Judge Benton noted, "generally excellent").

The hearing in the case had resulted from a suit brought by the Hartsville chapter of the National Association for the Advancement of Colored People. Lawyers were provided by that organization, and the suit went to trial in Federal court with city and State school officials as defendants.

The evidence was practically open and shut, as Judge Benton

noted in his decision. Overcrowded classroom conditions, poor sanitary facilities, low faculty standards, inadequate buildings, and general neglect were shown by NAACP lawyers to be characteristic of the Negro school system. The State Attorney General, heading the defense battery, barely contested the charges. His plea was for time to remedy the admitted evils.

Judge Benton held for plaintiffs, ruling that the city and the State must within one year "demonstrate conclusively" that steps had been taken to "equalize tangibly and intangibly" the two school systems. If this could not be done, he ruled, Hartsville white schools would have to "accept Negro students" at the expiration of the year.

The ruling did not overthrow the time-honored concept of "separate but equal" schools. Judge Benton was careful to point out that it actually reaffirmed it. He was even more careful to note that the weight of the evidence precluded any other possible decision in the case.

But, coming as it did at a time when for weeks the headlines had been full of State politics, the cold war, the opening of baseball season and the spectacular discovery of a Non-Virgin Club in one of the eastern cities, the news was singularly startling. It might have been expected; it should have been; but who but lawyers follows the progress of civil suits in Federal court?

It was the immediacy of the thing. In the time it took to read a headline mothers could visualize their children side by side in class with pickaninnies. In the time it took to read the full story the entire breakdown of segregation could be imagined.

And if segregation went, could social equality and intermarriage be long in coming? Would not golden-haired, blue-eyed Susie be doomed to a thick-lipped husband and a kinky-haired child?

So at least, on that day when Judge Benton's ruling was disclosed, it seemed to many. Hartsville, as any fool could plainly see, was on the verge of having its schools invaded and taken over by the niggers, the first victim of a well-organized, new drive by the NAACP and the Yankees to "tell us how to run our business."

Could this be anything but the beginning of the end? Not just for Hartsville, but for everybody?

First reports of the decision appeared in the morning papers exactly ten days after the primary election for United States Senator. By ten o'clock a poll would have shown it to be the leading topic of conversation in the State. By noon afternoon papers were on the streets, their editorial pages full of scholarly and reassuring analyses of the actual importance of the ruling, their front pages black with the shocking news of its sensational possibilities.

At 2:00 P.M. a press conference was scheduled for the Bright Leaf Room of the Stonewall Jackson Hotel.

This was a production as carefully edited and staged as a radio program. It had been planned for weeks. When the time arrived for curtain call, the cast was already on stage.

At one end of the long ballroom stood most of the volunteer and paid workers for Colonel Pollock, properly hushed and reverent and tired-looking.

At the other end, grouped pleasantly in easy chairs under the huge tobacco-field mural, sat Colonel Pollock, solemn and pink-shaven and dignified and every inch a deeply concerned man; his wife, Martha, groomed and charming and serene and not a little breathtaking, her skirt carefully covering her knees; and their son, Fred, scowling slightly, but handsome and decorative—a fit family indeed to present itself for the favor of the home-loving public.

Behind the Colonel, at rigid attention, stood the tall, Prussian figure of Joe Harrison, whose square jaw added not only popular favor but a flare of outraged determination to the group. It was, he told Bill Tucker later, one of the high points of his not un-exciting life.

Tucker himself leaned against a window sill, also concerned and serious, but, as became a professional, careful not to intrude himself upon the principals. There might have been found in his face a touch of irony, a touch of mockery.

But it was not his face that would be photographed, nor would it even be watched closely. Tucker was a stagehand.

"All right," he said, "we've got a minute to go before they let the herd in."

Colonel Pollock took a last look at the sheet of paper in his hand.

"Can I smoke?" Fred asked.

"Better not. It won't last long."

"You just keep quiet," the Colonel told Fred. "All you have to do is sit there and keep quiet."

Martha Pollock's eyes met Tucker's, briefly, coolly. They had not spoken since he had left her at her house two days before. The glance made him uncomfortable; it was too much like hearing his own voice on a phonograph record.

He was not particularly worried about what had happened on Colonel Pollock's sofa. He was reasonably certain that he was not the first to cuckold the Colonel, and he knew very well that Martha had made no great battle for what remained of her virtue, had in fact summoned him to her house in reasonable expectation of sacrificing some, or all, of it to him. He wished that the whole thing had never happened, but he did not blame himself for it.

As for any reprisals by Martha, Tucker had no worries at all. She'd keep her mouth shut. She couldn't afford not to.

"You ready, Martha?" he said.

Her cool eyes flicked over him again.

"Why not?"

Tucker waved his hand toward a man who stood at the central doors of the great room. "Brace yourselves," he said.

The reporters flowed into the room, nearly two dozen of them, arranging themselves before the little family group, talking among themselves, speaking to the Colonel and to Martha, waving hands at Joe Harrison. The radio men busied themselves with tape recorders, and the photographers turned the room into periodic white glares of light. Tucker thanked his stars that television had not yet penetrated the State's political methods.

He watched the Colonel, who was good at this sort of thing, be hail-fellow-well-met until everyone was set. He admired the cool ease of Martha, knowing as he did what a pill she swallowed, even as she smiled and nodded and made herself gracious and feminine. He kept a wary eye on Fred who occasionally managed to plaster across his jaws the reluctant posture of a smile. He did not look at Joe Harrison at all.

"Is everybody all set?" Joe finally called in his best Sunday baritone, the one befitting his position as arranger and conductor of press conferences.

"Shoot," one of the reporters said. Another flash bulb popped

and the voices dropped from a chattering babble to a few discon-
nected words to a final, waiting silence.

"I think the Colonel has something to say we've all been waiting
to hear," Joe said, his voice resounding and important. "Y'all know
where the phones are and you'll find copies of the statement on
that table back there."

He placed his hand lightly on the back of the Colonel's chair.

"Colonel Pollock," he said, putting into the words a mixture of
fervor, reverence, and awe.

The Colonel cleared his throat, shifted in his chair, and dropped
his eyes to the paper on his knees. Another flash bulb went off
and Martha Pollock's beautiful head turned slowly toward her
husband.

"Some months ago," the Colonel said, "I announced my inten-
tion of seeking, subject to the recent primary, election to the
United States Senate. Since that announcement a rigorous campaign has been waged in which I believe I have made a clear and
unequivocal stand—" pause—"for traditional Americanism, the
free enterprise system and the principles of Southern Democracy.

"I have been roundly attacked for that stand. These attacks continue daily. But despite them the people have failed to make conclusive their choice for a United States Senator."

Hurry it up, Tucker thought. You're not reading the Gettysburg
Address.

He listened only casually to the speech. It had been written
weeks ago, polished continually ever since. He could repeat the
words along with Pollock. He let them pass over his head without
notice until the Colonel boomed into full stride.

"And now in our own State we have the spectacle of the wild-
eyed liberals and the parlor pinks not only insinuating themselves
into all phases of our lives, but striving to infest our schools and
churches and homes with their foreign ideology—" pause again,
wearily—"to break down the very principles which our fathers
bled and died for, which they so wisely gave us that we might grow
strong and prosperous."

And fat, Tucker thought. Like you.

He half-listened as the Colonel called Jefferson, Jackson, Robert
E. Lee, and Our Forefathers to witness the greatness of Southern

Democracy, as he indignantly rejected the idea that the nation's children might inherit a nation changed one iota from the nation their fathers had founded.

Another flash bulb went off and the Colonel galloped into his peroration.

"On these things I stand. I call upon all Americans, all freedom-loving, right-thinking citizens of this great State, to stand with me. Tomorrow I shall ask the State Elections Commission to prepare for a second primary."

The reporters stirred, their movements breaking the scribbling silence. Several of them began to push away from the front ranks.

"I have unbounded confidence in the wisdom of the people. I know they will stand now for America as we have known it—for freedom as we conceive it. I put my trust in our great people and in Almighty God."

He put the paper down and looked up, still grave, still concerned, and reached for Martha's hand.

Tucker did not hear the applause, did not see Joe Harrison heading those reporters with no deadlines to worry them toward the table where drinks and food waited. He hardly saw the Colonel and Martha circulating casually through the crowd, the pretty girl passing out copies of the Colonel's statement. He was unaware of the popping glare of the flash bulbs, of the constant ebb and flow of voices in determined duel with each other, voices seeming to blend into one incoherent but insistent voice.

He leaned alone against the window sill, his arms crossed before him and thought of how the years had ground together to bring forth this moment, of how time in its vast tide had spewed it forth upon the beach.

I have been a long time coming to this place, he thought, a long time hearing these words, seeing this happen.

But the years had ground together and it was done now. There was no way to go back if he had wanted to. There was no exit from this vast room he had sought, only a threshold upon which he now stood alone, a threshold which, once crossed, would close relentlessly behind him.

But I will not be lonely, he thought. I will not be lonely there in my vast room.

For I will have myself.

I will have myself and I will have Vivian.

Vivian will be coming back now, coming back to me, and I shall take her by the hand, by her warm hand, and draw her with me into my vast room.

Into my vast room where I will never be lonely again.

Chapter Twelve

The soft smoke of Tucker's cigarette curled over Vivian's shoulder. She sat staring through the window of his car, through the haze of the smoke, amazed and perplexed at what she saw.

It's like another world, she thought. A world I never saw before. This was Melon Festival in Union Springs. The wide, dusty streets of the little town, baked to a sort of colorless glaze in the scalding sun, festooned with bunting and banner, bustled with self-contained fervor. Storefronts boasted huge welcome signs. Windows were filled with great piles of green watermelons and yellow cantaloupes, with 4-H and Grange and Home Demonstration Club displays, Kiwanis and Rotary and Ruritan exhibits. Merchants and clerks sweated profusely, their big yearly opportunity gleaming like a promise of wealth around them.

The people flock to festival like insects drawn to neon. They cluster on the midway, sprawling gaudily across the vacant lot near the river; they knot along the floor of the huge warehouse, crammed with displays of the fruits of the country; they gather in long lines to sign up for the new car to be given away at the grand parade; they are drawn, pulled in like gasping fish, to the shooting galleries and the bingo stands and the penny-toss and the chili-smelling eateries; they listen to the hurdy-gurdy music, the rasp of the barker, the sly whisper of the con man at his crafty trade; uneasily, they watch the hips of painted girls sway in musty hula skirts; they board the Ferris wheel, the merry-go-round, the swings, the shoot-the-chute, and the caterpillar, and the shrill screams of girls are soothed against the crinkled white shirts of bold young men.

A man sits silently on the sidewalk by the bank, holding in his fingers a leather cord at the end of which a moth-eaten monkey dances, while beside the man the pennies of children rattle into his cup. The ladies of the Baptist Church offer beneath the striped and shaky tent of McKeithan's Funeral Parlor, now pitched above the sparse grass of the Sunday school lawn, sandwiches and ice cream and lemonade. There are the trailer vendors of sugary clouds of cotton candy; the floating colors of children's balloons; and in the arms of the triumphant, the coveted China dog, immortal symbol of festival time.

Down the sidewalks come the country people. Through the alleys and back streets they move, over the sun-yellowed grass of the courthouse square, in and out of stores, restaurants, soft drink stands, beer joints. They come to buy and they come to sell; they come to play and they come to look, to walk and to listen—and all of them come to talk, all of these in festival time:

. . . Young men bold and loud in the afterglow of cold beer and cheap white whisky . . . fathers, their sun-reddened faces passive beneath sweat-stained hats, their eyes squinted against the sun-glare . . . old men, their voices slurred and thin with age, hands showing boned and skinny in the sun . . . and girls, too, oh the girls like bright flowers growing in the streets, like flowers blooming in festival time . . . who will someday be like their mothers, a little tired, a little drab, a little faded, talking quietly in that last longest oldest refuge of women: their own kind and their children . . . Negroes shuffling, shambling, careful to go to the rear of the store, ancient hat in hand, before buying . . .

All of these in festival time.

Vivian came from a prosperous region where farmers were gentlemen whose wives drove station wagons and bred dogs, from a land where even a high-school diploma was not necessary if you could scrape along on ninety dollars a week at the aircraft plant, where day laborers owned television sets, and opportunity lay all about if you had enough guts and luck, where everybody seemed to have enough guts and luck.

She was a stranger here among the rustics. She had never seen the South come out of the branch heads. She had never seen the red-necks come to town in festival time.

So she sat and stared, perhaps alone in pure silence among that great convocation of people talking. For in festival time ghosts, too, come to town. Shades of long ago slant darkly over the sand-hills, over the creeks and the green, green trees.

And out of this past, out of a time which never faded, out of a great clock whose hands have never moved, whose hands forever span the years to nowhere, come the people of the country South, the backwoods South, the brush-arbor South—timeless, slow-moving, ill-fed, ill-housed, ill-clad, prey to all the dark moods and passions, all the hates and hurts and beliefs of a land and a heritage blighted, diseased, cursed by an old black evil, an evil and a heritage they never saw, never knew, only accepted in some deep and bitter resignation, only accepted out of that deep and bitter resignation because acceptance alone surpasseth understanding; not resistance, not struggle, not even defeat; only acceptance.

Vivian knew little of the history and economics of the South. She did not understand that time had mired down here in this backwater for nearly a hundred years. She only knew that the people she saw were out of a different mold. A youth looked at her through the window of the car; she felt a chill slice along her spine.

"Big crowd," Tucker said. He flipped his cigarette into the street.

"Yes."

"You look funny. Odor getting you?"

She shook her head.

"No, it's just that—I don't know. Bill, they're all staring at me so!"

He chuckled, sliding lower in the seat, his long legs tangled around the steering post.

"Fair enough. You're staring at them, too."

She shook her head again. "I guess so. But there's something odd about these people. I—feel it."

"They're folks. More or less."

"When they look at me, the men I mean, there's something—almost perverted about it."

"Perverted? These people?"

"Maybe that isn't the word. But—not normal anyway. Not healthy."

"I wouldn't call them perverted," Tucker said. "But I wouldn't

· 184 ·

call them normal either, not the way you mean. And, my God, certainly not healthy."

He pulled at his cigarette.

"This is one of the most backward sections of the State, maybe the whole South," he said. "These are ignorant folks. Poor as hell. Dirty, too, I guess. And generally speaking they never had a chance in this world to be anything else."

Vivian looked again at the people trudging solemnly by. The way they spit, she thought. You'd think the gutters would be running with tobacco juice.

"But it's not like this all over. Not by a long shot. You've got farm agents and PMA and Grange and 4-H and REA and the welfare people and all that. They've done wonders, almost in no time. In some sections—especially if they've got tobacco or peanuts for a money crop—the farmers make real dough, live well, send the kids to college."

Tucker nodded at the street again.

"But not these people. You still hit this—" he pointed—"too often. The land's no good and too few people own too much of it. The farm agent's a political hack and the county commissioners are penny-pinching fools and crooks to boot, and there's not enough pull in Capital City to get roads built or schools or welfare money—hell, I could name you a thousand reasons for it."

He laughed shortly.

"They all add up to nobody giving a damn."

I never saw him show such feeling before, Vivian thought. Except that one night— She shut her mind against the memory of that night at his apartment.

"Why don't you do something about it?" she said. "You're a politician. You've got pull. You could help."

He threw up his hands in mock horror.

"Please, lady, please. I'm just a poor boy trying to get along."

"You mean there's nothing in it for you. Don't you?"

His smile wavered.

"Aren't we a little blunt today? You're liable to hurt my feelings."

"Sometimes I dislike you intensely, Bill Tucker."

The smile came back in full force.

"Everybody does, honey. But you'll learn to love me. Give it time, give it time."

"Don't bank on that!"

"Besides—" business of spreading hands and raising eyebrows— "you said one person, an individual all by himself, couldn't do anything. You told me—"

"Oh, you always get around me!"

"I get around everybody. Natural talent for end runs."

She started to flare back and suddenly felt laughter bubbling up. She tried not to smile, but slowly the corners of her mouth lifted and they were laughing together. I'm positively immoral about this man, she thought. I ought to be ashamed to be seen with him.

And look at us. Hardly a night since I came back that we haven't had dinner together or been somewhere. I haven't done a bit of work I've been so busy with him.

"You can't make a silk purse out of a sow's ear," he said. "What I like you best for is most of the time you don't even try to."

"You can make a silk purse out of a sow's ear, and the only reason I *don't* try, Mr. Tucker, is because I don't think you're worth the trouble."

"My illusions are shattered. Beyond recall."

"You don't have any."

And that is as true as can be, she thought. You are as hard a case as they come. If there were not something about you, some intangible something, like when you were talking about those people and you couldn't keep the feeling and the pity out of your cynical face, if there were not that something maybe I only imagine, that tells me you're not all iron and steel and chromium. If there were not that—

"One illusion I have," he said, looking at his watch, "is that it's high time that motorcade got here."

"That'll be a laugh. These people never heard of politics, did they? Or Colonel Pollock?"

"Are you kidding? They'd rather vote than eat. And they'd rather talk about voting than vote."

"Well, you'd never—"

Down the street, the *thump thump thump* of a bass drum started up and, faint and thin, the music of a brass band came on to them.

"Here they come," he said. *"Hail the Conq'ring Hero."*

"That's *Dixie*. And it's off-key."

The people were lining up along the curbs now, pushing out into the street. Their faces showed no enthusiasm, no real curiosity, only a sort of dull wondering at what was next planned for their enlightenment. The band music came nearer. Tucker and Vivian got out and leaned against the rear of the car. People pressed close around them, and Vivian was uncomfortably aware of a strong smell of manure from a thin man standing next to her. The sound of voices was stilled now, the crowd waiting.

"What's goin on?" the thin man drawled at his neighbor, a man in overalls.

"That er Pollock. Runnin fer Senator."

"Him, eh?"

Around a corner, a block or two away, a convertible poked its shiny nose. Swaying above it was a blue and gray banner, reading, in letters easily visible to Vivian and Tucker:

PROTECT YOUR HERITAGE—VOTE FOR POLLOCK

"Some heritage," Vivian said, and Tucker grinned. The thin man looked solemnly at her and Vivian met his eyes. He shifted a wad of tobacco to the other side of his mouth and looked back at the convertible. His look had sent that same little chill tickling down her back.

Another convertible followed the first. Two men sat up on the rear of the back seat. This car had no banner.

"The Mayor and the solicitor," Tucker said. "They're supposed to be neutral. Like you."

The band followed this car. It was a high-school outfit, clad in bright yellow.

"All the way from Bartow I bring those kids," Tucker said, "and they still play off-key."

Another convertible came around the corner, this one bearing two more men, one a familiar blond figure, erect as an English horseman, the other fat, bald, waving genially with both hands.

"Joe and Cousin Hadley. Nothing neutral about them."
The banner over their car read:

NO ANSON, NO FEPC—POLLOCK!

"I'm agin that er FEPC," the thin man said. "Be dog if I ain't."
"Nigger-lovers," the man in overalls answered. He put a finger against one nostril, leaned over, and blew his nose on the street. Then he blew his other nostril. Vivian wanted to brush germs off her bare legs.

The first convertible passed slowly and she saw the eager face of the boy driving. She looked back in time to see the car carrying Colonel Pollock and Martha nose slowly around the corner. The biggest banner of all flapped above them, reading:

A VOTE FOR POLLOCK IS A VOTE FOR REAL SOUTHERN DEMOCRACY

"Ol Massa himself," Tucker murmured.
Now they could hear a slow wave of handclapping pass through the crowd, a few whistles and cheers, even a rebel yell. Probably planted, Vivian thought.

The Bartow High School band puffed past, blowing hell out of *Dixie*. It *was* a good tune. Vivian felt her blood running faster at the sound of it. She waved at Joe Harrison. He nodded stiffly, surveying the crowd like a conqueror.

Colonel Pollock was waving both hands over his head now as his car came on up the street. Behind him one more convertible, packed with what Vivian took to be important local supporters, had fallen into line. It bore a final banner:

ARE YOU FROM DIXIE? VOTE FOR POLLOCK

Vivian heard Tucker chuckle.
"I bet Martha just loves this," he said.
Mrs. Pollock was waving too, Vivian saw. Her smile was somewhat fixed, but her expression was pleasant enough. Pollock was standing up now as the clapping and yelling swelled, waving with one hand, leaning on the other. His jovial face beamed in all directions.

"Fat, ain't he?" the man in overalls said.

Behind the last car a truck was now pushing along the street. In its open bed a string band played hillbilly music. A Boy Scout troop marched behind the truck, valorously trying to keep step with the band far ahead of them, its music growing fainter all the time. A bespectacled scoutmaster fluttered around them and the flag-bearer fought hard to hold Old Glory upright. It must have weighed, with its staff, twice as much as its determined bearer.

"How's he stan on them civil rights?" the thin man said.

The Colonel's car was past now, and Vivian gazed without interest at the important local supporters. A few ragged children ran after the cars, cutting up for the crowds on the sidewalks.

". . . white man all right. Feller was tellin me he . . ."

The band music had faded to a faint *thump thump thump* again and the scouts straggled past, no two of them in step. They could hear more cheering down the street as the Colonel passed.

"Looks like the show's over," Tucker said.

"And a very uninspired show, if you ask me. He'll have to do better than that, Tucker."

"Hell, he hasn't said anything yet." He took her arm. "Wait'll you hear his speech this afternoon."

Vivian was silent. She could imagine the speech from the banners that had waved over the convertible. I am suffering for my profession, she thought. I truly am.

The crowd was breaking up now. The thin man moved away with his friend in overalls. Vivian wondered if she only imagined that the smell of manure lingered after them.

"You don't want to hear the Mayor's speech of welcome, do you?"

"Heaven forbid!"

"Then let's get something to eat."

They pushed across the sidewalk into the hotel.

"Why weren't you in the parade?" Vivian said. "An important man like you."

He leered comically.

"I'm the unseen hand," he said. "Also I hate to have a lot of people looking at me."

"But mostly you're the unseen hand?"

He nodded. "Mostly I am."

She stopped and looked around.

"Powder my nose," she said. "Will you wait for me?"

He waved a hand. "Take your time. The Mayor has fourteen pages of welcome to read. I *told* Joe not to write it so long."

She hurried toward the ladies' room. She needed refuge. All of a sudden it had been a little too much to take. Those banners and those people and that fat man waving at them, almost obscene in his blatant appeal to their ignorance. But most of all she had suddenly not been able to swallow Tucker's bald admission of the way he worked, the things he arranged.

I'm the unseen hand.

Sometimes I can't stand to be around him, she thought. Just all of a sudden, like now. Not just for some one little thing in particular. Just for everything.

And yet—the way he talked about these awful people, for instance. The way he looked, the soft sound of his voice.

She pushed open the door. I've got to think, she told herself. I've got to get some of this straightened out.

✻

"Mr. Mayor, distinguished guests, my fellow Americans. The welcome you have given me here in this wonderful community has warmed my heart."

Vivian felt her whole body prickly with sweat. She held a newspaper over her head to shield her face from the blistering sun. Her bare legs felt coated, as if a thin layer of dust had already settled on them.

". . . to see so many of the great citizens of this great region in attendance here is indeed . . ."

The voice, made slightly nasal by the public-address system, boomed out over the crowd. By standing tiptoe, Vivian could see the speaker's platform, a wooden affair in the middle of the baseball diamond of Union Springs Memorial Park. Or rather she could see the bulk of Colonel Pollock, from the shoulders up, and a row of bunting hanging limply above his head. The rest of the men and women on the platform were below her line of vision.

I wonder if the unseen hand is up there? Vivian thought. That cynical crook.

She had planned to circulate through the crowd while the Colonel spoke, observing the reactions of the listeners, especially the women. It had seemed a good chance to get a firsthand impression of a given speech's effect, and she had thought, through a little judicious questioning, to get some colorful notes for what was beginning to look like a dull thesis.

She nudged experimentally to her left and came up hard against a broad, overalled back.

"I'm surrounded," she muttered aloud.

A dull face looked over the shoulder of the overalled back. Faded eyes blinked at her and she turned hastily away.

She did not listen to Colonel Pollock's standard opening. She had heard him speak many times, usually hearing different versions of the same old thing. She looked at the faces around her, wondering about these passive, soft-spoken people. He won't get much reaction out of these statues, she thought. Not in this weather.

". . . regretfully, as a final effort to protect that heritage I hold dear, I have agreed . . ."

Sounds like something new, Vivian thought.

Tucker had talked a lot about this speech today. It had to be more than just Pollock's first big speech since he decided on a second primary. It had to be something new.

A woman holding a sleeping baby edged in beside her, languidly waving flies from the baby's face. Vivian's nose told her its diaper needed changing.

". . . to protect our homes, our churches, our schools, our pure American blood . . ."

She was listening fully now, unmindful of the sweat trickling down her body, the dust in her nostrils, the glaring heat of the sun, the low, shuffling undertone around her.

". . . Southern traditions, framed and protected and fostered by our great Southern statesmen, from Jefferson to that small band of outnumbered heroes who even today battle stubbornly for their homeland in the hallowed halls of Congress . . ."

Cheap whisky fumes came over Vivian in waves. She felt, rather than saw, a man swaying behind her. The smell was nauseating and she moved ahead as much as possible. If he gets sick . . .

". . . with a heavy heart that I tell you our State is not fully represented among those heroes. One hand is missing; one hand is dedicated, not to those things we want in America, but to the destruction of them."

An airplane droned overhead. Some heads craned upward. But Pollock had the crowd's attention now, Vivian saw, and his voice had taken on a vibrant power she had not heard in it before.

". . . consistently opposed the very foundation stones of Southern Democracy—States' Rights, Free Enterprise and *segregation of the races!*"

The handclapping was louder now and a yell or two went up. That's the flattest he ever put it. That's pretty strong, even for him.

"Friends, I remember with warm love the old colored woman who tended me in my youth. I recall with delight the great soul of old Rufe Benton, who took me on my first hunting trip. Even today, I hold no man closer to my heart than Jed, who has worked for my family longer than I have been alive . . ."

He's got them listening now. He's talking their language, all right. I didn't know he had it in him. Look at them. Look at the poor fools waiting for him to light into the darkies. They know it's coming. They know what he's going to say. They can't wait to hear it.

". . . would they have asked to sit at my table? Would they have sought to ride with me on a bus? Would those wonderful old darkies, of which so few seem to be left, have thought of calling at my front door?

"Ah, my friends, what wonderful relationships we of the South established with our Nigras in those blessed days. We cared for them when they were sick, provided for them when they were hungry. Here was true democracy, friends, democracy in action— *Southern* Democracy, I choose to call it."

I always wondered just what Southern Democracy was, Vivian thought. And now I know.

The applause was furious. The man in front of Vivian put his fingers to his lips and whistled shrilly.

"Dead right, ain't he?" his companion said.

"Talks like a white man. Damn if he don't."

". . . today what do we see at every hand? We see the Nigras, our good and faithful friends of other, better days, spurred on by Northern agitators and Communists and fellow travelers, assaulting the very gates of our homes, our schools, churches, and families. And what are they asking, my friends? What do they seek?"

Vivian looked at the rapt faces around her, saw a man spit a wad of tobacco from his mouth to free himself for yelling, saw eyes squinting against the sun from faces as tense and waiting as a set trap, saw elbow nudge neighbor, saw women nodding in some faint, plodding approval. Behind her the baby had started to cry.

". . . and the sum total of all this, of these so-called civil rights bills, this FEPC and antilynch and all this other Yankee tripe, the sum total of all these unreasonable, ungrateful, un-American demands upon their old friends and protectors, is simply this, friends, simply this—*complete social equality* and the *abolition of segregation! And you know what that means!*"

The last sentence was almost unheard as the crowd roared in protest, the sound of it deep and full, almost frightening to Vivian, lost and alone in the middle of it. She was fascinated by the faces around her, the red faces, the stubbled faces, the old, leathery faces, the doughy faces of the women—faces lit now by some inner blaze, some old compulsion, some dark passion; roaring out, stirred, alive in some way not apparent before, answering to some long-dormant seed of discontent and hatred.

Vivian knew now what she had sensed in these people. It was hate, naked, glaring. And it was fear, crawling, malignant. It was hate she had felt coming out of them, hate she had known in little chills dancing along her spine. She felt it now, all around her, like a prairie fire before the wind. But it was fear that underlay it, hid silently beneath the surface, fear like the clinging suction of quicksand, fear of some black, monstrous evil, some horror too old to name—the ancient, abiding terror of the black man's blood.

". . . put no blame on our Southern Nigras. They know their

place, they know they have nothing to fear from us, only protection and care to look forward to in their old age. It's the Communists and the Yankee labor unions and the parlor pinks stirrin them up, friends, turnin their love to hatred, destroyin that age-old tradition of race separation for the equal good of both . . ."

Vivian saw the face of the woman with the baby turned up to Pollock as to a vengeful god, the mouth slightly open, the hair lank and loose, the eyes lost in far and fearsome glory. And she saw, beneath that face, the baby, forgotten now, sucking contentedly at the woman's udder-like breast, kneading at it with tiny, cruel fingers. The woman was not even aware of the feeding baby, Vivian saw, nor of her exposed breast. She was lost in the hell-fire pouring down on her. Vivian felt naked at the sight; she wanted to cross her arms protectingly over her own breasts.

". . . and in all of this, in all of this which would destroy life as we have known it, which would send us reeling into the darkness of race suicide, destroy that purity of blood which is our greatest heritage and strength, in all this CIO and Communist and foreign agitation, this stirring up of enmity between ourselves and our good old darkies, the hand of one man can be seen. Oh it's a clever hand, friends, a shrewd hand, an insidious hand, like the hand of that other so-called Christian, Judas Iscariot himself!

"It's a hand that will send the South in blood to the cross, as surely as the kiss of Judas sent Him Who knew no evil there. It's the hand of a man who asks you now to return him to the Senate . . ."

I can't believe what I'm hearing, Vivian thought. I can't believe he's saying all that.

Yet it was plain enough. It could be read in the faces around her, in the clenching hands, the gritted teeth, the flashing eyes.

It was not to be doubted. He was saying all of those incredible things. She was hearing it, watching these people lap it into their blood streams, watching it fan their dormant, lurking fear into hatred.

On and on the voice shouted, insistent, urgent, unceasing, lost occasionally in a roaring outbreak, emerging again at a higher pitch, ceaselessly stripping the mob of all individuality, until it stood as one man, naked and unashamed in its fear, its hatred.

"Damn niggers!" the man in front of Vivian shouted. "Nigger-lovin Yankees!"

Suddenly a fury beyond anything she had ever known shook Vivian to her soul. She felt rushing to her lips words she did not know she knew. She wanted to strike out, to feel her fists thud home in yielding flesh. She stood in the middle of the massive crowd, shaking with wild, passionate rage, not at Pollock, not even at Tucker, but at the people who milled like cattle around her.

"You fools!" she screamed into the uproar. "You crazy fools!" She could not hear her own weak voice.

Oh, you fools, you fools! You don't deserve anything but that scheming liar up there yelling at you, who'll fleece you like lambs when you give him what he wants, you suckers, you crazy suckers. You're like children, like that baby back there sucking its mother dry, you'll believe anything he tells you, swallow any lie he gives you just so it gives you somebody to hate and hurt and despise so you can feel like somebody. You'll believe anything that tears you open and lets the fear come dripping out to turn to crazy yelling hate; you'll yell for them and vote for them and make gods out of them because you're so afraid and so stupid and so ignorant you couldn't live if you didn't have something to hate for that very life you spend in fear.

"Suckers!" she screamed, and laughed wildly as her voice disappeared again in the roar. And felt the tears, warm and salty, start from her eyes.

". . . I don't stand on my record, friends. I stand before you today on my *opponent's* record, that record of villainy and deceit and foreign ideology! I urge you to repudiate that record now, to stand with me to preserve Southern Democracy for our children's children, to save our heritage . . ."

I can't listen any more. I'll be sick. I've got to get out of here.

She began shoving her way through the heedless crowd, elbowing, pushing her way through the row on row of packed, rumbling people, screaming bitterly into their animal roar, feeling the sour taste of futile words clogging her throat, stepping on feet, uncaring, unnoticed, her breath like a tight band across her chest, her tears flowing free now, shoving and scrambling and straining to get away, get back to air and sanity.

". . . strike down this evil, this abomination before God! Make America again a place where decent, white . . ."

She was out the gate and running, running hard down the street, heedless of the sun, not noticing the pain stitching her side, the rivulets of sweat down her neck, under her arms, between her breasts, not thinking of the hair flying about her head, only wanting to be away from the sound of the voice, the rumble of the mob, the stench of the corruption and disease and evil.

On the soft, warm grass before the courthouse she stopped finally to rest, falling almost limply to a low rise of lawn. A few passers-by on the now-deserted streets looked curiously at her.

I didn't know, she thought. I didn't know that was in me.

You didn't know what was in them either, a voice from inside said to her.

You didn't know what was in Pollock.

You didn't know what was in Tucker.

Did you?

No, she answered. I didn't know. But now I do. Now I've found out.

And what are you going to do about it?

Go away, she told the voice. I'm going away.

Far away? Where you can get it all out of your mind? Tucker and Pollock and the mob out there?

Yes. Where I can get everything out of my mind.

Where there isn't any hate and evil?

Yes. Yes yes yes.

There isn't any such place. Not in this world.

Chapter Thirteen

The telephone rang while Vivian was packing.

She leaned across the bed and reached for it. She had finished her bath and wore only her slip. The sun had gone down, but it was still hot in her room, and the overhead fan only stirred the mushy air.

It must be Tucker, she thought. Panic slipped through her. Then she squared her chin and picked up the phone.

"Hello?"

"Vivian? This is Bill."

"I don't want to talk to you, Bill."

"What?"

She felt her nails nick her palms. She pulled her knees up under her and knelt on the twisted bedspread.

"I said I don't want to talk to you."

The phone buzzed eerily. Like a ghost, she thought.

"The speech today," he said, his calm voice cutting off the buzz. "That it?"

"That ended it, Bill."

Again the faint, eerie hum.

"All right. I won't bother you then."

"What did you want?" She had not meant to say that or anything like it. But there had been something in his voice—he had *wanted* to talk to her.

"Let it go," he said. "I was just going to ask if you'd like to ride out a little, get cooled off."

She felt something absurdly like hope. There had been an almost-buried note of pleading in his voice.

"But I guess that's out," he said.

"I guess so."

"Listen, Vivian, I—I'd like to talk to you. I really would."

There was more than a plea in his voice now. There was something of fatigue, something old.

"What's the matter?" She was almost ashamed of the way resolution was draining out of her. But there's something different, she thought. He never sounded like this before.

"I've been in a hassle," he said. "Fred Pollock got himself in some girl trouble and I had to get him out of it."

"That boy ought to be whipped."

"He needs something, all right. Will you meet me downstairs, Vivian? Please?"

Please, she thought. Tucker saying please.

"All right. Give me a minute to dress."

"Sure. I knew you'd come, Vivian."

"You take a lot for granted," she said, and hung up.

As soon as she could no longer hear his voice, she regretted accepting. Running right back, she thought. As soon as I could think of an excuse.

They met in the lobby. He did not mention their telephone conversation as they walked to his car.

"That lousy Fred," he said. "Some cheap hooker got him up in her room and tried to shake him down."

"Because of the Colonel?"

He nodded. "She figured she could make Pollock pay off nicely if she got Fred up there and pulled the torn pajamas gag or screamed or something. Only she didn't know Fred."

"What did he do?"

"Well—he was drunk. You know. He slapped her around a little, not too bad, and called me to get her off his back."

Vivian made a disgusted little sound.

"Yeah. Nasty. I paid her off enough to shut her up. That's all she wanted to begin with."

"Such nice people," Vivian said.

"Don't be too hard on Fred. A kid like that, everywhere he looks all he sees is lousiness. Like this girl. Like his own father, in a lot of ways. And if you knew his mother like I know his mother—" He shook his head.

"He sees what everybody sees. Don't make excuses for him."

· 198 ·

"Only Fred hasn't got any guts," Tucker said. They reached his car and he held the door open for her. "He can't take it. Neither can most people. Most of them have to find something to get it off their minds. Fred found whisky."

Vivian did not answer. But the words stayed with her as they drove out of town, away from the crowds still clustered on the streets of Union Springs.

Maybe that's it, she thought. Maybe I can't take it either.

She heard again that voice which had whispered within her: *Far away? Where there isn't any hate and evil?*

Yes, she had said. *Yes yes yes . . .*

I'm so mixed up, she thought. So turned around and mixed up.

How are you supposed to know? I ought to have learned something by now, something to show me what I ought to do, what I ought to think and believe. But I haven't. I don't think I have learned one useful thing in my whole life.

Lights flickered along the highway. They were the lanterns of melon and produce stands where farmers offered to passing motorists the fruits of their labor.

The highway was straight and the country flat; as far ahead as Vivian could see, the yellow lights gleamed mellow and soft. As Tucker's car whisked smoothly past the flimsy stands, she saw the melons heaped high on the ground, the peaches rich and orange in their baskets. She saw the youths, the children who tended the stands, lounging lazily on the ground, about them the flickering glow of the lanterns. At one stand someone had cut a watermelon, and she heard laughter as the car passed the eating men.

"Where are we going?" she said.

"Just riding. Maybe down by the river."

She watched, in the glare of the headlights, dark, fantastic shapes springing across the flat pavement, saw the lights coming toward them, slipping past, the uninterested faces watching from beneath the hanging lanterns.

Her head dropped limply against the back of the seat and she let her hands lie loosely in her lap. A great lassitude crept over her. She felt the muscles of her body go limp and flaccid, felt

· 199 ·

even her toes relax, felt her whole being a mass as soft and pliable as sculptor's clay.

It was a strange feeling, at once sensuous and uncomfortable. It was unaccustomed; yet, at the edge of it, lurked some long-lost familiarity.

I have felt this way before, she thought. Somewhere. Sometime.

And yet it is so—new. Strange. Like remembering something out of a forgotten dream.

She struggled to remember. But her brain shared the lassitude. She drifted, like a log floating aimlessly on the sea. Outside the flat fields rushed past, the dark pierced only by the never-ending lanterns. A faint yellow tip of the moon reached above the horizon.

Tucker opened the ventilator in the window at his side. Cool air rushed in and she felt its touch rustle across her face and arms, her bare legs, felt the cool lift of it under her light skirt, a chilly little shiver along her thighs.

This was reminiscent, too, in that far, dim, lost familiarity. The stroke of the air seemed to free her brain; out of the lassitude, out of the aimless floating upon the great waters, she remembered.

There had been a moon then, too, a yellow crescent rising like gold from the glittering sea. There had been a breeze then, falling like a passionate sigh across the beach to the little balcony. And there had been—unmistakable now, a memory as clean and sharp and precise as the blade of a fine penknife—this lassitude, this giving up, this surrender of nerve and muscle and fiber.

Yes, she thought. It's the same now as then.

It's funny the way things go out of your mind. Things you thought you'd never forget, you thought had marked you in some way forever. It's funny how quickly they go away and get lost.

She felt her mouth quirk in an unbidden smile. And that's supposed to be the most important thing that ever happens to a girl, she thought.

And of course it *was*, at the time. Although the main thing

I can remember about it now is afterward I was so terribly afraid I was pregnant.

She felt the car slow. They turned on to a side road. A melon stand stood at the junction and she saw a vacant face follow their passage. The sweet smell of fruit was cloying in her nostrils.

The side road was narrower than the highway, unpaved, and the fields were close about them now. She could see the white glow of cotton bolls in the moonlight, smell the breeze-born odor of crop spray.

Well, to tell the truth, maybe things haven't been the same since then, even if I haven't realized it. But not because of him or because of—what should I call it? Taking the plunge? Breaking the ice?

No. It was just the particular time that changed things, made my whole outlook different. I was so eager and so terribly young, so terribly ignorant. I was in the Navy and it was going to be the war that ended war and I was a part of it and I was so awfully important.

And then Dad died and Mother married again so soon, too soon, and there was that operation I had and finding out I wasn't so important and neither was the war and—they were such little things really, except Dad. But it all sort of went to pot for me at once.

And then there was that night at his hotel at Daytona, looking across that beautiful water at that beautiful moon; I can still remember how beautiful it was and how the whisky felt inside me and his hand so light and easy and gentle . . .

The flyboy and the virgin. I lost my virtue to a pair of silver bars.

But he was gentle and kind and easy and patient. Thank God for that. I remember how I almost loved him that night, almost loved him for his gentleness and kindness, almost loved him out of that lassitude of mind and body and soul, that great emptiness he filled so sweetly.

I remember how I almost loved him that night and the next night and—how many more? Not so many. Because one night it came to me that it wasn't just gentleness and kindness and sweetness any more, that somehow that big, dull, listless void was gone, all swept away, and it wasn't the flyboy and the virgin any more; it was silver bars and concubine, man and mistress, sustained now on whisky and flesh and lust and nothing virginal about it at all, not on either side.

So right there it ended. Gently, the way it started. And then I worried and regretted and repented and thought about what I'd heard about fallen women and made all sorts of vows—and gradually forgot it, gradually came to where it wasn't even something to think about, it wasn't even anything, this that had come out of the disintegration of everything, that maybe, somehow, put things back together again by making me face up to what I had to do—pick up and go on and do the best I could to be decent in an indecent world.

Now why did it all come back to me tonight?

You know why.

I don't. Not for sure.

It all came back because everything has gone to pot again. That's why. Isn't it?

I don't know. I tell you I don't know!

Because there's that great, empty space in you again.

Shut up! she screamed to herself. Shut up!

Well, nature always fills a vacuum. You know that, don't you?

The moon was higher now and it was lighter outside. The faint dashboard glow threw a lean shadow across Tucker's face. He turned his head and she could see the faint smile on his lips.

"You know," he said, "the good thing about you is I never feel I have to talk."

"People talk too much. I talk too much."

The car slowed again, turned, and moved ahead. They were on another paved road now, passing through trees; she saw the matted undergrowth of swamp country. Moonlight fell only in isolated patches through the foliage.

Indians had hunted here and the bones of Spanish explorers lay rotting in the earth. For this country was old; its trees had sheltered pioneers. It seemed to Vivian, peering in fascination through the window, that specter shapes floated among the moonspots, that ghosts were risen to hunt the wood again. Savage, silent, brooding, the trees watched them pass.

It's too dark, Vivian thought. Too dark and old and deep.

A fox bounded across the road. The woods loomed, in black silence, all about them; the headlights seemed to dim in the face of the thick darkness.

The road curved and through the trees Vivian saw a glitter from black water, running deep. The road angled toward the glitter and then they were driving along the edge of the river, the bank sloping gently away from them to the quiet flow of the water.

It was not a wide river. In the moonlight now bright about them, she could see the opposite bank, a wall of undergrowth rising starkly from the water. On the black, glittering surface a log slid smoothly past. They were driving upstream.

The car slowed and Tucker steered it off the road into a little clearing overlooking the river. The silence, when the engine noise died away, was a live thing. She could barely hear the *lap lap lap* of the water and that was all.

"I haven't been out and parked in a car with a pretty girl since—"

"Since when?"

"A long time." He put his hands to his face and rubbed at his eyes. She heard his dry, tired breathing.

"God," he said, "it's good to get away from them all, isn't it?"

For a moment, in the deep stillness, in the dark flow of the river, she had forgotten what Tucker was. At his words she felt as if she had waked from a light and fitful sleep.

"You can't get away from them all," she said. "Don't hand me the martyr act, Tucker."

"Pollock's speech today. That hit you where you live, didn't it?"

"It was disgusting."

"It was necessary."

"For what? To get him elected?"

"You don't think he could be elected town constable any other way, do you?"

"No. And I don't think he'll be elected a Senator, either. Not any way."

"That's sentiment."

"All right. I'm sentimental, then."

He laughed.

"I am too. Sometimes I am."

I've had enough of this, she thought.

"I'll tell you what you are, Tucker. You're a cynical opportunist with more intelligence than integrity and more cunning than intelligence. I never fully realized it until today. I should have, but I didn't."

"You forgot one thing."

"What?"

"I'm honest. Where it counts. With myself."

"I'd laugh at that if it weren't so sad."

Anger had slipped out of her. It isn't any good, she thought. I can't talk to him.

"A lot of people would laugh, maybe. Not you."

"Tell me about it, Tucker. Tell me about this honesty of yours."

"Everybody's born honest," he said. "There's that much to be said for people. They start out clean, every one of them."

His voice was patient, husky, faintly condescending, the voice of a grammar-school teacher.

"Yes," he said, "you start out clean and beautiful and glistening, right out of your mother's womb, as clean and shining as you're ever going to be. But you don't have time to get your eyes open, to even breathe or let out a yell, before they get hold of you. And they won't ever let you go. Not unless you make them."

"They," Vivian said. "Everybody talks about they. Who is they, Tucker?"

"Everybody—" his voice surprised, even indignant at the interruption, the question—"give a few, take a few. They is everybody."

Let him talk, Vivian thought. Let him talk and then I'll have my say. And then it'll be done.

"They go at you easy at first. So easy maybe you don't even know it. Then a little harder and a little harder. They rip a little here and tear a little there, harder all the time."

The voice was not schoolteacherish now. Passion had crept into it. In the moonlight she saw his hands twist savagely on the steering wheel.

"Not with their hands or teeth," he said. "Not with anything you can strike at, not with anything you can see. Nothing like that, oh no. A word. A smile. A wink or a nod of the head. They rip you wide open."

Vengeance was in his voice now, vengeance and rage. She flinched at the words coming out of the moon-speckled darkness.

"Then, if you let them, they get down to it finally, they strip everything away and leave it bare and open and raw, that thin little gristle right down there in the middle of everything you are, all there is left of you, all there ever was of you worth spitting on—that one thing they have to destroy, that they can't live with, that one last thing they have to tear out of you the way somewhere, sometime, it was torn out of them—that thin little gristle of honesty."

Abruptly Tucker's hands jerked away from the steering wheel. He slumped a little.

"Christ," he said, "I'm talking like a goddam poet or something."

A thickness had surrounded Vivian. It was as if the river had risen and rolled over her, as if she had seen Tucker, his hands and profile, had heard his words, through the black waters.

Without knowing why, without moving from under the thickness, she put her face in her hands and began to weep. She felt her shoulders shake, her throat constrict.

She felt his arm go around her shoulder, his lips touch her hands.

"I shouldn't have said all that, I guess. I never said it before." His hand stroked her shoulder gently.

"It seemed like I had to tell you. I never cared before, but I just had to make you see."

A gigantic spasm whipped through her, wrenching her from his arm, hurling her back against the door.

"But I don't see! I don't, I don't!"

He was leaning toward her, his face fair and clear in the light from the moon, a hint of puzzlement working across it.

"I'm just trying to keep them from tearing me down. You *must* see that!"

The brief tears had stopped now. She could feel the skin of her face, sticky and drawn.

"I *have* to get where they can't get at me, Vivian. No matter how."

It seemed as if a cool hand touched her brow. Suddenly she was as calm and exact and direct as a precision machine.

"Even if it makes you one of them?"

"No. Not ever. Because no matter what I do, no matter what I say, I know what it is I'm doing, what it is I'm saying. I know exactly. No matter what, I stay honest with myself. And that's the difference."

"That's no difference. I saw that mob today. I was there. I saw what you did to them."

He laughed, harsh and quick.

"Wolves. Wave a nigger at them and watch them tear him to pieces. Just a pack of wolves."

"You sing a different tune now. This morning they were just people who never had a chance."

"So they never had a chance." He shrugged. "I told you I could be sentimental sometimes. Well, they're still wolves."

"With your help." I won't let him get away with this—this fantastic nonsense.

"Listen, Vivian." She saw his hands clench again. "I have to have power. Don't you see that? Power is the one thing that can save you from them. Not money, not possessions, not learning, not anything else, not even when they're the trappings of power. Just the power itself. The power to be your own man."

"No matter how you get it?"

"No matter how you get it."

"Well, let me ask you this then." She leaned forward now, almost enjoying the trap she was laying, her brain feeling nimble and quick. "When you get this power, if you do, then what have you got, Tucker? What have you got then?"

"Myself. I've got that little gristle down inside of me, safe and warm, where nobody can touch it."

Damn him, she thought. He always has an answer.

"Well, I'm no philosopher, Tucker. But if I were, I bet I could punch a hole through that the size of your head."

"A philosophy," he said, "is a way to fill in time from womb to tomb and not go nuts. It's a thing you play with. It doesn't do you any good. It isn't power, it's just a toy."

"I can't argue with you. It's no use even to try. You're so smug and cynical and conceited. You're so right, aren't you, Tucker? You're so damned honest."

In something near amazement, she saw him flinch at each word. She saw his body absorb them like blows.

"For God's sake, *listen* to me, Vivian! You think I like what I have to do? You think I do it because I'm smug and cynical? My God! It makes me bleed inside! It makes me want to howl like a dog."

Vivian shook her head. "Do you know what you're saying?"

His laugh was like the screak of chalk across a blackboard. There was hysteria in it, she thought, lurking, hidden, like a snag in the smooth, glittering river.

"I get up every morning and look in the mirror and tell myself what a crime I'm committing against Ralph Anson to get the power I need. I tell it to myself every day, so I'll never forget, so I'll stay honest about it. But I still want to howl like a dog."

"Then why, Bill? For God's sake, why?"

Low now and implacable, the voice almost a whisper, a whisper of pain and agony and desolation. "Because I have to! I have to preserve myself, stay ahead of the wolves. This is the only way I know."

"Then it's not worth it, Bill. It's not worth it."

He spun away from her and put his hands on the steering wheel again and leaned his head against them.

"If only I could make you see, Vivian! If only I could make it as plain and clear as it is to me . . ."

Nothing is clear any more, she thought. Nothing in this world. Her voice softened. "It has to come from inside, Bill. You can't just *make* me see it. I'd have to feel it inside of me. I'd have to feel—things tearing at me the way you say. Maybe I have. Of course I have, everybody has. That's why I don't understand you, I guess. It seems to me we're all in the same boat."

"Yes. It would have to come from inside. Everything that's worth anything has to come from inside."

"And I ought to tell you, Bill. I don't think you'll win. I don't think you're going to get your power."

He lifted his head from the wheel and looked at her.

"I'll win. That mob this afternoon. They told me I'll win. They told me I'm right."

"No. You won't beat Anson. Not like that."

His smile was almost the familiar, cocky grin. "Now you're getting sentimental again."

"Maybe."

"Sure. Because you know that's the one way anybody will ever beat him. Because he's an honest man too."

"Of course he is. That's why I *know* you're wrong. He doesn't have to lie and steal, does he?"

"He's got more guts than I have. He's got more guts than anybody. That's his power. That's all the power he needs."

I would like to see a chart, Vivian thought, of the way his mind works. I would like to know what has warped it into a pretzel.

"I can't hurt him," Tucker said. "I can commit crimes against him and bleed inside for them, and the crimes are bad. Necessary, but bad. But as for Ralph Anson, he'll go on being honest and kind and gentle until hell freezes over. No matter what. You can't hurt him because he has already got the power. A power of self."

"And you can't have that kind?"

"No," he said. "I haven't got the guts. I wish to God I did."

Silence came over them now, broken only by the *lap lap lap* of the water, the occasional whisper of a stray wind in the trees, the scrape of a match as he lit cigarettes for them both, the sound of her shoe sliding along the floormat, the sudden whir of a cricket striking up its song.

The silence lasted a long time. They sat through it, scarcely moving. They smoked two cigarettes apiece, watching the gleaming arcs flip through the dark as they tossed them out the window. Another log went by on the river, a long shadow in the moon-glitter.

Then Tucker took her hand. She felt the roughness of his palm.

"Vivian."

"Yes."

"When this is over, the election I mean, I—want you to marry me."

"What?"

He laughed. "You can do better than that, can't you?"

"You—you surprised me." After all this, she thought. After everything, to ask me that here, tonight—

He tugged gently at her hand.

"Listen," he said, "after the election, after we win, I'll have what I'm after. I'll be the man to see in this State. I'll have everything I'm after. If I have you too."

She could not believe the stark admission of the words. But she had to. She had heard them with her own ears.

She wanted to hurt him then, to beat at him with words and fists and ridicule.

"If I were like you," she said, "I'd ask what's in it for me."

He nodded.

"It's a fair question," he said.

For a moment she thought he had not understood the words. But then she saw his hands, twisting hard again at the steering wheel.

"I can give you an answer, too. I can tell you you'll get someone who'll be honest with you and gentle. That's a hell of a lot to get."

She felt goaded by his calmness, his massive refusal to be goaded himself.

"And how do you know I'm not one of them, Tucker? How do you know I won't tear a chunk out of you too?"

"How do you know anything? I know, that's all."

She laughed. Now, she thought, the hysteria was in her own voice, not his. Hysteria was a turncoat.

"Honest and gentle and trusting. All of that. But how about love, Tucker?"

She saw his lips move, as if he argued with himself.

"I haven't been around love for a long time," he said. "The kind of love you're talking about is a stranger to me. I'd like to try it."

The anger, the urge to hurt, left her. My kind of love, she thought. He wants my kind of love, the kind he thinks I can give him. And I'm sticking pins in him. Because he has me baffled and worried and afraid, I'm sticking pins in him.

He leaned closer to her.

"You might as well say yes, Vivian. Because I'm going to have you."

A lightning bolt of pure terror struck her mind. Fear paralyzed her. She felt the chill of death in the marrow of her bones.

He's after me too, she thought. He wants me too. No matter what.

She fought the fear with all her strength. It became, in the dim, strange byways of her consciousness, an opponent, huge, massed, relentless. In doing so it became human, it took on identity and outline; it ceased to be fear at all.

It ceased to be fear and became Tucker; now she must fight Tucker, who would come after her as he went after everything he wanted, with no holds barred, no rules drawn. She must fight him and she knew that she was ill-equipped for the battle.

Well, the almost-forgotten voice inside her said, a hint of glee in it, if you can't beat 'em, jine 'em.

"Take me home," Vivian said. "Take me home now, Bill."

Chapter Fourteen

There was no use hesitating like a school girl. He'd be long gone by now. There was no danger of his being down there at this late hour of the morning.

Still—

Oh, what if he is, Vivian thought. I can't stand here all day.

She started down the stairs into the lobby with a firm step, her chin high, trying not to look for him in the crowd below. Of course he's not here, she told herself.

At least, I hope he's not. Because I don't want to see him again, not any time soon. I don't want to see him until I can get my mind made up. I *can't* see him until then, I *can't*—

She started to run back up the steps, but resisted the impulse. Even if he were still in Union Springs, she ought to be able to avoid him in all this crowd. It was silly to be afraid.

She reached the marble floor of the hotel lobby and the crowd closed about her. She pushed her way determinedly toward the dining-room entrance, trying not to look at faces, keeping her eyes straight ahead, little sparks of apprehension flickering all through her.

Because it wasn't so silly after all. It wasn't so silly to be afraid of a man you ought to despise but to whom you felt a strange pull. A man who said, "I'm going to have you."

The dining room was crowded and at least a dozen people stood in line ahead of her. The colored headwaiter, smiling through the glistening sweat of his face, told her he'd seat her just as soon as he could, if she'd just wait a little.

Looking around, she saw a woman get up and leave a red leather chair. She plunged into the crowd again and arrived at the chair an instant behind a heavy-set man who carried a morning paper and smelled of hair tonic.

Vivian looked at him stonily, then at the chair. He glared briefly, mumbled something, and stalked off.

Sometimes, Vivian thought, arranging herself comfortably in the chair, I wouldn't take anything for being a woman.

She leaned forward, trying to catch the headwaiter's eye, to let him know where she was. As she did so her bag slid from her lap to the floor.

She leaned further, reaching for it. A man's arm, in faded seersucker, went past her knee, also reaching for the bag. Her mouth went dry with fear and she looked up, quickly, dreading to see—

"Ben!" Thank God, she thought. It's only Ben. "I thought you'd be around somewhere."

He handed her the bag with a little bow.

"I was observing," he said, "the marvelous feminine technique in action. Pre-empting the only vacant chair in the room."

His homely face carried gaiety with it, she thought. Even if he'd been pretty blue the last time she saw him, before he took off for the western part of the State. ("To ring some influential doorbells," he'd said.) It made her feel almost light-hearted just to see his face, owlish and grinning at her.

"It was nothing," she said. "Any beautiful girl could have done it."

"Waiting to meet some dazzled swain, I suppose?"

"No such luck. Just waiting to get in the dining room for breakfast."

He looked over his shoulder, pursed his lips.

"Conservatively, my dear, there are ten thousand souls in this madhouse today. Uncouth to a man. You'll be lucky to get a hot dog."

"I'd settle for one, the way my stomach feels. You look like the cat that swallowed the canary, Ben. Good hunting in the west?"

He sat down on the arm of her chair and she noticed how badly his pants needed pressing.

"Frankly, young lady, I'm happy as a mule eating briars. And not because of the hunting, good as it was."

"Do I smell a campaign secret?"

"You do. As sweet and fragrant as the lily bloomin in the valley."

"Don't be poetic. Just tell me the secret."

His face became serious. "It really *is* hush-hush, honey. Promise to keep it in your own little bonnet?"

"If I didn't want to know so badly, that would rate as an insult, Ben."

He leaned closer, his arm about her shoulder.

"The Senator," he said, "is going to fight back."

"You mean—"

He nodded. "Since yesterday. For one thing, I told him he had to answer that crap or I was through."

But what can he say? Vivian thought.

And she began to see, for the first time, the real depth of the pit Tucker was digging. Ben didn't see that mob, she thought. He doesn't know.

But maybe—well, if anybody could, it was Anson. If anybody could find the answer, he could.

"Wonderful, Ben! Listen, I heard that speech yesterday. I'm on your side now. All the way."

"Hell. You were all along. I knew it even if you didn't."

It was absurd how grateful she felt for the words. Feeling the way Ben felt, it was almost a profession of faith.

"Thanks, Ben. I guess maybe I knew it too."

"Sure." He grinned at her again. "Look, there's a joint just down the street." He pushed back the seersucker sleeve, glanced at his watch. "I haven't eaten either. Want to try it?"

"Best idea yet. Let's go."

She stood up and Ben took her arm.

"You look damn good today, Vivian. You look damn good every time I see you."

"Good old Ben. You never fail me."

They began to elbow through the throng milling around in the lobby. That was the best thing about Ben, she thought. He could say things like that in that light, easy way, and be

sincere. Nothing pushing in it, nothing intense. Just easy friendliness. And sometimes a girl could go crazy just from the lack
of that kind of companionship from a nice, intelligent man.

"I got news for you," Ben said, waving genially at a friend
across the room. "We're going dancing tonight."

"Oh, Ben, I've got to work. I really have!"

Now why did that pop out of me? I have all the time in the
world to work. I don't have to work tonight any more than I
did last night. And dancing might be fun.

He regarded her in mock bitterness.

"I've got so much to do, Ben. But thanks for the thought."

He was about to reply when a voice called, "Kirby!" It was
loud enough for everyone in the lobby to hear.

"Oh God," Ben said. "I was afraid of that."

A short man with a cigar lunged toward them and seized
Ben's hand. He pumped it twice, as if he were churning butter.
The cigar moved up and down with the handshake.

"We got to see them kids." His eyes swiveled disinterestedly
over Vivian.

"Now, Sheriff?"

"Four-H is a big thing in these parts, Kirby. Can't afford to
miss a trick. Not with Pollock pushin that Minute Men outfit."

"Hell," Ben said. He turned to Vivian. "No breakfast for Ben,
honey. You heard the man."

"You go on, Ben. I'll see you later."

"Sure about tonight?"

She nodded. "But thanks anyway." The short man clutched
Ben's arm, seized his hat, tipped it to Vivian with a jerk, and
began to move away. Vivian watched them and thought Ben was
trying to free his arm.

Politicians! she thought. Deliver me.

She moved into the crowds still thronging the sidewalks. Bigger
than yesterday, she thought. Simply mobs. Ten thousand, Ben
had said.

Ben. Sweet old Ben. And I lied to him, deliberately, about
tonight. It isn't that I don't want to be with him. I just got
through thinking how nice it was, that easy friendship of his,
not always trying to push you toward some bedroom door, in

that automatic way most men have, just because you're a female and not decrepit yet.

It's Tucker. There isn't any use denying it. Because I'm not a big enough fool even to try to deny that somehow, not meaning to and certainly not wanting to, I'm in pretty deep with that man. Pretty deep.

But maybe not too deep, not yet. Maybe not so deep that I can't think about it, get it straight, get it all laid out in order, and then get away from it. Maybe not that deep.

But a little too deep for Ben Kirby.

She pushed down the hot, jammed street. Twice she had to go off the sidewalk to pass idling strollers before she finally paused in front of an unprosperous-looking restaurant. *Purity Café*, the faded letters in the window said. A real greasy spoon, she thought.

An obviously bored townsman, methodically chewing a toothpick, pushed open the screen door of the café and stepped out onto the sidewalk. Vivian heard him belch under his breath as she caught the door before it closed. The smell of onions followed him.

She stepped inside, holding a hand behind her to keep the door from slamming. It was a relief to get out of the sun.

Which didn't mean, she quickly realized, that it was cool in the Purity. Two lazy electric fans hanging from the ceiling made languid passes at the kitchen odors of grease and greens and meat, and a large floor fan in one corner picked the odors up and hurled them in waves through the humid atmosphere, across the tables and booths of defenseless diners. None of the fans achieved any cooling effect.

Vivian hesitated, looking through the crowded room for an empty booth. Behind her band music blared faintly. That would be the Tractor Exhibit starting.

There seemed to be no empty booths or tables. Vivian glanced experimentally at the one vacant stool at the marble-topped counter. A bald Greek behind the cash register blinked at her; his eyes, above fat bags of pink flesh, looked lashless and watery. He nodded slowly at the stool, thin brows arching faintly.

Not in this tight skirt, Vivian thought. She watched a huge elbow swing into the space a body would occupy on the empty stool. And most especially not between those farmhands or whatever they are.

She smiled regretfully at the Greek and shook her head. She was turning to leave when she heard her name called. Mrs. Anson was beckoning to her from a booth near the far wall.

I'm in luck, Vivian thought, waving as she hurried toward the booth (knowing inside of her, almost shocked at the knowledge, that she was "in luck," not only because she had found a seat in a crowded restaurant, but because she had found opportunity to learn about Bill Tucker from one who knew him; she knew that and made up her mind in a second to use the opportunity, use it to find out things she had decided she had to know).

She ducked around a Negro carrying a huge tray of dirty dishes and arrived at the booth.

"You're a lifesaver," she said. "Thanks so much for asking me over."

Mrs. Anson laughed, and Vivian liked the sound of it, unaffected, with a tinge of real mirth.

"Isn't this crowd awful?" she said. "This was the only place in town I could find to eat. All the others were overflowing."

"I found that out."

Vivian sat down on the opposite side of the booth and put her bag beside her. "I waited half an hour at the hotel before I gave up and came over here."

"I wish I thought they were all here because of Ralph," Mrs. Anson said. "But I'm afraid even my husband can't outdraw the festival."

"It's really amazing, isn't it? This little town. I bet there aren't a thousand people who live in it. But Ben says there are about ten thousand people here today. And there must have been that many yesterday."

"Oh, were you here yesterday too?"

Vivian nodded. "The radio said it was a hundred and two. Presumably in the shade. It was pretty grim."

"Well, *Colonel* Pollock certainly heated things up."

Vivian noticed the emphasis on the military title. I'm afraid I'd be a little sarcastic too, she thought. If anybody had talked about my husband like that, I'd—

But after all, what can she do? She felt an impulsive pity for Mrs. Anson.

"All this must be very hard on you. It must seem so unfair."

The Senator's wife smiled.

"I'm beginning to learn that the word 'fair' isn't in the political vocabulary. Besides, it's nothing new. People like Pollock have always fought Ralph. We're used to it."

"I don't think I'd ever get used to being talked about like that."

"You can get used to anything, child. A lot of things you never learn to like. But you can get used to them."

A waitress put a glass of water on the stained tablecloth and handed Vivian a menu. She brought a strong odor of perspiration and cheap perfume with her.

Vivian glanced quickly at the menu. The waitress slapped a ragged pad down on the table, planted an elbow beside it, thrust out a hip and leaned there, looking at her insolently.

Vivian looked back at her and unavoidably stared straight down the front of the stained white uniform. She quickly looked away.

"Just bring me toast and jam and coffee," she said, "and a glass of orange juice."

The girl scratched at the pad and moved off, swinging her hips.

"I thought they only did that for the men customers," Vivian said. "That woman didn't have a stitch on under that uniform."

Mrs. Anson had finished her dinner and was leaning back, smoking a cigarette.

"I guess they just get in the habit in a place like this. Now there's a good subject for your thesis. What effect do you suppose the campaign will have on her?"

"I'll tell you a secret, Mrs. Anson. I'm beginning to hate that thesis. Because I'm afraid I don't think much of women. Present company excluded. And the more I see of politics, the less I think of it too. Or is it 'them'?"

"Goodness, I don't know. Aren't we a fine pair of teachers?"

"Oh, do you teach?"

"I used to, a long time ago. Why, I even taught Bill Tucker."

"I suppose that's one pupil who didn't turn out quite the way you would have liked."

Mrs. Anson leaned forward to snuff her cigarette.

"I don't know. Ralph and I think Bill has done pretty well, everything considered."

Her quiet eyes did not flinch as Vivian looked at her in faint surprise. These Ansons, Vivian thought, are either saints or fools. Maybe both. After what they've taken from him!

"I'm beginning not to care for him very much," Vivian said.

"Oh, I like Bill. So does Ralph."

Vivian felt a pang almost of disappointment. Which proves what sad shape I'm in, she thought. What I really wanted was to hear him cussed out, but good. And that's a mighty weak way to get myself out of this—whatever it is I'm getting myself into.

The perspiration and cheap perfume odor hit her again and the waitress put the orange juice, toast, and jam in front of her.

"Getcher coffee in a minute," she said, already moving away.

"You look a little surprised," Mrs. Anson said.

"I am. Everybody knows Tucker is the brain behind Pollock. I mean everybody who knows anything about it at all."

"Everybody but the voters, you mean."

Vivian smiled. "Everybody but the voters."

Mrs. Anson lit another cigarette and Vivian noticed the nicotine stain on her fingers, the quick, jerky lighting of the match. She's nervous, she thought, a lot more so than the last time I talked to her.

"It's not too surprising. Not when you consider how long we've known Bill."

"It's surprising to me. You've got reason to despise that man."

"You have to know Bill, I guess, to understand it."

The waitress returned, put down the coffee and the check, and departed without a word. Vivian reached for the sugar bowl.

"Tell me about Tucker," she said.

It's really a familiar story. But I think you have to go back to Florence to get at it, to really understand it.

The Slope is the old part of town. There are houses there that were standing before the war. Our war, I mean. There are new houses, too, but all of them are pretty nice, and there are lots of trees and grass and the ladies grow gorgeous azaleas. That's where most of the people with a little bit of money live. And a few with a lot of money.

Down beneath The Slope are the mills. That's where the mill people live, too. Ralph and I live there, but we have a nicer house than most. Ralph's business is close by and we never saw any need to move.

In a town where you have two levels, I don't mean physically but socially, you always have some bad feeling, but it's worse than usual in Florence. We had bad times there, back before the unions got so powerful. Really bad. I guess you've read about some of the strikes we had.

In our worst time, the big strike in 1928, some people were killed that time, all the merchants sided with the mills and wouldn't sell to the strikers. They even extended credit to the strikebreakers Mr. Sprague brought in. And of course most of the merchants live up on The Slope too, with the mill owners and executives.

People remember those things a long time. You'd think they'd forget, but they don't. I've heard children who weren't even born when all that happened swear they'd never buy from some merchant because he wouldn't sell to the union that time and fed the strikebreakers instead.

It's not as bad now as it used to be, but when Bill Tucker was growing up you never knew when there would be a fight or a strike or something. People from The Slope wouldn't go near the mill section after dark.

It was worse on the mill kids than on anybody else. They had their own grade school but the high school—where I taught history—was on The Slope. I've always thought that was the main reason so many mill children quit after grade school. A lot of them just couldn't stand going to school with the children from The Slope.

And those that did go to high school wouldn't half try or take part in any of the activities. A sort of passive resistance, I think you could call it.

But Bill Tucker wasn't like that. Not that boy. I had him in my ninth-grade home room and taught him several other times. I know.

There he was, right from the mills, as poor and patched up as any of them, but he was the star baseball player, the best debater in school, valedictorian in senior year—I don't know what all. He did everything he could. And did it well.

You don't know children if you think that made him a hero with the other mill kids. Do you know they called him a sissy because he studied? They wouldn't have anything to do with him. He was sort of a tribal outcast because I guess it looked to them as if he'd deserted and gone over to the enemy. They just wouldn't have anything to do with him, except for George. I'll tell you about George in a minute.

I suppose his own kind turning against him wouldn't have been too bad if Bill really had gone over to the enemy. That's what he was trying to do all right. He had sense enough to know, even then, that the other mill kids were all wrong, even though their reaction was natural enough. Even then he wanted to get somewhere, be somebody more than a mill hand.

A lot of that was his father's doing. Bill told me once, he couldn't have been more than fourteen at the time, he'd rather starve before he'd ever go into the mill. I think he would have too.

So it would have been all right if he'd really gone over to the enemy. But he couldn't do that because the enemy didn't want any part of him. Here was this mill stiff trying to butt in where he wasn't wanted. Not only trying but actually taking over what they considered their due. If they ostracized the other mill children, they made life hell for Bill Tucker.

I remember an essay contest on American history. The boy and girl who won were to get a trip to the State Museum as a prize. Bill won, of course, he always did, and the girl winner was Katherine Sprague. Her father owned the mill where Bill's father worked.

Do you know that creature absolutely refused to go on the museum trip if she had to go with Bill? He finally had to go right by himself. It tickled all the other kids to death.

And the worst of it was, I know for a fact because George told me, Bill wrote her essay for her. And then for her to act like that!

Children can be perfect savages. They really can.

Of course he *was* from the mills and hadn't had many advantages. His clothes were patched and secondhand, and he didn't have any ease or social grace about him at all. He tried—I think maybe he wanted that sort of thing more than all the rest, to be included in the dances and parties and things, to have a girl and all—but he didn't have anybody to help him and no way to learn except by copying.

After a while whatever chance he might have had to make any friends was gone forever. It wasn't all his fault, but some of it was. He never learned that how the other kids felt about him was natural enough, that he was different from all of them, that anybody different is going to suffer. If he could have accepted that, he would have been all right. But he never could see that, and he took it all personally and built a big wall around himself.

The only friend he had was George Grace. George was a mill boy too, and he and Bill grew up playing together. George was big and strong but not very bright, I'm afraid. He was one of those people with sort of an instinctive awe of intelligence and learning. He knew Bill was smart. Bill would write themes for him and George would get A's on them. George knew Bill was smart, all right, smarter than anybody else in school, even than most of the teachers, and I think George almost worshiped him because of that. He never went back on Bill. Maybe because of the themes, but I like to think not.

George was a sweet boy—he was killed in Italy—and he never really grew up. But Bill treated him like dirt. I guess he couldn't afford to let anyone crack that hard shell he had grown to protect himself. Or maybe he just couldn't let anybody think anybody could crack that shell.

There's one thing I remember that points all this up. Bill was a baseball star, I told you, and he made George go out for the team too. I don't think George was very good, but he made the squad.

Just before the season opened in their senior year, the team met to elect a captain. George nominated Bill. Ralph is a great baseball fan and he always said Bill was the only real ballplayer on the team, that he really deserved to be captain. I know he wanted to be. He never said so but he always wanted to be top man.

Well, whether he deserved it or not, the only vote he got was George's. The only vote. Not even his own because he told me later he knew what was going to happen and he just didn't even vote at all. And Ralph told me how Bill came to his shop that day and told him he'd like to work that spring instead of playing ball. It took Ralph the rest of the afternoon to talk him out of quitting the team, and the paper was four hours late getting out that day.

That's one part of the story. What rounds it out is that Bill didn't speak to poor old George for two weeks, simply because George had nominated him.

People don't change much, do they? Children grow up and get fat and bald and maybe rich, but all that's on the outside. I think whatever it is inside of all of us that makes us want to do whatever it is we try to do—I think whatever that is inside of us gets mauled and beaten into shape pretty early, don't you? And I don't think it ever changes much, once it gets settled in you.

I think Bill found himself outside the fence with his own kind, because of his ambition and ability. And he found himself just as much on the outside with people like those from The Slope. Because he broke all the taboos on both sides. He threatened all the sacred cows.

So he got on the outside and he's still there, still in that hard shell, still not letting anybody crack it, or at least not letting anybody think they've cracked it. I don't think he's any different from the child I taught history, the same one who didn't get elected captain of the ball team. Because he still wants to be captain of the team. Because he's still outside.

That's why Ralph and I don't despise him, the way you say we've got reason to. We had a soft spot for him when he was a child and we haven't changed and neither has he. We've still got a soft spot for him.

Too soft, I guess.

"I don't mean to excuse him for everything," Mrs. Anson said. "You answer for your own sins. But it gives me a little more understanding of him. It's what keeps me from hating him."

"You're right," Vivian said, reaching into her pocketbook for a cigarette. "It doesn't excuse him, but it does make you understand him a little bit."

Mrs. Anson smiled.

"Bill wouldn't thank me for telling you that. He was always so proud. But you seemed to want to hear it."

"I think you're a very big person, Mrs. Anson. And the Senator, too."

"Not big enough, I'm afraid. But thank you."

There was sadness in her eyes. She must be going through hell, Vivian thought. Pure hell.

The urge to say something comforting filled her, and she wondered if there were any such thing to say.

"You'll have the last laugh, though. Everybody thinks Mr. Anson will win. Except Tucker."

Mrs. Anson laughed. Vivian was surprised at the harshness of the sound.

"The last laugh is never worth anything. I just wish Ralph were out of it all."

There was nothing to say to that, Vivian thought. Even her own last words had an unpleasant ring to them.

Except Tucker.

Mrs. Anson glanced at her watch.

"I've got to be going! Ralph speaks in half an hour."

"I'm going too. May I come along?"

"Do. We'll fight this crowd together."

They paid their checks and left the café. The crowd inside had thinned, but the streets were more thronged than ever. There was now a current among the people, flowing toward the ball park, where the Senator would speak, on the same platform from which Pollock had opened his campaign the day before.

If I ever get away from all these people, Vivian thought, maybe I can feel clean again.

She remembered the mob, igniting like a fuse under the whiplash of Colonel Pollock's onslaught. I wonder how they'll be today. I wonder how they'll take Senator Anson. The fools probably won't even listen to him.

He won't give them anybody to hate.

The two women worked themselves into a comparatively clear stretch of the sidewalk and were able to slow down. It occurred to Vivian that it was odd that Mrs. Anson was with her, that she had been eating alone and was now on her way on foot to hear her husband speak.

As if she had read Vivian's mind, Mrs. Anson said, "Perhaps I should have stayed with Ralph and gone to the park with him. But—"

She turned her head, almost blurted the words.

"I can't stand those—those politicians. I know Ralph has to deal with them but—everywhere we go they turn up with some proposition, some deal—I just had to get away from them for a while."

"I know," Vivian said. "I know the kind you mean."

So they were in the Anson camp, too, not all clustered around Tucker and Harvey Pollock. She had a vague idea of county and precinct organization, but somehow she had not supposed that Senator Anson was involved with that. But of course he had to be. Tucker said a man got elected at the precinct level and that if he didn't have an organization at that level he damn sure wasn't going to, get elected.

So of course Senator Anson had an organization too. There was that little man with the cigar who'd taken Ben to the 4-H meeting. Practically a prototype.

She knew what Mrs. Anson meant, all right. The men who made up that kind of organization—she'd seen plenty of them yesterday—were grimy types in the main, delivering support for favors, votes for patronage, in just the same cold-blooded, calculating, disinterested manner in which stocks were traded in the market place.

And Tucker was one of them, on a grander scale perhaps, but flesh of their flesh for all that.

All right, she thought, no use thinking about that. It's too obvious to require thinking about. It's an established fact. He can wear all the labels.

But there are the other things too and those are the things you do have to think about.

That warm strength I can feel in him and that terrible night in his apartment when it seemed to give out, when something came out of the dark and took it away from him; the flashing gaiety with that desperate quality to it; the way he spoke of these people as if they were truly his people; the grimy little tale I have just heard; and there is finally (shall I ever escape it, be free of it again?) the voice within my ear, piercing like a sword: "I'm going to have you, Vivian."

All that to think of. All that and so little time to think. So little time to think about so much.

Because tonight the festival is over and I can go back. Tonight Union Springs will be behind me.

A woman elbowed against her and she had to stop to get her balance again. Thank God for that anyway, she thought. I'll be leaving this place.

But tomorrow—

Tomorrow there is so much to think about.

Chapter Fifteen

Ｉt was terrifying, Vivian thought, to look at all their faces.
They formed, she decided, a great, unappetizing pudding. There
were no eyes or mouths or noses to be seen anywhere in all the
hundreds, perhaps thousands, of faces turned up to the rickety
platform, stretching away from the front of it. They seemed to
dissolve, to merge; Vivian felt that if she should fall among
them from the platform, she would drown, slowly and horribly
and with small sucking noises, in a gigantic bowl of oatmeal.

I don't see why either of them wants to be Senator, she
thought. I don't see why anybody wants to stand up and face
these people and try to please them. All these people and that
one big pasty face gaping up at you.

She shifted on the hard undertaker's chair, trying to achieve
what small comfort she could in not being herself a part of the
crowd, as she had been the day before. At least she was in the
shade, she could sit down, she did not have to feel their sweaty
bodies pressing around her; if Town Councilman Thompson's fat
leg occasionally nudged slyly at hers, it was a small price to pay.

You fat clown, she thought, laughing almost politely at one of
his heavy, whispered jokes, if a little nudging makes you happy,
you just go right ahead and nudge. You fat clown.

Vivian was not listening at all to the school superintendent,
who was introducing Senator Anson. She sat on the back row
of the platform, squeezed between Councilman Thompson and
a thin-faced woman from the County Welfare Department, whose
stomach growled. She was hot and perspiring; she felt all over
herself a thin powdering of dust.

"He'll talk forever," Councilman Thompson croaked. "Always does." He sniggered hoarsely and his sly knee gouged at her again. He smelled of beer and bay rum.

But the school superintendent was already booming into his windup. He half-turned from the crowd, made a sweeping gesture toward the people on the platform, and declaimed, ". . . give you that great statesman—that Christian gentleman—that true man of the people—Senator—Ralph—ANSON!"

Vivian watched Anson stand up, take one hesitant step forward. She heard the crowd break into unexcited applause. She watched the Great Face blink its eyes and twitch, waiting for the Senator to speak.

It won't do any good, she told herself, watching him clasp hands with the school superintendent. There's no answer to Pollock.

The Senator stood alone before the speaker's stand now. There were no notes before him and his head turned, slowly, as if he were looking for friends in the audience.

Vivian looked at the Great Face again. She shuddered. I'm glad it's not looking up at me, she thought. That I don't have to answer to it.

The applause died away as unexcitedly as it had started. The Great Face waited, impassive, gelatinous.

"My friends," Anson said, "I take real pleasure in being . . ."

The leg nudged at her again. "Who's he think he is?" Councilman Thompson wheezed. "Presdunt Roosvelt?"

Vivian shook her head impatiently.

". . . time of crisis. We see millions of the world's people turning their backs on democracy and its suffrage, its majority rulings and its guarantees of freedom and processes of law, to embrace the tyranny and regimentation of the Communist dictatorship . . ."

Councilman Thompson's pudgy fingers plucked at Vivian's arm. He leaned close, smiling fatuously. "Four-dollar words," he said, in a stage whisper.

"Shut up," Vivian said, quite distinctly. Councilman Thompson stiffened. His knee swung sharply away. The woman from the Welfare Department frowned at Vivian.

I don't care, she thought. I want to hear this.

". . . despite those who despair, untold millions hold to faith in democracy. Even the Communist dictators have to tell their victims that tyranny and bloodshed are only steppingstones to a larger freedom, a more real democracy . . ."

His voice was high, almost reedy, so thin that Vivian could scarcely hear him. The loud-speakers pointed away from her; she leaned forward, cocking her head, straining to catch his words above the shuffle of feet, the scrape of chair-legs against wood, the low, careless mutter of the Great Face.

". . . in this time of crisis between the false appeals of totalitarian dictatorship on the one hand and the ways of freedom and democracy on the other, is it not our best hope to make American democracy and human freedom work?

"Does not our best hope lie in strengthening the ideals of that democracy so that not only will the might of the Communists batter to no avail at its principles but so that this nation can raise a standard to which all peoples can look for freedom, justice and peace?

"The greatest need in America today, in all the free world, is a reassertion of our belief in a deeper and wider use of the ways of democracy."

Vivian looked out over the Great Face. This pudding, this bowl of oatmeal, was the American democracy of which he spoke. It was human freedom too, and the people who made it up were the people he asked to raise a standard. They were the people he asked to reassert a faith.

They were the people who had, in frenzy and hate and fear, howled like animals under the fiery proddings of Harvey Pollock. They were the people who had risen in evil wrath at a specter they could not even touch.

He is too far ahead of them, Vivian thought. He is asking too much.

". . . many of us overlook the fact that the ways of the American dream, like the teachings of Christ, have never yet really been tried. In fairness to the hope that they may yet be, we must not, in complacency or disillusionment or despair or fear, deny the great promise of the American dream . . ."

And, as though a spotlight had been turned on each, Vivian saw the faces in the crowd. The Great Face faded and was gone.

He is only asking faith, she thought. And faith is no miracle. Anyone can have faith. Even me, even Councilman Thompson.

Anyone can have faith. If they are not complacent or despairing. If they aren't afraid.

". . . freedom is not a frail plant that must be safeguarded with intolerance or terrorism. In olden times, when colleagues in the Sanhedrin feared the subversive power of new and fervent programs, the great Gamaliel said:

" 'If this counsel or this work be of men it will come to naught, but if it be of God you cannot overthrow it.' "

Vivian scratched desperately at the surface of his words and it seemed to her that underneath she touched something firm. It was not a thing that could be described beyond this: in a broken and sickly world, it offered solidity.

In this solidity there was a measure of hope. Looking at the faces, now separate and individual, Vivian felt some invisible weight fall from her. She felt that never again would she see the Great Face.

". . . in this critical age it is well if the American people do not permit their well-grounded distrust and hatred of the Communist system to undermine our free institutions. We must keep perspective and balance. Let us be strong in our own democracy, our own freedom.

"If we fail in this, what good is victory on the battlefield? If we fail in this, we fail everywhere; we may unnecessarily sacrifice our democracy in the name of safety. We may, in our concern for the word, lose sight of its definition.

"Let us not be free with labels. Let us not call un-American those who stand by the Bill of Rights; let us not brand as agitators those who express the needs and aspirations of mankind, of whatever color of skin, whatever creed; let us not name subversive those who see faith in the American dream as a more searching answer to communism than the congressional probe; let us not smear in the headlines those who stand in need of a fair hearing.

"Let us send the traitor and the criminal conspirator to prison —but let us not, in the process, besmirch many patriots with the epithet of Communist."

This is more than an answer to Pollock, Vivian thought. More than an answer and less than an answer too.

Because Pollock's words are for the Great Face. They raise goose bumps and blood pressure and hackles, but they will fade. They are louder words than these, but somewhere, in some mind, Anson's words will imbed themselves forever.

". . . for my part I have been called many things. I have been labeled in *Pravda* a tool of Wall Street and a lackey to special interests. I have been derided in the *Daily Worker* as a living lie, a man of loud words and faint deeds. I have been called an agitator and a Red and, by inference, a traitor.

"In the face of this, I do not retreat from any position I have taken for human freedom.

"I shall continue to oppose, wherever they may appear, communism, fascism, terrorism, and every other form of tyranny over the minds of men.

"I thank you."

"No onions," Ben said. "Just mustard and chili."

The counterman grunted. He flipped a few drops of chili on the two hot dogs, made a pass at them with a wooden mustard dip, and put them, wrapped in waxed paper, on the greasy counter.

"Forty cents, Jack."

Ben put two quarters on the counter.

"And two cokes."

The counterman grunted again, opened two cokes, and put them beside the hot dogs.

"That'll be another dime, Jack."

"I got an extra pound of flesh," Ben said. "You want that too?"

"Huh?"

"Skip it." He laid a dime by the two quarters, handed a hot dog and a coke to Vivian, and they moved away. "Thanks, Jack," he called over his shoulder.

Vivian took a small bite. The roll was cold.

"I hate anybody calling me Jack," Ben said. "Makes me think of the Army."

They worked their way to the fence surrounding the ball park and leaned against it, eating the unappetizing hot dogs, watching the crowd ambling out the gates, moving unhurriedly back to town.

"If he could have just mentioned Robert E. Lee," Ben said. "Maybe that would have got a rise out of them."

He threw the half-eaten roll to the ground. "Sometimes I want to puke, if you'll pardon the word."

"I knew it would be that way," Vivian said.

"Christ, Vivian! He could have been talking into a rain barrel!"

"Maybe somebody listened. I did."

"You and maybe two other high-school graduates. It just didn't get through."

"No."

"He just didn't give them any hell. They never heard anybody talk like that before."

"I guess not."

"It was a goddam good speech, though."

"Yes."

"It said everything there was to say."

"Everything."

"Christ," Ben said. "It wasn't even worth the effort."

Vivian's hot dog followed his to the ground. She took a sip of the coke.

"Yes, it was. It was worth the effort, all right."

"I don't know. Everything is just so fouled-up, it looks like. They didn't even listen! That's what hawks me."

"I'll tell you something," Vivian said. "Something funny happened to me out there today."

"Well, I wish something funny would happen to me."

"Seriously. Yesterday I was out in the crowd, listening to Pollock. When they started yelling, when he really got them going,

I thought they were beasts. I thought they were inhuman, Ben, a sort of mass of meat all infected with some loathsome disease. I almost got sick I hated them so much."

She spoke calmly, with more assurance than Ben had ever heard in her.

"You know what I thought today, Ben?"

He shook his head and pushed his hands into his pockets.

"I thought they were beautiful."

Her hands came up and she began to straighten his bow tie. She kept talking, in that low, certain voice.

"It was like he put a soft light on them and they were men and women again instead of just a mob. I saw all kinds of people, Ben, good ones and bad ones, old and young—all kinds. I saw people like me, like you, even like Tucker."

She gave the tie a final pat and smiled at him. He thought it made her lovely, the soft smile and the glow in her eyes and something new and warm about all of her.

"And if they're just people—why, then there must be hope for them, don't you think? For all of us."

"There always was. Sometimes I wonder if hope is enough."

"It's about all any of us ever have."

He took her hand.

"I like hell out of you, Vivian. Even if you can't vote."

They laughed and he took her arm. They moved away from the fence. The crowd was pushing back to town now, anxious to see the Grand Parade. A square dance and a huge fireworks display would end the festival that night.

The dust of many feet stirred above the ball park and the sounds of many voices babbled about them. The sun was still hot; the sky still blue; far away they could hear the sound of the merry-go-round calliope.

"Did you see the latest handiwork of our friend Tucker?"

"What?"

He took a folded paper from his coat pocket, opened it, and handed it to her.

It was a cartoon, a caricature of Senator Anson luring a white girl into a saloon filled with Negroes. The caption read: WILL ANSON INVITE YOUR DAUGHTER TO THIS PARTY?

"That's the worst one. They had it and one or two others circulating around. Hundreds of them."

He pointed at the ground and Vivian could see the pieces of paper strewn about.

"I ought to be boiling about it. But it doesn't seem like so much any more. I guess I'm getting used to it."

"I don't believe Bill did this, Ben."

"I like you when you're idealistic, honey, but let's not be silly. You know damn well he did it. Or had it done."

"I don't have to believe it. Not till he tells me so."

He took the paper from her and put it back in his pocket.

"I thought so."

"Thought what?"

"You're in love with that bastard. Aren't you?"

They walked along in silence, perhaps half a block, before she answered.

"I don't know, Ben. I really don't."

"Wouldn't you know if you were?"

She laughed, a trifle harshly.

"That's romance you're thinking of, mister. And if I'm in love with him, there's nothing romantic about it, believe me."

"I don't see how you *could* be. A girl like you."

"I don't either."

"Dammit all to hell, anyway."

She laughed, more gaily this time.

"It's not that bad, Ben."

"Listen, I know Tucker. I've known the guy since college. I even *liked* him once. A long time ago. He's not for you, Vivian. He ought to find some snake to mate with."

She turned and faced him. He felt her hand warm on his arm.

"Don't you think I know all that, Ben? Haven't I got eyes? It's just that—there's more to him than he shows the world. I keep thinking maybe I can reach it."

His face softened and he smiled at her.

"Okay, honey. You'll have to find it out for yourself."

"Of course."

They moved on again. The crowds still pushed along and children dashed about, shrieking and laughing. An airplane buzzed lazily overhead, a black speck against the cottony white-ness of a cloud.

"I hope you're not in love with him," Ben said. "For your sake."

She squeezed his arm.

"But I'm afraid you are. It's in the way you talk about him."

She shrugged. There was certainly some new composure about her, Ben thought. She had always been poised, assured, but never so much as now. He felt the hurt, heavy as lead in his stomach.

"I'll say one thing for the bastard. He's had some breaks that would kill a mule. Like that lousy Katherine Sprague."

She looked up at him, faint surprise showing in her eyes, around her mouth.

I knew that would get next to her, he thought.

"That's the second time I've heard her mentioned today," she said. "Tell me about her, Ben."

When I heard Katherine had ditched him I wasn't surprised, just like I hadn't been surprised when I heard he was trying to make the grade with her. I was there when it started between them, and I could have told you right then how it would turn out.

The way I heard it later, Tucker chased her for a year or two, right after we left college. He made the big pitch for her as hard as he could. It didn't buy him a thing. She finally married some home-town playboy and Tucker was out on his fanny.

I first met him at the University; we were in freshman dorm together. He was a loner; he spent his free time studying, and he worked in the cafeteria and I practically never saw him. I hardly knew his name. At the dorm he had one of those god-awful roommates with sideburns who was always getting you off in a corner to talk about Engels or Lenin or somebody. I never dropped in on him there either.

The next year I pledged a fraternity and all I knew about Tucker was that he had become the star of the baseball team. He was still just a name to me, until junior year; then he was still a baseball star and also one of three juniors to make Phi Bete.

You would have thought the guy was Horatio Alger. Because he was still working in the damn cafeteria. You know how people are about that sort of thing. He'd got rid of the Bolshevik roommate though.

Upshot of it was, every frat on the campus woke up and got after him. Our bunch offered him a free ride and made the grade. I mean he didn't have to pay initiation fees or dues, just his board. I never liked that sort of thing. Now, I don't even like fraternities, but that's beside the point.

Right from the start, Tucker let it be known what he thought of a crew that ignored a poor freshman and then bought him when he got to be a big wheel. And that was just a sample. He was cynical and conceited, he never had a good word for anybody, and in general he was as hard to get along with as a guy can be. He even committed the cardinal sin—he laughed at the initiation ceremony.

Nobody cared much after the first shock of his golden personality; they got campus prestige from having him around and that's all they wanted. That's what a free ride's for. You buy a name to drop.

But he interested me. He was dead right about the free ride—but he took it. He laughed at the secret ceremonies—but he went to them. He didn't have any use for the fraternity—but I'd swear he was proud to be in it.

I think it was just that he had made it; he was in, he had cracked some forbidden circle. Coming from what he did, to be a member of the wealthiest, most social frat on the campus—that was what he was proud of.

Anyway, the two of us had a beer now and then, and he loosened up with me. We weren't close; he wasn't close to anyone. But we got along. And before long I noticed him copying me. Just little things, clothes, manners, speech. He knocked off a lot of his corners that way, copying me, and God knows I'm no Chesterfield.

Well, came spring and graduation and the cold cruel world just around the corner. Time for a party, some of us decided. Eat, drink, and be merry. Tomorrow we all had to go to work.

So we rented ourselves a big cottage at the beach, lined up some dates and a couple of congenial chaperons, laid in a stock of whisky you could float a rowboat on, and got ready to have us a ball.

There were seven couples in on it, but at the last minute one of the guys fell out. It was going to be a four-day house party and it was costing us plenty. The six of us that were left couldn't make the rent without the other guy. We had to have somebody to fill in for him.

The only guy in the house who had the dough was Tucker. He hit a home run in the last game of the year and some old grad slipped him a hundred for it. He was welcome like a catfish in the punch bowl, but no rent, no party. We swallowed the catfish.

To keep from having a stag around, one of the guys called his date at some girls' school and asked her to bring along a friend for this big baseball star we'd persuaded to come. A real swell guy, he told her, and Tucker stood there and laughed at him when he said it. He knew he had us over a barrel. But the girl said okay, she'd dig up somebody.

Did you ever see two taxicabs run head on?

It was like that when Tucker and Katherine Sprague met on that blind date. They backed off and started blowing their horns at each other.

I shouldn't say met. They'd known each other all their lives. She made it clear in about two minutes flat that her father owned the mill where Tucker's father worked. And he made it clear he'd just about as soon cuddle up with a corpse as with her. Great beginning.

The first day I thought there'd be a big blowoff. They couldn't seem to find one pleasant word to say to each other. I expected Tucker to pack up and go, and maybe he should have.

When night came on, we just walked out and left them to fight their own battle. Everybody went blanket-partying on the beach. And when we got up the next morning everything was okay between them. More or less.

I don't know what happened, but we could hardly recognize

Tucker. He was long-gone on that woman. He was on her string, believe me. She knew it too, and made him know it and everybody else know it.

I think it must have been something like the fraternity. He had too much sense not to know what she was, right to the penny what she was worth. But she was something he had to have. She was everything he had never had, had never had a chance at.

She was beautiful and she had money and clothes and the assurance they can give. She had all the ease and poise and arrogance, all the confidence in her beauty and her money and herself, all the certain, undisturbed ways that make people like her the nearest thing we have in this country to aristocracy, the nearest we had better get to aristocracy.

And she had this quality, this aura of something about her. Call it wickedness. But more than that. A sort of delicious wickedness that made you want to be wicked with her, made you want to go down with her to whatever dark places she knew.

She was the one who suggested we go swimming in the raw, and did it. She was the one who got a game of strip poker started and paid off when she lost, right down to the point where the other girls made her stop. She outdrank us all and never seemed to get drunk. And I know for a fact that in four days three of the guys laid her on the beach. But not Tucker.

Tucker just tried to keep up. What else could he do? He never touched anything but beer before that week end, but he drank plenty after the first day, after whatever happened between them, trying to keep up with her. Where she led he followed.

She played with him. She could get everybody, even me, to laughing at him. Some little remark about his clothes, or something she'd remember from high-school days. Or a gag about cotton mills, or the little bit of a mill-town accent he still had. And she was always making a play for one of the other guys, right in front of him.

I thought at first it was just her way, just that arrogance, that delicious wickedness of hers. Then I began to see it was more than that; there was system to it. Deliberation. I began to see that her ways with him were calculated as coldly as a game of chess. I began to see the pleasure she took in making Tucker come to heel.

The last night of the party I found out why. I think I did.

That night after everybody else was in bed, more or less separately, I was sitting on the porch of the cottage. I was thinking about all the money I'd spent and how hard I'd tried to have a good time, and I was wishing I hadn't come and wishing it wasn't almost over. The night-before-it-ends feeling.

I was sitting there about half-asleep and I felt her behind me. I *felt* that atmosphere about her, whatever it was, and I didn't even have to turn around to know who was there, looking at me.

"Go to bed," I said. "I'm thinking."

"About what?"

"About life." Honest to God, that's what I said. She laughed a little whisper of a laugh.

"How about death?"

"There is no death," I said. "We'll all come back to life as whisky bottles."

"Death is for old women." I felt her hand on my shoulder, light, easy, but with something peremptory in the touch of it. I looked up at her.

She had on pajamas and a light robe, and she wasn't showing off her bosom the way she usually did. She even had her hair rolled up. I could tell she hadn't come for fun and games with me.

And maybe this will tell you the kind of woman she was: I was disappointed. Knowing her for what she was, the way I did, remembering the three guys who had already had her, I had let her get to me a little bit too. I felt disappointed and sick and angry.

"You never get drunk like the others," she said.

"No. Not entirely."

"You watch me, don't you?"

I laughed. "Not all the time," I said. "Not when you're in bed."

That laugh again, still a whisper.

"And you like Tucker."

· 238 ·

"Nobody likes Tucker. Go to bed, will you?" I felt something coming, something I wouldn't like. I was still angry, still sick.

"Then you won't tell him?"

"Tell him what, for God's sake?"

"You know."

"I come out here to think about life," I said, "and you hand me a goddam riddle."

"You won't tell him what you see? When you watch me."

"I might. I see plenty."

"It won't do you any good to tell him. Not him."

"Nor you either."

She didn't say anything for almost a minute. I listened to the waves breaking down on the beach. I wished I was down there with them, feeling them coming in all the way from Europe, knocking me down and washing me off and leaving me in the clean, wet sand.

"My father's a big man," she said.

"I'll bet."

"One of the biggest in the State."

"I never said he wasn't." She'd lost me, somewhere in there.

"Tucker's father beat him once. I saw him do it."

"I'll tell him what I see then," I said, "if that's the way it is."

"Yes. Tell him I'll break him. I want him to know what I'm going to do. It will be better that way. Because he won't believe it until I do it."

I felt sick again. I was revolted at this buried twist in her. "You lousy bitch," I said. I never called any other woman even half of that, not before or since.

She didn't hear me say it. She was already gone. I watched her walking across the porch, and I thought that Tucker would have been better off if he had never left the cotton mill.

That house party was the last I saw of him up to these last few months, during the campaign. I went on from the University to law school at Georgetown, then to the Justice Department for a hitch. Then four years in the Army and back to Justice, and eventually on to the Senator's staff.

So everything else I know about Tucker and Katherine Sprague is hearsay. But I could have predicted it all, every damn bit of it, after that house party. She was right that night, you know. She won the big cigar on both counts. In thinking I'd try to warn Tucker off. In knowing it wouldn't do him a damn bit of good. All it got for anybody was a black eye for me.

Chapter Sixteen

I'd better enjoy this while I can, Colonel Pollock thought. No more time for it after tonight. Not till election.

He sat by an open window in the library of his home, relaxed in his favorite chair, a highball in his hand.

Colonel Pollock looked ahead to the days of last-ditch campaigning with a strange expectancy. It would be hot and tiring and dusty and monotonous. It would be a dry throat and indigestion and a constant headache and sore feet and aching hands. No sane man, the Colonel thought, would even consider going through it.

Not if he weren't sure he'd win. Not if he'd never heard them yell the way they yelled for me yesterday.

He could still hear the roar of that crowd at Union Springs. He could still feel the way the power had come on him, had swept all through him. His hand tightened around the highball glass.

That crap Anson gave them today, he thought. Who does he think he is? He ought to know better than to expect them to listen to that sort of mess.

He sank deeper into the chair. Last night before I hit the road again, he thought. Might as well enjoy it while I can.

Too bad Joe has to spoil it with whatever it is he wants to talk about. Nothing much, you can bet on that. A gripe on Tucker or one of his half-baked ideas. The man's an ass. Valuable, all right, but a complete ass just the same. Still—best not to offend him.

The Colonel settled more comfortably into his easy chair and reached for a pipe from the rack beside him. He selected a blackened briar, then regretfully put it back. Better watch the old throat, he thought, many speeches as I'm going to have to make.

Pollock did not, at the moment, look like a senatorial aspirant. His slippers were old and worn, his trousers unpressed; there was a conspicuous hole in his undershirt. His stomach bulged over the top of the trousers and sweat trickled along his heavy jowls and fleshy neck. His shirt lay across the desk beyond the window.

But by God, he thought, that's just what I am. Candidate for the United States Senate.

He heard the sound of a car pulling up outside. He quickly heaved himself out of the deep chair and put on his shirt and tie. He knew full well what Joe's reaction would be to seeing his idol in his undershirt, a torn one at that. It was a pain in the neck, but you had to watch out how you handled the guy.

He was such an *ass*.

Joe entered the room as if he were on his way to a Cabinet meeting. The scowl on his square-jawed face only made him look like a disappointed job seeker, but Pollock knew it was his serious look.

Oh my God, he thought, I've got to smooth his ruffled feathers again. I never saw such a man for getting his bowels in an uproar over nothing.

"Well, Joe," he said, rising and holding out his hand. "I can always count on you to be working even this late." His voice croaked a little, strained from his heavy speaking schedule.

Joe shook his hand firmly. The Colonel could sense excitement through his palm.

"This is no time to let down, Colonel." It was a pronouncement, the Colonel thought. Not just one of the usual clichés but, coming from Joe Harrison, definitely a pronouncement. It almost attained the status of a decree.

"Sit down, Joe." The Colonel moved toward the little bar. "Nightcap?"

"I need one, Colonel. I sure do."

He's really in the wind, Pollock thought. Despite himself, he felt a touch of curiosity. Maybe something was up, after all.

"How you like your bourbon, Joe?"

"Presbyterian."

Pollock chuckled. "Don't say that word. It'll cost us votes."

"What?"

My God, Pollock thought. What an *ass*.

"Skip it, Joe." He handed Joe the drink, took his own back to the leather chair.

"I'll get right to the point, Colonel." Joe leaned forward, his face still scowling, his eyes glowing intensely under the Prussian haircut.

"Please do." God, yes, Pollock thought. By all means.

"I've been working on something that's knocked me on my butt." Joe took half his highball in one gulp, not taking his eyes from Pollock.

The Colonel waited calmly. It was probably nothing, but you never could tell, and in any event, Joe had to be handled right. You had at least to pretend you considered his ideas important.

"It's about Tucker."

This has been brewing a long time, Pollock thought. The stupid bastard has just got to be the whole show.

"I think Tucker is a Red."

Pollock's first impulse was to laugh. He struggled to keep his face unchanged. What Tucker had once told him about never letting yourself be surprised was true enough; what he had found more important was not to let it show when you did get surprised.

"That," he said, his voice even and flat, "is a little hard to credit, Joe."

Joe waved a hand, brushing all objections aside.

"I told you it knocked me on my butt." He finished his drink. "Thing is, we can't take any chances."

"Where'd you get this idea?"

Joe's voice was properly modest.

"I got to noticing things. Little things. Like he's always making remarks about Anson. And cracks about you. Just little things, but they add up."

I'll bet, the Colonel thought. Of all the harebrained ideas. That ambitious snake a Red!

"I thought we couldn't take any chances," Joe said, taking the Colonel's silence for agreement. "You know how these Reds worm their way into things. So I've been checking up."

Oh my God, Pollock thought, if Tucker gets wind of this, we've all had it.

"And what did you find?"

"Plenty," Joe said. "And I think I can find more. I know I can."

Pollock could not keep his surprise from showing this time. He sat straight up.

"You mean—"

"Yes. I mean it's true."

Well, I'm a son of a bitch, Pollock thought. He slowly relaxed into his chair. I'd better get this all straight, he thought. It's too crazy to be made up.

"Tell me what you found, Joe."

"Colonel, the thing got me so worried I did something I wouldn't think of ordinarily. But as long as there was a chance— well, you've got to fight fire with fire these days." He looked squarely at Pollock, the scowl almost etched on his square face. "I went through his private files down at the office."

"I hope you can justify that action," Pollock said sharply. If Tucker ever finds out, he thought, there'll really be hell to pay. This crazy man is putting us all on the spot.

"I took the chance, sir. It was my duty." Joe took a large envelope from his coat pocket. "You will have to be the judge."

Pollock looked at the envelope, almost fearfully. Suppose he has got something, he thought. He can't have, the stupid ass, but just suppose he has—

Joe pulled a sheaf of typewritten papers from the envelope. He handed it to Pollock.

"I found this in the file," he said.

It was, the Colonel saw, a college theme or term paper or something. Tucker's name was scrawled plainly across the title page in a round college-boy hand not even reminiscent of the crisp, slanting signatures the Colonel was used to seeing every day.

The title of the paper was: "The Significance of Lenin."

Down in the lower left-hand corner were the words "Economics 52," followed by the date, 1936. Above this in red pencil was written the single word, "Excellent!" Beside this was the firm signature of someone called Dr. Harold Essley.

"The University's been trying to get rid of Essley for years, Colonel. Everybody knows he's pink as they come. Voted for Wallace."

It was very near to being hilarious, Pollock thought. Joe spoke like a man who followed the Grail, instead of one who skulked through people's private papers, turning up a schoolboy's immature maunderings.

But on the other hand it was not really funny at all. Nor was Joe Harrison.

Well, I'll be damned, Pollock thought, what am I going to do about this guy?

"Have you read this thing, Joe?"

"I quote: 'Among the giants of our century, Lenin stands supreme.' Lead sentence."

"What else do you have, Joe? You know this doesn't prove a thing." There was an edge of impatience in Pollock's voice.

"It does to me. But I found this too." He took a typed letter from the envelope. "He's got personal correspondence on file all the way back to when he was in college."

Pollock grunted. He looked at the sheet of expensive bond paper. The letterhead was that of something called the Soviet Aid Society, Washington, D. C. It was addressed to Tucker at the State Highway Division and it contained one sentence: "This is to acknowledge gratefully your check for $100 in response to our appeal of August 9, 1943."

Jesus Christ, Pollock thought, what's wrong with him? Does he expect me to swallow this?

"Look, Joe. You have to have more than this."

"I'll get it, sir."

"Now, listen—"

Wait a minute, Pollock thought. Wait a minute. Maybe I'm the one who's stupid.

"How are you going to find anything else?"

"I know a man who can find anything, for enough money. He's already on the job."

I'll be damned, the Colonel thought. Maybe I ought to be as

simple-minded as this guy. Sometimes a thing is so plain you can't find it with radar. Then an idiot comes along and stubs his toe on it.

"You haven't got much time, Joe."

It was a mistake. Pollock knew it, the second the words were uttered. Joe's brows shot upward.

"None of my business, Colonel. But have you promised Tucker anything?"

The straight way out was the best way out. Besides, things are changed now, the Colonel thought. All of a sudden. They damn well are.

"You know I have, Joe. I had to."

Joe's face set grimly. "I was afraid of that. Well, it'll have to be a fast job then."

Pollock was thinking rapidly. He had to play his cards just right. Joe was so simple and so unimaginative, you had to put on an act for him all the time. Joe didn't know how uncomplicated he was; he could never have accepted anyone else who was as simple. You had to be what he expected you to be if you got anywhere with him.

"This is a severe blow," Pollock said, passing his hand over his eyes. "I trusted Tucker."

"I never did, Colonel." He wants *that* on the record, the Colonel thought.

"Of course, we haven't proved anything yet."

"I will. You leave that to me."

Pollock stood up and stalked angrily to the fireplace.

"What could have been the man's object in this?"

"Proves what we've been saying all along. You never know where these lousy Reds'll turn up."

Pollock went over to him, slowly, like a man bent under great responsibility.

"If it's true," he said, "he's got to go. That much is certain."

He put his hand on Joe's shoulder.

"I'll have to count on you, Joe."

The light of holy battle lit Joe's face. There was a shade of mistiness in his eyes.

"I'm on your team, Colonel. All the way."

Pollock nodded slowly, still clasping Joe's shoulder. The son of a bitch is about to weep, he thought.

"Get me proof, Joe. Real proof. Before the election."

"As good as done, Colonel."

Pollock took his hand from Joe's shoulder. He walked slowly to the window.

"It shakes your faith," he said. "An awful thing like this."

"Not really. Not your faith, Colonel."

"I suppose not. But sometimes—" Pollock sighed wearily. "Joe, I owe you more than I can say. This has—I still can't quite believe it!"

"I can. Where there's that much smoke there must be some fire."

Pollock turned quickly. I can't take any more of this character, he thought.

"Look, Joe, this hits me pretty hard. I wonder—would you mind—"

"Of course not. I've got to go anyway."

Pollock went with him to the front door.

"I know I can depend on your discretion, Joe." He put his hand on Joe's shoulder again. "But let me know before you do anything—ah—publicly."

"Colonel, you can absolutely depend on me. I'll handle it just like you would yourself."

There was no doubt of Joe's sincerity, Pollock thought. The man actually believed Tucker was a Communist. Or he had convinced himself that he did, which probably hadn't been too hard. Joe was just not a man to play second fiddle.

"Good night, Joe."

"Good night to you, Colonel. And don't worry."

It was a relief to close the door on that square, broad back. Too much stupidity, like too much alcohol, left a hang-over.

You should never let a man be too valuable to you, the Colonel thought, settling again into his leather chair, reaching for his unfinished drink. You're bad off when you can't get along without somebody. When you don't know how to get rid of somebody.

Of course, I can't get on without him yet. Not till after election. But if I pay his price, do what I promised, pretty soon the tail will wag the dog. Once Tucker wins this election for me and I come across, he's got me. He'll have me then and he knows it.

But he doesn't know *I* know it.

He thinks I'm his front man. That's what makes it so rich. Me and Joe Harrison against Tucker. Would that hand him a laugh if he knew!

Which is exactly why he won't find out. Which is exactly why I let him think I'm dumb. Which is exactly why this crazy thing might work out.

Because if you are a real smart boy, like Tucker, there are never any other smart boys around. You are always the only one.

A Communist. Tucker a Communist. It's perfect.

He put his head back and laughed out loud, the sound of it deep and rich in the heat-stilled silence of the room.

I ought to pin a medal on Joe, he thought. My God, the significance of Lenin.

※

The heat gathered about Vivian like a low fog. She could almost see it creeping through the window of her room.

Out that window, over the rooftops and the listless trees of Union Springs, high, dingy clouds banked ominously, spreading into colossal shoulders at the top. The sun was too near the horizon to add its rays to the heat, but now, in early dusk, the air had gone dead. Not a breath moved; the heat rose out of the baked earth, damp, clinging, almost odorous, oppressive in its weight.

Vivian lay in her slip on the bed, feeling her limp body sunk deep into the smothering mattress, feeling the heat of it seeping into her pores, expanding inside her, checking even the flow of perspiration. Her flesh was warm to her own touch, almost feverish, yet her skin was as dry as old dust.

The room was nearly dark. Night was almost upon Union Springs and only the massive, malignant cloud reflected the last glow of the sun. On the floor by the bed Vivian's bags were packed, except for a small traveling kit. Her zipper notebook was untouched on the desk. She was ready to leave Union Springs in the morning with Ben Kirby.

She stood up, almost painfully, took her toothbrush and tooth-paste from the traveling kit, and padded her way barefoot toward the bathroom.

The first rocket went off outside. It seemed to burst almost at her window sill, although it was really much higher. Startled, she turned quickly and saw it exploding into a dozen greenish balls. They hung in the thick air a moment, sending their bilious light flitting about the room, then sank slowly toward earth. Before they had passed her window, the balls had winked into the gathering darkness.

They ought to warn you, she thought. You jumped a foot.

In the bathroom she methodically brushed her teeth. The tap water was sluggish, warm. She looked at herself in the mirror. Her hair was untidy, her bare shoulders seemed to slump forward; even her eyes looked bleary and unfocused.

This is enough. This has to stop.

So it's hot. Unbearably hot. So you've been through a wringer for two days. So you feel all jammed up inside.

Why don't you do something about it?

For two solid hours you've dodged around in this oven, packing, taking a bath, lying there on that bed smoking cigarettes and trying to make your mind go blank, lying there pitying yourself and cursing the heat and dodging it all the time. Dodging what you have to face, sooner or later.

She snatched a comb from the glass shelf in front of her, quickly ran it through her hair. She went into the bedroom again. She placed a straight chair before the window, turned the small electric fan to blow over it, and slid her cigarettes under the pillow of the rumpled bed, out of reach. She had been smoking too much.

For a moment she considered covering her near nakedness. Then she shrugged. If anybody wants to climb up three stories in this weather to play Peeping Tom they deserve to see anything they can see, she thought.

She sat in the chair and put her feet up on the window sill, legs slightly bent, knees carefully together. Another rocket went up, its course marked by a trailing streak of sparks. For a moment the air seemed filled with pink fireballs, dropping a lurid glow over the store roofs below, drifting slowly downward, flickering one by one, then by twos and threes, into extinction.

All right, she thought. Think about Tucker. That's what you stayed in this hole for, when you could have left long ago.

The one thing that hits me in the face, right off the bat, the one thing I can't get away from is that I ought to despise him.

Because Tucker is a crooked politician. He lies. He cheats. He steals when necessary, he connives and schemes and bribes, and all with that air of utter, cold detachment, as if it were all as routine as driving his car or typing a letter.

And as if all that weren't bad enough he glibly—no, not glibly —he excuses it all as something he "has to do" to protect himself.

I ought to despise him.

But I don't.

And there is my answer, no matter how I slice it. There isn't any middle ground with Tucker. Nobody is merely Tucker's friend. Nobody could merely like Tucker. Except the Ansons, and maybe they aren't quite human.

A whole bevy of rockets went up. They overlapped and burst, the flat sounds of the exploding powder slapping through the open window at her, the sky momentarily flashing red and green and white and blue, the yellow sparks spurting briefly, the whole conglomeration of color casting over Vivian and against the awesome backdrop of the tremendous, shifting storm cloud one long flicker of light and shadow, challenging briefly the night now falling full across the land.

This is the only part of the festival I've enjoyed, Vivian thought. They should forget the tractors and concentrate on the fireworks.

She caught her breath and held it, thinking she felt the faint stir of a breeze over her body. But it did not come again and the waiting only made her more conscious of the heat.

All right, Vivian. Keep your mind on your business.

So if I admit the fact—and obviously I have to admit it; I even get jealous as a cat, just thinking of the way he felt about that Sprague woman—if I admit it, the next thing is, why?

A huge firecracker went off beneath her window, booming like a sharp clap of thunder. She jumped and one foot slid to the floor. Her thoughts tangled wildly for a moment. Another rocket went up and she watched it flare and die.

Anyway, she thought, her mind zipping unbidden back to its main theme, Tucker lives within walls. And it's a woman's job to break down walls. They have to be broken from inside, crumbled into dust by love and warmth and tenderness and appreciation and beauty. And that makes it a woman's job.

Because that's what a woman is for, to enter a world where men in all their brawling, grasping, scheming vigor have thrown up a chaos of hurt and evil and discontent, to enter such a world and bring to it, if only for a moment, a little beauty, a little warmth, a little love.

That's what I think a woman is for, anyway. A woman who can't do that is no woman at all. Even if she can bring helpless children into that same world.

It was Katherine Sprague's job and she never knew it, never cared. And now it's my job, mine alone, to bring to Tucker all a woman can give, all the love and tenderness and beauty she has, and maybe bring this to him, too: the end of his fear.

She felt her trickle of thought widen into a flowing stream, until it was no longer thought, until the river of it possessed her completely, gripping heart and mind and soul, until all of her was emotion, all of her was feeling and being, all of her was Woman:

I shall open up the gates and lead him forth among his enemies. I shall cast about him the warming cloak of my faith and my hope and my prayer. I shall lead him safely through the valley of evil and bring him forth into the mountains and make him to lie down among the trees, a whole man again.

I shall offer up to him the ripe comfort of my breasts and the flesh of my body. I shall gather about him—

She sat straight and still, suddenly feeling the vast river of her offering empty swiftly from her, feeling fear pierce down like a dagger to her stomach.

What if it's too late? she thought.

What if I can't do it?

She remained rigid, paralyzed, feeling at last the warm trickle of perspiration over the whole of her body.

And there came to her again that soft and tender glow she had seen spread that day about all the people before her.

He is only a man, she thought. It can't be too late.

Because there is always hope. There has to be hope, even for Tucker.

All she could see now from her window was the colossal loom of the cloud, its edges diffused and dim against the sky. As she watched, the first flicker of lightning spat from it and quickly died.

Three doors down the hall, Ben Kirby watched the same bolt of lightning. He sat at a small writing desk, looking over his shoulder. He could not look back at the desk, at the scattered papers lying there waiting for him.

God, he thought, we don't have enough trouble already. If the newspapers get hold of this we might as well sign the peace treaty.

He pushed back from the desk and stood up, feeling fatigue all through him. He began to walk aimlessly around the room. He wondered why he should be so tired, after his first good night's sleep in weeks.

That idiot, he thought. That lousy idiot.

He fumbled for a cigarette. He pulled a crumpled pack from his pocket and felt again for matches. He could find none.

He put a cigarette between his lips, walked to the dresser, and looked at the littered top of it. No matches.

"Damnation," he said. He felt in his pockets again. Still no matches.

He went to the desk and hurriedly shuffled through the papers lying there, not looking at them. He found no matches.

In the bathroom it was the same story. He felt a slow, leaden rage stir in his belly, moving upward.

He almost ran to his open suitcase, ransacked it hurriedly. He jerked open the drawer of the imitation maple telephone table.

Walking grimly, like a man going to a funeral, he went to the closet. He felt in all the pockets of the jacket and the single pair of trousers hanging there.

There was no other place to look.

He backed out of the closet, looking wildly about him. A great pressure formed behind his eyeballs.

He could endure frustration no longer. In the simple dilemma of having no matches, the accumulated bafflement and despair of days drew to a head within him, a pasty white head, and burst like a pus-filled boil.

He took the cigarette from his mouth and hurled it to the floor.

Almost in the same motion he drove his fist, the entire weight of his body behind it, against the dark paneling of the closet doorjamb.

He felt the pain flow swiftly up his arm. He felt the solid thump of it against his shoulder. It seemed to dash the rage and the pain and the hate from all of him.

He put his knuckles to his mouth and tasted his own blood. It was bitter but he felt better.

"There," he said. "There, by God."

He shook his head a little and went to the desk again. The crumpled pack of cigarettes lay on top of the papers. He pushed it aside and as he did so saw a book of matches tucked in the cellophane wrapper.

He was not surprised.

Nothing surprises me now, he thought. Nothing ever will again.

He picked up the letter again. It had been sent down to him from Anson Headquarters in Capital City by special messenger. It had arrived less than half an hour before.

For a moment Ben thought of taking the letter in to the Senator. He decided against this almost immediately.

Time enough tomorrow, he thought. If this old fool doesn't jump the gun on us.

He read the letter through again. It was almost unbelievable.

Wilson Holloway, he thought. Wilson Holloway.

You stupid old fool. You and your kind will ruin us yet.

You and your kind and Pollock and his kind. I don't know which is worse.

He tipped back a little in the chair, the yellow light of the cheap hotel lamp making the papers before him the color of old parchment. He felt bitterness dripping into his stomach, thinking of Holloway.

Holloway, who was among the wealthiest men of the world. His wealth was not only vast, stable, it was inherited; in the tight circles of Eastern society, even of Boston society, his wealth was unquestioned.

But Holloway himself was not received in those same circles where his treasure ranked so high. His name was never mentioned in staid old homes and clubs without apoplectic snorts and full-blown curses. Of late years his name had even begun to provoke remarkably similar snorts and curses from august members of Congress.

For Holloway was an admitted fellow traveler and a self-proclaimed angel, financially and spiritually, of the American Communist Party. He was by all odds the most famous of native Communists. (Although nobody had yet pinned him down as a card-holder, the word was freely applied to him and had never been denied.)

He had been involved in three congressional investigations, contributed heavily in time and money to the 1948 Progressive Party, spoken violently of American imperialism and war-mongering, energetically and loudly defended party leaders on trial under the Smith Act and footed a share of the legal bills, visited Moscow, financed innumerable strikes, congresses, and peace rallies, warred sporadically with Westbrook Pegler, and entertained, among others, the Right Reverend Arthur Hewlett, Earl Browder (some years ago), Andrei Vishinsky, Harry Bridges, and a whole succession of Soviet and satellite diplomats, soldiers, and newsmen. Darker deeds, if any, had yet to be disclosed.

His money had come to him as a matter of course, grown to staggering proportions from the few watered stocks of an earlier Holloway who had once seen a vision of iron rails stretching beyond the horizon. That growth had been accompanied by avarice and selfishness and cruelty and callousness and bloodshed quite as staggering as the wealth which had finally accumulated in the family's vaults.

Of both, the wealth and the acquisition, Holloway was extremely conscious. Did it not devolve upon him to make such amends as might be for both? Were not those who snorted at the mention of his name brothers under the skin with those earlier, bloodier Holloways?

Did not Marx, furthermore, clearly sound their death knell? Had not he, Wilson Holloway, seen with his own eyes the happy people of Moscow, freed at last from the Capitalist heel? Could there really be any doubt that Marx had the right answer, that all the poor, helpless peoples of the world were at last to be sheltered warmly under the protecting wings of communism?

Could he, possessor of wealth, vessel of guilt, withhold his all from the struggle?

His life was his answer. Into communism he threw the same sort of furious activity his forebears had devoted to building railroads and amassing money. They had bequeathed him money beyond the needs of a thousand men, visited him with guilt weighing like an anvil upon his weak nature; but of their native abilities, their brains, their ingenious ruthlessness, they had left him only the remnants, diluted, fading, blooded out.

Thus equipped, Holloway approached communism as great ladies used to approach tenement houses at Christmas, with a basketful of food, a handful of pennies, and a mouthful of platitudes. He had never understood communism; his life bore witness to that. For him, it was enough that it seemed to offer absolution. If he could contribute little intellect and no ideas, he could contribute money, he could lend an impressive name.

Of practical politics he was as ignorant as of practical communism. There had been no elections of more than local import for thirty years in which he had not taken an interest; he had learned nothing from any of them. He had been heard to declare that some day, possibly not in his day, but some day, the Communist Party in open competition with Democrats and Republicans, would elect a President who would, of course, proceed to collectivize the nation, after suitably amending the Constitution to permit it.

Remembering that famous statement, Ben Kirby did not find the letter in his hand so fantastic. It was almost to have been expected, Ben thought; it was almost a natural vapor rising from the mixture of wealth and guilt and zeal and ignorance and watered-down blood that was Wilson Holloway.

You will ruin us, Ben thought again. You and all the guilt-ridden intellectuals who think communism wants what you want, who think communism cares about people.

You and your kind will ruin all of us who are not satisfied, who want to make the world better, who think there are new ideas still to be discovered.

You will ruin us because you don't know that nobody can force the world to be better. You don't know that nobody can decree justice or proclaim equality. You don't know that communism is not even interested in these things.

You will ruin us because you can't see that justice and equality are individual. They are inside people.

They are lonely and deep, but they are there.

You will ruin us because you in your blindness and your ignorance and your guilt and your misplaced zeal bring down upon us the Pollocks and the probes and the hysteria. You will ruin us all and, that done, you will be ruined yourself.

Ben rubbed his hand wearily across his face.

What are we going to do now? he thought. What can we do?

The words, so neatly typed on the expensive stationery, mocked him. They were engraved on his battered brain.

The Honorable Ralph B. Anson
United States Senator
Senate Office Building
Washington, D. C.

Dear Senator Anson:

I hope this letter will be forwarded to you speedily by your Washington staff and that it will find you in good health and spirits.

I have before me the morning edition of our paper, which reports that you will be engaged in a second primary. Some of the remarks you made in your recent campaign have confirmed my long-held opinion of you, which you may remember from correspondence of some years ago, before you entered the Senate.

I must preface further statement by asserting firmly that you are in error in speaking of "Communist tyranny." Sir, I have been in Moscow and was shown the life of that city and its people by official government guides. I may say, unequivocally, that there is no tyranny in Moscow. In Communist zeal for the liberation of oppressed peoples, I have noted excesses, of course. Surely, however, these are no more numerous than were those of the French revolution.

With that reservation as to your views, understandable in the light of the content of our Capitalist controlled press, I fully endorse your continued candidacy for the U.S. Senate. Your numerous speeches have shown you to be a man who believes in freedom, democracy, and equality. You have proven your courage, your eloquence, and your humane belief in a peoples' world.

With your consent I would like to send my endorsement of your candidacy to the press of your State. I would also like to send your campaign treasurer my personal check for $2,500.

I would appreciate by return mail a list of the papers in which you desire the statement of support to appear and an address to which my check may be sent.

I can only hope that to your great humanity and intellect you may yet add a real understanding of and sympathy for the Communist vision. To that hope I am willing to make public profession and private donation.

Sincerely,

Wilson Holloway

Ben choked with wrath. The stupid son of a bitch, he thought.

Can't he see the difference in him and Mr. Anson? Doesn't he know just wanting the same things isn't enough?

Doesn't he know anything?

He put his head down on his arms. How are we going to stop him? he thought. How can we stop him?

Festival was over.

Now it was silent in Union Springs, silent and dark. Its people, tired but exultant, had gone to bed. About them was the night and the heat and the storm coming, the black roll of the river and the endless stretch of the waiting fields.

The old cars and the wagons and the mules had left Union Springs, straggling steadily, reluctantly, out onto the country roads, through the flat, passive fields, past the lantern-glow of the watermelon stands, past the clean, bare yards of the Negro houses, past the looming, ancient trees, past the ghostly outlines of barns and outhouses—going home, the old cars and the wagons and the mules and the people going home from festival, back to "the place," back to the plowing and milking and chopping and cooking and cleaning, back to sweat and struggle and silence, to the smell of earth after rain, of manure spread in the fields. Going home.

Vivian still sat by her window, looking down on the empty square. She still listened for the rumble of the crowd, the shuffle of their feet. But they were gone and she was all that was left.

She was still sitting there when the storm came and, for a few hours, broke the heat.

Chapter Seventeen

Soft night sounds had lulled Tucker into half-sleep. He was drowsy, content; each separate little noise, each cricket-whir, each low engine-hum, the occasional yowl of a cat, a quiet footfall along the street, sent a delicate chill rippling along his flesh.

I wish it could always be like this, he thought. I wish I could always be so full and drowsy and easy all over. If only things would never change and I could go on like this, just like this, for always.

Vivian moved slightly in his arms, with a little sigh. I wonder if she's asleep, he thought, moving his elbow slightly where her weight came upon it. He started to whisper her name, then stopped.

Let her sleep, he thought. I'll wake her soon enough.

A breeze moved about the house, refreshing, unfamiliar in the summer night. Last night's storm had broken the heat wave. He felt the stir of air moving through the narrow opening of the window over his bare shoulder, on the back of his neck.

I never really believed it would happen, he thought, luxuriating in his whole being in the closeness of her body and his, the soft nest of the bed, the unaccustomed coolness of the breeze and the night. Even now I don't know how it did happen.

Ever since that night at Union Springs—God, it seems a long time ago!—I thought she was finished with me, with whatever little bit I had hoped there might be between us. And then to have her come to me. To have her now like this. To hold her and know her like this, with the night and the world outside and the closeness in here.

Involuntarily his arms tightened about her, his hands touched her soft flesh. She stirred again and turned her head, and he

knew she was awake. The very darkness became different somehow.

"You went to sleep," he whispered.

"Um . . . mm . . . m."

She stretched and he felt her body straining under his hands.

"This is nice. Spoon style."

He chuckled.

"This is nice too," he said.

"Stop that."

He kissed her neck, felt a shiver run along her body.

"You're so soft," he said.

She laughed lightly, the sound of it tinkling through the half-
dark of the room.

This is the way I used to feel, she thought. At home, a long
time ago. When I'd wake up and it would be rainy and wet
outside and I'd know I was inside and warm and cozy in the
bed, where I could hear the rain and the sounds from the kitchen
and feel the soft weight of the covers on me and know I didn't
have to get up, that I could just lie there and listen to the rain.

I haven't felt this way in a long time. And it isn't even rain-
ing.

She felt his beard rake along her bare shoulder, the scratch
of it delightfully male and rough against her skin. It was a reminder of his strength, his roughness, of the way he had taken
her as if she belonged bodily to him.

But he was gentle too, she thought. There was in his male-
ness a touch of gentleness that made his roughness wonderful.
He took me, but he gave himself to me too.

She squirmed closer against him, smelling his warm, male odor,
feeling the hair of his chest prickly against her shoulder blades.

"Bill?"

"Ummm?"

"You know what I think sex is?"

She felt his teeth touch her ear.

"Nope. But I think it's marvelous."

"Marvelous. But what I mean is why God invented going to
bed together."

"For you and me, baby. Just for you and me."

She put her hands on his, clasped around her breasts.

"I think God made sex so two people can tell each other the things they feel, the things they can't put in words. There has to be some way, something besides talk. A way we can commune together."

"A communion. I like that."

"The beginning of one. If it's right like it is with us."

"It's right, all right. It's the rightest thing that ever happened to me."

"To us."

"To us then."

"Because that's what it is now. Not just you or me."

"No. You and me."

She turned in his arms and found his lips with hers, not passionately, not demandingly, but simply and firmly, sweetly. They lay together, their faces inches apart, their heads dark against the single pillow, their breaths caressing one another.

"I have to tell you, Bill. It has to be all straight."

"What?"

"You—aren't the first for me."

His lips touched hers again.

"I know. And you didn't have to tell me."

"It has to be all straight. It didn't mean anything, then or now, but I want it to be straight between us."

"All right. Then I guess I ought—"

Her lips stopped the words.

"I know," she said, after a moment. "Just your starting to tell me makes it all right. Makes it straight."

They lay for a long time, not moving, not speaking. Their eyes, accustomed now to the dark, searched the dim outlines of the other's face. Occasionally, as if by some signal, their lips touched in that gentle promise, that tender bond.

She did not know how long they lay that way before he spoke.

"You got a sexy nose," he said.

She laughed up at him.

"What's sexy about my nose?"

"Just is. Gets me all het up."

He took his face from the hollow of her neck and lay on his

back beside her. He felt on the nightstand for cigarettes. She sat up beside him, then pulled the sheet up to her chin.

He lit two cigarettes and gave one of them to her.

"Listen," he said. "I'm going to make an honest woman out of you. Right after the election."

He said it lightly, but he felt his breath catch, felt a turn of fear in his stomach.

Suppose she won't, he thought. Suppose she never meant it to go that far. Suppose—

"Mrs. Tucker," she said. "I think I like that."

Relief almost choked him.

"So do I, baby. I sure-God do."

She lay back beside him, feeling for his hand.

"A woman costs a lot to operate," she said.

"They pay for their keep, though."

"They're funny beasts. They like to have their own way and they're always butting in on men's affairs and—"

"They're nice to have around. I always wanted one."

"Even for always?"

"Especially for always."

"All right. Don't say you weren't warned."

He kissed her. "Baby, I—"

"Oh, shut up, Tucker. Don't pretend you're the romantic kind. Hand over that ash tray, will you?"

He put it on her stomach.

"Let's see you make it go up and down," he said.

"That would be vulgar. Do you think we'll set the bed on fire?"

"If we haven't already, a couple of cigarettes won't do it."

They laughed. By God, he thought, a man never knows how much he's missing.

"What about your mother, honey? She mind your marrying a politician?"

"She'll be glad to get her old-maid daughter off her hands. She might even give you a Cadillac or something. What about your folks?"

"The hell with them."

"Bill!"

"Listen, never mind my folks. They don't have anything to do with this."

She took the ash tray and put it on his stomach. She leaned up on one elbow and looked down at him, holding the sheet around her.

"Why do you say that? What's wrong?"

All right, he thought. Sooner or later you'll find out anyway. It might as well be now.

"Let me just tell you about the last time I saw my old man then. That tells it all in a nutshell."

"All right. I want to know everything about you, darling."

He laughed.

"Then I hope you got a strong stomach, honey. I sure-God do."

Funny thing about most politicians is they always stay registered to vote in the old home town. Most of them have to, because of residence requirements, but even the ones who aren't running for anything and never will, do it that way too.

You take any election day, you can't find a politician in Capital City. Not a one. They've all gone home to vote and get in touch with the grass roots and all that. Even me.

So the last time I was down in Florence was the day of the first primary, when Mr. Anson licked the Colonel. I had a lot to do here that day, of course, so I started early. I wanted to be down there time the polls opened.

That part was all right, but where I made my mistake I decided to go by home for breakfast. I thought maybe—well, I should have known better.

They don't go to work in the mill until eight o'clock any more, and it was just a little after six when I got to the house, but the old man was sitting out on the porch, like he was waiting for me. Now I think about it, maybe he was.

I've seen him sitting there like that a thousand times. He had his chair tipped back against the wall, but he wasn't relaxed. He never relaxes. His feet were right flat on the floor and he had his arms crossed and his head cocked in a funny sort of way he has, as if he's listening for something.

I got out of the car and started toward the steps, and I could see he wasn't even looking at me.

But I felt just like I used to when I'd come home after cutting school or getting in some sort of scrape. He'd always be sitting there, waiting for me, and I could always tell, the minute I saw him, if he knew what I'd done. He nearly always did.

I felt like that that morning, going up the steps of my own house with him sitting there, not looking at me. I felt like any second he was going to get up and start burning me with those eyes of his. Like I'd done something and he knew and was going to whale hell out of me, the way he used to.

I'm a grown man now, but I actually had to force myself up those steps. That's the kind of man he is. At my age, he can still do that to me, make me feel that way.

"Hi, Pop," I said.

He didn't say anything. He didn't look at me. He didn't even move. I might have been part of the porch rail.

I stood there looking at him and listening to the mill. There's nowhere around there where you can't hear it. You get used to it if you live there, you hardly even notice it. But I heard it that morning. Just the way I wake up at night and hear it sometimes, just as if I were still there living with it.

"How's everything?" I said.

I knew by then he wasn't going to answer. I knew it as soon as I saw him, I guess.

"Where's Mom?"

He wasn't going to answer that either, and I don't know why I bothered to ask. I started to go on in the house. He still had that listening set to his head, he still sat there stiff as a board, not even an eyelid moving. It came over me to say something to shake him out of it, to make him move, make him look at me. It came over me to hurt him if I could.

I had my mouth open when I knew I couldn't do that either. Nothing in the world could shake that old man. Least of all me.

"All right," I said, "the hell with you." I went on in the house. Mom was in the kitchen where she always is. She was bending over the old stove, and I didn't have to ask where was the electric range I'd sent money for at Christmas. I knew there never had been an electric range I could buy for that house.

"How bout some breakfast, Mom?"

She turned around, not surprised a bit as far as I could see. She hadn't changed. She had done all the changing she was ever going to do a long time before that.

"Billy."

That was all she said. I went over and put an arm around her and patted her shoulder.

"You set to the table," she said. "I got the fire goin already."

We talked about the weather and things like that while she fixed eggs for me. It was always like that with Mom. You'd never have known she didn't cook for me every morning. As long as she could, she'd pretend everything was okay, that nothing had changed.

She had a cup of coffee while I was eating.

"You been all right, Mom?"

"I been fine, Billy. Just fine."

Sure, I thought. You've been fine. You'll be fine till the day you die and maybe even then, far as you'll ever let on.

We talked some more, just rambling on about people I used to know but didn't any more and what had been going on in Florence, and I told her she still knew how to fry the best egg in the world and she said she'd had enough practice at it, she ought to, and I said that's the truth, I guess.

But I couldn't keep away from it, not for long. I had to say something sooner or later. I gestured at the porch.

"Still down on me, eh?" It was like talking around a wall until I asked about him.

"You ain't what he hoped, Billy."

That was as near to taking me down as she'd ever come. But it wasn't that way, not really. She was just saying what we both knew.

"All right," I said. "So I wouldn't take the goddam job he had for me. So I wanted to live my own life. What did he expect?" In the back of my head I could hear my voice all those times I'd said the same things before.

"You hadn't ought to take the Lord's name in vain, Billy."

"All right. Just what did he expect, though? Just tell me that."

She put down the coffee cup.

"That union, Billy. You know how your pa is."

It was a kind of ritual I went through with her, every time I came home. It was almost as if we had a script written for us and all we had to do was follow it.

"I know he wanted me to take a job with it. Mom, how can you get anywhere working for a union?"

"I spect he never figured on it that way."

"He never figured anything any way except his way."

"He's got his lights, Billy. I reckon he does the best he knows how to do."

"Never mind," I said. "I know all about him. You don't have to tell me."

I looked around at the kitchen. Like Mom, it hadn't changed a bit. The same drab walls, the same bare, board floor.

Christ, I thought, he doesn't have to take my money, but he does all right for himself these days with his union running the show. He could use his own money and fix up some for her.

"It's just you ain't what he set his heart on, Billy."

Nobody else has ever called me Billy. William, Bill, Tuck, even Willy. Lots of things besides those too. But Billy is hers and it gives me a funny feeling every time she says it. The old man now—I don't think he ever called me anything. I was just a vegetable to him. I didn't rate a name.

"Look," I said. "Look, Mom. What did you set your heart on? What did you hope I'd turn out to be?"

She peered at me in that watery way of hers, as if she needed glasses. She did need glasses, and I'd personally taken her to a doctor one day when the old man wasn't home and had them fitted and made up for her. But she had never taken to wearing them.

"Why, I never thought, Billy. I always knew you'd be about like your pa."

I don't know what I'd have said to that. Because just as she said it we heard the front door slam.

Both of us just sat there. I told you what that old man could do to me. I could feel my back getting stiff while we listened to him rummaging around in the bedroom. When we heard his steps coming toward the kitchen, I almost wanted to run.

He came in the kitchen door and stopped. I could see Mom looking at him, past me, but I didn't turn around. I could feel his eyes on me. I could feel them like two candles at the back of my neck. I could feel my shoulders drawing up. I felt like a cat backing away from a dog.

He took two more steps and I knew he was standing over me, looking down at me. Then his arm went by my shoulder, so slow I could count the wrinkles on those bony old fingers. He put a package, wrapped in white, on the table in front of me.

The fingers lingered on it, spread wide, and then the arm began to go slowly back past my shoulder. I could hear him breathing, but I wasn't watching his arm now. I was looking at the package.

I took it in my hands. It wasn't tied and the white paper unrolled easily. Inside was a loose stack of bank checks. My bank.

I didn't have to count them or ask what they were. They added up to about eight thousand seven hundred dollars. It was every single dollar I had ever sent them since I had left college. Not a single check had ever been cashed.

Of course, I had known they'd never been cashed. But still—

And then I saw the inside of the paper they'd been wrapped in. It was one of those leaflets we put out in the first campaign. What it said was "Vote for Pollock." That and a lot of stuff about Anson.

All right, I thought. So there's that, too. So of course there's that and he can add it to his score now. But it all goes back to that goddam job. With his goddam union. It all goes back to that.

I pushed the checks toward Mom.

"Don't you be a fool, too," I said.

She looked at me, then at the checks. Not at him.

"We can make out, Billy."

I stood up. "All right. That's that."

I turned around and he was up close to me, looking right at

· 267 ·

me. Nobody ever looked at me like that before. Not even him.

"Don't come back," he said. "Don't never set foot here no more."

"Fine," I said. "That's fine with me."

"Sam—"

Neither of us looked at her. There was no need to. We both knew how she felt. And we both knew what she would have to do, no matter how she felt, no matter what either of us said. She would have to stand by a whole lifetime with him.

"You ought to wear those glasses some time, Mom," I said. "Just for me."

"Scab," the old man said. "Don't never come back, you dirty scab."

Know what a scab is, honey? To an old union hand like him? A scab is a strikebreaker, but he's more than that. A scab is filth, pure filth. A murderer isn't in the same league with a scab, not in my old man's circles. Neither is a rapist and not even a nigger. A scab is as low as you can get.

So I left on that. Without another word. Without even looking back. What good would saying anything else have done? Or looking back? I had it all carved on my mind like nail scratches in soft, wet lumber. I had said everything I was ever going to say to him.

Like I said, that was the last time I saw them. Or probably ever will.

No. Don't worry about my folks, honey. I don't really have any.

⚜

Vivian shivered.

"I'm chilly." She turned on the bed lamp. "First time in two months."

She got out of bed swiftly and went across the floor to a chair where his clothes were piled. This must prove it's all right, she thought. I'm not embarrassed to run around in front of him buck naked. Not much.

She slipped on his shirt, buttoned two strategic buttons, and pushed back the sleeves. The shirt was much too big for her, hanging halfway down her thighs.

She tugged at the tail of it, pulling it tight against her, and looked down at herself.

"Like my legs, Tucker?"

"Gorgeous. I like all of you."

She laughed and jumped back in the bed. She put her arms around him and kissed him, then pulled herself away, smiling at him.

"I'll be your folks, darling. I'll be mother and father and wife and daughter and son and bedfellow and everything else, too. You wait and see."

"Just be my wife, baby. All I ask."

She put her forehead on his shoulder. "Oh, Bill, Bill, I'm so damn sorry—you've had so much to hurt you."

He stroked her tousled hair.

"Take it easy, baby. I'll live."

"You just wait. I'll make it all up to you."

"I know you will."

"I'll be everything to you. Just wait and see."

But there's one little matter, she thought. Maybe I ought to let it ride, Bill, darling, but I can't. Because I'm a woman and you're my man now, and if you're going to have all of me I've got to have all of you, too. I've got to have every little bit of you.

She snuggled down close to him, putting her arms around his chest and squeezing. It wouldn't do any harm to be a little devious about it. It might be too early to be too direct. You never could tell.

"Tell me about the union job," she said. "Wasn't it any good?"

"It was all right, the way those things go. The textile boys are a pretty big outfit now, and the old man knows most of the big wheels in it. He had me lined up as some kind of district representative. Organizer, what it boiled down to. Great future, you know."

"And you didn't want it?"

He snorted. "Hell, no. I might as well have buried myself."

"You wanted to go into politics? Even then?"

"I wanted something where I could get somewhere. I had a good deal lined up with the State. So I told the old man no soap."

"I guess he wanted you to do it pretty badly," she said. "The union must mean a lot to him."

"Well, it didn't mean a thing to me. I wanted to get away from that mill. A long way away."

And that's not all, she thought. That's not all you wanted.

She chose her words very carefully.

"I don't guess Katherine Sprague liked the idea very much either."

Tucker sat straight up.

"Now who in hell told you about her?"

"Ben." They always think we don't know anything, she thought. The big apes.

"Well, damn his eyes. He ought to keep his nose out of my business."

Her voice was very small behind him.

"I asked him to tell me. I was terribly jealous."

"Were you?" He grinned at her, delightedly.

They can be as simple as monkeys, she thought. Maybe that's why we love them so much.

"I still am, too."

"Hell," he said, "that was all over a long time ago."

"Was it?"

"My God, yes."

"Well, I don't care, I'll bet she was the main reason you didn't take that job."

He lay back beside her. She saw his face tighten, his eyebrows draw down in the faintest of frowns.

"Not the main reason. One of the reasons, I guess. I had a lot of reasons at the time."

"Tell me about her, too."

He shook his head.

"Nothing to tell. I told you it was all over a long time ago."

Time to get tough, she thought. The big ape.

She put her face above his and raised her voice a little.

"There is so something to tell, Bill Tucker. You were in love with that woman and I won't have you in love with anybody else. Now tell me!"

"But you said—"

"I know what I said but this is different. You tell me all about Katherine Sprague right this minute!"

He bit his lip, not looking at her. Then he turned his head and grinned.

"Keep your shirt on," he said. "It's the only thing that keeps me away from your bare bosoms. Tell you what. Let's go out to the kitchen and grab a sandwich and I'll tell you all about it. I always get hungry after I—"

"Oh, shut up."

"Well, don't you?"

"I haven't had as much experience as you. But now you mention it—"

"Let's go. We'll eat while I tell you the story of my life."

"Not that. Just about that woman."

He was out of bed now and putting on his robe. Vivian decided his shirt was enough covering for her. Won't do any harm to keep him interested, she thought, looking down at her legs. Panting a little. Just in case he gets stubborn.

They went into the kitchen and peered at the contents of the refrigerator.

"I got olives," Tucker said. "Lots of olives. You know about olives?"

She pushed him away from the open door of the refrigerator.

"Who needs olives?" she said.

Chapter Eighteen

I t's funny you asked about Katherine because the last time I saw her was that same day I've been telling you about, when I went home to vote. When it rains it pours. But what happened should give you an idea of how things stand with her and me.

I knew most of the folks hanging around the polls that morning and most of them knew me. But not many of them spoke. Hell, that's Anson's home town. They weren't having any part of me. They all figured I was just what the old man had called me, I guess.

But I wasn't selling Fuller brushes. It didn't bother me. I spoke to a couple of guys, went in, let them look me up in the book, voted, and figured that was that.

I dropped the ballots in the box and went back outside. They still weren't shining up to me and I still wasn't selling Fuller brushes, and I was thinking it had been a long ride just to mark a couple of X's and get called a scab. About that time this convertible pulled up in front of City Hall.

Katherine got out of it. I hadn't seen her to talk to in a good many years, but she was the kind you can pick out of a crowd any time. Not as good-looking as you, but she had the goods all right.

Hell, I didn't want to talk to her. I didn't want anything to do with her. But there I was, in broad daylight, with no place to duck. The convertible pulled off, and she turned and saw me before I could move. She didn't blink an eye and I didn't expect her to.

"Why, Bill Tucker!"

"The same," I said. "Older and wiser but otherwise the same."

She laughed, the way she always laughed, half with me and

half at me. And half not laughing at all, if anything can have three halves.

"The great man returns."

"In disgrace, too. I seem to be highly unpopular."

She looked at the people standing about. They were all looking back at her. There had never been any secret about it back when I was making the big pitch for her. They all knew the score between us, and I expect a few of them were getting a bang out of thinking of that, the way they felt about me.

"What do they know, Bill? I'm kind of proud of you."

"You disappoint me," I said. "I count on you to be unchanging."

"Listen," she said. "Harry had to drive over to Georgetown this morning and dropped me off here. Why don't you give me a lift home?"

"Why don't you walk?"

"Don't be rude. I'll be out in just a minute."

That seemed to settle that. She hurried inside. I lit a cigarette and hung around like the others outside the building.

I guess Ben must have told you most of it, if he told you anything at all. I mean about when I was in love with Katherine.

I guess I was in love with her. I don't know. I was young and on the make for a lot of things besides women and she had them all. But I guess you'd have to say I was in love with her.

That was the first year or two I was out of college. I had gone to work for the State and I didn't have two dimes to rub together, and there I was courting the quality. Those were some years.

I broke my back and my pocketbook trying to make the grade with her. I should have known better, but name me somebody who knows better when it comes to women.

It ended just the way it had to, the way I knew all along it would have to, but wouldn't really admit to myself. She married Harry Watts. His family is about number two in Florence so that wasn't surprising either. Harry had just what it took for Katherine. Me, I didn't even get a bid to the wedding. I wouldn't have gone if I had.

Because by then I knew what she was. I knew she was an

arrogant bitch who collected men the way other people collect stamps and match covers. She was cheap, too, cheap and nasty, but I'll spare you that. And above all, she hated me.

Those were the days I remembered that morning outside City Hall in Florence, waiting for her just the way I used to, wondering, just the way I used to, what was coming next. I knew her pretty well. I knew something was coming.

A feeling like I had for Katherine doesn't pass away lightly. I think maybe part of it stays with you always, especially if it happens to you when you're very young. Maybe you don't even know it's there, but sometimes it'll come at you in the night. It all comes back to you in the night even when you know it's ended, finished, done, and better so. Sometimes you wake up sweating.

It was almost that way with me that morning. I wasn't sweating and it wasn't night. But seeing her brought back all there was to remember about the Katherine days.

I was leaning against a fender of my car when she came out. I watched her all the way down the steps and over to me. Watching her, I felt sorry for her husband. There was something about her, even if you didn't know her, that told you she always had her way. Maybe the way she looked like she owned everything she saw and was thinking of selling it.

I wouldn't hit a hog in the ass with Harry Watts, but I felt sorry for him that morning, watching her come down those steps. I sure-God did.

"I wasn't sure you'd wait," she said.

"Yes, you were," I told her. "You knew goddam well I'd wait."

I held the door open and she got in the car.

"Only you knew it for the wrong reason." I slipped in beside her.

I started the engine. She was just looking at me, not saying anything. She had that much sense, to keep quiet when she wasn't sure what was going on.

"You still think I croak when you smile, don't you? I got news for you. I stuck around just to find out what was on your mind, not to look in your beautiful eyes."

"How do you know anything's on my mind?"

"Any time you act nice something's on your mind."

I drove off, wondering why the hell I bothered letting her have it like that, after all those years. I couldn't touch her. Not in a million years. She was a lot like the old man. Nothing could touch either one of them.

"You're a little vicious these days, aren't you? You've changed, Tucker."

"Wish I could say the same for you." Which maybe was a little childish on my part.

I knew where Harry Watts' old man had built their house for them. It was on a nice lot old man Sprague had given them. They'd had it tough, those two lovebirds. I took the shortest route I could remember.

"But you're right," she said. "The minute I saw you, I wanted to ask you something."

"All right," I said. "What something did you want to ask me?"

"I've been thinking lately. I've been seeing your name in the paper and all, and it reminded me. I've been wondering how it would have been if I'd married you."

That was blunt enough. But it didn't surprise me. I think I'd known something like that was coming, as soon as she had asked me to wait for her.

"Was that what you wanted to ask me?"

"Not exactly. I wanted to ask you if you were happy."

I turned onto a street that leads up onto a big hill where all the moneybags live in Florence.

"Who's ever happy?" I said. "That's just a word people use. But I know this. I'm goddam glad you didn't marry me."

"I bet you are."

"I could tell you how it would be if you had, all right. It would take some crude language though."

That got the best laugh out of her yet. I wanted to slap that superior face up against the windshield.

"You know, Tucker, you have a very tough outside and I guess you are a very tough man. But you are also a little bit of a stuffed shirt."

"You ever see a tough guy who wasn't?"

"I don't know many tough guys. Just you. Maybe that's why I wondered how it would have been with us."

I pulled up in front of her house. It was a pretty sharp little hut. Picture window and white clapboard and azalea bush and a little green postage stamp of a lawn. I could see a Dutch oven in the side yard.

And somehow it hit me too, all of a sudden, more than it ever had before. How would it really have been? Suppose it had been me, living graciously with her, oh very graciously indeed, on her old man's money, in that house, right out of *Better Homes and Gardens?* Suppose it had all turned out that way?

"You tell me," I said. "Are *you* happy?"

She opened the door and got out. Her looks had hardly changed at all, and I could have shut my eyes and imagined it a long time ago when I didn't know a thing about her but the way she looked and the way she felt in my arms. Behind her that perfect house made a perfect backdrop for her, the perfect young matron, the perfect leader of the younger country-club set.

"You poor bastard," she said. "You've been wondering that all these years, haven't you?"

Well, sure I had. I'd never realized it before, but I'd been wondering just that ever since it ended between us. It was a bitter pill, but I swallowed it.

"Yes," I said. It was what she had wanted to know all along.

"You know I always get what I want."

"Yes."

"If I had ever wanted you I'd have had you."

I heard children's voices calling and two little girls came running around the corner of the house, calling to her. It was almost shocking to realize they were hers. They were very pretty and very chubby and they looked happy. I wondered if they would grow up to be like their mother.

"Maybe once," I said. "Maybe once you could have. But you and me, we know better now. You've beaten me the last time."

The children reached her then and saw me and stopped suddenly, staring. She did not look at them.

"Are you sure?" she said.

I put the car in gear and drove away. It was the second time

I'd driven away from something forever, the second time that morning. I was leaving Florence for good.

And I was leaving Katherine for good, too.

For Tucker, something had gone out of the night, something comfortable.

Katherine, he thought. Even talking about her can spoil things for me. Spoil even this.

"I wonder," Vivian said. "*Are* you sure?"

"No. You can't be sure of anything."

He reached across the table and took her hand. "Except you and me. I'm sure of that. Whatever there was with her once won't make any difference to us."

She smiled. "The competition doesn't scare me. But I do blame her for most of your troubles."

"Baby! I'm sittin on top of the world! What troubles have I got?"

Vivian had drawn the Venetian blinds, and the kitchen was cozy and private and smelled richly of coffee. The night was still cool, the little breeze still taunted them, whispering through the blinds; by the electric range Grace Coolidge lapped busily at a saucer of milk, her silken tail rambling luxuriously.

"I mean the way you feel about things. All these things you're doing."

"Now, look." Tucker put down his coffee cup. The remnants of their snack littered the table between them, two small plates, the remains of a loaf of bread, a jar of mayonnaise, a jar of mustard, two table knives. "Let's worry about my morals some time when we've got our clothes on."

"It's not your morals. It's what you're doing to them."

"I've never hidden what I am, Vivian, or what I'm doing. You knew what I was when—"

"Well, if you think I like it just because I went to bed with you, you'd better think again!"

"I didn't take it as an endorsement," he said. "But after all—"

"Oh, Bill, it's just that there's so much good in you and you've gone so wrong somehow!" She got up and came around the table and stood behind him, bending over, her arms around his neck, her cheek pressed to his, her long, bare legs soft and tan below the tail of his shirt.

"I think I understand a lot of how you got that way, darling, a lot about all the things that have hurt you. Like that Sprague girl. They hurt me too, they make me want to kill people. But you can't do that, Bill. You can't let yourself get cold and hard and callous. Don't you see that makes you as bad as all those people that hurt you so badly?"

Gently he stroked the soft arms about his neck. I hope she never finds out, he thought. I won't ever let them get to her.

"Baby," he said. "Don't worry about me."

"I want to make you whole again, Bill. I will too, you wait and see!" Her arms squeezed him tightly.

Some sort of a miracle, Tucker thought. It must be. That this marvelous creature can feel this way about me. That anywhere there is such feeling. Warmth. That she should come to me now when what she has to offer is all that's left for me to want.

The depression his talk of Katherine had brought on suddenly vanished. He let his hand fall to his side, slightly behind him. It found the smoothness of her thigh.

"You'll make me whole, baby. Maybe you already have."

Her sigh against his cheek was almost a sob.

"You don't even know what I'm talking about, Bill."

His hand squeezed her thigh.

"I only know we're right, you and me, I mean. That's right, honey, the way it ought to be."

"I hope so. I want it to be. So much."

Grace Coolidge lifted her head and looked at them contemptuously. She began to wash her face with delicately moistened paws.

I wonder where the Visiting Cat is, Tucker thought. By God, I never have got around to naming that animal.

"Will you kindly stop seducing me?" Vivian said. "You're rubbing my leg raw."

He grinned up at her.

"A very wise man once said history is made on a woman's back. I think it was Papa Dionne."

Her lips touched his ear.

"I like history. It's my favorite subject."

Catlike, he came to his feet. He felt her in his arms.

"Let's make a little history," he said. "Now."

She pushed at him.

"We've already written a couple of volumes. I've got to go. It's two o'clock."

"Go? Are you nuts?"

"If you don't care about my reputation, I do." She disengaged herself from his arms. "Much as I like—history, my friend, it's too late for even fallen women to be running around practically naked in a bachelor's apartment."

"Even if the fallen woman is going to marry the bachelor?"

"More than ever. I have to keep *some* of my charms for our wedding night, don't I?"

In the bedroom he first listened complacently to the sound of her shower, grinning at her yelps when the cold water came on, then contentedly watched her dress. It was not a thing he had ever paid any attention to in the casual affairs he had allowed himself. On those occasions the main thing had always been just to get whoever the woman was the hell out of there as fast as he could.

Now, however, watching Vivian's graceful, unabashed movements, he was conscious of a closeness about it, of an intimacy that brought a new warmth to the room.

She's mine, he thought, everything I ever dreamed of in a woman and she's mine.

He held the thought suspended with his breath a moment, watching the feminine ease with which she drew on her stockings. The greatest thing about her, he thought, was the absolute closeness to her he could feel, as if they were merely two interrelated parts of the same person.

"Bill, would you light me a cigarette?"

He reached for his pack, found it empty.

"Sorry, honey. All out."

"Look in my pocketbook. I think I have some."

He stretched, reaching for the pocketbook, which lay on the cluttered top of his dresser. His groping fingers tipped it off to the floor. Cigarettes, lipstick, compact, Kleenex, comb, coins, myriads of other items, all scattered over the rug.

"Butterfingers," Vivian said. "Look at that mess."

Tucker hastily began to pick up the things and drop them back in the pocketbook.

"What in the name of God you need with all this stuff, I'll never—" He stopped suddenly. His fingers darted to a square piece of paper which lay by a key ring. A few pencil lines sprawled across it.

"Now what the hell is Kirby doing in Boston?" He picked up the paper.

Vivian was already beside him, fully dressed now. She snatched the paper from his hand.

"What the hell are you doing reading a note to me?"

"It was lying open. I couldn't help seeing it."

"Not much, you couldn't. I don't like that, Bill."

He looked at her in surprise.

"What's the matter with you, honey? All it said was he'd give you the notes he promised when he got back from Boston. What's so private about that?"

Vivian bit her lip. There was a little frown on her forehead. Quickly, Tucker put the rest of her things in the pocketbook, stood up, and handed it to her. He put his hands on her arms and looked down at her. She looked away.

"Now look, honey. We don't have any secrets, do we?"

She shook her head. "It's just that Ben trusted me not to tell you. Or anybody. I forgot the damn note was in there."

Something's going on here, Tucker thought. What in hell is Kirby doing way up there? What's she so upset about?

Play this smart, boy. Maybe you're on to something. Play it smart and slow and easy.

"Trusted you not to tell what?"

"That he was in Boston. And now you know anyway."

Tucker shrugged.

"That's *all* I know. It doesn't mean a thing to me. Forget it, kid."

"No." She twisted free and walked to the window. She fumbled in the pocketbook for the forgotten cigarettes. "I know the way

· 280 ·

your mind works. You'll keep thinking about it and wondering and asking questions and poking around, and you'll find out a little bit here and a little bit there and you'll go jumping all over the place, not understanding a bit of it. No. I've let the cat out of the bag."

Easy, boy, easy now. Let it break your way.

"I don't even know what you're talking about, you know."

"But you will. Before long." She whirled to face him, as if she had made up her mind to something. The unlit cigarette was between her fingers and the frown had been replaced by an anxious look. Her eyes almost begged him. "If I tell you about it, the truth I mean, will you promise to forget it?"

Tucker scratched his head.

"How in hell can I say that till I know what you're talking about?"

"Take my word for it. You can do that, can't you? Just believe me when I tell you Mr. Anson didn't have a thing to do with it."

Jesus, he thought, it's big. I can feel it.

"You're a couple of miles over my head, honey. But I promise to forget anything you tell me, if that's what you want."

She seemed to sag a little, as if in relief.

"I only want to tell you because I don't want you to get it all mixed up. And I know if you promise me, I can trust you." There was still a faint note of anxiety in her voice.

Tucker went to her, took the cigarette, and lit it. He kissed her lips, lightly, before he placed the cigarette between them.

"You can trust me, honey." He grinned. "Maybe nobody else can, but you can."

"Well, listen, you know Wilson Holloway?"

My aching ass, Tucker thought.

"Sure. Who doesn't?"

"Well, he wrote Mr. Anson. Ben told me about it." She shook her head. "This ought to teach him to keep his big mouth shut."

"Stop worrying. It was just an accident I saw the note. What did Holloway say?"

"You swear you'll forget about it if I tell you?"

He put his hand on her cheek.

"I wouldn't lie to you, baby. Not to you."

She smiled back. The anxious note faded from her voice.

"He said he was going to send an endorsement of Mr. Anson to all the papers in the State. I think he wanted to send money, too."

What a windfall, Tucker thought.

"No kidding? Old Holloway, eh?"

"Yes. Ben said he and Mr. Anson were flabbergasted. He said it would be the kiss of death."

Tucker grinned, shaking his head a little.

"It sure-God would."

"So that's why Ben went up there, to talk him out of it. He didn't want to take any chances and he went in person. He was terribly angry."

Tucker took the cigarette from her fingers and took a puff at it.

"He had a right to be. That would finish Anson off, sure as shootin.'"

"You promised, Bill. You promised me you'd forget about it."

I know I did, Tucker thought. Goddammit. I know I did.

He looked down at her. Her eyes were wide and still trusting, the deepest blue he had ever seen. Her teeth worried at her lower lip. The smooth skin of her face was a little flushed.

By God, he thought. She trusts me.

She trusts me and we've already got the election in the bag. I think we have.

Maybe I will forget it. I don't know what I could do about it anyway.

And she trusts me.

He put his arms around her and pulled her gently to him.

"I haven't heard a word you said, baby. I been too busy re-membering my history lessons."

Jerry Cooley, Tucker thought. Jerry Cooley.

Gray light was coming in the window of his apartment. Before long the sun would be up, big and hot, smothering the earth.

Jerry would be the man, Tucker thought, if I were going to do anything about it.

He lay on the living-room sofa, where he had fallen, fully

clothed, when he had returned from taking Vivian home. He had lain there a long time, thinking about her, while the night faded away around him.

His thoughts had been of Vivian herself, not of what she had told him, until like a leaf floating from a wind-shaken tree, the name of Jerry Cooley had flitted into his mind.

Cooley had formerly done publicity work in the State Highway Division, where Tucker had been Chief Statistician for so long. He had owed not only his job to Tucker but the several Merit System reclassifications which later pushed him into the higher pay brackets.

A young man with an eager brain and a not-too-obtrusive pushiness, Cooley had been a good press agent. If he owed his quick rise through a deadwood-loaded bureaucracy to Tucker, he owed his success in performance of duty to himself. When he left the State, it had been for a lucrative public relations job in private industry.

His office was now in Boston.

The hell with Jerry, Tucker thought now. I promised her I'd forget it. And I don't really need it. We've got plenty riding for us already.

And yet—

Dammit, it never pays to miss an opportunity. Any opportunity. You never can be really sure how things are going in a business like this. Suppose Pollock's guff isn't going over the way I think it is?

That's silly. You know they're eating the nigger stuff with a spoon. We're in like Flynn.

But just suppose. Well, suppose nothing. I promised Vivian and she trusts me and that's all there is to it.

Old Jerry would be glad to help though. He knows who paved the way for him. But—dammit, I promised her.

Tucker shook his head and got up from the sofa. Got to get some sleep, he thought. You don't have a night like this very often. Or a woman like that. How perfect can things be? It even turned a little cooler, just for us.

He chuckled to himself, unbuttoning his shirt. You never

know, he thought, what lies behind a ladylike exterior. She's really stacked.

He thought, almost happily, of Katherine Sprague. That bitch doesn't know what it can be. She's been missing out all these years, her with her dirty words and her dirty mind, and she never even knew she was missing out.

He stretched luxuriously. He could still catch a few hours of sleep before he had to talk to those Grange people at the office.

It won't really matter if I don't get there at all. Everything's all set now. The real work is done. Just a matter of sitting back and letting things ride themselves home.

He brought himself up short. Now that's a damn fool way to look at it, Tucker. You know better. That's exactly how elections are lost, thinking you've got all the angles covered and then sitting back and letting things ride. And there's a week left to go.

That's why I wish I hadn't made that damn fool promise to Vivian. It would be smart to pull a little insurance deal right at the last. Sort of plant an ace in the hole.

But she'd be plenty mad if I did. She'd drop me like a hot potato.

The hell she would. She loves me, doesn't she?

God knows why, but she loves me. Look at tonight. She's too decent to be the way she was with me tonight if she didn't love me, all the way, with everything she has.

By God, he thought. I could pin it on Joe anyway.

He'd be glad to get the credit. I could say he found out Ben was in Boston and got hot on it and smelled out the whole deal before I knew what was going on.

Tucker sat down abruptly. His brain was clicking smoothly now, as if he had had a good night's rest. In the twinkling of an eye a plan formed in his mind, complete, self-contained, like the final solution of a jigsaw puzzle.

It would work, he thought. There's just enough time. And if that doesn't cook Anson's goose for sure, nothing ever will. That would be insurance, all right.

But I promised her.

He snapped his fingers impatiently.

It was just too bad.

Because he saw very clearly that he couldn't afford to go soft now. He couldn't afford to overlook this God-given opportunity. It would be the last thing needed to cinch the election, to make victory his for sure. He owed it to himself to take advantage of it.

Come to think of it, he owed it to Vivian, too.

It's all for our future, isn't it? Mine and Vivian's? That's what the whole damn lousy mess is for, isn't it?

Besides, he thought again, I can always pin it on Joe.

He stood up and went to the telephone. He picked up the receiver, suddenly clapped it back in the cradle.

Would she really give me the boot?

If she found out, I mean? Does she love me enough to forget it if I break my word?

He shook his head.

She's got to. She's just got to.

And anyway I'm doing it for her. I'm doing everything for her. I just can't afford to let this pass.

He picked up the receiver and dialed 112.

I can see to it she never finds out, he thought.

The phone buzzed busily in his ear, suddenly clicked loudly.

"Long Distance." The voice was cheerful, even at that early morning hour.

"Operator, I want Boston, please. Mr. Jerry Cooley in Boston."

Chapter Nineteen

Even the old-timers could not remember a spell of weather as hot as those last days of the Pollock-Anson campaign.

There was something frightening about it, something ominous. The sun hung above the earth, a glaring red ball, scarcely seeming to move across the brilliant sky. It had rained but three times the entire summer; three rains scattered helplessly in the middle of what seemed a century of sun and heat and sweat.

Dust rose from the parched land and there was no wind to carry it away; it spread between earth and sun a thin, choking veil, dimming at last the brilliance of the sky. Through this filter the sun's rays seemed only to treble in intensity.

Prosperous corn yellowed and stood gaunt along the row; even the sun-thriving cotton faded and drooped, day by day, hour by hour. Night fell on schedule, bringing each twenty-four hours a promise of relief, of a freshening evening breeze, of morning dew gleaming damp on the dying grass. But there was little relief, even at night. The sun sank below the horizon, darkness came on, pale stars gleamed; yet no breeze stirred, and the dust hung still, its fine gray shadow powdered across the land. The heat remained. And the rain did not come a fourth time.

But, strangely, in that sun-scorched wasteland of dust and heat, in that ominous vacuum of listless, perspiring people, the senatorial campaign rolled on, more powerful and disturbing than ever. Where intense interest in the first campaign had been manifest in huge crowds at partisan rallies, in hot debate at every street corner, a deeper, wider, if less obvious, concern now marked the second.

Crowds were much smaller. (Who could brave heat that wilted cotton in the fields?) Discussion seemed to be at a standstill.

Campaign workers found volunteer help scarcer every day. A casual observer would have said both candidates were wasting their breaths. It was just too hot to bother with politics.

True, in a sense, but it did not go far enough, it did not probe beyond the scant crowds, the apathetic talk. For, if the sun seared across the people like a branding iron, another fire had touched them too—the fire of fear.

It had started that panicky day of the decision in the Hartsville School Case, when every white parent had held for a moment a fearful vision of dark skins side by side in the classroom with his children. It had started then, springing quickly from the fertile, well-manured fields sown by Harvey Pollock and his hammering speeches about the Communists and the fellow travelers and creeping socialism and the Threat to the American Way of Life.

It had started then, that day, nourished well in that fecund climate, and now that same Harvey Pollock raged the length and breadth of the State, sounding in four or five speeches a day the call to arms.

How he did it, in that heat, no one knew. Even Tucker felt grudging admiration. In shirt sleeves, the sweat streaming from his fat face, over all of his body, he howled doggedly on, hitting and running and hitting again and again and again, now to two or three farmers at a country filling station, now to hundreds in an air-conditioned theater, now to thousands over the radio, hitting and hitting and hitting again at the jellied, quivering fear of the people who listened, howling not so crudely as Talmadge and Bilbo and McDowell, not so piously as his Reconstruction ancestors, not so viciously as the Klan, but somewhere in between, somewhere in that dreamlike state where a Negro is not a nigger but a Nigra, where segregation is neither an evil nor the will of God but a necessity, where an opponent is not a nigger-lover nor a Communist but a pink.

Colonel Pollock used a simple approach; he was not against Negroes advancing themselves. He was not against Negroes at all. It was not that. It was just that his opponent was too much *for* them. His opponent wanted to go too far.

It could not be called race-baiting, not in the old sense. It was too clever for that.

The newspapers saw through him, to a large extent. They chastised him editorially for injecting racial issues into the election. Yet, by the very nature of what men call news, his words at the same time drew bold and disturbing headlines. His crowds were small; his speeches were apt to be almost singsong; his arguments were incredibly vulnerable to reason. But fear worked for him, an able servant, sly, creeping, almost irresistible.

Ralph Anson answered when he felt the need. He answered without heat and without rancor. He did not answer often.

In the breasts of the few who listened, really listened to him, an intense, passionate admiration grew. These unfrightened few, in those last days of the campaign, were the most diligent and devoted workers in either camp. Being unafraid, being reasonable, they knew what they were up against.

They felt that Ralph Anson was calmly pitting truth against fear. They knew it was written that the truth shall make men free. But they also knew that frightened men are deaf. They worked with desperation hanging over them, desperation not less brutal than the blistering sun.

A nationally syndicated columnist also sensed the nature of the battle. A professional underdog-supporter, he wrote a scathing denunciation of Harvey Pollock. Like a twanging bowstring, resentment vibrated across the State. Another damned outsider sticking his nose in our business, people said.

Nearer home, the *Capital Times* wrote of Anson: "Some men can lead an entire generation to higher ground."

But, that summer, people were reading headlines, not editorials. And Harvey Pollock was saying in those headlines that Anson favored abolition of segregation. That amounted to intermarriage, for all practical purposes. Anybody knew that much.

In answer to a direct question, Anson declared, to the utter despair of Ben Kirby, "I shall never participate in any filibuster for any purpose. That is not a proper tool of democracy."

Pollock observed that it had been a tool, proper or not, that had upheld Southern Democracy more than eighty years. Now take the Communists, he bellowed. They favor an antilynch law.

Senator Anson, according to the *Congressional Record,* was also on record for such a dastardly measure. Anyone with eyes, the Colonel said, could certainly see the significance of *that!*

The desperate struggle Hartsville faced to protect its heritage and its young children, the Colonel repeated in speech after speech, was a preview of what was in store for all the South if people didn't wake up. Up to this point, he would add, Ralph Anson had hastened, rather than hindered, the coming fray.

This was no time, he observed, to weaken America by either advocating foreign ideologies or stirring up minorities at home. What was needed was solidarity in defense of everything everybody held dear. No time now for new ideas; hang on to what you've got.

Anson, almost as indefatigable as his opponent, still inclined to talk about foreign policy. He talked also of freedom and democracy and of one world, but he made it sound like he meant those things for the niggers too. He spoke of the necessity for fair hearings for those accused of subversive activities, on the very day that Pollock shouted that such people should all be shipped right away to Russia, where they belonged.

After Union Springs Anson seldom mentioned racial issues. A close study of what he did say, of his congressional speeches and of his earlier record, would have disclosed that he favored an antilynch law, repeal of Senate Rule 22, abolition everywhere of the poll tax, and "universal" suffrage. He was not for FEPC; it contained, he had said in a Senate address, an "unhealthy element of thought policing . . . two evils can never make a right. . . ." In no public statement had he ever said he favored the immediate end of segregation.

No one bothered to make a close study of his record. His workers did the best they could; in speeches, pamphlets, newspaper ads, personal letters, mimeographed circulars, by every means of communication they commanded, they told the truth about Ralph Anson, desperately, defensively, despairingly.

But it was just too hot.

After all, people told each other, it could be that he's just what Pollock says. Why take chances?

They had always thought of Ralph Anson as a champion of "the little guy." He was better known for his views on wages, working hours, and pensions than on who was, or was not, entitled to sit on the front seats of city buses. That was how they had always thought of him, but now that Pollock mentioned it —well, there *was* a lot of smoke.

This Anson had funny ideas. You couldn't get around that. He probably wasn't *really* a Communist but he *might* be. You couldn't tell nowadays. And Pollock said he was all for this civil rights stuff.

Well, brother, that's all *I* need to know about a man. I ain't aimin to vote for no damn nigger-lover, no matter how pretty he talks. These lousy pinks always hand you this guff about brotherhood an all. The bastards.

So it went, that summer. Pollock's achievement was undeniable. From a position 40,000 votes behind a popular, respected candidate, he had forged in an incredibly few days neck and neck with a man whose very patriotism was now open to question, whose loyalty to the deepest beliefs of the South was openly challenged. Every political observer conceded at least part of the gain. Few predicted victory for Pollock, not yet. The smashing vote given Anson in the first primary could not be forgotten.

Except by Tucker. He hardly ever thought of it again, after that Sunday he had spent, alone in the chaos of the Bright Leaf Room, committing to memory the unofficial returns. Those last days he was everywhere. He had no time to remember, if he had wanted to.

Tucker spent hours at the telephone. In calls to nearly every precinct in the State, he never once dealt with a man whose face he would not have recognized, whose first name he could not call. He spoke to few who did not "owe him something."

He made suggestions, issued orders, demanded results, received reports. No detail was too small, no idea too insignificant; not for Tucker. His was the final say-so on the speeches Joe Harrison wrote for Harvey Pollock; his were all the ideas they contained, even some of the phrases.

Tucker's combination was effective: it had Joe Harrison to grind out its frightening message; it had Zeb Ruggles and Steve Gary to write the checks, together with the industrialists and business-men and lawyers and doctors they influenced; it had a solid nucleus of sure votes in Cousin Hadley's obedient counties; it had the old, loosely powerful State machine, galvanized and revitalized by Tucker; it had brains, realism, courage; it was absolutely without scruple.

But most powerful, most important of all, it had fear for a weapon, fear and its ugly partners, ignorance, hatred. Fear it created. Fear it used.

Fear, in the long run, it relied upon.

✄

The polls opened at 6:30 A.M. It was Saturday morning.

It was Saturday morning, Election Day, and it was going to be another scorcher. The air lolled heavy and mushy about a man's head, even at that hour of the morning. Folks were sweating like mules before the sun was well up. Not even a hint of a cloud softened the glass-blue of the sky; a man could feel his skin dusty and gritty to his touch.

Some folks walked or came in their own wagons or cars. A lot more of them were hauled. The politicians saw to it there was transportation for the voters. Groaning cars would ply the roads all day. (This day an time, iffen a man got a mind to vote, looks like he ain't even got to shake a leg.)

Of course the whisky stores in the few wet counties were closed. Nobody could sell beer or wine either. That's all right, though, most folks thought (except the old-timers), because even if it does hurt business a little a man ought to be cold stone sober when he goes to vote.

But a man could always wet his whistle if he looked sharp. The politicians saw to that, too, especially in counties like those administered by Cousin Hadley, where the worth of a vote could be reckoned to the last dollar and the last cent. There was usually a designated place where spirits flowed, genially if not lavishly. Some folks even brought their own "white," but these were mostly wild young men who had no proper respect for the day.

Reporters anxiously watched for trends, a word they used know-

· 291 ·

ingly. One of them got off an early dispatch to his afternoon paper, describing the voters as "grim-faced and determined." A more casual observer would have thought this reaching a little too far for color in a routine story.

Other reporters duly noted that large groups of Negroes were voting—large, that is, for the comparatively small number of their race considered eligible under State law. The reporters also saw, but did not say in their stories, that the Negroes were no smarter politically than they had ever been. They voted almost en masse, early in the morning, in long, quiet, low-voiced lines, almost as if their groups had been organized. Within an hour afterward, white people extended in lines three times as long from the doors of the polling places.

The reporters and most of the voters received fresh Pollock literature, too, material that had not hitherto been used in the campaign. Most of it was routine, but one circular, handed out in bulk at every polling place in the State, made headlines in most afternoon papers.

The circular carried a blurred photo of Ben Kirby taking leave of a lean, well-dressed old man on the steps of an elegant home. It also featured much large, excited print. The whole thing caused a great deal of talk and headshaking around the schoolhouses and filling stations and City Halls and country stores where polls were kept.

Another strange thing was reported by registrars and poll keepers. Although voting was lighter than in the first primary, they said, an unusually large number of people who had not voted then were voting now. The total vote traditionally fell off in a second primary; that much was not surprising. But obviously something had happened to interest many who had paid little attention to the earlier election. This *was* unusual; second primaries generally were merely contests for the supporters of eliminated candidates.

Was something going on, then?

Well, the hell with it all, the reporters decided. It's too damned hot to bother with. We'll know tonight anyway.

"Well, boys," Cousin Hadley said, "all our bridges burned flatter'n a fritter. Like the old nigger says, either we is or either we ain't."

Zeb Ruggles nodded, not taking his eyes from the big blackboard propped against the wall of the Bright Leaf Room. Two men were chalking figures on its gridlike face.

"Too late to worry now, all right." He shoved his hands in the pockets of a pair of weather-beaten slacks. "This is always the time I start worrying the most, though. When there's no time left. When you get to thinking maybe in spite of all the work you did and all the money you spent, they went and voted the way they damn please anyway."

"Shoot, boy. When they ever do that?"

"Forty-eight," Steve Gary said. "That's what they did in '48, wasn't it?"

Cousin Hadley eyed him wisely. He plucked a highball from the tray of a passing waiter and held it up to the light, surveying its color critically, his bulk a solid island in the shifting sea of people around him.

"Forty-eight was like any other year, Cousin. Smartest side won. Just like they always do."

"I don't know," Gary said. "You look at how many votes Anson got that first time. You—"

"Well, hell, we put in everything we had," Ruggles said. "No use worrying now."

"Course not, Cousin." Hadley suddenly plunged into the mob, his ponderous form bulldozing people from his path. Ruggles and Gary watched him pound a limp-looking party on the back with one hamlike hand and save the same man from collapse with the other. His welcome roared above the sound of all other voices.

"That Cousin. Always the big hello for some poor guy."

Gary frowned. "I suppose it takes all kinds."

It was early yet. The polls had been closed less than an hour. Only a few unimportant returns had trickled in to be chalked on the big board before which they stood. But the crowd was already sizable and the liquor supply was beginning to show hard

usage. Mounds of sandwiches and potato chips were mostly untouched as yet.

Many of those present were campaign workers or various political job-holders and hangers-on. The real crowds would not begin
to come in for an hour or so yet, the amateurs, the voters, the
people. With them would come the yelling and the singing and
the drunks. With them, in the event of victory, would come the
hysteria of celebration.

Now the crowd stood in close knots of people, talking quietly,
professionally, eying the scattered figures on the board, greeting
friends calmly. The heat was beginning to rise, but not until
later would it become suffocating, the air saturated with tobacco
smoke and whisky fumes and B.O.

"Zeb, listen. What do you really think?"

Ruggles chuckled.

"Goddammit, Steve, if I told you I'd already seen tomorrow's
paper and we won, you'd still worry. Wouldn't you?"

Those hard little eyes of his, he thought. Gary never really
laughs, never sees anything but black and white, win or lose,
profit or loss. Everything can be put on a balance sheet. Those
hard, seeking little eyes.

"It's all right to worry," Gary said. "Trouble with most people
is they don't worry enough. Don't care about anything, seems
like."

Poor worried little rich man, Ruggles thought. Hard tight little
millionaire.

"I think we're in," he said, "if you really want to know. I
don't think we can miss. Unless we outsmarted ourselves somewhere."

Gary nodded. "I wish I could be as sure. I've got too much
tied up in this thing. Too much to lose."

"Hell, so have I. Buck up, Steve, the world won't come to an
end, no matter what happens. Never has yet, anyway. How bout
a sandwich?"

"No, I'll watch the board a little longer. Something ought to
be in soon."

Ruggles touched his arm and elbowed away through the crowd.
It had been a long drive to Capital City and he had missed

dinner. He took a couple of wafer-thin ham sandwiches and a paper cup of coffee and moved toward a quiet corner. Might as well take it easy now, he thought. No rest for the weary later on.

He had taken only one bite when someone touched his shoulder. He turned to find the glowing face of Joe Harrison beaming at his side.

"Hello, Mr. Ruggles. All set for the great night?"

"Ready as I'll ever be. In the bag, eh, Joe?"

"It better be," Joe said. "It goddam well better be." He let one eyelid droop in a confidential wink.

Joe oozed with restrained exultation. He gave the effect of executing a perpetual little dance step. The bastard, Ruggles thought. The sly little bastard.

"Listen, Joe," Ruggles said. "That business this afternoon. I go along with the crowd, but I don't buy a word of it."

Joe's lips pursed delicately and his face disapproved of Ruggles. You disappoint me, his expression said. You are disputing the Gospel.

"It's all in the record, Mr. Ruggles. You saw it yourself."

All right, Ruggles thought. When the wind blows from the west, you face the east if you have any sense. You face the east but you don't have to like the view.

"Listen, Joe. My business is riding with the winner. I know my business, so I'll ride with you. I'll go along. But you be sure of one thing, Joe. You be sure you're covered, all the way. If you don't, he'll smash you. And if he doesn't, I will."

"He's a Red," Joe said. "What I did was for the good of the country, we can't have—"

Ruggles laughed. He waved the sandwich in Joe's face.

"For Christ sake, Joe, get off the radio. You think I swallow that pack of lies you trumped up?"

Joe's hair bristled above his Teutonic forehead. "I don't have to take that, I—"

The casual air melted from Ruggles. His spare frame seemed to jerk upright and his voice snapped out, brittle and commanding. His face became absolutely blank. His board of directors would have recognized the change in him; few others had ever seen it.

"You'll take it, mister. I need you but you need me more. I wouldn't forget it if I were you."

Joe turned away, his lips pouting like a child's.

"Remember, Joe. You better be sure. Leave him an opening and you're a gone goose. And so is the Colonel."

Joe did not look back. There was something faintly heroic in the square set of his burdened shoulders.

Son of a bitch, Ruggles thought. I haven't flown off my rocker like that in a long time. That stiff-necked bastard rubs me the wrong way. And this deal today—

He relaxed against the wall. It was too bad. It was a hell of a thing, all the way around.

But that's sentiment. And in a lot of ways, it's Tucker's own fault. Hell, didn't I warn him myself not to underestimate Pollock? But he wouldn't listen.

If it was just me, I could put the quietus on it, quick. But there's too much at stake. In the big picture he doesn't matter that much. In the big picture the important man to us is Pollock. And you have to look at the big picture all the time.

A murmur of excitement swept through the big room. People began to move toward the door and there was a sudden burst of applause, some cheering and a great many whistles.

Pollock, Ruggles thought. The Great White Father arrives. Colonel, damn your fat ass, I take off my hat to you. You are a bigger and smarter bastard than even I thought you were.

He smiled, half-regretfully, half in amusement.

It just goes to show how much a man knows. Even Joe Harrison was smarter than I thought. In the end those two turn out to be the smartest of all. It just goes to show.

I am damn glad I'm just one of the pocketbooks. Because nobody double-crosses cash. Nobody outsmarts it either. Everybody has to have a pocketbook.

Colonel Pollock was striding to the center of the long room now, smiling, waving, nodding to right and left. Applauding people moved aside to clear a path for him.

"Speech!" somebody yelled. And "Speech! Speech!" came the echoing cry from all over the room.

Pollock stopped, shook his head helplessly. The cheering became louder now. The candidate put both hands over his head and waved, turning his body in all directions, his beaming face taking in everyone.

Zeb Ruggles saw Tucker standing near the Colonel, arms folded across his chest, a somewhat forced grin in the correct position on his face. Cousin Hadley was beside Tucker, his bull roar coming clear above the steady sound of the cheering.

Pollock gestured for silence. The noise died slightly and Pollock gestured again. As the yelling dropped to a low murmur his hoarse voice called clearly, "No speeches now, folks—" The murmur swelled into protest and again the Colonel stilled it with a gesture. "I'll wait until I have something good to talk about!"

No one could halt the explosion of sound which followed the words. Christ, Ruggles thought, you'd think he'd already won. They better save their breath.

The Colonel waved again, then began to move toward the big double doors which led down the hall to his private office. He shook a hand at every step, slowly making his way along, pounding a back, laughing, greeting friends, waving genially at the crowd.

He's getting good with a crowd, Ruggles thought. That big grin and the way he waves those arms around. He's going to go a long way, now we've got him started. It was a good day for us when Tucker pulled him out of the hat.

Not so good for Tucker, but a good day for us. We can get along with a man like that. He talks our language.

Pollock turned at the door for a final wave at the crowd. Then he slipped out the door, the elephantine rear of Cousin Hadley hulking after him, the high-pitched, ecstatic yelling following both of them.

I wonder if Tucker knows yet?

I think I'll sound him out. Way things are going around here it won't hurt to keep one leg on each side of the river. Just in case.

Because they are going to have to count ten over him before I feel easy about Tucker.

He swallowed the remnants of the ham sandwich and put the paper cup on the floor. When he looked up he could no longer see Tucker. As if Pollock's arrival had been a signal, the mob was beginning to flow into the Bright Leaf Room. Already Ruggles could feel his eyes smarting from the tobacco smoke.

He pushed and shoved his way toward the center of the room. Progress was slow, for, like Cousin Hadley, Zeb Ruggles knew many people. Even more wished to know him. His hand was feeling greasy and bruised from handshaking, his shoulder ached from pounding when he finally reached Tucker.

It was characteristic, Ruggles thought, that Tucker should be standing alone by a window, looking out upon the street. In a crowd, the man had the quality of melting away from people, of turning in upon himself, so that he could be standing unnoticed by your side while you searched for him among the people milling about you.

It was probable, Ruggles thought, that Tucker knew more of the people in the Bright Leaf Room than anyone else, not excluding the omnipresent Hadley. Yet he was noticed by fewer of them than even such an unobtrusive little man as Steve Gary. Tucker had more responsibility for the entire occasion than anyone else. It was virtually his creation. Yet he stood alone, an aloof, seemingly uninterested figure, his hands clasped loosely behind his back, staring away from what he had wrought.

It was even, Ruggles decided, essentially proper that he should stand so, solitary and unmoved, unintegrated with anything. Because when you got down to the basic, bedrock Tucker, all you found was a ghost. His work was done by other hands. His words fell from other lips. His triumphs glorified other men. Even his weapons were unseen. There was not a thing about Tucker a man could lay his hand on, except his body.

"Don't jump out that window," Ruggles said. "We might win yet."

Tucker grinned at him. "Did I look like a prospective suicide, Zeb?"

"It would be a hell of a dramatic thing, wouldn't it? In the midst of the maddened throng, out through the window plunges Tucker. You could have a worse end, I suppose."

"I could. And I probably will."

"Undoubtedly. Maybe at the hands of some Ansonite."

"Not to change the subject, Zeb, but I'll make you a bet."

"What's that?"

"Anson will concede by nine o'clock."

"Done. It won't be before ten."

"Nine. I feel it, Zeb. I can always feel these things."

"I hope you're right. This thing has been a masterpiece so far. You called your shots all down the line, Tuck."

Tucker looked at the crowd, now pressing into every corner of the room, eating, drinking, laughing, yelling, just standing. He took a cigarette from his pocket and Ruggles saw, in sheer amazement, his hand tremble as he lit it.

"All my life," Tucker said. "Every god damned stinking minute I ever lived I was building up to this."

His head turned slowly, looking at the people.

"Because I'm going to win. At last I'm going to win."

"Listen," Ruggles said. "You know what my old man told me once? He said nothing ever turns out quite as good as you think it will. And nothing ever turns out quite as bad as you think it will either."

Tucker put the cigarette in his mouth and looked through the rising smoke, blinking a little, at Ruggles.

"Your old man had a lot on the ball. Some people hated his guts, but he had a lot on the ball."

"Well, he was right that time."

"Only thing is, that's just something you tell yourself. You know it's true, but you have to have it proved to you all over again, every time. You never really believe it."

"Just thought I'd pass it along."

"You know something, Zeb. Something you think I don't. What's on your mind?"

Christ, he's sharp. I hope to God Joe and the Colonel covered all the angles.

He punched Tucker's chest with a friendly fist. "Not a damn thing, Tuck. I'm just running off at the mouth."

Now I've got him to wondering if something's going on, Ruggles thought. I ought to have my ass kicked.

"Here comes Gary," Tucker said. "Looks like he ate a bad oyster."

Gary came up to them as if he had to catch a train. His voice was precise, a shade impatient.

"When can we expect some significant returns, Tucker?"

He talks like the Alsop brothers, Ruggles thought. Poor little rich man worried about all that money.

"Not long." Tucker pointed toward the board. "Here's something now."

A man was standing on a chair before the board, waving for silence. Ineffectual at first, his efforts gradually brought response. The crowd quieted and moved swiftly in around the chair.

"Listen!" he yelled. "First big county! Complete returns—" Brief cheers and handclapping interrupted him but were quickly shushed.

"In Toombs County—for Anson, five thousand seven hundred and forty-one—" a few scattered boos and hisses—"for Pollock, SEVEN thousand . . ." The sudden booming roar of the throng around him drowned the rest of his words.

Tucker, Gary, and Ruggles watched the first real demonstration of the evening. It was a happy scene, not yet hysterical, not even what reporters call "wild." But the spirit was there. There was already, in the fetid, humid, body-smelling air, a faint aura of victory.

As the noise died somewhat Gary turned to Tucker. "We took that county last time. Did we gain anything today?"

Tucker peered at the board to get the exact figures, now plainly chalked there. He pursed his lips.

"About eleven hundred twenty-odd, I make it."

Gary shook his head. "I'd hoped for more. We spent a lot in Toombs."

"Oh, hell, Steve," Zeb said. "You remind me of this ol nigger down home. Ol Catfish Brown. I let him have ten bucks one time, for a week he said. Bout a month later I ran into the ol devil on the street. 'Catfish,' I said, 'what about that ten dollars?' He looked at me as surprised and hurt as if I'd hit him.

'Whut ten dollahs is dat, Mis' Zeb?' 'You know what ten dollars,' I said. 'That ten dollars I let you have for a week bout a month ago.' Wellsir, ol Catfish bust out laughing fit to kill. Laughed and laughed and laughed. 'Mis' Zeb,' he said, 'ain't you shamed? Heah you is plaguin me bout ten dollars an all de time I owes *hunduds!* ' "

Gary smiled, a little grimly. He always smiled, a little grimly, when someone told a joke.

"And here you are," Zeb said, "worrying about a few votes. Why, man, there's thousands where those came from!"

"Oh, I'm not really worried. It's just—"

"Excuse me, will you?" Tucker said. "I want to talk to a guy I see over there."

"Sure, Tuck."

Gary and Ruggles watched him push away through the crowd.

"I never did trust that man," Gary said. "He never showed any respect for anything."

"Not even you."

Gary nodded gravely.

"That's it exactly. I always felt like he was laughing at everybody, even me. I won't be sorry to see the last of him."

"I wonder," Zeb said. "I wonder if any of us ever will."

Chapter Twenty

That was a warning, Tucker thought.

That was a warning if I ever heard one.

He dodged a large woman who had wavered into his path. She was gesticulating airily with a half-empty highball glass and from her high-piled blond hair a long, limp coil hung down the back of her neck, like an abandoned noose.

"Where's the Sentor?" she said loudly. Her breath wheezed alcohol fumes across his face.

"Who?" Tucker said. "What Senator?"

"Sentor Pollock. Whoinell you think?" She peered at him in tipsy outrage. "Where is he?"

"Jesus, lady, you're in the wrong place. This is the Sanitation Department annual outing. No Senators here."

He ducked swiftly into the throng, ignoring the indignant hand falling heavy and demanding on his shoulder, the loud voice tipsily commanding his return. I hate a drunk woman, he thought. Especially a fat, drunk woman.

The room was now packed almost solidly with bodies. The smoke and noise were all about; either could almost be touched. Before the blackboard returns were being announced more rapidly now. As each pair of figures was called off, a fresh roar went up from the jammed room. Tucker did not listen to the straining voices reading out the returns. The voices around him told what he needed to know.

From long habit, however, Tucker could not ignore the actual figures. He was a man who believed in cipher, in fact; there was an incorruptibility about numerals which appealed to something unanswered in him. He pushed himself near the blackboard and for long minutes peered at the rapidly growing rows of figures. Then he turned away. In his mind the picture was clear.

Pollock was well in the lead. Not a wide lead, but a good lead. Three counties had already switched to him and in several others, where Anson had trounced him soundly before, he trailed by narrow margins only. In the few counties he had taken in the first primary, Pollock had this time rolled up huge majorities. His lead now, at this early hour, was over six thousand votes.

It was true that Anson's heaviest backing had been in many counties as yet unreported. But it was also true that still to be heard from was Cousin Hadley's rigidly controlled empire; still to be heard from were most of the flat, low, sandy counties of the east, the coastland, the counties where the Negroes outnumbered the whites, the counties of poverty and ignorance and run-down farms and worn-out land, worked-out people; still to be heard from were the fields where fear had been sown most thickly.

Now, Tucker thought, the reporters can talk about a trend. Now they can see the way the wind blows. Just the way I saw it six months ago.

Funny. I've waited a long time for this, longer than anybody knows. And now its happening. It's happening just the way I thought it would, just as if it were a house and I had taken my two hands and built it exactly the way I wanted it.

He looked at his hands, watched them clench into white-knuckled fists.

But something is wrong. Something is all wrong. Everything is going just the way it's supposed to and yet something is wrong. Bad wrong.

Maybe—Vivian. Maybe she knows by now. She must have seen the papers. Or Ben could have told her, shown her. Hell, she's bound to know by now.

He stared at people around him, recognizing their faces, speaking to a few, nodding at others. And suddenly he was lonely.

It was nothing new. He had been lonely most of his life, had even gloried in loneliness, finding in himself, in the certain strength of his purpose, the fine, clean-edged blade of his understanding, his comprehension of a world as it was and would be, some infinite joy at once beyond and forsaken of happiness, some negotiated peace not peaceful nor even comforting, but definitive.

But this was different. Into his loneliness had entered the quality of uncertainty. There was Vivian. There was the veiled warning of Zeb Ruggles. There was something else too, and this was the worst of all, because he did not know what it was, only knew beyond a doubt that it was something, that it was real, impending.

I want to get out of here, he thought.

He wanted to be away, far away, where he need not see them, need not hear the voices straining only to be heard above other voices, need not touch moist and heated flesh, need never move again among the futile attempts of men to justify their fears; where, finally, he need never look again upon the faces of fat, drunk women.

He made a quick move, almost a lunge, to his left and felt his shoulder strike against a man's back. He turned and a solid wall loomed before him, lined and stained along its surface by a tiny pattern of plaster cracks cobwebbing from floor to distant ceiling; he turned again and the white grid chalked across the blackboard rose like bars before him. He felt a man step on his foot, felt another pressing against his back.

Something near panic scratched at him with long, sharp fingernails.

I want to get out of here, he thought. I've got to find a way out, I'll suffocate here. I'll—

He lunged again, to his right this time, and felt his whole body drive against a soft, depthless mass, felt his frame recoil, felt closing about him now the absolute terror of entrapment, the final disintegration of no escape, of encirclement and obliteration.

"Whoa there, mule!"

As abruptly as it had come panic dropped from Tucker. The voice was as welcome as the first sudden sound of an auto engine on a winter morning. It was unchanged, unchangeable; it took Tucker from behind the grid of white bars, bodily, and left him, smiling, on the teeming floor of the Bright Leaf Room.

"Jesus Christ, Cousin. You're soft as a cotton bale."

"Bout as big, too. You in a hurry or something?"

"Just dodging, Cousin. Just dodging."

"Well, lissen. Colonel says his missus'll be along any time. Wants you to meet her down front of the hotel."

"Martha? Hell, yes. Anything to get out of this nuthouse." Hadley puffed blue cigar smoke at him.

"Cousin," he said, "you know we clobberin them folks up there, don't you?"

"Cousin, I got ten bucks says it'll be over by nine."

"Good bet. Been a good bet all along. All the way."

A blaring voice over their heads interrupted them.

"Clinch County—for Anson, twenty-four thousand eight hundred and ninety-one—for Pollock—lissen to this one now—for Pollock, TWENTY-NINE thous . . ."

As if a spring had been released, pandemonium broke loose in the Bright Leaf Room. The impact of the sound almost sent Tucker reeling; grown men jumped up and down, screaming hysterically, their faces red, their mouths and eyes gaping; women threw their arms around total strangers and screeched with joy; in the middle of the floor a snake dance began to form and in one corner the strains of *Dixie*, punctuated by drunken profanations of the rebel yell, rose shrilly above the uproar. Sheer animal joy rolled across the mob.

Hadley and Tucker stood apart and watched. They were excited themselves; the spirit of the unrestrained bodies around them was contagious. But they looked upon this biggest news yet as essentially a matter of business, a dividend declared as expected. To them it was not a pep rally. They could feel their pulses beat faster; they could not tag on to the end of the snake dance now undulating across the room.

"That was their county," Tucker said, when the noise had abated somewhat. "That one hurt them. Bad."

Hadley nodded, rolling the cigar across his fat lips.

"God, this congregation down home, Cousin. Holiness. Had this ol barn of a church made out of planks off ol boxcars. Well, seems like the folks what built it got all messed up. Put in two windows to one side of the pulpit an only one on the other, kind of unbalanced. Wellsir, got to thinkin bout that thing down there and first thing you know that church was split right down the middle. Half the congregation wanted to close up one window an balance it off. Other half wanted to put in a fourth window.

"Pretty soon the preacher upped an called this meetin to get the thing settled. Them folks argued for an hour, one way then the other. Didn't get nowhere. Preacher couldn't get a soul to give a inch.

"This one ol feller, he set in the back pew an didn't open his mouth. Just set there an listened while the rest of the congregation argued it out. Well, long bout the time it looked like somebody was fixin to get hurt, up rose this ol boy back there an hollered up at the preacher. 'Preachuh,' he hollers, 'what's the Lawd's word on this thing?' Preacher hauled off an pounded his fist down on the pulpit. 'Charlie,' he bellers, 'far's I know the Good Lord just don't give a hoot.' 'Well, then,' Charlie yells, 'I move we leave them windows like they dang are.'"

Tucker smiled sardonically. Hadley did not laugh at all. They might have been two sales managers, repeating an anecdote about a good territory.

"That's what they done, too. Seems like folks most always leave them windows like they are."

"You always did understand politics, Cousin," Tucker said. "Well, I'll get on down and wait for Martha. Don't let them sell us any wooden nickels while I'm gone."

"Nobody puttin nothin over on ol *Cousin*," Hadley said. He put the cigar in his mouth and rocked his huge frame back on his heels, his hands going into his pockets, his eyes benignly meeting those of Tucker. The emphasis on the last word had been unmistakable.

Stronger now, pushing at him out of that strange shiftiness of his insides, that odd floating sense not so much of worry as of bafflement, Tucker felt the off-key something again. Forcing his way through the close-packed people toward the doors leading to the elevator bank, he felt it all around him, vague as it was threatening.

Somebody's got the knife out, he thought. Ruggles, Hadley— they both know something. Something they can't quite keep to themselves.

Sudden rage enveloped him. The bastards, he thought, I haven't got enough troubles already—Vivian—

Jesus, he thought, I wish I knew what she's thinking.

Ben Kirby could feel the acquisitive eye of hysteria sizing him up; the shrill gaiety of approaching despair had already descended upon him, leaving his head light, his eyes unnaturally wide.

"John, my boy," he said, placing a conspiratorial hand on the arm of the man beside him, "how would you like to be in the U.N.?"

The man's eyebrows went up.

"Great," he said. "Just great. I speak a little French."

"Then you have all the qualifications, John. All the qualifications. Just like Colonel Harvey Pollock."

"Listen, are you fried already?"

"Sober as a judge."

"Well, let's you and me go get fried."

"All right, John. A splendid idea. Just as soon as I clear this U.N. appointment for you, I'll—"

"You better go see Pollock," John said. "See if you can line it up for Mr. Anson."

Ben shook his head.

"You don't understand, John. You're a bookworm. You don't understand practical politics is your trouble."

John nodded at the blackboard, where two frantic figures tried to keep up with chanted returns. "I understand blackboards though, and that one up there says Pollock is ten thousand votes out in front of us."

Ben nodded amiably and winked at him. "Doesn't mean a thing, John. Don't let it worry you." His voice dropped to a cloak and dagger whisper. "I can remember when we were *forty* thousand votes ahead!"

"That's what I mean," John said. "Let's get fried to the elbows."

"Not yet, John. Give it time."

"Goddammit anyway."

"Exactly," Kirby said.

The two men stood somewhat apart from the crowd squeezed into Anson Headquarters. They were old and close friends and both quite willingly had given up more lucrative jobs to work for Ralph Anson as executive assistants. John Walters had remained in Washington during the campaign to keep the office going, while Ben had served as campaign manager.

They stood now, looking over the quiet, patient people in the Formal Gardens, the Stonewall Jackson's second biggest ballroom. It was a different crowd from that which had crammed into the same room the night of the first election. Then they had been a cheerful, steaming, yelling throng, flushed with victory and certainty. Now they simply waited, patient, hopeful, but subdued, apprehensive. To them, tonight, nothing was certain.

They were the same people, to a large extent, but they had learned much since the first night they had gathered. They had learned more than they wanted to know and this was graduation night.

May you all stand there, Ben thought, may you all stand there, the faithful and the unafraid, and let it come down upon you, that which has happened. May you all see it and know it and remember it forever. May the Lord at least let us have that.

"I want to get drunk," John said.

"Go on, then. Get drunk as you want to."

"Maybe I better not. Maybe there might be something I can do."

Kirby shook his head.

"That's the trouble with you. You just don't understand politics."

And neither do I. I wonder if I ever will. Certainly I have been disillusioned and that in itself is hopeful, that there is anybody left to be disillusioned.

"Reckon we ought to go talk to the Senator, Ben?"

"Hell. What could we say to him?"

They listened to returns being read from another county. When the figures were announced, a spasmodic cheer went up from the crowd, dying quickly into that patient watchfulness, that hope without confidence.

"What do you know? We took one."

"Great," Ben said. "Now he's only eight thousand ahead of us."

"You're a cynic. You don't believe in the impossible."

"I believe in Calhoun County, John."

"What is Calhoun County besides a county?"

"Our last hope. Our last chance for a big majority."

"How much chance would you say we had?"

"A big majority there could save us," Ben said. "That's all I know."

Yet faint hope plucked at him as he listened to his own words. He knew, without saying so, that it would be a political miracle, like a boat floating upstream, if even one county held out against the Pollock trend strongly enough to overcome his lead. Yet miracles had happened before. Even Harvey Pollock had accomplished something like one.

If he can, Ben told himself, in the last extreme of loyalty, Ralph Anson ought to be able to pull off a dozen.

He wanted desperately to believe in such a miracle, to believe in anything that might call a halt to this nightmare. He could not yet bring himself to accept defeat and that which had brought defeat. Even less, standing staring at the blackboard, could he accept that it might yet be averted. It was too plainly the will of the people.

And, even more than he believed in Ralph Anson, Ben believed in that curious phenomenon, the people. He did not understand them nor know very much about them. But he believed in them, not in their wisdom nor their sanctity, but in their right to decide. He did not believe that even a miracle could thwart the will of the people.

"Here comes that sexy schoolteacher," John said. "You been fighting a tough war."

Vivian, Ben thought, the old hurt bubbling into his chest, drowning even the brief, fleeting irritation at the careless remark. Even Vivian, he thought. To the victor belongs the spoils. It is almost too much that in addition to taking everything else from us Tucker has also taken her from me.

She stopped in front of them, searching their faces as if to find there some shred of comfort. Ben thought there was something haunted in her eyes, as if what she saw happening were not a mere event, however disastrous, but rather some entwining horror within her.

"I can't believe it," she said.

"You were there that day in Union Springs. You should have known."

She shuddered.

"I know. But I thought maybe it was just those particular people, that place. I didn't—" She stopped. "At least, I didn't want to think it would be the same everywhere."

"Nobody ever lost an election in these parts cussin out the darkies," Ben said.

"That college you teach in," John said. "They need a good economics man?"

She smiled, a little faintly.

"I got an M.A. in economics. Looks like I might have to use it at last."

"Have you given up?" Vivian said. "Really and truly?"

"There's always Calhoun County," Ben said. "Do you believe in miracles?"

She knows it, he thought, watching the droop of her shoulders, the tiny sagging lines peeling away from the corners of her mouth, seeing almost in surprise that Vivian Reynolds was not a young girl any more, seeing the look of tiredness about her eyes, the shadow falling swiftly over all of her. She knows who did it, who pulled all the levers, whose handwriting is on the wall.

And quickly, out of his own fatigue and despair and disbelief, out of that lurking fog of hysteria, out of his hurt and disillusionment and perhaps too out of that old, familiar, painful lump in his chest, that lost sense of something gone by in the night, never to return, out of all that, anger, blind and unrestrained, "What are you worrying about? You've got Tucker, haven't you?"

She flinched and the anger, trebled now by rage at himself, at his outburst, drove him on.

"The great Tucker. He'll hold your head and listen to your troubles, won't he? You got nothing to worry about."

"It's not all his fault, Ben. You don't understand."

Her voice was soft and there was no anger in it, no reproach.

He hated himself and could not stop, hysteria now clutching eagerly at him.

"Listen," he said. "I am getting god damned tired of this poor old Tucker he had a bad environment it's not all his fault routine. I am getting god damned tired of anybody thinking that crook is anything but the lousy crook he is." His fingers closed on the folded paper in his jacket pocket. "I am getting god damned tired of this sort of thing."

He put the paper in her hand. He felt John's uneasy movement at his side and then he looked away.

Kirby heard her breathe four times, very distinctly. There is so much lousiness in all of us, he thought. Maybe it is a wonder any of us manage to be as decent as we are.

"I didn't tell him, Ben."

He heard his voice crack like a child's.

"I know, lady. I'm sorry."

"He found out from me, but it was an accident. I was stupid and he found out."

"I'm sorry. I was just so damned tired when I said all that."

In the long run, he thought, we are all reduced to making excuses for ourselves.

"He promised me. He said he wouldn't do anything like this." There was a note of wonder in her voice.

He looked out over the docile crowd. It was beginning to thin a little, he saw, and that meant some of them could not believe in Calhoun County either. Returns were still being called, bringing a small injection of excitement with each new announcement. Few of these were significant. Pollock maintained his steady, sizable lead.

If he takes us in Calhoun, Ben thought, if the son of a bitch wins there—

"I would have staked everything I had on him," Vivian said. "He promised me, Ben."

It is all such a damnable mess, such a lousy mixed up mess. It started out clean and simple and black and white and now it's not just an election any more, it's all mixed up with love and hate and fear and faith and hope and—it's all such a mess now.

"I don't know what this is all about," John said. "But I got an idea. Let's all go get drunk."

"Listen," Ben said. "Listen, Vivian. Maybe you were right. It's not all Tucker's fault, it can't be. Everybody had a hand in it."

"I don't know," she said. "I don't know about that." There was a grim ring in her soft voice and Kirby looked at her in surprise, saw the smooth curve of her lips draw down into a thin, straight line. "All I know is he promised me."

⚹

It can't be anything but that, Tucker thought. I'd be in on anything else myself.

They think they're going to ditch me, now I've won it for them.

He flipped his cigarette away and watched it fall into the gutter. He stood leaning against the entranceway of the Stonewall Jackson, unnoticed by the people hurrying past into the hotel. Traffic was heavy on the broad city street and the headlights of cars made the night almost as bright as day.

Tucker could feel his shirt clinging under his arms. It had been hot all day and, as usual, night had brought no relief. The air was dry, scented with dust, and lay heavy against his skin. At least, he thought, I'm not in that oven upstairs.

So they think they're going to toss me to the wolves. At least Cousin ought to know better than to try it.

He watched a car pull up under the portico of the hotel. Two men and a woman got out. They were well-dressed and the car was big and expensive.

". . . want to hear Harvey's acceptance speech," one of the men was saying.

The doorman got in the car and it whisked smoothly away. The three entered the hotel. As they passed Tucker heard the other man say, "Damn good to have a businessman back in there."

They must have heard it on the radio, Tucker thought. So even the radio people think he's in now, do they?

Businessman. I wonder if it was the businessman or that little rat Harrison dreamed up this scheme to lay the ax to me. Or maybe even Cousin.

Did they actually think I would be stupid enough not to figure they might decide to get rid of me? Did they actually think they could beat me at my own game?

I should worry about them. If I can just get by with Vivian —Vivian—

It's a funny night. Here I am wondering what the hell Vivian is thinking and what particular piece of stupidity that gang of thieves has put together for me, and I am hardly even realizing everything else that's happening.

He glanced at his watch. In maybe less than an hour— He grimaced. Even now the bastards won't let me alone. When I've earned the right to—

But the hell with that. If they have to be shown, then I'll have to show them. That's all there is to it.

A taxi darted out of the honking stream of traffic and moved smoothly in to the curb. The driver leaned back to push open the rear door.

Tucker moved away from the wall, across the wide sidewalk toward the car. Fred Pollock stepped casually from the rear seat.

"Hello, Fred."

Fred glanced at him, briefly, almost negligently. "Hello," he said. He turned his back to Tucker and extended his hand to his mother. She came through the low door of the cab gracefully, with all the casual assurance of beauty and wealth and position and arrogance.

"Hello, Tucker," she said. "I'll bet Harvey sent you down."

"I might have come anyway, Martha. You never can tell."

She turned and dazzled the cab driver with a smile. Fred handed him a bill.

"Thank you," Martha said. "I enjoyed hearing about your little boy."

"Thank you, ma'am," the driver said, grinning fatuously. He waved and the cab dashed away in a cloud of exhaust fumes.

"Well, you brightened up his life, didn't you?" Tucker said.

"Cab drivers are fascinating people. Don't you think?"

Tucker laughed.

"That's what I like about you, Martha. You find so many people fascinating."

"Listen," Fred said. "I got to see a bellboy I know. Will you wait for me a minute."

"We'll be in the lobby."

Martha caught Fred's arm.

"Fred, you know what you promised."

He looked down at her hand.

"I know. I'm not going to get drunk, Mother dear. Only a little tight."

"Well, I know what you want to see that bellboy for."

"Christ," he said. "You don't think I could take this without a drink, do you? Haven't you been listening to the radio?"

"Go on, then. Go on and make an ass out of yourself like you always do."

"I'll try, Mother dear. I really will." He turned away and walked rapidly into the hotel.

Tucker took Martha's arm.

"Come along. You are about to see the remarkable spectacle of Colonel Harvey Pollock in absolute triumph."

They went through the broad doors of the Stonewall Jackson into the spacious lobby. It was carpeted in red from wall to wall. Overflowing the huge room, crammed and jammed into every available inch of floor space, ponderous, overstuffed furniture squatted in silent obeisance to Grand Rapids. Relieving this scene of splendor were several potted palms, strategically placed where there was no room for a sofa or a chair.

A dim mezzanine ran around all four walls at the second floor level. From those vastnesses of the hotel rising above the lobby, the sounds of partisan revelry floated, drifting down from the Bright Leaf Room. The lobby, too, was crowded, thronged with the overflow from the headquarters of both candidates. Cigar smoke drifted blue and hazy in the rays from the dim overhead lights.

"I feel a headache coming on already," Martha said. "Listen to that noise. Last time I didn't get over it for two days."

"It won't last much longer. Your boy is in like Flynn."

They paused by one of the potted palms, near the elevator bank. Tucker lit cigarettes for them both.

"And so is Tucker. You're in like Flynn, too, aren't you?"

He nodded, blowing smoke from the corner of his mouth.

"Everybody wins," he said. "Except you."

"That's a dirty dig." Her voice was unruffled, almost uninterested. "You and I ought to be past all that. After what we've been to each other."

Tucker laughed out loud.

"All right, Martha. You want to be friends, we'll be friends."

She nodded.

"Besides, what makes you think I'm losing anything?"

Tucker flicked ashes into the potted palm. Everything changes, he thought. You can't put your money on anything. Last time I talked to her she offered me twenty-five grand a year and a roll in the hay to put a knife in the Colonel's back.

"You've changed your tune, haven't you? Any of my business why?"

She measured him with cool eyes. The bluntness of her stare made Tucker shiver. She has no pity, he thought.

"It took me awhile to catch on," she said. "But then I saw it. I saw that if Harvey is going to be a great big Senator he won't want any bad publicity. Will he?"

"No. He won't."

"In fact," Martha said, smiling faintly now, her even white teeth delicately touching the full, red curve of her lower lip, "he'll do almost anything to avoid bad publicity."

"I expect he might."

"I only tell you this because we're such old friends."

"I appreciate that. You don't know how much."

"You were so worried about me the last time we really talked about it."

"You just thought I was," Tucker said. "Actually I had a stomach-ache."

She laughed, fully and freely, and men standing in the lobby turned their heads at the sound of it.

"And just to think," she said, "I almost bribed you to lose the election!"

"You never came close, Martha."

"Oh, well, now that we understand each other, you must be sure to call on me in Washington. I'll give you a—warm welcome." Something lurked deep in her eyes, in the corners of her scarlet, smiling lips. That much, Tucker thought, she means.

She's like Katherine. She can bring out the worst things in you with just a look or a word. Not like Vivian—Vivian—

God, he thought, I keep coming back to her. I've got to see her. Soon. I've got to find out. Because if I'm going to lose her for a few lousy votes—

But I won't lose her. I can't.

Chapter Twenty-one

I hear the asses braying," Fred Pollock said, behind them. "Has Ass Number One mounted his throne yet?"

"In about a half-hour," Tucker said, "if you mean what I guess you mean."

Fred ducked under a scrawny fringe of the potted palm and joined them. He carried a paper sack in his hand.

"Look out, Washington. Big wind coming."

"You just be quiet," Martha said. "I'm getting a little sick of your smart talk."

"I'm just a little sick of *everything*, Mother dear."

Her voice was suddenly bitter.

"At the ripe old age of nineteen. What a wise man of the world you are!"

He yawned, taking a wide, bored glance around the lobby.

"You can be tiresome, too, Mother dear. Even if you are beautiful. And by the way, I'm twenty now."

For a moment Tucker thought Martha would strike the boy. Then she shrugged and turned away. Why, she has *some* kind of feeling for him, he thought. Whether love or pity or blood-tie or whatever, she does have a feeling in her for him.

The pity he had felt so often for Fred Pollock touched him again. There was something reluctantly honest inside the boy, something which saw through the sham of Harvey Pollock, through the sheen of his mother, something which could not accept unprotested what it found in them, even if the protest was negative and vacant, invoked in weakness.

A fresh outburst from above hurtled down at them.

"Tell you what," Tucker said, "before you two start pulling

hair, let's go up and let the photographers snap a little happy family stuff."

"Look, Tucker. Is Fat Boy really in? Is it a sure thing?"

"It looks that way."

Fred shook his head wonderingly.

"I really wouldn't have believed there were so many fools."

"Takes one to show them up."

Martha's laughter rang out again, mocking now, not calm any more, not bantering.

"You two," she said. "You two big smart wonderful men. Standing there talking like nobody knows anything but you. Well, let me tell you something, you big smart wonderful suckers."

Her words were rapid and little sparks of contempt snapped in her eyes.

"You think he's a fool. You laugh at him and call him names. Fat Boy. And neither one of you knows a damned thing about him. Well, I know him."

Something turned over in Tucker's stomach. Dammit, he thought, nothing is going right tonight. Nothing is going wrong, but nothing is going right either.

"I know him, all right. I know just what he is, just what he can do, just what he *will* do. Do you think I don't? Do you? Well, go on and laugh at him, laugh all you want to. Because sooner or later you won't be laughing any more. Not at Harvey Pollock, you won't."

Pure venom in the words. It's hard to know whom she hates the worst, Tucker thought. The Colonel or me. Or maybe even poor Fred. Or maybe there's plenty to go around and cover all of us.

"I used to laugh at him. Just like you. Well, I haven't laughed for a long, long time. Because now I know—"

"All right," Tucker said. "So he's not a fool. Let's cut this out, Martha."

"God, Tucker! Good *God*, have you got a lesson coming to you!"

"Oh, hell," Fred said. "Let's go upstairs. I want to get a look at the asses."

She stared at them, and for the first time in his experience of her Tucker thought she was near tears.

"You make me sick," she said. "Both of you." She swung around and walked swiftly toward the elevators.

Tucker and Fred followed, more slowly. Her words had reminded Tucker of the problem he was sure he faced. She called the turn on Pollock, all right. She knows exactly how he'd try to play it.

Only she forgets he's dealing with Tucker now. She forgets Tucker is no fool either. She should know that, if anybody should.

Fred punched the button and the elevator indicator dropped rapidly. The car slid smoothly to a halt and the doors clicked back. It was empty except for the operator, a Negro boy in a red jacket and black trousers. He held a comic book in his left hand and he did not look up from it as they entered the car.

The doors flicked to behind them and the car jerked once, then moved upward.

Fred nudged Tucker.

"Think it's all right?" He nodded at the Negro boy, still engrossed in the comic book.

"What?"

"Unsegregated elevator. I've got the family reputation to think of, Tucker. After all—"

"Shut up," Tucker said. "Will you just kindly shut your mouth?"

The elevator stopped and the doors slid open again. The elevator boy still did not look up from the comic book. His long brown fingers caressed the polished wood of the control handle.

Tucker saw the fury drop like a mask from Martha's face. In an instant her whole appearance changed. She moved ahead of them out of the elevator, and graciousness and charm enveloped her.

In his absence, if possible, the Bright Leaf Room had become more crowded than ever. The noise assaulted his brain; every mouth seemed to be open, yelling, a tidal wave almost pushing him back into the elevator.

Down the long room, between the high walls, under the glittering chandeliers, people stood in solid rows, banked together like so many nameless, formless animals; there was no air for them to breathe, and for it they substituted smoke and fumes and odor. Single voices shouted into the mass of sound and were lost, became part of the general gabble of the mob. The heat was saturating; the shirts of men clung damply to their bodies and perspiration flowed more freely than alcohol.

About them all, above and below and around that great conglomeration of faces and mouths and eyes, of voices and sounds, of men and women taken up into one great unhuman organism, hung like a thundercloud the dry tinder of excitement. Volatile, tense, dehydrated of individuality, the mob waited. A single match would start the conflagration.

Into this phalanx walked Martha Pollock, casting before her in almost visible waves, that charm, that assurance, that arrogance she could don like a Dior original. Magically the crowd opened. She moved through them untouched, a cool and magnetic intruder among the commoners.

Smiling, speaking graciously to friends, nodding to right and left, for all the world like a queen casting largesse at the feet of her subjects, she made her undeterred way toward the door leading to Colonel Pollock's office.

Katherine walked that way, Tucker thought. Katherine and Martha. Two people born as far apart as can be. I would like to know what they know that I don't, how they came to have that inner certainty. That total absence of doubt.

He turned his head and his eyes took in, in one quick sweep, the figures sprawled across the big blackboard. But I don't need it, he thought. Whatever it is. Not any more. Because now I'll have the power.

A hand touched his arm and he turned his head. A pretty girl, flushed with heat and excitement, yelled something at him he could not hear. He took her arm and she moved along with him, behind Martha.

Finally they were through the big doors and out of the mob. The tremendous, pulsing sound of the yelling could still be heard, but it was dimmed now. An individual voice, where they stood, could be heard.

"What is it, Ellen?" Tucker saw the girl was a staff employee.

"I've got a message for—oh hello, Fred!"

Fred Pollock put his arm around her waist.

"I was wondering how I'd find you in this mob, baby."

"What was it, Ellen?"

"Oh, I'm sorry, Mr. Tucker. Miss Reynolds wants to see you. She's in the little office beyond the Colonel's."

"Thank you." He turned away. Fear laid a palsied hand on his heart.

"Listen," Fred said, behind him, "get us a couple of Seven-Ups, will you, baby?"

I'll tell her it was Joe's work. She'll believe me if I tell her I didn't do it.

He hesitated, his hand poised above the doorknob. Behind him the yelling, the singing, the cheering, pounded from the Bright Leaf Room. But it seemed to him that a certain silence had gathered close about his head, as if there were water in his ears; sounds came to him distant and filtered, a little hollow.

She'll believe anything I tell her. She has to. She loves me.

He put his hand on the doorknob, the smoothness of it moist against his palm.

She trusted you. She'll know. No matter what you say.

He took a deep breath and turned the knob. All right, he thought. Maybe so. But I'll tell her Joe did it.

She wore a high-necked, sleeveless dress, and as she stood dim and shadowed against the high darkness of the room there was an expectant air about her. In the dull light of a single floor lamp, her face was in shadow, but Tucker could see her hands moving, pale blurs in front of her; he thought she seemed not so tall as she was.

"Vivian." The word clogged in his throat, came out a muffled croak.

"Hello, Bill."

He closed the door quietly, taking infinite pains with the catch. Still that faint silence hovered about him and her words echoed through it, like a voice disembodied.

"I'm sorry to bother you, I . . ."

"That's all—"

". . . know you're busy."

"Not at all," he said. "I'm not busy." He took two steps toward her and he thought she moved too. In the yellow, faint light, he could not tell if it was toward him or away.

"No, I guess you're not. It's all over, isn't it?"

He put his hands in his pockets.

"Well—I guess—just about."

He moved nearer. They were close now and he saw she was leaning against the desk. He saw the row of little tucks on her blouse, the soft tendrils of hair curling at her ears, sensed the faint breath of her perfume. She was lovely, he thought, and he felt a great sadness.

"I didn't think you would win, Bill. I didn't think you could."

He felt a smile tug at his mouth and wondered why.

"I know," he said. "I know you didn't."

She put her head slightly to one side and her eyes looked at him gravely. Her voice was thin, a little shaky.

"Do you think it helped you win, Bill?"

No use, he thought. I can't lie to her. I don't know why, but I can't lie to her.

"I don't know. Some, I guess. You can't tell about those things."

"I hope it did. I hope it wasn't for nothing."

"Vivian, I—listen, will you—"

She nodded.

"I know what you want to say. You had to do it."

"I thought so."

"I think so, too. I think you had to."

He felt his ears pop, as if the water had suddenly drained from them. Sounds came at him full-strength now, the subdued mutter from the Bright Leaf Room, the swish of tires along the street below, a footfall along the corridor, even the swift sigh of her breathing.

"You mean—you understand?"

She nodded. He saw the pale blur of her hands moving again. I could reach out and take them in mine, he thought.

"And it's all right?"

God, he thought. God, be good to me this once. Let it be all right.

"No. It's not all right."

Too much. You should never ask for too much.

He felt his hands rise helplessly, fall in slow motion to his sides.

"Then—you don't understand. Not really. You can't—"

Her mouth grimaced.

"I know everything you can say. You've already said it all."

He took her hands in his, feeling them cold and lifeless, the fingers as limp as those of old gloves.

"You're upset, Vivian, tomorrow things will seem different. To-morrow—"

"To whom? To me?"

"I know it looks bad, but tomorrow I can—"

Her smile deepened and he stopped, feeling the uselessness of the words. She made no effort to take her hands from his.

"Things never will look different to you, though. Will they, Tucker? It's always somebody else who doesn't understand."

"Will you be quiet?" he said. "Will you please just let me talk?"

"Should I?"

"Yes. I'm going to anyway." He pulled her to him, felt her body soft against him. "Have you forgotten everything, Vivian? Have you?"

Her words came muffled and low against his shoulder.

"I can't forget—I've tried but—I can't."

"You never will either."

"No."

"Listen," he said, "you've *got* to understand. You've got to see how . . ."

Her face was still against his shoulder and her voice, when she began to speak, was twisted and unclear. But she would not stop and neither would he; for a moment their words tangled unintelligibly and they talked on blankly, making no sense. Then he stopped and her low voice emerged above the faint, furious din of the crowd a few vast feet from them, the sound of it still muffled and twisted but her words clear now, intelligible, striking powerfully at him.

". . . listen any more. I've listened too much, believed too much. I can't listen any more. I can believe but I can't listen any more."

He felt her push terrifically against him, not so much with arm and muscle as in some ungoverned thrust of mind and emotion, some irresistible urge away from him. His hands relaxed and she swayed back, body free of him.

"I listened and thought and listened again. To you, to anybody who would talk about you, tell me what I wanted to hear —how you were hurt and hurt and hurt until you couldn't stand hurt any more, until you had to strike back at them all. Oh, I listened and God! in the end, how I believed!"

"Yes," he said. "You believed in me."

"Enough to look past it all, not to go blind to it, but to look past it, to think what I wanted to think. That I could help you."

Quite suddenly Tucker realized he was tired. His body reeked with fatigue and he felt his knees go to jelly. Sleep, he thought. If I could only sleep.

And knew it was not sleep he craved, not fatigue he felt. Knew that creeping over him, deadly, insidious, like some tropical flesh-rot, was despair.

God, he thought. Does a man ever get a chance to quit? Just quit?

". . . because I saw in you what I wanted to see and not what was there. That was my fault. Not yours. Because I was a woman first and then a person. Because I thought a person could be wrong about a man but a woman couldn't, not if he were her man—"

He saw her hands go behind her and then she was holding them out to him, grasping in them a piece of white paper.

"Take it, Tucker. Read it. Then tell me your story again. Like that night at Union Springs."

Just quit, he thought. Quit and lie down under the sweet trees and look up at the blue sky and feel the grass-itch under your shirt and let the feet walk on you and leave their prints indelibly in mud.

He took the paper and looked at it, read it, WHY DID ANSON'S ERRAND BOY VISIT JOE STALIN'S ERRAND BOY?

He tore it into small pieces.

"Tear it up," she said. "Like you did me."

"I'm sorry—I—hurt you, Vivian." It was amazing how puny the words were. Some words say so little, he thought. But they are all we have.

She laughed, almost gaily, and he felt claws at his intestines.

"You're sorry you hurt me. But what if I hadn't been hurt, Tucker? What then? Would you still be sorry?"

He put his hands to his head.

"I said I was sorry. I said it, didn't I?"

"And what else can you say? Is that what you want to know?"

"Yes! What else can I say?"

"That you wished you hadn't done it. That you wished you hadn't been too much of a coward to do one honest thing out of all the misery and evil you've made."

He shook his head. She can't talk to me that way, he thought. Nobody can. Not to Tucker.

"I'm honest. I'm always honest. I always know what I'm doing, I—"

"You never drew an honest breath in your life, you cheap crook."

Her hands clenched before her jerked up, then down, like tiny sledges on an immense anvil.

"The one thing honesty takes is courage. Sure you were hurt, hurt again and again, maybe more than most people. But you never got up and went on and took it and got up again and still went on. That's courage, Tucker, that's all it ever was and all it ever will be. Getting up and going on.

"But you never had it. Not since the day you were born. That's why I said you had to break your promise to me. You didn't have the courage not to."

He slapped her, hard, with the palm of his hand, then the back. He felt fire behind his eyes. God damn her, he thought, talking to me that way, God damn her, God damn her soul.

He seized her wrist and yanked at her, pulling her face up close to his, feeling the sharp edges of his teeth bite deep into his lip, the bone of his jaw protruding in rigid outrage through his flesh.

"Don't talk to me that way!"

The words were a scream. He felt them one by one hurtle through his aching mouth, felt with each of them ejaculate a little of the rage, a little of the flame, until with their passage there was no flame. There was no rage, either, and he let go her wrist.

Then he saw the marks of his hand on her flesh. He felt his fingers curl.

"You see?" she said. "You still don't have any courage. Do you?"

⊁⊰

They waited, rigid, in timeless silence.

They seemed fixed, almost transparent, looking with eyes that saw not so much as probed, breathing with lungs gone taut and aching, alone, apart, within the same room, the same silence, but not the same world.

I hear him breathe, Vivian thought. I hear cloth slide over flesh.

The quiet, Tucker thought. The dead.

Sound crushed the silence.

Their bodies crumpled before the blast of it and they fell away, moving without will in escape, the terrible mass of the sound a live thing, a thing of power and motion assaulting them. A thousand throats alone could not make that sound; a thousand dead fears had to be discarded first, dropping away to the floor in ignominious and abject defeat.

Behind them the door flung open; a man's head protruded around it like that of a striking snake, his tongue flicking at them, "Calhoun's in—carried it—seven thousand—have to concede now!"

As if they had never been there at all, as they had never needed to be, the head, the tongue, the voice disappeared; only the sound remained.

They adjusted to it; it was no longer living, pushing, surrounding them, it was no longer an eruption. It was merely the sound of many voices.

"Then Pollock wins?"

"Yes."

"God, it's funny," she said.

Yes, he thought. Funny. Because I want to laugh. I have done everything else and now I want to laugh. It must be funny if now I want to laugh.

"Funny he wins but you don't."

"I'll always win now. Always."

"No. Because it never was power you wanted, not really."

He shook his head, wondering if it would come free from his shoulders, hoping it would, thinking how strange if it should roll off and drop thudding to the floor and gape up at him with his own eyes.

"I don't know," he said. "I don't know. What good is anything else to me?"

I can't take any riddles, he thought. I've lost her and it's done, and Pollock is elected, damn his soul, and I can't take any stinking riddles.

"You wanted to win. To know you could win. Because you didn't have the courage to lose."

The door flung open behind them again. The same voice, still breathless, still shouting, "Just got word—goin to concede—he'll be right down!"

Tucker felt the skin of his face at the cracking point. If I could smile, he thought, it would split wide open and she could see inside my head. She could see the little things move.

"It looks like I know, then. I know I won. Don't I?"

She moved away from the desk now, for the first time striding away from him, whirling in the center of the room to face him again.

"You still can't see yourself. You still can't understand the very thing you told me that night."

"Just go on," he said. "Go on and leave me alone now."

"Not before I make you remember, Tucker. Not before you remember that thin little gristle you told me about. The one you said was what they had to get to in a man, what they had to tear apart."

Riddles. I am so damned tired and all I want to do is quit. Just quit and she won't let me. God damned riddles.

"That's why you've lost, Tucker. You wanted to get at that little gristle, yourself, the one down deep in Anson. That was the one thing you couldn't live with, wasn't it?"

NO, he wanted to shout, and could not form the word. No, oh God no, not—

"But you're going to have to, Tucker. You're going to have to live with it."

He put his hands over his ears.

She came slowly to him. She put out her hand as if to touch him. Then it fell slowly to her side again.

"I don't have much courage either, Bill."

No, he told himself. No No No.

"I'm going now. I guess I should be weeping and wailing, but I'm not. I hurt all over, Bill, inside and out. In one way I'm sort of dying. Like you said, I haven't forgotten, and like I said, I never will."

"I'm sorry I—hit you—" feeling the words thick and lifeless on his lips, rolling aimless from his tongue, feeling inside of him already the dead weight of not having her—"oh God, Vivian, oh Jesus God—"

He felt her eyes on him, quiet as her voice, felt all about him the sense of her, the very being of her.

"It doesn't matter, Bill. What makes you think we're any different, you and me? All that matters is to get up and go on. And learn something if you can. I learned something. I learned what a power one human being can be. One honest man."

He felt his tongue tight on the roof of his mouth, pulled it free with an effort.

"From Anson?"

"Yes."

"But he lost."

"No," she said. "He won. And that's what you don't understand. I don't think you ever will."

She turned, then, and walked to the door, her head high, the hem of her skirt swinging gracefully to her long, slim stride.

"Vivian!"

He felt the cry dredged up out of him by a giant hand, flung across the room with the last, despairing drop of strength in his racked body.

She stopped, her hand on the door. She did not look back.

"Don't beg," she said. "Please leave me that. Someday—if you need me—I won't ever forget, Bill."

"I—want you now, Vivian—please."

"I know you do. But you'd give that up," she said, "if you had a better offer somewhere else. You already have."

She opened the door and went out.

He heard the cheering again.

Ralph Anson came into the Bright Leaf Room a little after nine o'clock.

At his entrance the cheering stopped.

Anson paused, his head turning, looking about him. He blinked a little in the smoke, the fogged air. His collar was wilted and his necktie was askew; from his high forehead, above steel-rimmed spectacles, the lights caught a glint of perspiration.

The crowd gave way a little, pressing in upon itself, giving him room. He walked forward, toward the stout figure awaiting him. Ben Kirby walked behind him, stepping too precisely, too exactly, like a drunken man along a chalk line.

Anson smiled; he waved a hand almost casually. A spatter of handclapping flickered across the crowd and a yell or two went up, feeble against the hanging echo of the boomings that had gone before.

There was a smile of victory across the broad, glistening face of Harvey Pollock, a smile of victory in the eyes rimmed red above the pudgy cheeks.

I am waiting, his face said. I will take your hand in mine and forgive all and restore you to the grace of the multitude. Now that I have won.

Tucker counted each step Ralph Anson took. The planting of

the left foot filled him with fear; the right came down and re-placed it with denial.

She can't be right, he thought. She can't be. There has to be that much out of it all that was true, that I believed.

The thin applause died. The left, the right. The long waiting was upon Tucker now. Left, right.

Anson passed beyond the last gaping face; he paused and held out his hand, long, bone-thin, steady.

Flesh crossed flesh. It was over.

It went up then, the full, huge accumulation of the sound, of the cheering; it went up and filled the room, overflowed it.

Tucker saw Pollock's fat arms swing above his head, heard the sound fall away obediently. He felt his knees tremble as if they could no longer bear the weight of the fear, of the wild, des-perate denial.

"We are all," Anson said, "glad of one thing. Now we can be friends again."

The fear went out of Tucker. But he was not relieved, al-though the denial was gone too; his knees still trembled.

"It is traditional at the end of a primary to call for a closing of ranks in preparation for the general election. I do not now hesitate to make this call to you."

I have heard it all before, Tucker thought. Somehow, I know what he will say before he says it.

"I respect tradition. What is good in tradition is what is good in all of us. But I would remind you now of a wider call, the call to go forth unafraid to face the America tradition has given us. To face what is good and what is bad in our America."

I always knew what he would say. I should have known.

And I should have known what it was I wanted.

"Face this America as it is and make it a place where differ-ences may be resolved without hatred. Make it a land where tradition is not reaction, where hope for tomorrow is not revo-lution.

"May God preserve America. May God bless America."

They were silent at first. And then they applauded, lightly, re-spectfully. Because this was harmless; these were platitudes. Who fears platitudes? Who even listens to them, really listens?

Tucker saw Joe Harrison applauding. He saw Harvey Pollock applauding. He felt something strike his hands and looked down at them and found himself applauding too.

Then, above the noise of a thousand clapping hands, he could hear only the mechanical *slap slap slap* of his own palms coming together, as mechanically, as rhythmically, as a pendulum swings.

She was right, he thought. I applaud my own decay.

All right, then.

If that's the way it is. If she were right.

What is left?

The *slap slap slap* of his beating hands filled his ears. If there were an answer, he could not hear it.

Chapter Twenty-two

Ⅰt was time now to leave.

Tucker knew this, and, knowing it, knew also the end of his pain and abasement. It was as if he had undergone a total cleavage from all that had been, from all that had even been hoped or anticipated.

All of that simply no longer was. And with its negation, he saw clearly that he no longer had a purpose there in the big room among the celebrating crowd. Perhaps not anywhere, but certainly not there.

In a way, he thought, I have been set free. There is no longer any necessity.

He could not have felt this passing of necessity more positively if it had been the abrupt cessation of the pull of gravity. It was a heady feeling.

Almost lightly he began pushing toward the door. He heard Pollock's voice only as a larger part of the general noise, not deciphering words or meaning from it. He felt no irritation at the close-packed crowd through which he struggled.

After all, he was one of them now.

And Vivian.

Now I need her, he thought. Not just want. Now I need her.

Vivian. She will help me. She will come back to me now that I need her. Now that I know I need her as I have always needed her more than anything else.

He pushed and shoved on toward the door. Out there was something else, something new. Maybe it would be no better, but it would be something different and that was enough to settle for. Anything different.

People moved from his path, not looking at him nor even noticing him. They were listening to Pollock and roaring steadily back at him. They could not be bothered with Tucker, who was now very near the door.

Quite suddenly Tucker found himself facing the imposing bulk of Cousin Hadley, who gazed at him with bland, blank eyes. Tucker found, staring back at him, that Hadley was almost lashless, that his eyes were almost unmoving in his pouchy face.

There was something menacing about him. There was, in the blinkless stare, the ponderous stolidity riveted there in the midst of the moving, rootless crowd, a faint but profound threat. And, at almost the same time he became aware of this menace, came up short against that motionless mountain of flesh and stolidity, Tucker became aware also of Pollock, still speaking.

". . . will set up, as I said I would, an office right here in this city, an office whose doors will never be closed to you, where you may come, one and all, to tell me what you want done in Washington, to tell me . . ."

All right, Tucker thought. This will be a place to begin. Let him say it and then I can begin.

". . . to run that office, to keep it open to you, to act as my ears when I am not within your reach, to be my point of perpetual contact with you, I am appointing my friend and my close adviser . . ."

It will be a pleasure, a real pleasure. To begin here. To tell him to shove it up—

". . . almost my right arm—JOE HARRISON!"

A blackness closed on Tucker.

He had forgotten in the agony of his realization, the vague hints, the treachery he had felt in the very air so short a time before. In the vast upheaval he had endured, it had gone entirely from his mind.

Now the blackness closed tight around him, like a hangman's mask. Rage welled up from the bottom of his soul. He felt his hands clench into fists, felt his nails pierce his palms. Red touched the fringe of the blackness. He felt rage almost foaming in his mouth.

And then the black was gone and the red too, and finally

even the rage. He found himself cool and calm and precise; he felt necessity. As nearly as he could ever be, he was the old Tucker again.

He stepped close to Cousin Hadley.

"Anson," he said, squeezing the word between his teeth. "Yes. Even Vivian. Even myself. But I will be damned if I take it from you, Cousin. I will be god damned if I take it from Pollock."

Hadley blinked. His head bobbed back.

"Why, Cousin," he said, "don't you go blamin me now."

Tucker turned and began pushing his way back down the long room. He was not aware of the final, frenzied roar of the mob around him; he did not notice the people he pushed bodily out of the way. He saw only the stout man also pushing through the crowd, pushing his way toward the door at the other end of the room.

Bastard. Bastard. To think you could pull a cheap double cross on Tucker. For you to think I was that stupid and even worse that you were that smart. Bastard.

Pollock turned, far ahead of him, and waved a last time at the crowd. A last deafening roar went up and then he was gone. Almost at once the noise began to fall away.

Tucker felt a hand on his shoulder and swung around. Zeb Ruggles, perspiring and limp, looked at him.

"Well, Tuck, I guess—"

"Were you in on it, Zeb?"

Ruggles nodded.

"I warned you, Tuck. You know I did, a long time ago."

"I know it."

"I play winners, Tuck. Only winners."

"You sure?"

"I can't afford it any other way."

"I was going to make you Governor, Zeb."

"Look, Tuck. Listen—"

Tucker turned away. "The hell with it."

He pushed on through the crowd. It took him almost five minutes to get to the double doors opening into the hallway. The space before Pollock's door was deserted.

He'll be waiting, Tucker thought.

He will know I am coming.

✳

The door was locked. Tucker did not knock. He took out his own key and opened it.

"Hello, Tuck," Pollock said. He sat behind the desk, with one leg carelessly over the corner of it. He held a glass in his hand and he had loosened his tie.

Joe Harrison stood by the desk, looking over his shoulder at Tucker, his square chin waggling slowly up and down, as if he wished to speak but had no tongue. Tucker looked at him briefly.

"Get out," he said.

"Take it easy, Tucker," Pollock said.

"I want him out. Now."

Pollock looked at Harrison.

"What the man said, Joe. Run along."

"Now—look here—" Joe's voice croaked, half-indignant, half-fearful.

"Beat it," Tucker said.

Joe moved away from the desk, glanced once at the Colonel, then went out the door. It slammed behind him.

"All right," Pollock said. "You know damn well I couldn't go through with your deal."

"You thought you could awhile back. When you were nobody."

Pollock nodded.

"And now I think I can't."

"Why? Tell me that."

"Because I can't spend my time watching you. Fighting you. Because there can't be but one boss."

"You?"

"Me. You knew goddam well it was me or you, all the time. You thought it would be you, but you were wrong."

"You think I'm out of it now?"

"I know you are."

"What makes you think," Tucker said, "for one minute even that I didn't have you figured the day I first laid eyes on you?

· 335 ·

Do you actually think I didn't see this coming six months ago? From a cheap crook like you?"

Pollock laughed.

"You didn't see anything coming."

"Cut it out," Tucker said. "Just show me what you've got."

Pollock stood up.

"You didn't see anything coming because you were the great Tucker. You were the brain. The smart guy. You didn't . . ."

"I'll break you, Pollock. Right in half."

". . . think anybody could think and plan but you. You thought Pollock was a dope. Didn't you?"

"And now I'm damn sure of it, too."

"I will tell you something, Tucker. I will tell you once and no more. You thought you were using me. But I've been on your back all the way."

They leaned across the desk as if they would leap at each other. Tucker saw for the first time the bulging muscle under the glistening, stubbled jowl. He saw Pollock's lips flatten back against his teeth.

"Nobody uses me, Tucker. Not even you."

"A phone call," Tucker said. "Tonight. Tomorrow. A phone call and I could ruin a dozen men. You know that?"

Pollock's nostrils quivered. Tucker could feel the man's breath on his face. Tucker leaned further forward, his head bobbing a little with each word.

"And any of those men could ruin you just as quick."

"I know the way you work, Tucker. You don't have to tell me."

"You think I won't make that phone call?"

"You could. But I don't think you will."

"Show me," Tucker said. "Show me why I won't." He put his hand on the telephone on the desk.

Pollock straightened, slowly. He picked up the half-finished highball. Then he sat down abruptly, as if something had quite suddenly been finished.

"About the election. Is that how they could ruin me?"

Tucker felt contempt edging into him. For a moment there, he thought, I was afraid the slob had something worth listening to.

"How else?" he said.

"You can pin some of the deals we made on me?"

"All of them. If I have to."

Pollock nodded, pursing his lips.

"That would finish me, then. As a Senator."

"Absolutely."

Tucker was bored now. It was anticlimax. A man's final battle, he thought, ought to last longer. It ought to be his hardest.

"But I don't have to be a Senator."

Tucker felt a muscle tighten and jerk in his cheek.

"No," he said. "You don't."

Pollock put down the highball. He opened his desk drawer.

"You're holding a full house, Tucker. But we're playing with my deck."

He took a folder from the drawer and laid it on the desk.

"I call," he said.

Tucker took his hand off the phone and took the folder, not looking at it. He saw Pollock smile gently, almost sweetly.

"Sit down and read it, Tuck."

The touch of the folder in Tucker's hand was like a small defeat. I ought to throw it in his fat face, he thought.

He sat down and began to read. He read for five minutes, without looking up, without change of expression, turning the pages rapidly and without noise. Pollock sat still, moving only once to take a pipe from his desk and place it unlit between his teeth.

Tucker slapped the folder shut.

"Cute," he said. "Joe's idea?"

"Sure. You think it would stick, Tuck?"

Tucker crossed his legs. Now there is a good question, he thought, and I ought to know the answer.

Funny. This is so damned funny it isn't even real. Nothing real was ever this funny. This is so good I wish I had thought of it myself.

And the funniest thing of all is that in the long run I guess I really did.

"Crazy," he said. "It doesn't make sense."

He was amazed to hear his voice coming from over his own shoulder. He was not even sure it was his voice. He was not, at the moment, even sure that a man named Tucker was sitting there with his legs crossed looking at a man named Pollock.

Pollock lit his pipe with a small flourish.

"Think it over, Tuck. Tell me if it would stick."

Tucker wanted to laugh. Stick? he thought. *This*? On Tucker? And then he knew he did not know. He did not know whether it would stick or not.

"Take it one by one," Pollock said. "Then add it up."

Add it up. I've got to add it up.

"You feel all right, Tuck?"

God damn you, Tucker thought. I'll add it up for you. I'll add it up for you, all right.

"I feel fine," he said. "You want to know what I think of this?"

Pollock nodded, smiling faintly.

"Now this first thing," Tucker said. "Going way back here. This about my old man's union. Matter of fact, it was pretty damn Red at one time till they cleaned it out. I never was in it but I grew up with it. Not bad, that one. Not bad at all."

"I told Joe to leave it out," Pollock said. "But I guess it would go."

"In a pinch," Tucker said. "Now this about—let's see—James Wilton. Who the hell is James Wilton?"

"You roomed with him in college. Freshman year."

"Son of a bitch. I haven't thought of him since. Red as a Winesap apple."

"That's a good one, that is. Attorney General's been after him for years."

"I give you that one," Tucker said.

Christ, this is funny. A scream.

Sitting here and talking this way as if it were somebody else. As if it were real. Actually talking this way as if it were somebody else.

Me. Tucker. Pulling this on me and all I can do is sit here and say I give you that one.

Oh, Christ, if I start to laugh I won't ever quit. Christ, don't let me start to laugh now.

"How about the theme there?"

"The theme," Tucker said. "Immature stuff but you could do a lot with it. I give you that one too." His voice still seemed to come from over his own shoulder. I'm giving him everything, he thought.

Pollock chuckled.

"That Joe," he said. "You underestimated him too."

"Well, now, this collection for Soviet Aid. That won't wash. That was a whole office collection, not a hundred bucks from me. I could prove that one."

Pollock puffed thoughtfully at the pipe. "Scratch it, then."

"And this Supporters of the Abe Lincoln Brigade. Me on the letterhead. I can't make that one."

"We invented it," Pollock said. "Good measure."

"Oh. And that brings us down to this last one. How in hell did you even find out about her is what I want to know."

"Well—" Pollock took the pipe out of his mouth and looked it over, as if searching for some minute flaw—"Joe had to read a few of your letters and things. He managed."

Now that's not funny, Tucker thought. I'm going to remember that.

"I think it makes the whole thing. It's what pulls it all together. A girl you went with for two years and knew all your life and tried to marry swearing the reason she turned you down was because you had told her you were a Communist. How can you top that one?"

Quite suddenly the impact of the thing jarred Tucker to the soles of his feet. It was no longer even remotely funny.

"I could still ruin you," he said.

"Look, Tucker. Get wise. You could cause me trouble. But everything you say you're going to have to prove before a committee of politicians and in a court of law. Maybe you can do it. Maybe you can even get me booted out of the Senate. I admit that wouldn't help my reputation any. But I'd still have money. I'd have my bank. I'd still have a lot of things left, you stop and think about it. But you—listen, Tucker, I don't have to prove a thing to make you a Communist. I just have to suggest it. And I ask you this—if I make you a Communist what have you got left? What have you got left in this country this day and time?"

Bastards, Tucker thought. They always got a way to get at you.

It's not so bad just to take a licking. It's not even so bad to have Katherine reach back at me this one last, worst time, when she didn't even need to, when she had already licked me for good.

No. The bad thing is to be beaten the way you have beaten someone else. The bad thing is to know what you have done to someone else and to learn it by having it done to you, just the same way. That is the bad thing and the hard thing, even harder than having to admit that is what has happened.

He put the papers on the desk and stood up.

"Pot's yours," he said. "I fold."

The lobby was empty when Tucker stepped out of the elevator. A sleepy clerk eyed him from behind the desk. An uninterested bellboy leaned idly against an overstuffed sofa. From upstairs, in the Bright Leaf Room, the songs and shouts of the diehards drifted down.

Tucker listened to feet crossing the lobby, not sure they were his own. He went out the door, noticing that it seemed to swing open seconds before his fingers touched it.

It was cooler outside and darker. Tucker was grateful for the coolness and the darkness. The fresh touch of air about his face, his hot, gritty neck was as welcome as the solitude.

Traffic was not so heavy now and the sidewalks were shadowed and empty under the insect-shrouded street lights. A few faceless people moved past him. Around a corner a newsboy shouted into the cool and the dark the news of Harvey Pollock's victory.

So what do I do now?

What does a man do when his props give way? No matter how rotten they were, what does a man do when they go?

Get up and go on, Vivian says. Get knocked down and get up and go on, the best way you can.

Face what is good and what is bad, Anson says.

Get wise, Pollock says. Add it up.

But what does Tucker say?

Tucker doesn't know. Tucker doesn't have the answers any more.

Again he heard footsteps and wondered if they were his own; he decided they were. Down the long, quiet, dark canyon of the street he could see lights burning in store windows here and there. As he watched it, a theater marquee dropped into darkness. He passed a window in which ladies' shoes were mercilessly exposed to a glaring white light; the smell of onions came to him from a small, dim café. He heard the newsboy again, behind him now. A car with one headlight burned out went by him on the street.

Tucker stopped. So did the footsteps. I wish they'd go on, he thought. I don't like them following me. They don't have any right to follow me like that.

He was standing on a corner. The street ran emptily by him, narrowing away into the night. Over his head a traffic light turned from red to green and he saw the transition reflected on the concrete far below him about his feet.

What is so empty as a traffic light issuing orders to a vacant street? Blinking solemnly green here in the lonely night with only me to obey it.

Empty empty empty.

He went across the street, the footsteps following him. He wondered if he could see them if he looked back. He tried it, twisting his head quickly, glancing from the corners of his eyes. But he saw only the pavement, tinted red again with the changing traffic light.

He came to a large building fronted by wide stone steps. This was the Central Post Office and he went slowly up the steps, hearing the footsteps go up with him. The lobby door was still open. Inside the air was stale and dead. Pale lights clung lazily to the high ceiling and cast freakish shadows over the WPA mural straining from the far wall. A drunk slept peacefully and open-mouthed beneath a high-legged writing desk.

Tucker walked down the tiled lobby, past the *Air Mail* slot and the *Parcel Post* window, past the criminals and thugs looking bleary-eyed from the fly-specked photos, past the flapping, mimeographed Civil Service notices, *The Navy Needs Men Like*

You posters, the thousand numbered eyes of the postal boxes, past the stained governmental walls with their air of old and forgotten urgencies, their reek of tobacco juice and disinfectant and cigar smoke, to the row of three telephone booths, standing like upended coffins beneath the bulging mural.

He entered the first of these and closed the door behind him; the ceiling light clicked on. He put a nickel in the slot, listened to it bounce as it hit bottom. Slowly he dialed a number.

By the square black box of the phone, a shaky hand had written a name and number on the wall and enclosed them in a lop-sided heart. Tucker leaned closer, squinting in the dim light, hearing the first raucous ring of the phone.

Marty, the shaky hand had written. 6129.

Marty, he thought. Martha.

The phone rang again.

Martha.

By God. Martha Pollock.

A third ring.

I forgot all about her.

He heard the receiver picked up, the sound echoing faintly along the line.

There's his weakness. Martha.

"Hello," Vivian said. Her voice was sleepy, a little strained, as if she were not sure hello was the right thing to say.

And Fred. Fred too. I must have been blind not to see I could get at him that way. If I play it right. Plan it right.

"Hello. Who is it?"

He looked at the mouthpiece of the phone. So it had come down to this. So it had come down again, as it always did, to a choice.

"Hello," Vivian said. "Hello, hello."

Only there isn't any choice. Not really. No matter what they say. Not for me there isn't.

Because I made my choice a long time ago. It's like opportunity. It only knocks once and if you flub it then you flub it for good.

"Hello," Vivian said again. "Who's calling?"

He hung up. The lopsided heart seemed to grow larger as he

looked at it. In my own way, he thought, in my own way I think maybe I am getting up and going on.

Not the best way I can. The only way I can.

He left the booth and walked quickly, no longer hearing his own echoing footsteps, back past *The Navy Needs Men Like You* and the tattered mugs and forgers and embezzlers and out of the post office and into the cool dark again.

There was a lot to be done and he was eager to be at it. It would be his kind of work.

The kind I'm good at, he thought.